Martina Murphy has been writing for as long as she can remember. She is the author of two  versions of her name! Her languages and include the Impac long-listed *Somethi* is a qualified drama teacher. two adult children and tw

Also by Martina Murphy

YA novels:

Livewire
Fast Car
Free Fall
Dirt Tracks

As Tina Reilly:

Flipside
The Onion Girl
Is This Love?
Something Borrowed
Wedded Blitz

As Martina Reilly:

The Summer of Secrets
Second Chances
Wish Upon a Star
All I Want is You
The Wish List
A Moment Like Forever
Even Better Than the Real Thing?
What If?
Things I Want You to Know
That Day in June
Proof

As Martina Murphy:

The Night Caller

THE
BRANDED

MARTINA MURPHY

CONSTABLE

CONSTABLE

First published in Great Britain in 2022 by Constable
This edition published in 2023 by Constable

A CIP catalogue record for this book
is available from the British Library.

ISBN: 978-0-34913-499-4

Typeset in Bembo MT Pro by Initial Typesetting Services, Edinburgh
Printed and bound in Great Britain by Clays Ltd, Elcograf S.p.A.

Papers used by Constable are from well-managed forests and
other responsible sources.

Constable
An imprint of
Little, Brown Book Group
Carmelite House
50 Victoria Embankment
London EC4Y 0DZ

An Hachette UK Company
www.hachette.co.uk

www.littlebrown.co.uk

For Conor and Caoimhe
with lots of love xx

Prologue

15 July – Sarah

The thing is, Sarah thinks, as she crosses the top of her road and heads in the direction of Westport, it's her mother who needs to be taken into care, not her. She can manage fine.

Her mother had finally pissed her off big-time last night. Rolling in from the pub, dragging some skanky man behind her. Both of them falling onto the sofa in front of her, both of them oblivious to the fact that Sarah was trying to watch *Love Island* on the telly.

She had asked them to get a room.

Her mother had started shouting at her: 'I pay the rent on this place. This is my room.'

Sarah had never loathed anyone as much as she did right then.

And so here she is, on the run. But she won't make the same mistakes she did before. First off, the weather-forecast man, the one her mother fancies, says a heatwave is coming, so it means she isn't going to end up wet or bloody frozen, begging for money on some street corner. She'll be out sunning herself, so she will. Getting a tan. And school is out, so no worries on that score. No

1

social workers turning up on her mother's doorstep wondering why she isn't attending.

The first time Sarah had left home, she'd been taken by social workers because her mother had had a bit of a meltdown in a shop over the price of crackers. They'd put her into a home with smiley foster parents. But that had been weird, too calm and false and always on edge. She'd run away on them, spent some nights in a shelter, but BIG mistake.

Sarah will take her chances on the streets for now, sit on the bridge in Westport and look pathetic and sad. Good training for her acting career when she's going to be famous.

It's the thing that keeps her sane, knowing that one day this part of her life will be over.

This will be an adventure.

Chapter 1 – Day 1

The first of August is the hottest day of the summer so far. The sky is a bright and cloudless blue, the sun is white, and the whole land, as far as the blue mountains in the distance, is a mass of gold and brown due to the hosepipe ban, which has been in force for the last two weeks. On either side of Johnny and Katherine's garden, dried-up fields stretch on as far as my eye can see.

The glass of sparkling water I'm holding has lost its sparkle, as have I. Both of us are too hot to be out here, but Johnny and Katherine have insisted on having about two hundred people to their granddaughter's christening and, in this southwest-facing back garden, the sun is relentless. There is no relief to be found either in their house or in the marquee.

This whole christening is a farce, I think, as I sip the tepid water. Neither Luc, my son, nor Tani, his girlfriend, is religious, but if the child didn't get baptised, it'd be the talk of the district for months to come. My mother, who is normally pretty tolerant, was even anxious for it to go ahead.

'God Almighty,' she'd said to me one night, 'if they don't get the child baptised soon, she'll walk up the church one day and do it herself.'

I'd stayed out of it, hoping that Luc and Tani would stay strong, but even they couldn't withstand the pressure, and as Tani said the last time I saw her, 'Sure a party is a party no matter what way you look at it.'

'On your own?' Johnny Egan, Tani's dad, lands in beside me and I try not to blush. It takes everything I have to sound normal when faced with either him or his wife. I'd gone out with Johnny for a few years in school before Katherine had arrived, super shiny, down from Dublin and snatched him from me. Years later, my ex-husband, Rob, had lived up to his name and robbed Johnny and Katherine of most of their savings. And if that wasn't bad enough, my eighteen-year-old son had got together with their eighteen-year-old daughter and subsequently made her pregnant. A litany of horrors.

'My mother has gone to get us both another drink,' I answer, my voice mercifully even. Looked at objectively, Johnny hasn't aged well. Sometimes being top dog in school is a curse. To me, Johnny looks as if he's still trying to hold on to whatever it was he'd once had because life hasn't delivered on its earlier promise. His tan is too deep, his trousers too tight and I recognise his shirt, a blue and yellow flowery affair, from Luc's wardrobe. But there is still something there, on my part anyway, maybe because he was my first love. Plus, he's a lot friendlier to me than his wife is, though that may be explained by my having been the first girl to show him a bra. 'Good party.'

'It is in its arse,' he fires back, blue eyes laughing down at me. 'When did you ever get to be so polite, Lucy Golden?'

My heart gives a *whump* as my cheeks light up. For feck's sake. I wish I could say it was a hot flush, but it's not. It's the way he smiles: it brings me back to when I was fifteen. I miss being

4

fifteen. But, Jesus, Lucy, I chide, this is not the same man you used to fancy like mad. This is the man who picked a stuck-up cow for a wife, so how nice can he actually be?

'I'm enjoying it.' I sound like a nun.

I spot my mother picking her way towards us in her high shoes. Her mission to get me another drink has been aborted because she has Sirocco – my eight-month-old granddaughter – beautiful child, horrendous name – in her arms and has commandeered Luc to carry the drinks.

He looks even hotter and sweatier than me. He's wearing the suit he wore for his Debs, which was a bad choice on a day that's hitting thirty degrees. I feel suddenly sorry for him, catapulted into this adult world before he was ready.

'Hello, Johnny,' my mother calls, 'didn't ye get a lovely day for it? The baptism was beautiful. Isn't that new priest an awful eejit, though?' She smiles at Sirocco as she says it. 'An awful eejit,' she repeats, in a high-pitched voice, making Sirocco coo and gurgle. Turning back to Johnny, she adds, 'Where was he going with the amount of water he threw over the poor child? I thought he was waterboarding her.'

Johnny laughs, and once more I'm catapulted back to fifth year in school and the sound of Johnny clattering along the corridors. My ears were hyper-attuned to every move of the boy back then. God, I haven't felt that way about someone in such a long time. I wonder if I ever will again.

A trickle of sweat runs down my face, and as I go to wipe it away, my fingers find the track of my scar. The ugly puckering of skin that I earned courtesy of Ellen McKenna, the wife of one of my informants. In a trial, about ten years back, he'd been offered witness protection for his testimony. His wife refused to go and had blamed me for breaking up her marriage and leaving her son fatherless. In retaliation, she'd come to the station and thrown acid in my face, resulting in scarring for me and her son losing both a father *and* a mother. I pull my hand back, not wanting to draw attention to it.

I am aware that my mother is saying something to me and that I have zoned out. 'Your phone,' she says, probably for the third time. 'Your phone, Lucy.'

Not today, I think. Today's my day off.

I pull it out of my bag and see that it's Dan, one of the detectives I work with and probably my closest friend on the force. It must be important because I'd told him not to ring me at any cost.

'Shit.' I hold up the ringing phone. 'I probably have to get this.'

I move away to a quiet corner of the garden to take the call. I could kill Dan for this. I know Luc understands it's my job but that doesn't make it any easier to leave him any time there's a crisis. And today of all days . . .

'Dan,' I say, flicking on the phone. 'This better be important.'

'They've found a body.'

'Where?' In the background someone has started singing a terrible version of 'The Fields of Athenry'.

'Lough Acorrymore. I'll swing by and pick you up. That party sounds particularly painful.'

'You have no idea.'

'I'll rescue you in twenty minutes,' he says, and hangs up.

I rejoin Luc and my mother. Johnny has moved to talk to Milo McGrath, Katherine hanging onto his arm, like he's her property.

Tani is talking to Luc. My mother is occupied with a neighbour who is cooing at Sirocco.

'I've just about had enough—' Tani breaks off, as I join her and Luc.

'I'm so sorry. I have to go – it's pretty important.' I hope they can't hear the relief in my voice. It's been hard, this party, seeing Luc trying to fit in with this new part of his family. Hoping he'll stay true to himself. 'I'm so sorry, Luc.'

'No bother.' Luc gives me a wry grin. 'I wish I could go home.'

Tani giggles.

'Don't be so ungrateful, Luc.' I feel I have to chastise him. 'Tanita's family believe in God, so just go with it.'

It's unfortunate that the singer chooses that moment to stop. My voice seems to rise above everything. Heads turn in our direction and Luc starts to snigger.

My mother, who has heard, pretends nothing has just happened. 'God is a great fellow altogether,' she says.

Now Luc shakes with suppressed laughter. I hand him my car keys so he and my mother can get home and I make my escape.

Chapter 2

I find a shady spot, under a tree, opposite the house to wait for Dan. Everyone is at the christening, so there isn't a sinner on the road. I pull my blouse away from my body because it's sticking to me something rotten and you can definitely see my bra underneath. The heat is oppressive. Nothing moves in the dead air – it's as if all the birds and insects have given up and retired until things cool down. The roads shimmer in the haze and the sun burns my skin. I pull some lotion from my bag and plaster my legs with it. The smell of summer.

I wonder about the body that's been found. Something tells me it's not going to be a slam-dunk open-and-shut murder. Dan would never have called me for that. He'll fill me in on the drive, I suppose. Nothing stirs in the hot afternoon so I can hear Dan's car from miles away, the purr of the engine as it grows closer, see the swimming image of it cresting the hill and the heat that radiates off it as he pulls it to a stop beside me.

'Hot, is it?' He grins as I climb inside the blessedly cool interior. 'Belt up. We're heading out to Lough Acorrymore.'

'Lough' means 'lake' in Irish and Lough Acorrymore is the reservoir for Achill Island. Though to call it a reservoir is to do it a disservice. It's a low-lying lake surrounded by stunning cliffs. You can reach it easily enough by car, which is a relief for us. At least we won't be hiking for miles to view a body, which could happen in a place like Achill.

'Tell me what's going on,' I say to Dan, as he heads towards the island.

'William rang. He hadn't much information. Just said that a tourist who was fishing in the lake snagged his line on something. He tried to pull it in, but about three metres from shore the line snapped. So, our fisherman waded in, couldn't find it and decided to ring the local lads.'

'Over something his line snagged on? I'd say that went down well at the station.'

'The lads creased themselves laughing, I heard, but Kev said he'd go and take a look because he was hot and he wanted a swim.'

'Aw, God . . .'

'Yep. So, he arrives at the lake and dives in.'

'Kev Deasy dives?'

'A boy of many talents,' Dan says. 'After a bit, he managed to grab what was a suitcase, hauled it ashore and found a body inside.'

'Holy Jesus.'

'I know, you'd swear we were in Dublin,' Dan says, only half joking. 'Kev then called for assistance and got the scene sealed off. He also called in Joe. He wasn't too happy because he was away on a dirty weekend with his wife, who I'm sure was glad to be rid of him. Can you imagine?' Dan makes a face and I laugh.

Joe Palmer is the pathologist and as contrary as hell. He's rude and abrasive but good at the job.

'Any details yet on the body?'

'No. But it'll be a media circus if we don't get a move on. With the amount of tourists milling about, word is bound to get out. Before we know it we'll have bloodhound Stacy on our backs.'

He says it as a joke. Stacy is a local journalist who has recently been promoted to senior reporter on *Island News* mainly because of the exclusives she'd managed to wrangle from me over the last big case I'd handled. She is as persistent as a mosquito and refuses to ring the garda press office, like every other journo.

We cross onto Achill, take the main and only road towards Keem Bay, but before we get there Dan takes a right, marked 'Reservoir', and follows the twisty narrow trail until we're stopped by a guard, who tells us to park and walk the rest of the way. 'Big cordon,' I remark.

'Yep.' He holds out some dust suits for us. As ever, only the XXL ones are left. I pull mine on and complain that no one considers women on the force. As usual, it's met with silence.

'The Cig here?' Dan asks, as the guard logs us into the scene.

'Yep.'

The detective inspector is William Williams, whom I'd got to know a little during our last big investigation together. He's a bit of an enigma, ploughs his own furrow, doesn't do the bonding stuff and scares the life out of newbies. But he's direct and fair and there's no side to him. I really respect that.

'It's good that William is there,' Dan says, watching as I try to wrestle the dust cover over my stilettos. 'I suppose that means he's been appointed SIO.'

I hope so. He's a good man for managing an investigation. Nothing gets lost. '"Tell them what to do and why,"' I say, quoting his famous line and actually doing a fair impression of him.

Dan snorts out a laugh. 'If the garda career fails, go into taking the piss out of William. There'd be a lot of lads who'd pay to see it.'

'I'll keep that in mind.'

The cordon is wide, extending from the road down to the entrance of the car park to the lake and about fifty metres on either side. Scene-of-crime officers are busy and a diving team has just arrived.

'Right,' I say to Dan. 'Let's see what we've got.'

A little later, Dan and I are by the lakeside, staring at the decomposed body of what appears to be a young teenager, wrapped tightly in thick see-through bloodied plastic, lying in a foetal position in a medium-sized suitcase. It's the kind of suitcase that people immediately notice at airport arrivals carousels, hard shell, bright blue. The body appears to be naked, tiny-boned, with brown hair. Blood has leaked from the plastic all over the interior of the case.

She's surprisingly dry after having been in the lake.

We are quiet for the longest time.

'Fuck's sake,' Dan whispers eventually. 'It's a kid.'

'She's quite well preserved,' Joe Palmer, the pathologist, says from behind. Even he doesn't sound as abrupt as usual. Maybe the man does have a heart. He comes to stand alongside us. 'Whatever troll threw her in there didn't realise that a waterproof case like this would do us a favour.'

'Can you tell us anything at the moment about the body?' I ask.

'Not much until I get her moved. That plastic she's wrapped in hampers the view but she appears to have been beaten about

11

the face – see the cheek, smashed there? Now, some of that injury could be due to the bag being bashed about by the currents, but this lake,' he turns to look out over it, 'is not famous for its currents. And the case is hard shell, so she'd have been partially protected.'

'True,' I agree. 'Anything else?' He's being amazingly cooperative. Maybe the weekend with his wife has softened him up.

'Just that she's not in bad condition so there will be plenty of forensics. This should be an easy solve for you, Lucy. No excuse to fuck things up.'

I should have known he was lining me up. 'I'll be at the PM,' I tell him, 'so you'd better not fuck things up either.'

Dan sucks in his breath. The big pussy is far more terrified of Joe than I am. But though my words are feisty, my heart has started to rocket about in my chest as Joe's eyes narrow.

'I'll see you then, Detective Sergeant Golden,' he says. 'Now, if you'll excuse me, I'm off to do my job.'

'Arsehole,' I mutter, as I turn back to the girl. I crouch down, covering my mouth against the smell. She looks about fifteen. Who are you? Who is missing you? Whose heart will we break when we contact them to say you're here?

'We need fingerprints, if we can get them, and DNA as soon as possible, and a picture of that suitcase for the conference tonight,' I say.

Dan nods. 'Someone is bound to be missing her.'

I straighten up, my legs creaking with the effort. 'You go and organise those pictures. Talk to William and see what the story is. I'll take off the dust suit and have a chat with our fisherman.'

Chapter 3

The fisherman is from Cavan. He's twenty-two but looks younger. His name is Peter, only he pronounces it Pater, in the flat vowels of that county. He smiles uneasily at me as I approach and makes room for me to sit alongside him on the smooth rock he has found. I do not present a dignified picture of a responsible detective as I try to lower myself into a sitting position with high heels and a short skirt. I can't even pull it down once I sit, and my thighs bulge out on either side. I don't know how I'll get back up again. I pull my notebook and pen from the waistband of my skirt.

'I know you've had a shock, Peter,' I say.

He flicks a wary glance towards the suitcase.

'I'd appreciate it if you could talk me through what happened. I'll take a few notes – it's procedure. You'll need to make an official statement later, though.' I nod encouragingly at him. 'Off you go, in your own words. Tell me what happened.'

'Right,' he says, and pauses, thinking about what to say. I like that sort of witness. They tend to be clearer in their stories. His accent is a creamy drawl. 'I packed up the car this morning at about five-thirty to come and fish. I like to go somewhere different every week, you know, and sure this seemed as good a place as any.'

'And you got here at what time?'

He rubs the bridge of his nose, his hand trembling, and I feel sorry for him. He's only a young lad. 'Maybe nine or thereabouts,' he finally says. 'I don't know for sure. And when I got here, I was on my own and I set up the rods. Put the flies on them, that sort of thing. Do you fish yourself, Guard?'

'I don't, no.'

'Aw, 'tis great for the head, like.' There is a silence after that, as if he's suddenly realising that fishing will be changed for him now. 'Anyway,' he goes on, after a bit, 'I fish for a while, like hours, you know, and sure the going is slow. It's probably the hot weather – the levels are very low in the rivers and that. Anyway, then I cast out, a bit further this time, and with a different hook on the line and I feel this weight. Now, I knew it wasn't a fish because there was no to-ing and fro-ing like you'd have with a fish, but I also knew now that it wasn't a rock because it was coming in with the line, very slow, mind you. So, anyway, I'm reeling it in and I decide to lift the rod up in the air, to get a look at what I have and sure, I seen a suitcase. I got a quare shock, I can tell you. But then the line snapped, and I thought, well, I had two choices, continue fishing or ring yourselves. I did try to go in after it but I couldn't find it. And it was suspicious, I thought. So I rang Achill station and that lad there,' he points to a tall, skinny guy, with a rapidly reddening bare back, standing just beyond the cordon – Kev Deasy, I realise, 'he arrived out and he just stripped off, down to his boxers and dived right in. It took him no time at all to find the case. Then he made me get out of the way while he opened it. I never saw a fellow go as white and then I looked and . . .' His voice trails off and he shakes his head. 'It's a terrible thing.'

14

'It is.' I ask him some questions about who he saw and what he saw, but the body looks as if it's been in the water for at least a few days if not weeks, so it's unlikely he saw anything of significance. Finally, he gives me his contact details and stands up.

'Thanks, Peter, we'll be in touch.'

After he leaves, I stagger to my feet and move towards Kev. 'That was some find.'

He trots towards me. 'Poor kid,' is all he says, his usual sunniness damped. 'Can you imagine doing that to anyone?'

'Have you sun cream on?' I ask.

He bats the question away. 'I tan, so no need. Will William be heading up this investigation again, Luce? Would you say he'd let me on the team?'

I'd say he's top choice. He'd been the surprise find of our last investigation, smart as a whip, able to look at things and turn them upside down. I smile. 'If you get a shirt, maybe.'

He beams. 'I'll go and find one.'

'I never knew you could dive.'

'I've been swimming in lakes since I was a kid. My mother used to call me Flipper.'

I splutter out a laugh and he grins good-naturedly.

I scan the area for Dan and spot him with William some way off. William is staring out across the lake, hands in his pockets. To the casual observer, he seems relaxed, but I know from experience that he's taking in every aspect of the scene. The man has an almost photographic memory for detail.

'I'll go and talk to the Cig,' I say to Kev. 'Sort out the incident room, see you back at the station.'

'Sure thing.'

★★★

15

'Hey, Cig,' I say, picking my way towards him in my bare feet, shoes in my hand, 'I didn't see you when I arrived.'

'I was talking to the SOCO team. Christ, I can't believe Kev Deasy followed up on the phone call. Things must have been slow.'

'And hot.' I smile, then ask, 'Have you been allocated SIO on this?'

'I have. I want you and Dan on the team.'

'Great. Thanks, Cig.'

'We have a team of seven and—'

'Seven? You'll need more surely.'

'Sorry?' He looks startled at my interruption.

'You'd need ten people at least, wouldn't you?'

He doesn't answer, just lets the silence build and, like an eejit, I rush to fill it. 'That child deserves the best we can give her.'

'I agree. That's why I've put you on the case, Lucy.' His voice is steely. He seems to be avoiding my gaze, though.

Dan digs a finger into my back, a warning to leave it.

'Look, Cig, we have no ID, no idea when she was murdered, no idea where she was murdered, no motive, no murder weapon, and have you looked at this place? There's no CCTV. Anyone from anywhere could have put her in the lake at any time. The body could have been there months, years, we do not know. Also—'

'She's been there at max two months,' he says.

'What? Sorry?' Then I do the unforgivable: I laugh. 'And how do you figure that?'

There is a yelp from Dan, which we all ignore.

'Cig,' I tag on weakly at the end. Then, softer, with a lot more respect, 'How did you figure that, Cig?'

I'm not sure if it's amusement I see in his eyes, but probably not. 'I've seen bodies like that before,' he says. 'She's not bad enough to have been in the water longer than a couple of months. And from pressing Joe, he reckons that any decomposition in the body took place mostly in the water, so chances are you're looking at a two-month time span at most.' He offers me a quick smile, eyes flitting away from me again. 'That's my thinking on it, Lucy. Anything else?'

I swallow hard. 'No, Cig,' I say.

'Good. Get back to the station and see how they're doing with the incident room. We've also got Kev, if he doesn't die of sunstroke, Larry and Ben from Ballina – you worked with them on the last investigation. Larry's great on the CCTV. Ben'll be good if he takes his mind off his spectacularly awful ex-wife. Those Keystone Cops, Mick and Susan, from Ballina, seeing as you're their biggest fan. So, including you and Dan, that's seven.'

I ignore the barb about Mick and Susan: if he thought they were Keystone, he wouldn't have them on the team. One thing I like about the DI is he gives people a chance, and even though Mick and Susan had fecked up on a case in court a few years back and had been the butt of jokes for a while, he's slowly allowing them back in. Not many people would do that.

'And IRC?' I ask.

'Incident room co-ordinator will be Jim D'arcy. Also we'll use any of the regular lads who want to get involved. Jordy comes in useful now and again, even if he doesn't seem to give a fuck. Get cracking.'

'Will do.'

Then, sounding as uncomfortable as I've ever heard him, he

says, staring into the middle distance, 'You might want to put a jacket on for conference.'

I look down. Holy Jesus. My blouse is saturated. 'Yes, William.' With as much dignity as I can muster, I turn away. When we're out of sight, I thump Dan.

'Ow! What was that for?' He rubs his arm, looking wounded.

'You should have told me about my top.'

'I was going to offer you my jacket but then I thought, Naw, if you talk to William looking like that, he'll agree to give you whatever you want.'

'Piss off.'

He laughs all the way back to the car.

Chapter 4

The incident room is hopping that evening for the conference. Aside from the team, there are off-duty guards and detectives from other districts because murder is always big, and the death of a young woman in a bag in a lake is bigger still. And if it turns out that our victim is a minor, that'll affect us all. Galvanise us too, I hope.

The air is stifling. It reeks of heat and body odour and coffee. Dan opens a window, which makes zero difference.

The boards erected at the top of the room will be used to track the details of the investigation. They'll fill with information as the days go by. Kev has also secured a projector for us.

'Thanks for coming in on a bank holiday,' William says, standing up. He speaks quietly but there is almost instant silence. He has that rare air of command that I think will get him to the top in this job. He stands tall, hands in his pockets, and surveys the room. He's wearing the same suit he had on earlier but it doesn't look sweaty or wrinkled, and he appears totally relaxed and at ease. 'So, lads, before we give out the jobs, a word about the case. As all of you know, the body of what we believe to be a very young woman or child was found in a suitcase in the water at Lough Acorrymore earlier on today. As of now, we have no ID and establishing her identity will be our first priority because until we do, or unless we do, we will not make much progress in this investigation. Once ID has been established, a family liaison officer will need to be assigned. This work is vitally important so, no matter how tedious, do everything with focus. Do not attempt anything if you're tired or hung-over.' Someone titters and William eyeballs them. 'I mean that,' he says, and the guard, a young woman, flushes. William flicks a glance at Dan. 'Dan?'

Dan turns on the projector and an enlarged picture of our victim appears on the blank wall behind William. The quality of the photograph is good, detailed, so that you can see, even under the plastic sheeting, every wrinkle and fold in her skin. You can also see how small the IP is. Calling any victim of violence an IP – injured party – is, in my book, such a euphemism for what has been done to them. Still, I know that the image sears itself into the minds of all there, which, of course, is the point. William allows the picture to do the talking before he resumes: 'Very young IP, as you can see. We have as yet no idea how she died. The PM will take place tomorrow, Detective Sergeant Lucy Golden will attend along with Garda Susan Blake.'

There is a tiny yelp from halfway down the room, which is quickly suppressed. Susan. She looks desperately at her friend and sometime partner Mick, who pretends he doesn't notice. No one likes PMs, especially not the ones that Joe Palmer presides over. He seems to take pleasure in making his observers uncomfortable. Hardened medical students have walked out on him. The trick with Joe is to remain blank and unimpressed. I am unsure if Susan will be capable of that.

'Jim is IRC,' William is saying, 'and I'm SIO on the

investigation. *Senior. Investigating. Officer.*' He stresses the words. '*Everything* goes through us. Got that?' People nod and he turns to me. 'Lucy?'

I'm not one for the big speeches. When I was a child, I'd hide away at my own birthday parties, not enjoying being the centre of attention. The problem with promotion in the guards is that a certain amount of public speaking is a requirement of the job. And the importance of doing it right can't be underestimated. You have to be clear and concise in what you say, so there are no misunderstandings. You have to instil confidence, make people believe that you know what you're doing – which you do to a point. But you can never predict an investigation. Indeed, tunnel vision is a bloody dangerous thing. So, every crime is a trip into the unknown but with certain procedures that anchor you. Luck is involved more times than you care to admit but mostly it's down to solid police work and good communication. Before I begin, I take a look at the picture of our girl to steady myself. I can't let her down. She did not deserve that death.

'What we have here,' I say and, to my relief, my voice carries, 'is what looks like the murder of a young woman. We don't know her age but we can be certain of one thing. She died before her time. Someone is missing her. Someone is mourning her. As William said, we need to identify her as quickly as we can and give her family closure. And after that, we need to find out how she died, and if someone is responsible for her death, make sure they pay for it.'

My words fall into silence so deep that I think I've been too strong, but then I see Susan nodding and know that I've hit home. Sometimes you use the last-seen footage of the victim or videos of them laughing with their children to humanise them, to underline the point that this person is not just a statistic to be counted as a 'solve' or a 'live' at the end of the year but a living, breathing person who was loved. All we have to show of this girl is a picture of her battered body in a bag. But it's enough. 'Now, as William also said, it's important that we identify her. After the PM tomorrow, we should have a number of other avenues to pursue. Anyone who has some free time or time off and wishes to lend a hand to the investigation, they'd be very welcome. Our resources are low.'

William darts a look at me but I ignore him as I take my seat.

William stands again. 'The first thing we'll be checking is the missing-person bureau. The woman is white, no older than mid-twenties. Mick, you're on that. With any luck, tomorrow after the PM we'll have a bit more information for you.'

'Grand,' Mick says.

'Our victim was found in this.'

Dan puts up pictures of the suitcase, as it was when it was found and the version that was downloaded from a website. 'As you can see, it looks fairly new and preliminary enquiries reveal that it's a recent model and has only been on sale worldwide for the last two months. It is however reasonably priced and has proved a popular seller. We need a list of how many were sold, where they were sold and, if possible. who bought them. Kev, will you chase that up? Try to get credit-card details, CCTV if any. You know the drill.'

'Sure.' Kev doesn't sound as chirpy as normal. It might be due to the sunburn glowing beneath his blue shirt.

'We'll be showing the picture of the suitcase at the press conference tomorrow,' William adds, continuing, 'We've asked for any fingerprints found, either of the IP or of the suspected offender, to be fast-tracked, so once we get them, they'll be run through the AFIS in the hope we can identify her or the perpetrator.'

I doubt our girl would have been old enough to have her prints on the automatic fingerprint identification system. Still, in a case like this, you try everything. If we get prints from the SO though, they might be logged.

'Once we get DNA from the IP,' William continues, 'we can run it through the DNA database. Fingers crossed, we'll get a hit. Ben, you'll be chasing forensics.'

'Sure.'

'Door to door,' William says. 'As ye know there aren't too many houses up by Lough Acorrymore, but a car driving by late at night might have been noticed. Who's on that?'

A couple of regular lads put up their hands, including Matt, who was on the last investigation with us.

'Knock on every door. If people aren't in, knock again. If it's a holiday let, find out names of anyone who was in it in the last two months. I don't want any telephone detectives here, so talk to them all in person. Have you got me?'

The regulars on the door-to-door nod.

'We should have an image of our victim in the next day or two as well,' William says, 'and that, too, will be released to the press. Someone knows this girl. Larry, you're on CCTV if there is any. The body was put in the water no longer than two months ago. After tomorrow, we might have a tighter time frame. Whoever dumped her there knew that place. It was chosen because it was isolated, hidden from view by the cliffs. Joe Palmer reckons the IP was placed in the water not too long after she died. We need footage of cars driving late at night anywhere on the island but particularly up by the lough.'

Larry looks pained.

'I know. It won't be easy.'

We go through the rest of the jobs and give them out.

There's a shuffling of feet and a murmur of conversation as people get ready to go. 'One last thing,' William calls, and I brace myself for his speech about not assuming anything. I thought we'd got away with it and I groan inwardly. I don't think I'm the only one. Instead, he surprises us by saying, 'Go home, get some sleep, boys and girls, because I think you'll need it.'

The parade to the door begins.

'See you tomorrow, Lucy.' William pulls his jacket from the chair, pats his pockets to check for his phone and bids us goodbye, ending, 'Enjoy the PM.' A quick rare grin. 'Look after Susan.'

'Susan will be fine,' I say back. 'You really should have told her she was coming with me.'

'Not at all. It'll be good for her.' He dismisses my concern with a wave. 'I'll expect an update in the evening.'

'Sure,' I mumble.

After he leaves, it's just me and Dan in the empty room, which seems suddenly shabby and too hot. I gather up my files as Dan flicks off the projector. I need a lift home from him.

'I think the Cig has a bit of a soft spot for you,' Dan says, as we descend the stairs to the ground-floor hallway.

To the right there are doors to the front desk and the kitchen, while on the left, there are two interview rooms and the back door to the car park. I push it open and am hit by a wall of heat. 'That fella has no soft spots.'

'He would have gone through any other detective for a short cut if they'd looked at him and made a pointed remark about resources being tight.' Dan laughs as he unlocks the unmarked

24

district detective unit car and I slide into the passenger seat. These DDU cars are a bit shite but, right now, I'm so tired, it's a luxury to be driven in it.

'I didn't know I looked at him,' I lie, closing my eyes. The heat is bloody stifling. 'Anyway, so what? If we get extra people to volunteer on the case, that's what we need. That picture affected him, did you notice?'

'No, I did not. He barely glanced at it.' The car chugs to life and Dan flicks on the air-conditioner.

'Exactly,' I say. 'He didn't once look at it. Isn't that interesting?'

'It's bloody cold, if you ask me.' He pulls out of the station and takes the Keem road.

'I think he wasn't able to look at it.' Then, as Dan shoots me a look of disbelief, I go on. 'Think about earlier. You know what he's like on a scene – he's usually down by the body, looking around, talking to the SOCO team. This time he was up the rocks, out of the cordon, well away from it. I thought it was odd, but then I thought he was just taking it all in.'

'So, William has some kind of aversion to looking at dead bodies of young girls. That's not unusual.'

'He's a detective. It's his job to look at stuff like that.'

Dan says nothing and for a bit we just watch the road unfurl in front of us. We pass groups of people, families on holidays, youngsters down for the surfing, locals, all making their way back from their nights out. Laughter drifts on the air, as do drunken good-humoured voices. The moon cuts a perfect circle in a sky studded with stars. It has truly been a spectacular summer for the west. We don't get the sun that often here, but when we do, it's the best place to be. I turn back to Dan. 'He's an odd man, isn't he?'

25

'William?'

'Yes.'

'Understatement.' Dan laughs a bit. 'Why the interest?'

'No reason. I just can't figure him out.'

'No one can. Better off saving your energy for the case,' Dan says.

'Like, he's weird and brusque and dismissive, but he's also . . .' I try to think of the word '. . . kind,' is the best I can come up with. 'He was so good to you when you were in hospital back there last Christmas.'

'Yeah, he was pretty decent, and me being with Fran didn't seem to bother him.'

'Why should it? It's not his business.'

Dan says nothing. His sexuality has always been something he has hidden. William found out he was gay on our last case but has never told any of the others. I think Dan was hoping he would, so that he could finally come out. But obviously William is not a man for the water-cooler gossip. And unless Dan actually brings Fran out one night, the lads will never know.

'I think we'll ID this girl pretty quickly,' Dan interrupts my thoughts.

'Yeah.' I turn the air-conditioner up to the max. 'If she was transported down in a car, there's a car boot out there that will be DNA heaven if we can find it.'

He doesn't say the obvious, that the car could be well gone by now, crushed in a yard or burnt out. Or bleached. We just have to hope.

'And she's young. Most people would report a girl that young missing. She'll be on file somewhere.'

We lapse into silence once we reach Keel. Dan is not a fan

of the road from there to Keem because it's twisty and narrow and very, very high. Hanging-off-the-edge-of-a-mountain high. And in the dark, with maybe a sheep or two wandering about, it demands concentration. Eventually we come down off the height and I can sense Dan unwind, like the coils of a spring. 'You're not that far from the lake yourself here,' he remarks, as he pulls in outside my house, which faces the great Atlantic.

Before I have a chance to respond, my mother, who has obviously heard the car, appears in the doorway looking a bit agitated. What now?

'Talk tomorrow after the PM,' I say to Dan, as I climb out of the car. He gives a *bip* of the horn and, with a wave to me and my mother, he heads back along the road.

My mother comes up behind me. 'You'll never guess what happened,' she says. 'Rob was here.'

Chapter 5

On the kitchen table there is a small square parcel, tied with a thin pink bow. The card, which had been Sellotaped to it, lies open.

'It was addressed to Baby Golden, so I figured it was Sirocco,' Luc says.

'Good deduction.' I try for lightness, but end up sounding tense.

'Rob must have dropped it off while we were at the christening.' My mother states the obvious. 'Isn't he barred from contacting you?'

'What time did you get back?'

'About eight.' She momentarily forgets her distress as she adds, 'Johnny and Tani had a row, then Katherine gave out to Tani and she stormed off. It all got a bit uncomfortable so everyone started to leave.'

Normally I'd be nosy and ask for details but this visit from Rob, my con-man ex-husband, is too disturbing.

'Rob was here between three and eight, so.' I pick up the card. A picture of a contented baby in a pink frothy dress with the words 'Welcome to the world, Baby Girl'. Inside is written, in

Rob's flamboyant swirl, 'To my Grand-daughter – A Gift from Granddad Rob'. It brings me back to the last time I saw that writing. He'd sent me a letter from jail begging me to visit. I hadn't replied, so he'd sent another, which I hadn't even bothered to open. After five years or so, the letters had petered out. But he'd been released last year, having served his sentence and, according to a detective I know in Dublin, he was, a few months back, living just outside Castlebar. But as Rob isn't a sexual offender they can't keep tabs on him. So, despite his horrendous crime, fraud on a major scale, for which he showed no remorse, he's not monitored at all. I cannot believe that the man has had the nerve to come to my house when we were away and think it's all right to do so. 'How did he know we wouldn't be here?' I wonder, turning the card over and seeing the price sticker on the back. It was a euro. He must have got it in a bargain shop, the cheapskate.

'It might just have been chance.' My mother puts a cup of tea in front of me and a large slice of christening cake. 'I helped myself to it as we left,' she confides. 'That Katherine one thinks everyone eats as little as she does.'

I push the cake away. 'He wouldn't take that chance.' I know it to be true. 'Did you post anything on social media?' I ask Luc.

'Well, yeah,' he shrugs, 'course I did. It's, like, what you do.' He pulls my cake towards him and takes a large bite. 'I don't know how he saw it, though.'

'You should make your accounts private.' I'm tempted to add that I've told him this countless times, but I don't.

'I did.'

'What?'

'I made it private, like you said. Ages ago.'

That fact that he listened to me actually makes me speechless

29

for a second or two and he smirks cockily at me across the table. 'Can I open the present?'

'No, you cannot!' My mother is appalled. 'It's going straight back.' She snatches it out of his reach and he heaves a frustrated sigh. Luc loves presents.

'So, he's not in your social-media contacts?' I ask.

'Not unless he's set up a fake profile and I followed him by accident.'

'What? Do you make a habit of following strangers?'

'No. Anyone can take over profiles of people you know and pretend to be them so, like, they don't appear to be strangers. That might have happened.' He sounds spectacularly uncon-cerned. He turns to my mother. 'I'll give it back, but it'd be nice to know what's in it, wouldn't it?'

I'm curious too. 'I suppose it doesn't matter if we're giving it back.' Though giving it back might prove difficult as I do not want to interact with him.

'If you open that present, it'll be a slippery slope,' my mother warns ominously, placing the box on the table and moving to the other side of the kitchen, as if washing her hands of the whole thing.

Luc begins to pull away the Sellotape.

'Just rip it open,' I say. 'If he asks, we'll just say we opened the present before the card.'

From the corner my mother huffs out her disapproval.

Luc rips off the paper to reveal a small box, which he opens. He passes it across to me. It's the tiniest little gold Claddagh ring. Typical Rob, ridiculously impractical.

'Put that on a child and she'll choke on it.' I roll my eyes.

'He can't even pick out a decent baby present,' my mother says, as I snap the box closed.

'Excitement over.' Luc stands and stretches. 'I'm going to call Tani, find out how she is after the row with her parents. See you tomorrow.' He leaves for his bedroom, already dialling.

My mother waits until he's out of earshot, then slides in beside me. 'What'll you do? Isn't he supposed to stay away?'

'I'll see what I can find out about him,' I say. 'I'll get an address, post this back or something.' I go to the press, take out a ziplock bag and pop the card and the gift inside.

Evidence. Just in case.

Chapter 6 – Day 2

Susan and I meet just outside the hospital morgue at ten the following morning. She's tied her plaited hair to the top of her head and she looks about twelve. Tall and thin, she has a perpetually anxious expression. 'I don't mind admitting that this is probably the worst moment of my life,' she says, sounding desperate.

'Any time spent with Joe Palmer is pretty gruesome,' I joke a little. 'Throw in a dead body and it makes for top-ten bad times, all right.'

Susan laughs nervously before growing serious again, 'The poor girl, though. She had a horrible death.'

'Which is why we're going to go into that morgue, ignore Joe's barbs and do the best we can for her, OK?'

'Absolutely.' Susan takes a deep breath and hitches her shoulders back. 'Too right.'

'I wouldn't breathe that deeply in here.' Joe comes up behind her and she flinches. He laughs slightly. 'Right, let's crack on, ladies.' He swaggers up the steps of the morgue, without waiting for us, the door swinging back behind him.

We are suited, masked and gowned, and Susan and I have made

good use of the vapour rub provided, though I have found over the years that just breathing through your mouth is the best thing to do. Palmer had eschewed the rub, giving us the kind of look that says he hates dealing with amateurs.

By eleven, we're ready to get cracking. Susan is standing well back. She'll be bagging and labelling all the evidence we need to send to the lab for forensics. The chain of custody needs to be impeccable or the case could fall apart. There is a SOCO photographer in the room to document the process with good-quality pictures. And alongside Palmer is the APT, a lovely man who has assisted Palmer for years and takes all Palmer throws at him with a grain of salt.

The body is carefully removed from the suitcase. Susan labels the suitcase and asks for a full forensic examination. With the water, it might be hard to salvage anything.

Then Palmer begins the painstaking process of removing the plastic that the body is wrapped in. Slowly, he peels it back, taking his time, revealing the girl underneath. Then he pauses, moves in closer and, with tweezers, picks up a screw with two nuts attached. 'Curious. It must have fallen in.'

Susan bags it.

Once the plastic is removed and fingerprints taken, the body is exposed. The smell worsens and Susan turns away. Palmer gently lays the body on its back and stares down at it for what seems an eternity. Light bounces off the tiled walls, the floor and shiny surfaces, and I wait, resisting the urge to appear in any way impatient. I know he's assessing her. We're all perfectly still, no sound, focusing on the body of the girl, looking so small and pathetic that my heart twists again. The smell crawls through the room and I try to relax into it. Susan looks pale behind her mask and goggles.

And then Palmer starts logging every part of the body, from the top of the head to the tip of the toes. He notes the injuries and their location by marking up a blank body map pinned to the wall. He measures her height, taking notes. 'Unidentified young female, slight build, five foot, mid-length brown hair, looks to be her natural colour though obviously we'll double-check that. Severe bruising to the forehead, cheek and chin, suggestive of fractures. X-rays will give us more information – we'll be able to tell if any of these fractures were caused before or after death. We'll also be able to log any fractures she got during life and you can compare that to medical records.'

Thank you, I feel like saying. I do know how to do my job.

'Track marks on the arms, suggesting drug abuse – we'll run toxicology. Also, I'll hazard that she was in the water about three weeks to a month. Normally if a body is found in water, the level of decomposition is half that of dry land. But the water temperature at the moment at the lake is twenty-one degrees and the water levels are low, so decomposition would be further advanced than would be usual. There is no sign of adipocere – that's a waxy substance that develops in bodies in moist conditions after about three months of immersion. Not happened here.'

I could actually kiss him for that. Though even four weeks will be a tough solve.

After the first few minutes, after the shock of the smell and the image of the decomposed body, I usually find that I can accept what I'm seeing without becoming too engaged, but this time the body is so tiny that Palmer's probing and commenting and swab-taking seem so brutal. On he talks, his eyes taking in every inch of this person. Then slowly, painstakingly, he goes through every mark on the body, every bruise, every cut, their position on the body, the width, the depth. The rise and fall of his voice is almost hypnotic in the silent room.

'I'm going to turn the body, to have a look at the underside. A bit of help, please.' His assistant helps turn our IP onto her stomach. It's not easy: they have to be careful as they don't want to cause any damage to the body. It's decomposing rapidly now because it's out of the water. The vapour rub is not half strong enough and, from the corner of my eye, I see Susan gag.

Please don't let her get sick.

Once again, Palmer stands stock still and assesses the body. 'Interesting.' He points to the victim's head. 'I'll bet that's our fatal injury, but we can come back to it later.'

He parts the hair and there appears to be a sizeable gash to the head. 'It might have occurred post mortem,' he says. 'We'll know more when we X-ray her and open her up.'

It's then I notice the tear along one arm, as if a chunk has been cut out of it. 'What's that?'

Palmer ignores me. He likes to do things at his own pace. I know now he'll leave it until last. 'No birthmarks, no major scars. And, oh, look, a cutting in her skin.'

I bite my lip and ignore his baiting.

He bends in closer, gets a magnifying-glass. 'That piece of skin was cut out,' he says. 'The edges are far too clean to have been done by tearing or animals. I'd imagine it was done after death as it would have been too painful to do while she was still alive – a cut away as clean as that would not have been possible.' He stares at it for another second. 'It's cut almost down to the bone. Maybe a birthmark or tattoo was removed to stop ID,' he says. 'Though you'd imagine they would have taken the fingertips off if that were the case. We'll take some skin from the edge, see if we have anything of interest.' Then, with the help of his assistant, he flips her back onto her front and calls for his scalpel.

Susan closes her eyes.

Hours later, after he's had his egg and onion sandwiches and we watched his assistant sew the girl back up, he says, wiping a hand across his face, 'All right, here's my guess as to time of death, cause of death and age range. We'll need Kim, the forensic anthropologist, to examine the X-rays and she'll be back to you in a day or two with more precise information. For now, though, my interim report will say that we're looking at a young female, sexually active, murdered by blunt-force trauma to the back of the head, which caused her to pitch forward onto her face, smashing her forehead, nose and chin. It occurred sometime in the last four weeks. Her age is approximately anything between fourteen to maximum twenty-two. That will narrow down with Kim's report. For now, I'm basing that on the fact that her third molar – they're the teeth at the back of the mouth – well, the third molar hasn't come in yet. The first two are there all right. The third generally comes in between eighteen and twenty-two years of age.'

'Even if she's been using? Would that not slow things down?'

He rolls his eyes, sighs as if I've just asked the stupidest question in the world. 'How you live affects your bones, your body, your organs. It does not affect your teeth. They might decay and fall out, go brown, but they'll always grow on schedule more or less.'

'Thanks.' I ignore his patronising tone. 'When will Kim get to take a look?'

And I've annoyed him. 'When she takes a look,' he snaps, 'she'll call you. Now, if you'll excuse me, it's been a long day.' He turns his back on me, pulling off his mask.

Chapter 7

'He hates us, doesn't he?' Susan says, after we've dispatched all the evidence to the lab, with detailed instructions on what we want, adding that we want it as soon as possible, like everyone else. 'Like *really* hates us?'

We're in a deserted coffee shop, close to the hospital, having a much-needed coffee and sandwich, though Susan has eaten very little of hers. She looks at me glumly.

'He's a grumpy bastard. I wouldn't let it bother you. You didn't puke, that's the main thing.'

'No,' Susan says. 'I'm talking about the Cig. He hates me and Mick, doesn't he?'

I'm not quite sure how to respond to that, so I go for a lie. 'No! No! He likes you. Hasn't he put you on the team?'

Susan eyes me, then says, after a moment, 'I'd be a terrible guard if I didn't see that for the whopping fib it was.'

'Sorry.' I stare into my coffee, wondering about the best thing to say. 'Look,' I begin carefully, 'he's a strange man. And yes,' I admit, 'he seems to pick on you and Mick a little, but maybe it's because he wants to test you.'

Again, that shrewd look.

'And maybe,' I shrug, 'it's because he wants to punish you for messing up in court that time.'

'I knew it,' she says. 'Mick was like, nah, he's forgotten that, but he hasn't.'

'But,' I go on hastily, 'my advice, for what it's worth, is to suck it up. Don't complain. Your best answer to him is to get the job done and you did great today, Susan, you really did. And I'll tell him that.'

'Thanks,' she says. 'That's what you did, wasn't it?'

I flinch and she notices.

'Oh, Lucy, I – I'm sorry,' she leans across to me and knocks over her coffee, which spills across the table. One of the staff hurries over with a cloth, glares at us and, in silence, wipes up the puddle that results on the floor.

'I'll not replace that coffee,' she barks, standing up and stretching, making her back crack so loudly we both wince.

'Fine,' Susan agrees meekly. 'Understandable.'

A final glare before she stomps back up the length of the shop. I know now why we're the only customers in the place.

'I meant that remark as a compliment,' Susan says, as we sit down again. 'I really admire that—'

'It is what I did,' I say, interrupting her. 'I worked my arse off. I knew I was good. I knew that what happened with Rob was not my fault. And it was William gave me the chance to prove how I could handle a case. He's fair. You just have to work hard.' I concentrate on finishing my sandwich, not sure what more to say and feeling a little exposed. Even after all this time, I think, people still remember that I was the guard with the crooked husband. I was the guard who couldn't see what was right under her nose. It follows me about like a bad smell.

'And he'll notice that, will he?' Susan asks. 'If I work hard.'

'I'll make sure of it.'

'Thanks.' She offers me a smile. 'Being a guard is the only job I ever wanted, Lucy.'

'Me too, ever since I read Enid Blyton's Famous Five books.'

'Well, I've wanted this job ever since my mother was killed in a hit-and-run.'

Her honesty is brutal. I choke a little on my coffee.

'Sorry if that's too much information,' she says, but she doesn't sound sorry. She offers me a tissue. 'It's just the guards were great to us at the time. They cared and I was . . . well . . . I said I wanted to do that for people too.'

'And you will,' I say. 'We will. We'll ID this girl and bring her home to her family. Right?'

'Right.'

'But first,' I say, standing up and grabbing my bag, 'we'll go and get some decent coffee.'

The station is almost empty when I get back. It's been a longer day than I had anticipated. Dan, who has left for the evening, has sent me a text to tell me to call in to the Cig before I leave. *He'll fill you in.*

The office William uses when he's working from Achill has the light on, so I knock on the door and poke my head in. He's at his desk, his tie loosened, and the top button of his shirt open. He's rubbing his eyes with the heels of his hands and he looks knackered. He closes his laptop down. 'Come in, Lucy.' He indicates a chair in front of his desk, and I sit. 'Shoot,' he says.

I fill him in on what Susan and I had gathered today and the forensics we'd requested. He nods, showing his approval of the tests I'd asked for.

'Joe will send an interim report through for the morning conference,' I finish. 'And in a day or so, Kim will weigh in with her findings.'

'I'd press her for them,' William says.

'I will. Dan says you've to fill me in on something from today?'

'One lead. We've had a bit of luck. One of the regular lads on the house-to-house says that a Lugs Larkin, a blogger chap, was out and about around four in the morning on the fourth of July and was almost knocked down by a car speeding past.'

Pity it didn't, is my first very uncharitable thought. Lugs is the biggest shit-stirrer. He runs a blog called 'My Boring as Shit Life', which has thousands of followers.

'Apparently he always wanders about late at night, looking for news,' William rolls his eyes in amusement at the oddities of people on Achill. He's a Limerick man, born and bred, with that unmistakable inner-city Limerick accent. He grew up tough, I'd say. A bit like Dan.

'Did Lugs say what kind of a car it was?'

'A black one, apparently, which really narrows it down.' William allows himself a grim smile. 'But it had a Dublin reg and he blogged about – I quote – almost being run over by an ignorant bastard of a Dublin Jackeen.' William's smile grows. Everyone beyond the pale hates the Dubs, mainly because they've won the football All-Ireland a bunch of times. 'He also has a video of the car, not great quality, though. There's another up on his blog now that someone else posted, so we've got that too. I'd like you to re-interview him and get a proper account from him.'

'Well, the timing ties in with Palmer's estimate that she was only in the water about a month.'

'Yes, which is good. Of course, it might not be the car, but we can put a call out and whoever it is, if they come forward, we might be able to rule them out.'

'Anything else?'

'Not as yet.' William waves me away. 'I'll let you get on home. See you at the conference in the morning.'

'Sure thing, Cig.' I turn in the doorway, about to wish him a good-night, but he's already forgotten me, his laptop open again and a look of what I can only describe as unguarded grief on his face. I close the door quietly.

Chapter 8 – Sarah

Begging on the streets was not working out as good as she'd hoped. First off, it is really fucking hot and she wears a hoodie because she does not want to be recognised by anyone. She had the thought, a week or so ago, a sort of scary yet hopeful thought, that maybe people were out looking for her. So, she has to keep her head down and, as a result, all she sees is shoes. Big shoes, small shoes, shoes with bows, sparkles, lace-up shoes, Velcro-fastened shoes. Who knew there were so many fucking shoes in the world? And everyone walks different. Fast, slow, hopping along – that's mostly little children. And people are so bloody rude, they talk across her. Stand each side of her and flipping talk. One time, though, two men were mouthing about a business merger, whatever that was, and the fella with shiny shoes and red laces dropped an empty Tic Tac box on top of her.

'You dropped your rubbish on me,' she said, unable to stay quiet.

The two looked at her like she was from outer space. Then the man who dropped the rubbish just shrugged and they walked away.

'I know you plan to take over Hibernian,' she yelled. 'And that you're going to wait until the share prices drop before you make your move and that—'

They gave her ten euro to shut up. And an apology.

That was a good day.

She didn't have a clue what she'd even said. But it paid to listen, it paid to listen.

She becomes aware suddenly that a pair of tattered Converse trainers has come to a stop directly in front of her. Now, how will anyone bloody give her money if some eejit is standing in front of her? She's about to tell the owner of the Converse to 'do one' when the person crouches beside her. Peers into her face. It's a girl, younger than her, maybe about twelve, in a filthy T-shirt that might have been white once and a pair of cut-off denim shorts.

'You look hot,' the girl says. 'You should take off your hoodie.'

'Mind your own business.'

'I've sun cream you can use so you won't get burnt.' The girl holds a tube of lotion towards her. 'Your face is burnt.' Her voice is light and airy. But her eyes dart about, like little baby fish.

'Then it's too late for the sun cream, isn't it?' Sarah snaps.

'I guess.' Without asking, the girl sinks down beside her, legs splayed out. 'I ran away from my care home.'

'So?' Though Sarah gives her a sideways glance.

'I stole this sun cream, you know. I'm good at shoplifting.' She makes it sound like she's good at playing the piano. 'We could team up.'

'No.'

'I'm Jenny.'

'I'm not interested.'

Jenny laughs. 'Fine.' Then she stops, as if it hadn't been a real laugh at all. And she doesn't move away. She just stays sitting there. Then, after a bit, she says, 'I picked you because you don't look high.'

Aside from Bernie, Sarah hasn't talked to anyone in two whole weeks. And she doesn't talk to Bernie: Bernie talks to her. And in two whole weeks, she hasn't touched anyone. This whole town is alive with sunshine and music and loudness and she has stood apart, watching it through a veil. Watching it trapped in her own head.

She sneaks another glance at the girl beside her. She's a tiny kid with a scared face, trying to look brave. Like her on the inside.

'I'm not high,' she says then, and it's like an understanding unfurls between them.

They both sit until the sun goes down, without speaking,

Chapter 9 – Day 3

The next morning, after the conference, Dan and I drive to interview Lugs. He lives in Bunacurry, so the route would tie in with anyone coming from the lough and leaving the island.

It's another stifling hot day – the air-conditioner in the car isn't really up to the job.

'I'm actually cooking,' Dan says, and I laugh.

He flicks a glance at me and asks, 'What's happened? You were a bit off in the conference this morning.'

I was hoping no one had noticed but, of course, Dan had. We've worked together for the last number of years and know one another pretty well at this stage. So, I tell him about Rob and his present, and of how I don't quite know how to handle it.

'Does he scare you?' Dan asks.

'No.' Then. 'At least, I don't think so, though I haven't seen him in a decade. Prison could have knocked the *faux*-sophistication out of him.'

'Look, pull over and I'll take the wheel. We've another while before we reach Lugs's place. You make a few calls, see what you can find out.'

I pull the car into a lay-by and switch places with Dan, grateful for the offer. Working a case leaves you very little time to have any personal life, never mind trying to sort it out. 'Thanks, Dan.'

'Aw, it's just the excuse I need to drive a car of this class.' We both snigger. DDU cars are not known for their glamour, though they have all the bells and whistles police technology.

As Dan pulls out, earning a blast of a horn from someone breaking the speed limit, I dial Peter Casey, the arresting detective in Rob's case. He was the one who told me Rob was in Castlebar so maybe he'll know more, though I'm sure if Rob had moved to Achill or Newport, Peter would have called to let me know.

'Lucy,' he says warmly, when he picks up the phone. 'How's it going? I see William is on another case down there with you. It's becoming a bit of a habit, isn't it?'

'If the gougers didn't come from all over the country to commit the crimes, there'd be no habit at all,' I say back.

'Ouch!' He laughs. 'So, you're not looking for a local, then?'

'I don't know, really,' I admit. 'But who I am looking for is Rob. Would you have any idea where he's got to? He dropped a present outside the house over the weekend.'

'Really?' Now he sounds like a guard. 'When was this?'

'Saturday. Me, Mam and Luc were out at a christening. He must have known somehow. And he also knows where I live too.'

'That's not hard, small place down there, and you did get a bit of a profile after your last case.'

A bit of a profile is understating it. The arrest of the Night Caller was big news. The media had nicknamed him that because he'd stalked and murdered young women who only ever tried to help him. I still get chills when I remember his impassive way of explaining his reasoning for the awful things he'd done. There was no remorse. He's in the Central Mental Hospital now, hoping to plead guilty but insane. He wasn't insane: he was pure evil.

'Is Rob still in Castlebar?'

'I don't know. The quickest way might be to ask the lads in the station there. They might have an idea. He's not monitored, Lucy.'

I hesitate and he gets it. 'All right, look, I've a few minutes free, I'll give them a call for you.'

'Thanks, Peter.' I don't want anyone to know I'm asking these questions. And news travels faster in the west than it does anywhere else.

'No bother. Keep the phone with you.'

He hangs up and I fill Dan in.

Then talk turns to other, smaller, cases we're working on.

We have just pulled up in front of Lugs's semi-derelict bungalow when Peter rings back. 'Lucy,' he sounds a little flustered, 'I have to rush off but, anyway, I rang the lads in Castlebar. I was talking to the sergeant there, Philip McCabe – d'you know him?'

'I do.'

'He dispatched a guard to check on the address I gave him and he confirmed that, yes, Robert is still living there. The guard reported that he was invited in, offered coffee and shown some of Robert's photographs.'

'How civilised.'

'He just said he was there doing a community visit, checking for problems in the locality. Anyway, that's your update.'

'And his address?'

'Aw, Lucy, you know I can't give you that even if I had it.' There's a moment's pause. 'But he's having a photographic

47

exhibition in the Ace gallery in Westport on Wednesday, the first of September.'

'Good to know. Thanks, Peter.' I hang up and look at Dan. 'He's still in Castlebar. If I can get his address, I can send the present back.'

'You might be better off ignoring it. If he stopped writing when he was in prison because you didn't respond, it might be the way to go.'

I've thought of that, but the truth is I'm too damn mad to consider it. 'If it was just me, I would, Dan, but it makes me so furious that he thinks he can come to my house and use Luc and Sirocco as an excuse to leave a present. He knows he's not welcome and he just came anyway.'

'Yes, but—'

'No.' I shake my head. 'This is one thing he won't get away with.' I open my door. 'Coming?'

Dan joins me on the path in front of Lugs's place. 'Let's go, boss.'

Chapter 10

Lugs Larkin's house is chock-a-block with newspapers, maga-
zines, books. They tower in the hallway; they block the entrance
to the kitchen; they teeter dangerously in piles against the wall.
Cats of various hues, sitting on top of the books, regard us dis-
passionately as we squeeze by. Lugs makes no attempt to explain
his chaotic surroundings as he shows me and Dan to the front
room.

'Sit down,' he says, as he seats himself on a surprisingly clear
leather chair. As Dan and I busy ourselves removing copious
amounts of paper from the other two chairs in the room, Lugs
says, 'I only keep the one nearest the telly clear. I don't get many
visitors so I've no call to use those two. I was thinking of selling
them. Do any of ye need a chair?'

'Not just now,' Dan says pleasantly.

'Are you from Dublin?' Lugs asks, recognising Dan's accent.

'I am. Dublin city. Why?'

Lugs makes a face, shrugs. 'No reason. Is this about the car I
saw that night, up on the main road there?'

'It is,' I say, as Dan takes out his notebook.

Lugs manages to confirm for us that it was definitely 4 July,

MARTINA MURPHY

that the car was average-sized and was either blue or black. And that it was speeding.

It's not much more than the door-to-door got from him yesterday.

'All right, Lugs,' I say. 'I'd like you to close your eyes.' At his questioning look, I add, 'We find it helps people remember things they think they've forgotten. We use it on important witnesses.'

He likes that. If he was a peacock, he'd have spread his tail feathers. He snaps his eyes closed.

'Good. Now, just relax, take it easy. We'll start with your morning routine. What did you do on the morning of the third of July?'

'What I always do.' He settles back in his chair, his hands folded on his lap, like he's sunning himself. 'I fed me cats.'

Dan covers his mouth to stop himself laughing.

I let him ramble on, colouring in his day. After a while, we are at four in the morning.

'I'm walking back from the town, turning up the road. It's warm, a really warm night, and then I . . .' His voice hitches, like he's remembered something. 'I see the lights of the car first. They're unusual, I think.'

'Describe them to me.'

'There's a stripe of lights running down the front of the bonnet. It looks great but then I have to jump into the ditch because the car careers along the road.'

'Describe the driver.'

'It's a man. A large man. There's someone in the passenger seat too. Then they're gone.'

'Describe the back of the car.'

'Red lights on either side. I took a video.'

'Can you see the registration number?'

'Just a 'D' for Dublin.'

'All right. That's great, Lugs.'

'Can I open my eyes now?'

'Yes. Describe those lights to me again.'

'I'll draw them for you.'

Without a bother, he reaches behind him and extracts a note-pad and a pen from the tower of rubbish on the table. Then he bends his head, tongue protruding out of the side of his mouth as he sketches. After about five minutes, having studied it, having looked at it from all angles, he tears the page from the notepad and hands it to me.

'That was what it was like coming towards me. I only took the video from behind.'

'Oh, those headlights are quite distinctive,' I murmur. 'Would you sign and date this for me, Lugs?'

He does.

It'll go into Exhibits.

I stand up. 'Thanks for your time.'

'No bother.' He stands now, too, and walks us through his obstacle course to the front door.

'If you think of anything or if anyone else posts on your blog about this car, will you let us know?'

'I will indeed.' A second, then he says, 'I hope ye catch the fecker that did it. The murder of a young girl is a terrible thing.'

'Thanks, Lugs, we'll do our best.'

Chapter 11

We have given a working copy of Lugs's sketch to Larry, who is currently studying another video that was posted on Lugs's blog. 'It's not a large car,' Larry tells us, 'if you study the distance between the front and rear wheels. And, look, some kind of fancy alloys.' He zeros in on a small section of video. 'I'll make that clearer, get a better image, and send it to the various companies. It's possible we'll be able to ID the car based on the wheel base, tyre size, alloys and that sketch.' He studies the drawing. 'Lugs could give up the blogging and become an artist,' he says.

'Thanks, Larry. See what you can find out by the next conference.'

Dan and I have just sat down to a cup of coffee in the kitchen when my phone rings. I glance at the screen. It's Kim. That was quick. She's the forensic anthropologist and a joy to deal with, despite her passion for bones and skeletons. She also has a thing for Dan, which makes me feel sorry for her.

I press the screen. 'Kim, hi,' I say. 'I'm putting you on speaker. Dan's with me.'

'Hey, Dan,' she says, 'how's life?'

'Grand, Kim, yourself?'

'Aw, sure, I won't complain. Who'd listen?'

'A shrink if you paid him enough, I suppose,' Dan jokes, and she laughs. 'What have you got for us?'

'Now that is a dangerous question.' She chortles, and as Dan obligingly laughs along, I glare at him. If Kim ever finds out he's gay, she'll be mortified, I'd say.

'I've got quite a bit for you,' she says then. 'You're lucky I had nothing much on so I got stuck in with your IP. I'm going to send you over a copy of the X-rays and my preliminary report tomorrow afternoon, but I thought I'd ring and go through it with you so you'll have it for the next conference.'

'Great stuff,' Dan says. 'Shoot.'

'Right, well, the bones were in great condition. Not there that long, you see. And well preserved in that bag. So, I know Palmer gave you an age range of fourteen to twenty-two, based on the teeth, but I'd narrow it down to fourteen or fifteen and that's based on a more in-depth look at the teeth, because the third molar hadn't even shown itself, really. Now, I won't get all techie on you, but just to say that the clavicle, or shoulder blade, is the last bone to stop growing. And by growing, I mean that all parts of the bones fuse together. You know that ad that used to be on the telly – I think it was for milk and it said, "A child's got more bones than a grown-up's got"?'

'Yep,' Dan says.

'Well, that's true, and what happens is that children's bones fuse as they get older. It's how they grow. Like the tibia in a small child is in five parts. In an adult, it's in one part. So, in our girl's skeleton, the clavicle wasn't yet fully fused. In most people it happens by around twenty-one years of age. So we know she wasn't twenty-two. Now, the tibia, the bone I was talking about

53

– they're the long bones in the legs and generally stop developing at around sixteen to seventeen years of age. The tibia of this girl was barely there. So, I'd say she was no more than fifteen.'

I swallow hard. The poor kid.

'I also found, on the X-ray, evidence of a broken ankle. This occurred most likely in childhood – you can tell because when a bone breaks, new bone grows to repair it and this bone is very evident if you know what to look for. The ankle injury was well healed. What wasn't so well healed was a recent break to the collarbone, not terribly bad but enough to cause a bit of pain. I'd imagine that this occurred some weeks before death, six maybe, at a guess. Now, as to the cause of death, Palmer was right. It was a blow to the head with a blunt instrument. It occurred perimortem, because when I examined the skull, there was no attempt by the bone to repair itself, and because the edges of the bone were cleanly broken, I can say with confidence it occurred at the time of death. That's in contrast to the broken cheekbones, which must have happened while she was in the water – with that break, you can see clearly that the bone was dry, that is, not alive when it happened.'

She pauses to draw breath, then launches in again.

'Now, it was blunt-force trauma because in the X-rays of injuries like that, there tends to be radiating concentric fracture lines and we have them on this skull. There are also bone flakes at the edges. In the skeleton itself, there was no evidence of any disease, so a healthy girl, except, of course, for slight tooth decay. But I understand Toxicology will confirm if it could be drug-related. There you go.'

'That's fantastic, Kim.' Dan has been recording her. He'll take notes for the meeting in the morning, then delete the recording. 'You'll send the written report through at some point?'

'Yes. I'm finishing up for the day here. Good luck with the case.'

'Thanks, enjoy your evening.'

She hangs up, and as I finish my coffee, Dan transcribes the information into his notebook.

'Give Mick a shout,' I tell Dan. 'Ask him to narrow down his missing-people search to fourteen-to-seventeen-year-old girls. Then tell him to ring the parents of those girls and ask if they had any broken bones as a child. Tell him to rope in Susan as well.'

'On it.' Dan starts to dial.

'And tell Ben to chase up the DNA on the bones.'

'Will do.'

We're getting closer.

Chapter 12

After I part ways with Dan, refusing an offer of dinner at his place, I stay in the station, talking to Jim and William about jobs for the following day.

By the time I finally leave it's after nine and I just want to take it easy while I can. The journey home is dominated by my fantasy of a glass of red wine, sipped at leisure in a bath full of bubbles, followed by a rom-com on Netflix. And, a little voice says, googling the art gallery where Rob is having his show.

But as I get out of the car, the shrill scream of a baby pierces the air.

What the hell?

In the hallway Luc is trying to comfort a very disgruntled Sirocco as she howls the place down. My mother has her arms around Tani, who seems to be having a bit of a meltdown too.

I feel like a stranger in my own house. Is it the weekend? Is it Luc's day for the baby? Before I can ask, Luc holds the baby towards me and I've taken her from him. She's all arms and legs, thrashing against me. She's harder to restrain than a suspect.

'You two go and get a coffee for yourselves, loves. We'll manage here,' my mother says to Luc and Tani.

'Thanks, Nanny.' Tani gives a tearful sniff and I gawp.

'Since when has she called you Nanny?' I whisper, as I try to take my jacket off while holding Sirocco hostage against my body.

'Since today,' my mother says. 'Jesus, give me the child – you'll drop her.' She takes the baby from me and I'm glad. I've never been a natural with babies. I like them when they can talk and tell me what's wrong.

'Isn't it a bit late for Tani to be here?' I throw my jacket over the chair by the hall door. It was originally bought for a 'pop of interest'. Now it's just a make-do coat-stand. I pull a funny face at Sirocco, who, I fancy, teeters on the edge of a laugh but opts for a shriek.

'Sirocco has come to visit us for a while and so has Tani.' My mother directs this to the baby, speaking in a high-pitched voice. Sirocco coos gummily. 'They arrived today in a taxi with all of their things and they've set up in Luc's bedroom.'

For a second I think I've misheard. 'They've moved in?'

'I didn't call you about it because of that murder you're solving. Isn't this place going to the dogs altogether? Murders everywhere you look.'

I ignore her attempt to change the subject. 'Why have they moved in?'

'I'm not exactly sure,' my mother confides. 'Tani was very upset and I got nothing out of her. She just told me she was moving out as she couldn't live at home. Luc said she had her reasons and for me to leave it and, sure, well, we have to trust him, don't we?'

'Do we?'

My mother looks at me in disappointment. 'It's up to you,

Lucy, but as far as I'm concerned, it'd be an act of cruelty to send Tani or Sirocco back to that house if it makes them miserable. Tani says the christening was the last straw.'

'Everyone fights with their parents – you can't just take off. They'll want her back.'

'Katherine came today. Started off all calm and civilised. But then, when Tani refused to leave and said she preferred living here, Katherine started shouting and asking her what she could possibly like about living here, which I thought was a bit of a cheek. Poor Luc was caught in the middle, God love him – he's not used to rows, is he? I tried to stay out of it, but after a bit, I had to tell Katherine to leave. You were lucky you were off trying to solve your murder, Lucy. I thought you'd have another one here by the time you came back.'

Solving a murder is probably going to be easier than dealing with the Egans, I think.

Luc looks uneasy as I come into the kitchen but he shifts a little nearer to Tani, protecting her or looking for protection, I can't quite figure out. She swipes a tear from her face and tries to pretend she wasn't crying.

That decides me.

I slide into a seat opposite the two of them. In the doorway my mother hugs a calmed Sirocco. 'Here's the deal,' I say. 'Tani, you and Sirocco are welcome here but you need to sort things out with your parents.'

'I can't,' she says. 'It's not up to me.' Then, on a gulp, 'It really isn't.' Then, 'Thanks. I know you're real busy and important and all but we won't get in your way.'

I suppress a smile. Go for the hard bit. 'And while I love

Sirocco,' I eyeball the two of them, 'I do not need another grand-child, thank you, so a bit of responsibility would go a long way.'

'Jesus. Ma.' Luc looks appalled.

'Fine,' Tani agrees. 'Thank you, Lucy.'

'And, Luc?'

'Jesus. What?' He's mortified, the tips of his ears bright red.

'Clean up that room of yours or the baby won't stand a chance.'

My piece said, I take a bottle of wine from the press, bring it out of the kitchen and into the dining room. My mother puts the baby down to sleep and joins me.

We clink glasses, and just when I think I can finally relax, she says, 'I heard Lugs Larkin is helping ye crack the case.'

Chapter 13 – Sarah

'Oh, Sarah, you've found a friend,' Bernie from the shelter says, when she arrives with soup the next evening.

Bernie is too jolly. It's like she's trying to be all motherly but doesn't know how. At least Sarah's own mother doesn't even try to fake it. She just sits smoking weed and picking up men and asking Sarah to do stuff for her. The only time she ever smiles is when a man pays her attention. Sarah hates men. She distrusts smiles. But then again, Sarah has a deep distrust of the human race in general.

Jenny hasn't lost that shine yet, Sarah thinks. One day she will. Everyone does. It just takes longer for some people.

'What age are you, love?' Bernie asks Jenny, while simultaneously offering Sarah a bread roll.

As Sarah tears apart the bread, Jenny answers, 'Nineteen.'

It's such a whopper of a lie that Sarah almost laughs aloud.

'You look younger,' Bernie says.

'Everyone tells me that,' Jenny replies.

Give the girl credit, she doesn't bat an eyelid. Sarah admires her for it.

Bernie digs into a pocket of her coat and hands Jenny a card. 'This one,' she thumbs to Sarah, 'isn't interested, but here's the directions to our shelter. It's just around the corner from here. You can come in for a hot meal at six and there are beds available most nights too. We provide breakfast in the morning.'

'Shelters are shite,' Sarah speaks up.

'With respect, Sarah,' Bernie is always patient, another thing Sarah hates about her, 'you haven't seen ours.' She turns back to Jenny. 'It's just a year old and it's really clean and safe.'

Jenny examines the card. 'A hot meal?'

'Yes.' Bernie says, 'and if you come, try and get your friend to tag along.'

'We're not friends.' Sarah crams the rest of the roll into her mouth and lies down, closing her eyes.

'Have you been on the streets a long time?' Bernie asks Jenny.

She is a nosy cow, so she is, Sarah thinks.

'Years,' Jenny says. Then, 'My dad killed my mother and he's in jail and my nanny took me in but she died and then I was in court for stealing only I didn't. And then I was put in care by the court so now that I'm nineteen I'm free.'

It sounds like she rehearsed it.

'And have you no relatives, love?'

'Nope.'

'Keep that card,' Bernie says, standing up. 'I'll see ye around.'

Sarah hears her climb into the van that bears the logo of the shelter and roaring off.

'I'm actually twelve,' Jenny says.

'I fucking know that, dumbo,' Sarah half grins in the dark.

'My dad did kill my ma,' she says.

'Don't mistake me for Oprah.'

After that Jenny says nothing.

Good, because Sarah doesn't need anyone to take care of.

Chapter 14 – Day 4

The following morning, having not slept a wink because of Sirocco crying on and off all night, I'm early for the conference. It's blessedly quiet in the station as it only opens to the public from ten. It's eight thirty now and soon the other detectives and guards will start arriving for the updates and to receive the job sheets for the day.

Larry and Ben are first, quickly followed by Mick, Kev, who looks dreadful, then Susan, a few of the regular lads, Dan, who takes a seat beside me, and, finally, William. He sits down on the other side of me, and I'm not sure if I imagine it, but he smells of drink. I glance sharply at him but he's busy wrestling with the sleeves of a light jacket. When he's done, he turns to the room, 'Right, Dan, can you go through Kim's findings, please?'

Dan stands up and relays what Kim told us the day before. 'To sum up, we have a fourteen- to fifteen-year-old victim, a possible drug-user, who had a broken ankle in childhood and an injury to her collarbone within the last few weeks of her life. She was killed by blunt-force trauma to the head.'

'Larry?' William looks to Larry.

Larry unfolds himself from his chair. At six foot six he is the tallest man in the room. He's also probably the broadest and the best-looking. I used to have a bit of a thing for him until I realised that he was not good partner material. A total man's man, the drinker, the pool player, the cigar smoker, the boys' poker nights out, a chaser of women. There was no soft, fuzzy side to Larry. He was a dogged detective, though, a much-sought-after CCTV specialist. 'Right,' he says, 'I've sent images of our car out and the lads hope to be back with the marque later today. Once we have that, I'll send it out to the car company and, hopefully, we'll get a model number. I also managed to get a partial registration of 221 D.' A grin. 'I managed to get that last night. I'm also looking at any other CCTV footage from the third and fourth of July along the route that the car probably took. At the very least, if nothing else, we'll be able to rule it out of our enquiries.'

Beside Larry, I see Jordy opening up a bag of toffees. He offers one to Mick, who accepts.

'Good work, Larry,' William says. 'Mick?'

Mick's head jerks up. He's mid-chew on Jordy's toffee. 'Sorry, eh, sorry, well, actually we had . . .' Chew, chew, chew. 'We went through all the missing . . .' He begins to splutter a bit, then cough.

'Sit the fuck down and finish off that toffee,' William snaps, rolling his eyes.

Susan's hand shoots up. 'I'll do the report,' she says. 'Mick didn't know he'd be next so you caught him by surprise.'

There's a bit of a gasp in the room. Beside me, Dan's shoulders start to shake. I think he's laughing.

William says nothing for a moment as Susan stays standing, her face getting a little redder.

William leans back in his seat. 'Off you go, then,' he says, with deep sarcasm.

This better be good, Susan, I think.

'Right. Well, Mick and I spent yesterday searching missing persons. We had nothing much to go on because we had no ID and the age range was massive. Then Lucy rang and asked us to narrow it down to fourteen-to-seventeen-year-old girls of which there were eight. We rang the contacts we had on all eight, which was hard going,' Mick nods along, 'but unfortunately none of those missing girls had broken their ankles as children.'

'You found out nothing, then,' William snaps.

'We found out that our IP was never reported missing.' Mick gets up now, toffee chewed. 'We'll have another look over it again, just in case we missed something.'

'I hope you haven't.' There's a warning note in William's voice and Mick swallows.

'We're pretty sure we haven't,' Mick says.

'Good work, guys,' I say, before William can get another crack in. He shifts in his seat but says nothing. It's a puzzle, though. Who would not report a missing fourteen-year-old girl? Maybe her circumstances were chaotic. But still . . . 'Ben, has the DNA on the bones come back?' I ask.

'Expected early today, Lucy.'

'Kev?' William says. He loves Kev.

Kev stands up. His shirt is sticking to him. He begins by going through what we already know about the suitcase.

'Excuse me,' William says. 'What the hell is wrong with your shirt?'

Kev goes redder than the sunburn that glows from under the

THE BRANDED

fabric. Beside him, one of the regular lads sniggers. 'Eh . . . nothing,' he says lamely.

'It's sticking to you. Have you a fever?' William barks.

'No, I, eh . . . Well, I got a bit burnt there the other day, like, and my mother said that natural yogurt is good for getting rid of the soreness and healing it and that . . .' He trails off as the room explodes with laughter. 'Fuck off,' he says, glaring around.

'You have yogurt on your skin and you put a shirt over it?' William is a bit dismayed at his little star. 'For God's sake, change after this meeting and get some after-sun or something normal. Jesus.'

'After-sun has chemicals, Cig, and—'

'You will not work with yogurt plastered all over your chest. Have you got me?'

Kev nods miserably. 'Yes, Cig.'

'Just get on with the report,' William huffs.

He's in a worse mood than normal.

'Right, well, I contacted the manufacturer of the suitcase,' Kev begins.

'Was that before or after you plastered yourself in yogurt?' Matt, one of the regular lads, calls and the room breaks up again.

'Enough.' William fights a smile, I think. 'Kev?'

'As I was saying,' Kev goes on, with a bit of grit, 'I contacted the suitcase manufacturer and they said that, yes, the suitcase went on sale here in early June. To date, they have sold two hundred. I asked how many did they sell between June and the fourth of July, and they said eighty.' A look up at us. 'I'm working on the same timeline as Larry for the dates. So I'm currently getting a list of shops where those cases were sold and I'll call up the managers and see if we can get payment details on anyone who bought one. And CCTV, if possible.'

'Hopefully, it wasn't purchased online,' William says. 'Stay with that today, Kev. All right, door-to-door?'

There is nothing to report on that.

And the phone lines have been eerily quiet.

'Let's hope that car proves to be the one,' William says, 'and that it wasn't just some tourist no one bothered to arrest for drink-driving.' He turns to me and Dan. 'We'll need to make a hell of a lot more progress if we're to ID this young girl. Jim will give out the jobs for today.' With that, he stands up abruptly and stalks out of the room.

It's as if we all let out our breath collectively.

Chapter 15

William pokes his head around the office door about noon. I'm helping Kev with the suitcase part of the enquiry and have just hung up on a shop that sold three. They have promised to look through their receipts to see if they can identify who bought the bags and when. 'It's the only thing that's priced ninety-five euro and eighty cent in the shop,' the chirpy sales assistant says. 'It'll be easy to find on the system.'

'I need someone alongside me in the press briefing today,' William says, hulking over me. 'Come on. I'll drive.'

No 'please' or 'thank you'. I bristle as I follow him to the car park. And he knows how I hate press conferences: I find it hard to keep my face impassive while we're questioned by people who are only looking for a story. Any story. It doesn't matter what that story is: win or fail, they've got their headline. They don't care about the victim.

'You just have to stand beside me and look serious,' he says. 'I'll do the talking.' He looks me up and down. 'You're presentable,' he says.

'As are you, Cig,' I say, and a small tic starts up at the side of his mouth.

Sitting alongside him in the car, I realise he has economy of movement that is almost graceful. The way he changes gears, the way he flicks glances at his mirrors, the way he accelerates. It's all done with such efficiency. He probably lives his life like that too.

As he indicates to go towards the lough, he says, 'We need to get an appeal out there, especially if what Mick says is true and there has been no young girl reported missing. Jesus Christ, who wouldn't report their child missing?'

He sounds incredibly sad about it and I wonder if the job is getting to him.

'Are you all right?' I risk asking.

He doesn't answer but I see his jaw tighten and he gives a stiff nod.

We say no more until he pulls the car into a small lay-by and we climb out to the waiting media.

It's in the middle of the conference, as William is outlining the case and appealing for witnesses to come forward, that my phone rings.

It is loud and shrill and stops William in his tracks.

Shit! I never turned it off.

William resumes talking after first indicating that I should take the call, though I can't miss the annoyance in his eyes. I walk off a little distance, turning my back on the group.

'Mick,' I hiss, 'what the hell? I'm at a press conference with the Cig.'

'Oh, shit.' Mick sounds dismayed. 'Does he know it was me on the phone? Oh, God, what—'

'No, he doesn't. Go on.'

'I did try to get Dan, but he was talking to Larry,' Mick sounds excited, 'so I thought I'd ring you. We might have an ID.'

Chapter 16

'Mick says the DNA database has thrown up a close-relative hit,' I tell William, as we drive back to the station. 'A James Devine. We think he could be a brother of our IP. He's from Pearse Grove, off Pearse Street in Dublin, and was imprisoned for five years in 2019 along with another man, Denis Dunne, for aggravated burglary. James got out six months ago after serving three years. They stole some jewellery, which was never recovered. Used a lot of violence. James hasn't come to our attention since.'

'Family?'

'A mother and a sister, Abby, whose age matches our IP. I told Mick to check James Devine's social media for any images of Abby or to see if she has any social-media pages herself.'

He nods. 'I want to know everything about James Devine and who this girl is before we go informing relatives.'

The file on James Devine is slim: he's only ever been in trouble once, but it was serious aggravated burglary. A woman, living on her own, was beaten until she opened her safe where her jewellery was kept. Denis Dunne took a necklace and, by all accounts, James got everything else. He was eighteen at the time. The jewellery was never recovered, James and Denis both testifying that they had sold it on.

James's mugshot shows a skinny boy with sticky-out ears and dark hair. His face is pale and long and he reminds me of a vampire. His eyes are dark brown with a sullen expression. His features seem not unlike those of our victim. Both small, both thin, both dark. Both with the same DNA. Abby, it turns out, has an Instagram account and her features could be a match for our IP. And, more tellingly, she hasn't posted in months.

According to the regular lads in Dublin, whom Ben contacted, James and Abby both live with their mother in a house in Dublin's city centre, though they don't believe there has been any sign of Abby in the last while. She has never been reported missing, though.

William tells me and Dan to get on the road. 'If any leads come up, I'll call in a favour or two from the boys in Pearse Street to help where they can. I know you'll be arriving just as bad news may be broken to a grieving mother, but you have to strike as soon as possible. Do it before they can react.'

And, though it sounds ruthless, it's the best way to solve cases. Catch people off guard.

Chapter 17

Dublin is more than three hours away, most of it motorway. It's fascinating to see the scrubby, boggy landscape change to a lush green, though there is a lot of parched dry land, too. In the car, the heat builds until we're driving with the air-conditioner up full blast. As we near the city centre, I let down the window on my side of the car and am immediately assailed by the traffic fumes as they lie heavy in the heat. I'd forgotten that about the city: I've spent so long in the freshness of the west, in its wide expanses, that I have no love left for this place, with its constant noise and bustle. When we arrive at the house, there is already a garda car parked outside.

Dan raises his eyebrows and makes a face.

'Give it ten minutes,' I say. I hate this part of the job, talking to the newly bereaved. No matter how many times I've had to do it, it never gets any easier. This girl was younger than Luc. As we wait, I study the house. You can tell a lot about people from their home, both inside and out. This one is functional. Two up, two down. It has a small front garden, grass cut, no flowers. A knocker. Clean but not polished to a high shine. Blinds on the windows. No car. Driveway with no weeds. This is a house

71

where people do what they have to do, where there are no frip-peries because there just isn't time for that.

Ten minutes later, Dan and I are on the doorstep. The family liaison officer, or FLO, comes to the door and steps outside. 'Miriam,' she introduces herself. 'You're the detectives from Mayo?'

'That's right. How are they?' I ask, in an undertone.

'It's just the mother. I'm trying to get hold of her son. She's absolutely distraught, as you can imagine.'

'Is she up to talking?'

'I think so. Go on in. I'll get some tea.'

The front door opens onto a small parlour. Miriam crosses into the kitchen. The two guards, a man and a woman, very young, are perched uneasily on a blue sofa. They are out of their depth with the grief in the room. Mrs Devine glances up as we enter. 'Have you come to ask me questions?' She looks ravaged.

'Yes. I'm so sorry for your loss.' And yet, I'm thinking, why on earth was your girl never reported missing?

She takes a moment before covering her eyes with a hand and beginning to shake. It's like the truth is slowly pouring into her, waking her body up, so the shaking grows more violent. Finally, an anguished cry splits her open. Miriam hurries back in, looks at the four of us staring uselessly at this broken woman. I desperately want to comfort her, but I also have to question her.

Miriam waits until the moaning softens and the shaking subsides, before placing her hand on the woman and just sitting with her, then finally saying, 'The detectives have some questions for you, Mary, if you're up to them.'

Dan gives a signal for the two guards to leave and they jump up, dying to get away but at the same time not wanting to appear too eager.

'We'll be off, Mary,' the female guard says.

She doesn't acknowledge them and they throw painful looks in our direction as they disappear out of the door.

Dan and I take their seats. We wait. Dan pulls out his notebook. We wait some more.

'I'll get that tea now,' Miriam says. 'All right, Mary?'

'Yes,' Mrs Devine says, though I don't think she even understands what's being said to her.

As Miriam bustles out, we allow some more silence to develop. Eventually I begin, 'Mary, as I said, I'm so sorry for your loss. We're almost sure it's Abby's body but you will have to identify her.'

'Yes.'

'We'll arrange that for you.'

Her gaze meets mine, but her face is blank with shock and I continue with well-worn words I've said too many times before: 'Detective Garda Brown and I, we want to catch the person who did this to Abby and get justice for you and your family.'

Her voice a whisper: 'The other two, they said she was murdered? That girl found in the suitcase, the one on the news?'

'Suitcase, yes.' Her accent isn't inner-city Dub.

'Oh, my God.' A silent tear slips out. A wave of permission. 'Then ask your questions.'

'All right, and I'm sorry if any questions upset you. We're just trying to do our job.'

'They won't upset me as much as this news has.' The honesty is devastating.

In that moment, Miriam reappears with four mugs of tea, one for each of us. 'I took the liberty of putting milk in for everyone,' she says, handing them out. 'Here you go, Mary. Even just hold it, it'll make you feel better.'

Mary takes the mug, one with a picture of a red balloon on it, and wraps her hands around it, like she's holding on to a life buoy. In contrast to her son and daughter, she's a stocky woman, small with a round face that looks as if it has seen a lot of hardship. Lines are etched deep.

'When was the last time you saw Abby?' I ask her, after a moment.

She physically gathers herself before answering. 'May sometime. Early May.'

'Three months ago, then?'

'Yes. Abby was always going off and coming back. She was my daughter and I loved her. God knows, I loved her with every part of me, but . . . she, well, she was a bit wild. She was taking drugs and she'd disappear for ages on me. I never knew where she was half the time.' Her voice fades.

'When did she start using?'

'I don't know. It sort of crept up on me.' She swallows her grief and adds, 'She was the sweetest little girl once. But easily led, you know. Easily led.' The words cause her to break down again. 'I don't know if it was my fault. Did I not give her confidence or—'

'You did your best, I'm sure,' Miriam says.

'You say she was missing for three months?'

'Yes, but I didn't think – oh, God.'

'Were there any tensions, problems at home before she left?'

'No.' Too fast, too abrupt. But she makes no attempt to change it. 'No,' she says again, softer. 'No tensions. James had got out of prison a couple of months before but that was the only change. And he's doing well. He's got a job.'

'So . . . nothing that you think might have triggered her running off?'

74

A moment. I'm not sure what it is – hesitation maybe? Or perhaps she's just thinking. Then, with a shake of the head, almost as if she's denying it to herself, 'No. Like I said, she had a habit of disappearing.'

'Was there anyone who might wish her harm?'

'I barely knew what was going on in her life. She had no friends around here any more, I know that.'

'Anyone who'd wish you harm?'

'No. My husband is long gone. He's not in the country.'

'We'll double-check that anyway,' I say. 'And James? Any enemies there?'

'I don't know. You'll have to ask him. But I doubt it.'

'Any names she mentioned? Who would she be likely to talk to?'

She gives us a couple of names, then says, 'She has a lot of pictures in her room. I can show you photographs. Her room was full of them.'

'That'd be helpful. We'll have guards who will come and examine her room later on, if that's all right?'

She nods.

'Did she have a mobile phone or a laptop?'

'Just a phone. She took it with her.' She gives us the number without prompting.

'Did you ever try to contact Abby after she went missing?'

'Yes, but she would never answer the phone to me. And then it just . . . died.' She stumbles on the word.

'And you never thought, after three months, to report her missing?'

'I just didn't think she was,' she says. 'I thought she was holed up somewhere. Abby could take care of herself.'

'Only she couldn't, Mary,' I say gently. I say it not to be cruel but to try to prise out whatever she's keeping from us. People keep things from us because they think it's not important, because they think it has no bearing on a case, but that's our job to decide.

She raises her hand to fend off my words, but I want them to hit her hard. Why would a mother not contact the police if she hadn't heard from her daughter in three months? Something's missing here.

'Mary, do you know who killed your daughter?'

'No. No. If I did I'd tell you.'

'Do you have any suspicions on who killed your daughter?'

She raises her head and looks at me. 'No.' It's like the slam of a door. We won't get anything from her just yet. I think she's protecting someone and the only person people tend to protect in cases like this is their child.

The front door opens and slams. A young man stands in the doorway. He glances at us before hunkering down in front of his mother, taking one of her hands in his. She flinches slightly.

'Ma, it's all right,' he says, rubbing her hand. 'I'm here. It's all right.' He turns to us. 'Are yous the guards?'

'Sorry to hear about your sister,' Dan says.

'Ta.'

'Is there anywhere we can talk to you?' I say. 'Your mother has had enough for now. Perhaps you can help fill in some gaps.'

'Right now?'

'The sooner the better,' Dan says. He turns to Mary. 'Miriam will stay with you until all this is over. We might need to come back and ask a few more questions. In the meantime, if you can think of any reason why she left or where she might have gone, can you let us know?' He hands her his card. 'Anytime,' he says, with meaning. He turns to James. 'Maybe we could talk in the kitchen.'

James, looking a little fearful, I think, stands up. 'This way.'

We follow him into a tiny kitchen that just about fits the three of us. It's a tired room, brown, uninspired but as tidy as the living room. There are no pictures here and the door has a hole in it, like it was kicked.

'Bad dent in the door there,' Dan remarks.

'Yeah.' James leans against the worktop and takes out a cigarette. Lighting up, he asks, 'What do you want to know?'

His head is shaved, his eyebrow pierced. He looks at the two of us, blinking rapidly.

'When was the last time you saw your sister?'

A small pause. 'End of April, before she left. She was always going missing.' He takes a drag on the cigarette, pulling the smoke right down into him.

'How would you know that? I believe you were only released from prison in March.'

'I do talk to my ma. She did visit me in prison. That's how I know.' The words are spat at us. He takes another drag on the cigarette, his foot tapping out a beat on the floor. He's as edgy as hell.

'How was Abby in the days before she disappeared?'

'Grand.'

'Do you know if she had any enemies?'

'I hardly knew her, like you just pointed out. She never came to see me in prison – Ma didn't like her being in there.'

'Do you have any enemies, James?'

'No.'

'None from prison?'

'I was never in trouble in prison. I steered clear of all that. That robbery . . .' he shrugs, takes a saucer from the press and stubs his cigarette out on it '. . . that robbery was a big mistake. I never should have done it.'

'Do you know any reason why your sister would end up in County Mayo?'

'No.' A pause. 'I don't have to talk to you, sure I don't.'

'No, but seeing as your sister was found murdered, I'd assume that you'd want to.'

Eyes blazing, he leans towards me. 'I have nothing to tell you. It's awful, course it is, but I have nothing that can help.'

'Did you or your mother not think to report your sister missing when you hadn't seen her for months?'

'We didn't think she was missing, did we?'

'After three months? She was fifteen.'

'There are a lot of kids on the streets out there,' he says. 'But you wouldn't know that, being from the country and all.' A snort. 'I'm done here. I'm going in to me ma.' He leaves the kitchen.

'That went well,' Dan says wryly.

'He's wary of us,' I say. 'It's the mother we need to talk to. She's the key to getting the truth. I'll have a word with Miriam.'

Chapter 18

After Miriam promises to do her best, we decide to canvass the homeless shelters in Dublin as Abby must have stayed somewhere when she was off grid. While we wait for some images to be ready, Dan grabs us a coffee and we sit outside the print shop, in the sunshine. The city is heaving.

'D'you ever miss it?' Dan asks, apropos of nothing. He waves a hand about. 'All this?'

He means Dublin. The city. The vibe.

'I thought I did, but no. You?'

'Nah, not really.' Then, softer, 'Though I will say it's easier to be gay and anonymous up here.'

He's eyeing me as if he wants me to say something. 'Maybe,' I answer, after a bit. 'But you haven't exactly given the lads in the station a chance. They might be grand about it.'

He laughs, but it's sceptical. 'I am afraid of very little, Luce, except what Larry Lynch might have to say about my choice of partner.'

'Larry's all mouth.' I wait a moment, then ask, 'You thinking about telling them?'

'Maybe. Not sure how to go about it.'

'Trust me, you'll find a way.'

'Shit.' Dan laughs again, then changes the subject, swirling his coffee around, staring into his cup. 'James is lying his hole off, as is his mother. They have extra information they're not sharing. Though whether it's for the same reason, who knows?'

Obviously our little personal moment is over.

'I agree,' I say. 'So, let's see what we have. A murder, no doubt. Brother a convicted violent criminal. Mother protecting someone, most likely the brother. A black car, maybe. We've been told by James and his mother that she left the house late April, early May. Her body ended up on Achill three months later. We estimate she's dead one month so she must have spent the previous two months somewhere. She had to be around Dublin at some point.'

'She also broke her collarbone in that time.'

'That's right.'

'And whoever did it wasn't local. Chances are Lugs Larkin would probably have recognised a local driving that car.'

'Someone who visits, then,' I say.

'Someone who knew the land. That lough is not the most obvious dumping ground, but if the water levels had been high, it would have been genius.'

Dan's phone bleeps. Our pictures of Abby are ready.

Time to do some good old-fashioned legwork.

James was right about one thing, I think, a few hours later: Dublin has a horrifying amount of young homeless people. They all have their patch, their safe doorway, or their place out in the open, picked because it has maximum footfall. Some are reasonably dressed. Others' clothes are held together by a thread.

Addicts and the mentally unwell and the ones who just want to be alone. Dan and I talk to as many as will talk to us, showing them Abby's picture. Did they see her? Did they see anyone like her? It's around three by the time we meet Carla. A woman in her thirties who sits on the Ha'penny Bridge wearing a brown T-shirt with the slogan 'Say "No" to Global Warming' and a pair of indecent shorts. Her feet sparkle in glittery sandals. She sees me looking. 'A girl's got to have something pretty,' she snaps, almost defensively. She's skinny as a bamboo shoot with too much dreadlocked hair framing a tiny face. In front of her is a sign that says, 'Please help. Money for a shelter needed.'

'They're pretty sandals,' I say, and am rewarded with a half-smile.

Dan shows her the photo of Abby.

She squints hard at it. 'Yeah, I think I seen her a couple of times. Is her name Abby?'

'Yes. Whereabouts did you see her?'

'Moore Street. I mainly remember her 'cause she looked so young. She used to stay in the shelter there. The nice one. "Home", it's called.'

'When would be the last time you saw her? Can you remember?'

'I don't know one day from the next, luv.'

'OK,' I say. 'The last time you saw her, was it hot? Had the heatwave begun?'

'No.'

So, she hasn't seen her in the last five weeks.

'Do you remember if you talked to her?'

'One time. She was a bit high. She was saying she was robbed – I don't know if I believed her.'

'Did she say what was stolen from her?'

81

'Didn't ask. You'll always get stories like that, luv. But she seemed real upset.' Then a thought strikes her. 'She was holding her arm too, like it was sore. Think she said she might go to a hospital.'

I take a note of that. 'Was she dealing to your knowledge?'

'I never knew if she was.'

'Did she say who robbed her?'

'No.'

'You say she stayed in a shelter on Moore Street?'

'I think so. I seen her coming out of there one morning.'

'Who did she buy her drugs from?'

Carla looks wary. A shrug. 'Dunno.' Then, reluctantly, 'They all have their patch.'

It's the closest we'll get.

'Thanks,' we both say together.

She shrugs.

'If we need to talk to you again, Carla, where would we find you?'

She laughs, a bitter sound, showing a mouthful of rotting teeth. 'Here, luv. I'm going nowhere.'

Dan throws some cash into her bowl.

'Isn't that police bribery?' she yells after us, and laughs.

The Moore Street Home shelter, which looks better than your average shelter, is only open from six in the evening. There is a phone number taped to the door, which Dan rings.

'I'll be right over,' a man's voice says, from the other end. 'I'm just in the Ilac. Hang on there now and I'll meet you outside the shelter.'

In less than ten minutes we spot a tall, youngish man pushing through the Moore Street throng. It's changed a bit, this street, since I lived in Dublin. It's still full of stalls and heavy with the smell of overripe fruit, but it seems more commercial now, less authentic.

'I'm Gareth,' the man says, holding out his hand, which we shake. It's a strong grip. Solid. He looks like a sixties throwback with the dreadlocks, the tie-dyed T-shirt and cotton shorts. His sandals are made of some kind of cloth. 'What can I do for ye?' He's all homespun charm and good looks. Straight teeth and smooth skin. His grin is sure and lazy. 'You're interested in the shelter, is that right?' The sunlight behind him makes a halo of his hair. He looks a bit like a modern Jesus.

'That's right. We're up from Mayo. Anywhere we can talk?'

'Sure.' Gareth pulls some keys from his pocket and unlocks the door. 'Your timing was good. The dinner-time volunteers will be here shortly. Come in.' Even the way he walks is pop-star nonchalant.

While he switches off the alarm, Dan and I take in the small reception area. It's clean, painted beige with brown tiles on the floor. A wooden counter runs opposite the door. To the right a narrow staircase leads, I suppose, to the bedrooms. A door to the left of the reception desk must go to the kitchens. It has a vaguely institutional smell of toilets and bleach, but there's also the aroma of food mixed in. Soup and stew mainly. Behind the reception desk is a picture. I cross towards it. It shows about fifteen people, all happily waving at the camera.

'They're our volunteers,' Gareth says. 'Most of them have been with us ages. The four in front, dressed up, are members of the board. And that,' he points to another picture, 'is an aerial view of our newest centre down your way in Westport. We're celebrating being a year old in a few days' time.'

'Congratulations,' I say. I've seen that shelter. It's never too busy – Westport isn't coming down with homeless kids. I turn again to the picture of the volunteers. Most are young, three men, one of whom looks half terrified to be in the picture, and about thirteen women. 'We'll need names and contact details for your volunteers so we can talk to them.'

'Eh . . . right.' He makes a face. 'Is that legal?'

'Yes.'

'Can you tell me what's going on?'

'If we could sit down?'

'Sure.' He indicates the door to the left. 'Let's go in here.' He leads the way.

The room hosts a small serving area behind which is the kitchen. Three long tables with benches fill the rest of the space.

'Nice,' I say.

'It's tight,' Gareth admits, 'but we try to serve as many people as possible. The volunteers come in at four to start prepping for dinner and the soup. We do a soup run to rough sleepers each night. Can I get yez tea? There might be a few biscuits left back there too.'

The B-word does it for us. While Gareth busies himself making tea and grabbing a packet of biscuits from the press, Dan and I sit at one of the long tables. This room is cheerier than the reception area. There's a window that faces onto the street. It's barred from the outside but still lets in plenty of light. A few inspirational framed posters hang at intervals along the wall. 'Only YOU Can Save Yourself' and 'Make your friends the family you wish you had.'

Dan pokes his finger into his mouth and pretends to puke as I glare at him to stop.

'Nice posters,' Dan calls out to Gareth.

84

Gareth hands Dan and me a cup of tea each and lays sugar and milk on the table. 'Biscuits are a bit stale but edible,' he says, putting down a half-finished packet. Then, turning a chair around, he sits, elbows resting on the back. 'What's this about?'

'We have reason to believe that this girl stayed here. Do you recognise her?' Dan shows him a picture of Abby.

Gareth takes it and studies it, frowning. Finally he says, 'No.' A shrug. 'But that's a nice picture. She might not have looked so good when I saw her.'

He has a point.

'We have a witness says she stayed here.'

'She could have. Some stay a couple of nights, some stay up to four weeks. I don't remember them all. We have a log book, though – you can check in that.'

'That'd be great.'

Gareth glances at his watch. 'It's ten to four. The dinner volunteers will be in soon so we have to hurry. What dates do you need?'

Dan tells him and we follow him back to Reception. He flicks on a computer and it hums and whirrs as it boots up. 'Ancient thing,' he says. 'Now, where were we?' He bends over the keyboard and presses some buttons, and soon we have printouts of sign-in sheets for various nights. 'Sorry it's not more streamlined,' he says. He studies the pages. 'What's her name?'

'Abby Devine.'

'Oh, yeah, she was here quite a few times, actually. The last time was the seventh of June. She might have stayed in other shelters, too, though we do keep places here especially for the younger homeless. It's a bit safer for them. Then we try to hook them up with social workers, the usual. Is this girl in trouble?'

'She was murdered,' Dan says, 'so anything else you remember would be very helpful.'

Gareth pales, opens his mouth to talk but shuts it again.

We bid him goodbye.

Chapter 19

Helped by the local drugs-unit sergeant in Store Street, Dan and I manage to trace a number of Moore Street dealers. They're mostly young with track-marked arms. They wear the 'narco bling' of the criminal youth, expensive tracksuits, watches and runners. They won't talk. They've been so long dealing with the guards, they know their rights, and they know they don't have to say anything. We get nowhere.

'Who's the guy that runs them?' I ask Janet, the sergeant.

'You won't get anything from him,' she says. 'And he's out of the country at the minute.'

That's that, then.

'Was Abby Devine ever on your radar for possession?' I ask, already knowing the answer. If she was, it would have been one of the first things we found out.

'No. Whatever got that girl killed, it wasn't her involvement in the drug trade, not to my knowledge anyway.'

'Thanks. And is there anyone we can talk to about James Devine? Who dealt with his case?'

'I'll find out for you, and get someone to ring you,' she promises, as she takes our numbers.

***

I brief William at about eleven that night. He's still in his office. 'We've asked the local imagery unit to assist,' I say. 'They know who has CCTV in the Moore Street area inside out. And we'll need people up there to carry out interviews with the volunteers and Abby's friends and that.'

'I've already been on to the lad I know up there. He says he can give us a small team to carry out the minor Dublin interviews. He'll send a DS down to brief us on progress in the next couple of days.'

'Anything happen here today?'

'Nothing as yet. Mick and Susan are working on contacting hospitals in Dublin to see if anyone remembers a young girl coming in with the same type of collarbone injury our IP had. It's an important job so keep an eye on those two. Don't let them fuck it up.'

'Thanks, Cig, they'll welcome the challenge.'

He rolls his eyes and dismisses me with a wave.

In the car park, my phone rings. It's Miriam. 'Lucy, Mary Devine was wondering if she could come down, have a look at where Abby was found.' She hesitates. 'I think it might help her talk to us.'

My heart hops a bit. So, she has information. 'When was she wanting to come?'

'Day after tomorrow.'

'I'll be here. See you then.'

Chapter 20 – Sarah

Jenny wasn't lying when she said she was a good thief, Sarah thinks. Her expertise is in shoplifting and pickpocketing.

'My mother taught me,' she says, as she throws a wallet on top of Sarah. 'She says every girl needs a skill.'

The wallet contains fifty quid in cash along with two credit cards.

'They're good for tapping,' Jenny slides down to sit beside Sarah, 'but, like, if you're caught on CCTV using them, you're fucked.'

Sarah nods, taking the cash and throwing the wallet and cards into the river behind her. 'We can buy chips,' she says.

'Or we can save the money for something better and get free food in the shelter,' Jenny suggests.

'No.'

'And a proper bed and a breakfast.'

'No.'

'Why not?' Jenny sounds like she might cry. She's been at this since Bernie brought them some left-over dinner a night back.

'Because I said so.'

'You're not the boss of me.'

'You go if you want.'

'I do want. It might be good.'

'Let me tell you about shelters.' Sarah leans towards her and Jenny pulls away. 'They're full of people on drugs, dangerous people who come into your room at night and try to do stuff to you. And—'

'Did that happen to you?'

'No.' She says it a moment too late.

Jenny, very wisely, doesn't comment. Instead, she says, 'This shelter, we all have our own room. We can lock our doors, Bernie says.'

'And you trust her, do you?' When has she been talking to Bernie?

'Yeah. She's nice, don't you think?'

Sarah doesn't know what she thinks. She doesn't know what nice is.

'You are so negative.'

'And you're only twelve. Grow up.'

'I've had bad stuff happen to me, but I don't think everyone is horrible.'

Is that what she thinks of her? Sarah wonders. 'I don't think everyone is horrible,' Sarah says. 'Just . . . not . . .' She can't find the words. Instead she swallows an unexpected lump in her throat. Jesus, what is wrong with her?

Jenny jumps up. She is so tiny, like a small bird or something. 'Well, I'm going to get dinner in it.' Defiantly, she nods at the fifty in Sarah's hand. 'Go buy your chips. I'll see you later.'

Sarah watches as she walks away, her fine brown hair swishing about her shoulders, her legs as skinny as a pair of pencils.

Aw, fuck it, she thinks. She can't let the stupid idiot go on her own.

Chapter 21 – Day 6

Two days later, at eleven in the morning, Mary Devine arrives in Achill with Miriam. I'm going to accompany them out to Lough Acorrymore. Just before we leave, I pick up my notebook and pen, hoping that along the way Mary Devine might open up about what was really going on in her house, because something was. And when people see the last place their loved ones were killed or buried, it loosens something inside them. Secret-keeping is seen as futile, and anger can take over, the need for justice. Come on, Mary, I think.

Even in the two days since I've seen her, the woman has caved in on herself. She walks slowly, stooped over as if she's been given a blow to her solar plexus, which, I suppose, in a way she has. Her clothes and general appearance have an air of shabby neglect. She and Miriam follow me to the car and take the back seats.

'The scene was preserved until yesterday,' I tell her, as I fire the engine. 'It's open to the public now, but we've restricted traffic today until you've been there. That way, you can be on your own.'

'Thank you.' A whisper.

I drive out of the station, car windows down, because this

car has crap air-conditioning, and take the Keel road to Lough Acorrymore. The island couldn't look more beautiful than it does today under the cobalt blue sky. The land stretches brown every which way, some of the bog cut, most of it left to grow back into the wild bogland it was for thousands of years. In front of us, the mountains rise and we drive towards them, taking a small, twisting road, with room enough for one car, up and up and finally down to the car park by the side of the lake. A guard allows us to park once he sees it's me. We are the only vehicle there, aside from the garda car, and as we step out, the peace of the place wraps itself around us, like a blanket. In front of us stretches the lake, still as a mirror, and rising, on every side, the mountains, lit by sun and shade. Beyond the mountains, the muted crash of the Atlantic.

Mary peers around with bewildered eyes. 'Here?' she says.

'This way.' I lead her towards the exact spot, the one where the fisherman was. We cross the small bridge that marks the dam. 'Just here.' I point. 'The fisherman was standing here when he felt a tug on his line. She was out there in the lake. Because of the weather, the water levels were very low. It's normally a lot deeper.'

Mary stands on the spot and stares out over the lake. Miriam and I take a respectful step back.

After a bit, Mary says softly, 'It's a nice place to be found. Nicer than if she was dumped in a bin or you know . . .' She trails off. 'It's peaceful, isn't it?'

'Yes,' I say.

'She liked nice things and places,' Mary says. 'She would have liked here.'

I swallow hard. Christ . . . I blink back tears.

'We'll be in the car if you need us,' Miriam says, and we move off.

In the car we watch Mary as she remains motionless, memorising this place, imprinting it on her mind. Even from a distance you can see how broken she is.

'What's your impression of her and James?' I ask Miriam.

'Mary loved Abby, I have no doubt. I'd imagine if she thought she was missing for real, she would have reported it. As for James,' she shrugs, 'he seems genuinely fond of his mother but he's already committed one violent crime so . . . I wouldn't trust him.'

'I got the impression when I interviewed her that she was afraid of him.'

'Afraid of getting him into trouble, I think.'

We watch as Mary starts back towards us. Miriam gets out and opens the door for her. She settles herself into the seat.

'Thank you,' she says, and means it.

I take my chance, turning around and eyeballing her. 'We really want to find out who did this, Mary. I promise you we'll give it all we have.'

Tears stand out, bright in her eyes.

'But if people aren't honest with us, it will hold us up. I'm not saying we won't find out things anyway, but it'll take longer and who knows what damage that may do?'

An imperceptible stillness in her now. A wariness, wondering where this is going.

'We rely on information, Mary, to do our job, and right now, despite everything, we don't have enough so if you know anything that might help us, then, please, tell me.'

She can't meet my eye.

'There was a reason you didn't report your daughter missing, Mary. What was it?'

'I told you. I. . .I didn't think she was missing.'

Miriam shoots me a warning look.

And then it clicks. Christ, it's so bloody obvious. Miriam said it herself. 'Was it because you thought reporting it would get either Abby or James into trouble?'

And there it is. Like a shining coin winking in the sunlight. That look. That flinch, like I've pinched her. 'Who would have got into trouble if you'd reported your daughter missing, Mary?'

It takes a second or two but then her expression crumples. 'He did nothing. I know he – he would never . . .' She brings a hand to her mouth and shakes her head, tears bright. 'He would never,' she says. 'And I couldn't tell on her . . . because . . . no.' Tears fall. 'No,' she whispers, 'no.'

'It's our job to prove who did it,' I say. 'No matter what you tell us, if it doesn't pan out, we have to let it go. You have to trust us, Mary.'

It's a long time coming, the silence stretches so that I can hardly bear it. But finally, 'I do trust you,' she says.

'Then come back to the station and tell me the full story,' I say. 'I promise you we'll tread carefully.'

'I thought I was doing the right thing, but now . . .'

Miriam places her hand over Mary's. 'Telling us what you know is the right thing and it's never too late.'

I turn away and start the car. Sometimes, I think, it is too late.

In the station, I ask if anyone is free to come in with me to talk with Mary Devine. Dan, who is mid-conversation with a shop assistant over the suitcases, isn't available, but Ben, who has just hung up on the forensics lab, joins me at the door.

'They're really on the ball in there,' he says. 'A few things. First, d'you remember the way the skin was cut from Abby's arm?'

'Yep. Palmer took some skin from around the area in the PM.'

'That's right. Apparently, the edges of the skin had been burnt.'

'Like from a gunshot?'

'I said the same thing but was told they can't make assumptions.'

'Did you push them?'

'You know what it's like. He just said it was burnt, that the girl's arm was burnt. At a guess, they said, no, it wasn't a gunshot.'

Weird. 'All right. What else?'

'The next is interesting. Apparently ye found a screw with two nuts on it wrapped in the plastic?'

'That's right.'

'Now, they haven't been forensically tested yet, but according to one of the lads in the lab, who is into electronics, he said, and he wasn't swearing to it, that it looks like the bones of a variable tuning capacitor.'

'A what?'

Ben takes out his phone and hands me the results of a Google search. 'Here. It's for tuning up radios apparently. Only the real geeks bother to make them.'

It's a website with instructions on how to make your own radio set and the image of the tuning capacitor looks identical to what we found in the PM. 'Excellent.'

'Also,' Ben says, 'there were fibres and a strand of hair found on our victim's clothing. They messed up wrapping her in plastic. The fibres haven't been tested yet but the hair was from a male.'

'Has it been run through the database?'

'Nothing.'

That's as expected.

'And the pot of gold,' Ben waits a second, relishing the moment, 'a perfect fingerprint on the blood found on the plastic. The blood was Abby's but the fingerprint most definitely wasn't.'

'Now that's great.'

We resume walking.

'How's the mother bearing up?'

'Come on and see for yourself.'

Mary Devine barely looks at us as we enter. Her gaze is fixed on a glass of water she's clutching. There's an uneaten sandwich on the table in front of her, but it looks so unappetising that I'm not surprised she hasn't touched it. The crusts have shrivelled up in the heat. I introduce Ben and he shakes her hand and offers his condolences. Then he takes off his jacket, loosens his tie and undoes the top two buttons of his shirt.

'I can't take this bloody heat,' he says to her.

She manages a smile. 'It's been hot.'

We all agree that, yes, it has. Then I explain to her that we will take a witness statement from her. I read her the declaration at the top of the C.8 form: '"I hereby declare that this statement is true to the best of my knowledge and belief and that I make it knowing that if it is tendered in evidence I will be liable for prosecution if I state in it anything which I know to be false or do not believe to be true."' Putting it down, I ask, 'All right?'

'Yes.'

Ben gets ready to write.

'All right, Mary,' I say calmly, 'just take it from the top.'

She looks confused.

'Anywhere you think is best to start.'

She takes a sip of water, hands shaking. 'You know that my James was in jail for robbery, don't you?'

'Yes.'

'Well, oh, God . . .' She shuts her eyes. 'He'll kill me. Promise you won't go jumping to conclusions because this will make him look bad and he's not bad. He's really not.'

'I promise,' I say. 'In telling us, you're doing the best for your daughter. You're helping her.'

'I know but . . .' She sips some more water. Puts the glass down and steels herself. 'All right. When James was arrested for the burglary that time, he told the guards he'd sold on all the jewellery, but that was a lie. That boy wouldn't have known his arse from his elbow. He had no idea how to do that sort of thing.' She looks at us as if expecting us to say something. 'It was his first robbery. I didn't know that he'd lied about it at first. But when he, you know, was in prison, I found it.'

'Where?' I'm sure our boys would have gone over his place at some stage. I can't believe they would have missed it.

'He put it in with some stew I'd made. I make dinners in bulk, you see, and freeze them. My neighbour lets me use her chest freezer. Well, when I defrosted that stew, there it was.' She gives a bit of an embarrassed laugh. 'Abby nearly choked on an earring. I don't think she realised the significance of it at the time. Not then. Anyway, I confronted James in prison. I told him I'd found the jewellery and he begged me to do nothing with it. He'd only hidden it, he said, because he thought that if the guards couldn't find the jewellery they wouldn't be able to charge him but, like, all the details of the robbery were on his phone, the bloody eejit.'

'Then what?'

'It was too late to change his statement. He'd have got into even more trouble so I hid the stuff in a drawer in my room, thinking, I don't know, that one day we could give it back or whatever, and then the years went by and the urgency seemed to go out of it and it was just there, in the drawer. I almost forgot about it. But . . .' she swallows '. . . it wasn't long after James got out of prison that he demanded to know where the jewellery was and I refused to tell him until he promised not to sell it and he said he wouldn't. I honestly don't know if he was going to but Abby saw her chance and one day, when James and me were out, she must have gone through the house, looking for it. She took the jewellery and ran.'

'And that's why you didn't report her missing,' I say softly, 'isn't it?'

'She would have got into big trouble if she'd been found with that stuff. I never thought she was missing. James isn't the same since he came out of prison and all I could think was that if Abby was flung into some place it would ruin her too. Oh, God, I should have . . .' She buries her face in her hands, takes a few shaky breaths, then drags her gaze to me. 'I just didn't want her to get into trouble. I thought she'd be back. There was no way she could have sold it, she knew no one. Except maybe a dealer or something.'

I leave it a moment, then ask, 'And James?'

The silence stretches. Ben looks up from the statement.

'Mary?' I prompt gently. 'In the car, you said that James would never? Never what?'

'He didn't realise that the jewellery was gone at first, neither of us did, but then he went mental,' she whispers, as if she's afraid he's listening. 'He swore he was going to find her.'

'And, to your knowledge, did he?'

A tear falls, plop, onto the table. 'I don't know,' Mary says. 'I went out looking for her myself, too, you know. I rang her friends and walked the whole of Dublin for about three days and I didn't find her.'

'When was this?'

'Sometime in May. Late May because in the beginning I thought she'd come back.'

'And when did James go out looking for her?'

'As soon as he found out. Early May.'

'Did James find her?'

There is a long hesitation. Then she says, 'He never said.'

'How long did he spend looking for her, do you know?'

'Not long.'

'Did he give any reason why he stopped?' The words fall into the room and land.

Her face has a haunted expression. 'No. But he would never—'

'How was his form around that time, after he stopped searching?'

'He was . . . I don't know.' At my look, she says, 'I don't!'

'All right. I've just a couple more questions for you, Mary. Can you tell me if Abby had recently broken her collarbone at all?'

'Not when she was at home with me, no.'

'All right, and had she burnt her left arm somewhere up around here?' I point to mine.

'No. Definitely not.'

'And, finally, did she know anyone who was into radios or making radios or any sort of electronics?'

'No.'

'All right. Thanks for that. We'll need to talk to James again, get his version of events.'

She swallows back a sob. 'He's a good boy,' she says.

Ben reads her statement back to her and Mary signs her name in a hasty scrawl, as if she can't bear to be near the document. Then we all stand up and accompany her and Miriam to the door of the police station. Stacy is up at the counter, all beaming smiles to Matt. On seeing us, she waves her notebook and calls, 'Just wondering if there's any more on the Body in the Lough case?'

Mary gives an audible gulp and stares at her.

'You know you've to go through the garda press office for that,' Matt says to her. Then he tries to impart with his eyes that she should keep her mouth shut.

'Your eye, Matt,' Stacy says coyly. 'Are you winking at me?'

Matt's face lights up like a furnace.

'Garda press office,' I snap. 'And don't come here again.'

William is leaving at the same time as I am. We walk out to the car park together. 'That's good work today with Mary Devine,' he says. 'Get to Dublin tomorrow, and if we can get the brother to talk, so much the better. Don't go—'

'Making assumptions, yes, Cig, I do know that,' I say.

'I was going to say don't go scaring him. If he's guilty, he'll be scared already and you might get something out of him. If he's not and you attack him, he might be too scared to tell us what he does know. But, yeah,' he nods, 'don't go making assumptions.'

'Sorry.' It comes out gruffly.

'We'll get the bastards who did this,' he says, with a grit that surprises me. He's normally pretty detached – I think it lets him

100

do his job well. 'Or die trying,' he adds, and he's not joking. 'See you tomorrow morning, Lucy.'

He slouches off across the car park, hands deep in his trouser pockets, head bent. He cuts a surprisingly lonely figure and I remember how disappointed in me he was after he'd offered me a chance to move to Limerick.

'Cig,' I call, before I've a second to wonder what I'm doing. 'Sorry about letting you down.'

He turns and quirks an eyebrow. 'Lucy?'

'About Limerick? About wanting to stay here.'

There's a moment when I think he's going to reply, but he merely raises a hand and shrugs. 'You had things to stay for,' he says. 'See you tomorrow.'

Chapter 22

I used to enjoy getting home from work because, no matter how bad the day, I could close my front door and shut it all out. Now, though, with Tani and the baby staying, there is no hope of any sort of peace. I love my grandchild, I do, but every night I arrive back, the baby always seems to be howling. 'It's her cranky hour,' Tani says each time.

Tonight I'm met by the sight of Johnny, on my doorstep, calling to Tani through the letterbox.

Nice arse, I think, then tell myself to stop it.

'Please, hon, please come and discuss this like adults.'

Inside Tani shouts a response that I can't make out. From somewhere else in the house, Sirocco howls.

'Hello.' I slam my car door. Johnny jumps.

'Lucy.' He straightens up, looking abashed, runs a hand through his dirty-blond hair. He gestures at my front door. 'Sorry about this.'

'Do not let him in,' Tani yells, through the sitting-room window. 'Please, Lucy. I have my reasons.'

'I only want to talk to her,' he says to me. Turning to the window, 'I only want to talk to you!'

Tani responds by pulling the curtains across. Johnny and I look at one another, both of us, I think, feeling the awkwardness of the situation. I shuffle from foot to foot under his blue-eyed gaze. The light from the setting sun softens his face and he could almost be twenty years younger.

'This is breaking my heart,' he says.

A picture of Abby flashes through my head, of how she will never get to talk to her mother again. That's heart-breaking. There is at least hope for Johnny. 'I'll have a word with her. I'm sure she'll come around.' I'm tempted to ask him what happened, but it's none of my business.

'She won't,' he says, sounding defeated. 'Tani is as stubborn as her mother.'

A second before he adds, 'Sorry, that was . . . disloyal.'

I don't quite know what to say. The moment stretches. I want him to leave but how can I just walk in and close the door? He looks wretched. It'd be like abandoning a needy animal on your doorstep. 'Well . . .' I jangle my keys '. . . I'd better get in.'

'Yeah.' He huffs out a sigh. 'Can you just tell her . . . tell her that . . . she can come home anytime?'

'I'm sure she knows that.'

'Still . . .' He shrugs. Then, with a soft, bitter laugh, 'Katherine will implode if she doesn't come back soon. I'll get the blame.'

'I'm sure that's not—'

'It is true. I mean, come on, Lucy, she's as jealous as hell of our old relationship and –'

'That was years ago.'

'– the fact that you have a cool job and –'

'It's not cool, in fact –'

'– Tani thinks you're great. That hurts her. And, sure, it's my

103

fault for being with you in the first place.' He stops. Winces. 'Sorry. I shouldn't have said . . . Sorry.'

'That was pretty epic disloyal,' I say.

'Yeah, sorry.'

Is it wrong to feel flattered?

Yes.

Yes, it is.

I am *pathetic*.

'I will talk to Tani,' I say firmly, trying to keep the pleasure I feel at his words from finding expression in my voice. 'And sure maybe you and Katherine use the time to go on a nice break somewhere.'

'Some hope.' He rubs a hand across his jaw and, with some embarrassment, says, 'And, eh . . .Katherine isn't keen on them, you know, sharing a room. People talk.'

Oh, yes, the gossip. The obsession with appearances that is Katherine. Though she's not alone. 'I'm not keen on it myself,' I answer, 'but this house isn't exactly made for two families. I've warned them to be responsible.'

He winces. I suppress a grin. Whoever would have thought that Johnny Egan would be so prudish? But it is his daughter we're talking about. 'Good,' he finally says. 'Thanks.'

'No bother. Take care.'

He slouches off down the driveway, a gloomy figure in horrible orange shorts. But with a very nice arse, thank you very much. 'What happened?' Christ, what made me ask that? 'Tani hasn't said much,' I blunder on, as he turns to face me. 'She gets upset whenever we raise the subject.'

A moment's hesitation before he says, 'In that case I'd better not say anything because it'll be the wrong thing and annoy her more.' Then, with a small shrug, 'She just . . . well . . , me and her, we don't see eye to eye on certain things.'

'Give her time.'

There is a moment of stillness and then his eyes meet mine and I fizz right through. I could be fifteen all over again. 'Tell her we miss her, will you?' he says.

'I will.' My voice is high and weird.

He holds my gaze. His eyes are bluer than ever in his deeply tanned face. Underneath the try-hard, the boy I remember is there. The boy I'd loved all through school, the boy who had broken my heart. He takes a step towards me, hesitates, looks at me as if seeking permission for something.

I cannot fancy the father of my son's girlfriend. That is fucked up. But my whole life is like that anyway. 'Well . . .' I say, hoping he'll fill the gap, but he doesn't. He just smiles a tiny bit, a lop-sided grin that makes my heart flutter.

'Bye, Luce. Thanks.'

'I'll do my best for you. With Tani,' I clarify, just in case he might think something else.

Christ, I am pitiable.

I watch as he disappears down the drive to his car, which he has parked on the road.

I let my breath out.

That was close.

Chapter 23 – Sarah

'It's so clean.' Jenny stands in the centre of the bedroom in the shelter and inhales. 'And there's a real bed.' She sounds like beds are on a par with unicorns. 'And curtains. With a flower. Isn't this lovely, Sarah?'

'It's grand.' Sarah is noncommittal. She hasn't any intention of staying – she is happy to leave and let Jenny meet her in the morning – but, actually, the bed does look nice.

'Will I put your names down?' the volunteer who'd shown them the rooms asks. Valerie or something, Sarah thinks her name is.

'Yes, Alexandra.' Jenny nods. 'I want a room anyway.'

'And you, Sarah?'

'I can lock my door at night?' Sarah checks.

'You can. In fact, we encourage it.'

'All right so,' Sarah says, and ignores the excited little whoop from Jenny. Honestly, for a thief she can be a pain in the hole.

Hours later, Sarah is still awake. She doesn't sleep, really, not since she was about twelve. She lies, staring at the ceiling. Outside the sky has gone inky black, but the stars blaze right out of it.

All is quiet, silence punctuated by the creaks of the building settling.

And then she hears the scrape of a door being opened. Not up here, but downstairs. It opens like someone is trying not to make any noise. A bleep as the alarm is disabled. Then the door closes, and footsteps cross the hallway and move on into the kitchen. And now a door opens on the landing.

Softly, Sarah unlocks her own door, depresses the handle and pulls the door towards her, so it opens a crack. Up the way Alexandra, still dressed, tiptoes downstairs.

Sarah wonders if she should join her. What if it's a thief and Alexandra has gone down alone? Sarah has never had much time for people who can't make decisions, who stand and wait for stuff to happen, people like her mother, and so, taking a breath, screwing up all her courage, she grabs a lamp and runs lightly from her room.

She catches a flash of Alexandra heading into the kitchen and she follows her down. From the kitchen door, which is ajar, comes the soft murmur of voices. So, it's not a robber. It's someone Alexandra knows.

Relief makes her legs shake slightly.

Peeking in, she sees a scruffy-looking hippie guy, his back to her. Alexandra has her head buried in his chest.

'You're very late,' she says.

'I'd a pile of stuff to do.' He kisses her. 'And I didn't want to be seen. We'd be in trouble.'

Alexandra kisses him back before pulling away. 'You have to be quiet,' she warns. 'We're full tonight.'

'It's OK. I'll just have to share your room, then, won't I?'

They laugh softly.

Sarah is transfixed. She should leave but she can't. Alexandra had seemed so serious and joyless, and now here she is . . .

'Come.' Alexandra takes the man's hand and starts leading him from the room. Sarah melts into the shadows of the door. The guy is kissing her neck, her shoulders.

Alexandra leads him upstairs.

Her bedroom door closes.

Sarah crosses to where he left his bag and a cardboard box in the kitchen. His haversack holds nothing but some clothes and a bunch of keys. In the box is a large old-fashioned radio.

The following morning, his bag has vanished, but the radio remains, squat, in the corner of the room.

Chapter 24 – One week after discovery

The detective sergeant, Ciaran Brady, assigned to us from Dublin stands up to address the room. 'We were tasked with interviewing Abby's friends and the shelter volunteers,' he says. 'There were fifteen volunteers in the shelter and we have made contact with thirteen. Of the two remaining, one is away on holidays in Spain and will be back this evening. We have arranged an interview first thing tomorrow, and the other volunteer, a Mr Adam Gray, was ill and said he would call us back to arrange an interview. He hasn't as yet. We have a Dundrum address for him and we'll call into it over the coming days if we still haven't heard. One of the volunteers interviewed, a Pearl Reardon, is the only one to positively identify Abby. She remembers seeing her on the morning of the sixth of June, which was the second last night she was in the hostel. Pearl says she remembers the date because it was her birthday. She says Abby was holding her arm and saying she was going to get it looked at. According to this volunteer, Abby said that another volunteer offered to bring her to the hospital. However, the volunteer is unsure if Abby just said it to stop her prying. Abby's friends, of whom there were three, had nothing to add. None of them had seen her since she left her home in late April.'

'Thanks,' William says, as the DS sits down. 'Let's have the rest of the updates.'

I stand. 'Today Dan and I will interview Abby's brother James, who has become a person of interest.' I outline what we learned from Mary the previous day and there is a quickening of attention in the room. When I finish, I sit down.

'Mick,' William barks, 'have ye had any luck on checking the hospitals in case anyone came in with a fracture that matched Abby's?'

'Uh-huh.' Mick stands up. He looks nervously at William, who stares back impassively. 'Well, I rang all the A and E departments in the Dublin area and there were a lot of collarbone fractures. It's quite common apparently. I sent them a jpeg of our IP's injury and that narrowed it down to four, but only one matching the victim's description was identified by anyone.'

'Good,' I say encouragingly.

'A young girl matching Abby's description arrived into St James's Hospital on the seventh of June. Apparently, she was with her older brother. She was meant to come back for a check-up but never did.'

'That ties in with what the volunteer said,' Dan remarks.

'Any actual proof that it was her?' William asks.

'Eh . . . not yet but the fracture is identical to the one in the picture. I asked them to check the details on the patient file and it turns out that the name and address the girl and the brother gave are false, as is the phone number. This girl said she was eighteen but the doctor remembers a young girl who didn't look a day over fourteen – he commented on it. I sent him a picture of Abby—'

'A picture?' William barks. 'A picture?'

'Sorry, Cig, twelve photographs, one of which was Abby, and

he pointed out a couple of girls, one of which was Abby, and he says that this girl he saw in the hospital was very similar. He put her arm in a sling but never saw her again. She had vanished.'

'I doubt she vanished,' William says shortly, making Mick pink up. 'Did you ask if the girl had any burns on her upper arm?'

'Eh . . . no.'

'Have you requested CCTV from the hospital waiting room?'

'Eh . . . that was my next thing.'

'Who was on shift that day and might have seen her?'

'Yeah . . . that's in hand.'

'A list of names and addresses of people who attended the hospital around the same time as this girl who gave a false name?'

'That's a good idea,' Mick says weakly.

William says nothing for a moment. The room waits. Dan kicks me under the table and I ignore him.

'So, we have a doctor who points out a number of girls, who says the girl he saw was "very similar" and who "thinks" she was younger than she said but nothing else?'

'The name and address were false,' Susan says.

'Probably to get out of paying the fee,' William snaps back. 'Moving on,' he continues, suppressing his irritation, 'Larry, I believe you have news for us about the car?'

'Yes, good news I think. I got this back this morning.' He reads from an email, his voice assured and measured. '"I can say with confidence that the model of car is a Peugeot 208, 2022. First, because the headlights in the sketch are the distinctive Peugeot 208 "claw" design. When I compared the alloys of a Peugeot 208 with the alloys in the image taken from CCTV, they match the model brought out in 2022."' Larry looks up. 'Here's Lugs's drawing, the alloys and the car together.' He pops an image up on the screen and it's the headlights that sell it. Good man, Lugs, I think. 'I'm running a pulse check for Peugeot 208s sold since the beginning of the year. It should be back today. I've also roped in someone to check with car-hire firms to get a list of names for anyone who hired a Peugeot sometime around the beginning of August.'

'Excellent,' William says.

'Huh,' Susan says, then winces. I don't think she'd meant to say it out loud.

'What was that, Susan?'

She flushes bright red. 'Nothing,' she says. 'I was just . . . making an observation.'

'Care to share it with the rest of us?'

'No.' Then, 'Yes, actually.' She stands up, straightens herself and eyeballs William. 'I said, "How come you didn't preface your 'excellent' with a whole lot of questions for Larry the way you did with us?"'

Oh, Christ.

Here it comes.

'Because Larry is an experienced detective,' Williams says, his voice like sugar, his eyes pinning Susan to the spot, like a butterfly in a case. 'He already knows it. He's not about to jump in making assumptions.' He pauses. His voice hardens: 'You and Mick are new and I don't need you two haring off and trying to make evidence fit your theory that this girl was somehow the same one as in the hospital.'

Dan snorts a laugh at that and it's my turn to kick him.

'Larry also managed to go to the nth degree with his enquiry,' William goes on, as Susan flushes, 'whereas you and Mick missed out fundamental steps. Will I continue?'

Mick is staring at his hands. His face looks like it's about to combust. Susan is stock still. I think she's trying to hold herself together. This is her moment, I think. Make or break.

'I see your point,' she says, with great dignity. 'Thank you.' She sits back down and looks at William expectantly.

His face is a picture. He hadn't expected that. He probably thought she'd cry or run out of the room or glare at him in a strop. 'Good,' he says, almost choking on the word. His gaze sweeps all of us, 'Anyone got anything else? Ben?'

'I'm looking into Abby's phone data, Cig. Without the phone, you know yourself we can get its location and any calls and texts made but not the content. It appears that her mother was right. There was no activity on her phone in the last week of her life so what I have is all Dublin-related. I haven't gone through it yet – it only arrived yesterday evening. I should have a clearer picture tomorrow.'

William nods. 'Good. Get James's records too. Phone lines?'

A young lad, I forget his name, who'd been given the miserable job of sifting through the phone information, stands up. 'No, Cig. The phones are dead quiet. It's weird.'

'It's the good weather,' William says. 'They've better things to do than ring us up with oddball theories. It might mean that whatever does come in could be useful. We'll release a picture of the girl to the press today. That should shake them up. All right, Kev, how you doing on the suitcases?'

Kev hops up and gives a rundown of what he's done. 'I've traced five people so far who paid with credit cards. None were around Achill in July. As for suitcases bought with cash, I've sent some lads out to harvest the CCTV from those shops. I've a few more credit cards to check up too. But nothing yet. It was a very popular suitcase.'

'All right, when the Pulse details on the Peugeots come in, cross-reference that with any names you have for the suitcase purchases. Long shot, I know.'

'Sure.'

'Jordy?' William says. 'Find out all you can about the jewellery that was stolen in the James Devine robbery. There must be images of it somewhere – ask the owner if you have to. Check the usual sources to see if it's been offered for sale. Maybe it's been melted down now or sold for cash, but I reckon if James Devine didn't know how to offload jewellery, his sister would not have had a clue. She'd have given it to a dealer or something.'

'Sure thing,' Jordy rasps.

'Anything you find, pass it on to Lucy ASAP.'

We get our job sheets for the day and the meeting breaks up.

And Dan and I are on the road to Dublin once more.

Chapter 25

Before we talk to James, we've arranged to chat to the arresting guard in his original case to get a feel for him. The guard, Vince, who was twenty-two at the time and fresh out of Templemore, remembers it well. 'It was my first arrest,' he says, handing me and Dan a coffee from the canteen in the station. 'And it was odd, because Devine was, like, the same age nearly as I was. Truth be told, I felt a bit sorry for the chap.'

'How so?' I take a sip of the coffee and almost gag. It's not a patch on our machine in humble Achill.

'Because he was young.' Vince takes a great gulp of coffee and reaches for a biscuit. 'And that Denis Dunne, the guy he did the robbery with, he was a head case. Talk about getting in with the wrong crowd. A violent fella altogether. He's still inside. I didn't get the impression, at the time, that James was the same sort.'

'He was obviously a good liar, though,' I say. 'He convinced you that he'd sold on the jewellery.'

'Aye,' Vince agrees, 'there is that against him but there's a difference between lying about something like that and murdering someone. If you've your eye on him for killing his sister, I can't see it, though prison might have changed him. It was a while back now.'

'Anything else you can tell us that might help?' Dan asks.

'He was close to his mother,' Vince says. 'That really stood out.'

We thank him and, leaving our coffees unfinished, we drive five minutes down the road to talk to James.

He has taken a half-day from work, agreeing to meet us at his mother's. He regards us sullenly as we enter the kitchen. The place is a jumble of unwashed dishes and half-eaten meals, the tidiness of three days ago gone, the disorder of the room reflecting the upheaval in Mary Devine's life. I go straight for it, hoping to shock him with the question but aware that his mother might have warned him in advance.

'You never sold that jewellery, did you, James?'

His answer is a stare. Then, 'I know it was me ma told you that.'

I'd have liked to arrest James based on the fact that he lied to us in his first interview, but William wasn't having any of it: 'Lucy,' he'd said, like I was two years old, 'you know that we can only arrest if there are lies in a written statement. Maybe he just misremembered things.'

'He withheld information,' I tried again. 'He told us that the last he saw of her was before she ran away.'

'And maybe it was.' William had looked keenly at me. 'His mother only said he'd gone looking for her. She had no proof that he'd found her. You know this, Lucy. You're scraping the bottom of the barrel.'

And he was right. I'd known it when I went in to him but still . . . James must have found his sister because he'd stopped looking. Wasn't that what his mother had said?

'Did you sell the jewellery or not?'

James, with deliberate slowness, pulls a cigarette from a pack on the counter and strikes a match, lighting up. After taking a drag, he looks at me through a fog of smoke. 'And if I say no?' he asks. 'That'll get me into trouble, won't it?' There is a tiny note of fear in his voice. I think that maybe Vince is right: that James is not the hard man he pretends to be.

'We are investigating the murder of your sister,' Dan says calmly. He's leaning against the door. The kitchen is too tiny for a table. 'If you made a false statement to the police initially, we will have to send a report to the DPP, but you won't serve any more time. It might help, though, if you're honest with us now.'

'She put that hole in the door,' James says, nodding towards it. 'She's dead but she wasn't a saint.'

We let that hang until it dissipates on the air. James shifts uneasily, knowing he's said the wrong thing. 'Just say yez're right and I never sold it,' he says. 'How'll that get yez further in your investigation?'

'That's not your concern,' I say. 'What I'd like to know is if your sister took that jewellery and ran?'

A long moment. Finally, he says, 'She saw it as drug money.'

Bingo.

'And what did you do then?'

'What anyone would do,' he says. 'I went looking for her.' He jabs his cigarette in my direction. 'She'd stolen my stuff.'

He has no sense of the irony.

'Did you find her?'

A moment. He has that look in his eyes, the one they must teach you in prison. The one that shows people like me that you're thinking four steps ahead. Like a chess move, figuring out

117

all the combinations and permutations of your answer. Finally, he shrugs. 'Yes. Dublin isn't that big and I knew where to look.'

'So, tell me again, when was the last time you saw your sister?'

James inhales, long and deep, buying time. Then he exhales. Smoke fills the air between us. 'About a week or so after she ran off. In May.'

'Where was this?'

'Moore Street.'

That would fit with what we've already been told. 'What time? Late? Early?'

'After tea. About seven, maybe.' A pause, then in a rush, 'I did nothing to her.'

'I never said you did.'

'You're thinking it, though. I know it looks bad, her taking my stuff and me going after her and not telling yez about it, but I did nothing to her.'

'When you found her, what happened?'

Another pull of the cigarette. His gaze slides upward. 'Nuttin'.'

There's a lie, right there.

'Nothing?'

'I had a look for my stuff but it was gone, sold.'

'Sold?'

'Musta been.' A shrug. 'It wasn't there.'

'What happened when you discovered that she didn't have your stuff?'

'Nuttin'.'

'Really? Your sister stole your jewellery, she offloaded it for probably next to nothing, and you just walked away? Come on. Help me out here.'

'You think I did it.'

'I'm not paid to think. I'm paid to investigate. You must have been hopping mad.'

'No.'

'Why bother looking for her, then? The jewellery must not have been that important to you.'

'I did nuttin' 'cause a fella ran me off.'

'What fella? Describe him.'

'It was dark.'

'But it was May. You said it was around seven.'

For a second he looks annoyed, as if I've caught him out on something, but he recovers. 'Maybe it was later than seven, then. Anyway, I don't remember what he looked like.'

'Height? Taller than you?'

He seems to think, or maybe he's pretending. 'Taller.'

'Accent?'

'Dublin, I guess.'

'How was he dressed?'

'He wore clothes.' A smirk. He stubs his cigarette out. 'I told him what I was doing, what my skank of a sister had done, but he told me to piss off. I wasn't there for a fight so I did. Now, I told you what happened. I found her, I left her. End of.'

'You left your sister to the mercy of the streets?'

I've pressed his buttons now. He leans towards me, eyes blazing. I see Dan bracing himself for trouble. 'Don't think you can judge me,' he almost spits into my face. 'I spent three and a half years in jail for a thing I did when I'd just gone eighteen. I never thought that robbery would get all violent. And since I got out, I've tried. You can ask my ma. I've been out nearly six months and ask yourself why I didn't sell that jewellery before now? Truth? I didn't know what to do with it. And when she took it,

I was . . .' he closes his eyes, bangs his fist against his head '. . . I was afraid she'd be picked up and it'd be traced back to me, right. I needed to get it off her. I knew what she'd done would come back on me.' A moment, then he adds, 'The only victims here are me and my ma.'

He almost had me with that speech. 'Victims?' Now it's my turn to snap. 'You're alive. Your sister was beaten, had bones broken. She was stuffed into a suitcase, a *suitcase*,' I repeat, 'and thrown into the middle of a lake. Her head was banged in. She was fifteen years old.'

He rears back, swallows and stares at the ceiling. It's an age before he speaks. 'Sorry,' he says, and I think he is sorry. 'I do know that. And she didn't deserve it but all I'm saying is—'

'Can I just clarify that you say you weren't planning on selling the jewellery when you came out?'

He's off balance by the question. 'No.'

And yet he'd asked his mother for it.

'And what about Denis Dunne? What about his cut?' Denis was the man who'd been involved in the robbery with James.

'Denis robbed a necklace to order. He was well paid for that. I was just along for the ride.'

'So, there you are, trying to go straight, and your sister runs off with your stolen jewellery, which could send you back to prison, potentially. You must have been panicked.'

'I guess.'

'And then you find her and realise she's sold everything to people you don't know. That must have scared you?'

He jerks ever so slightly. He's already admitted as much and he knows it. He can't deny it and admitting it makes him look bad. 'I didn't kill her.' He stands up, pushing back his chair. 'Now, I

120

don't have to answer your questions, so I'd like yez to leave now and actually catch the person who did kill her. Thanks.'

'I have one more question,' I say. 'Did your sister have any burns when you saw her last?'

That surprises him enough to answer, 'I don't know.'

'Do you know how she broke her collarbone?' Dan asks.

The tiniest of pauses before he shakes his head.

He's lying. Dan realises it too. 'So, you know that your sister had a broken collarbone, then?'

He stares impassively at us.

'Did you accompany her to hospital?'

Nothing.

'We will find you on CCTV if you did,' Dan says.

'Knock yourself out.' He's done now.

'Fine,' Dan says. 'We'll be in touch.'

Chapter 26

I run into a local Costa and get take-out coffee, which we sip in the car.

'No muffins?' Dan's face falls when I arrive back and hand him his Americano. 'I always get you a muffin.'

'And I always tell you not to.' I open the top of my cup and run my finger around the frothy rim. 'I don't need to be eating any more crap than I already do.' I turn to face him. 'What d'you think?'

'On you eating crap?' Then, as I roll my eyes, he says seriously, 'His story hangs but he's lying about something and he has a history of violence—'

'Not according to Vince, and he had good behaviour in prison,' I say.

'Yeah, but I'm thinking he went looking for that jewellery. He would not be a happy man to find out it was gone. There is no way he would not react badly.'

'Do you believe he was run off by someone?'

'He was light enough on the description. CCTV might answer it, though, if we get lucky.' We probably won't.

'Do you think he killed her?'

Dan swirls his coffee about. 'He had motive, to get the jewellery and stay out of prison. Or sell it and make a few bob for himself. Is it strong enough? I don't know. He'd have had to kill her somewhere else, get a suitcase and a car. He doesn't strike me as the organised type.'

'Maybe he had help.'

'Who?'

'I don't know. The radio fixer?'

'That's the piece that puzzles me. How the hell does that fit in?'

We slump into silence. Solid, hard evidence is thin on the ground. We have a few 'possibles' – a possible car, a possible date of death – but the only concrete thing we have is that a girl was murdered with blunt-force trauma. The only real suspect is James. If he did it, how on earth did he manage to get her down to Mayo? And why Mayo? None of it makes sense for James. He'd have dumped her in the Liffey or something, I reckon.

Later, as the car eats up the miles back to Mayo, Dan asks me what I'm going to do about Rob.

I'd been putting the question off, burying myself in work and home. 'I don't quite know yet,' I admit. 'The exhibition is on in September. I thought I might turn up and hand him his present back.' I risk a sidelong glance. 'What do you think?'

Dan doesn't answer at once, shows he's thinking about it. 'What good will it do?' he eventually says.

'It'll make me feel better for one,' I say. I indicate to overtake a car that's crawling along. When I've passed it, I add, 'I just want to. I think I just want to . . . I'm angry at him, Dan. Really bloody angry.'

'You should be,' he says. 'He ruined your life, but by confronting him, maybe you're playing into his hands.' He pauses. 'It's why I never visit home when I'm in Dublin. I wouldn't give my da the satisfaction of a row.'

Dan's dad used to beat him, seeing his homosexuality as a weakness. I wish he could see his son in his job. Dan is tough, can wither with a look, and though he appears laid-back, he can be bloody scary when he has to be.

'I did think, you know, that maybe he wants to provoke me. He could have lived anywhere in Ireland, Dan, but he chose to live near me. He befriended his son by covert means on social media, called out to my house when I wasn't there and left a present for Sirocco. He does want a reaction.'

'Yeah.' Dan nods. 'And you never wrote him in prison, never visited. Why would you bother now?'

'Because of Luc. And Sirocco. He needs to be warned off. If I don't, maybe he'll think we're all right with it.'

'He knows you're not all right with it.'

'What would you do, then?'

'I'd get an impartial someone to give it back to him, with a friendly warning.' A second later, he adds, 'I'll do it if you want.'

I turn to him. 'Really?'

He meets my gaze. 'I'd take pleasure in it, Luce.'

He's got my back, is what he's saying. If I wasn't driving at a hundred and twenty kilometres an hour, I'd wrap my arms about him and hug him. 'That'd be great.'

'Done so,' he says, with a grin.

'I want a full report, though.'

'You got it, boss.' He tips me a salute.

Outside, the land starts to grow scrubby.

★★★

124

At nine o'clock, just as I'm pulling into the station, my phone rings. Feck! I flick it on without looking at caller ID. 'DS Lucy Golden,' I snap, hoping to discourage anyone calling me unless it's important.

'It's William.' Brusque and to the point.

'Dan and I are just back. I'll be with you in a second.'

'I'm in Croy at a suspected suicide scene. Any chance you can come over and give me your thoughts?'

My heart sinks. 'Sure. Give me thirty minutes. Send me the address.' I hang up and relay the information to Dan. 'He didn't ask for you so just go and get an update from the lads and get off home. I'll give you a shout later.'

Dan looks pityingly at me. 'It must be hard being his very favourite detective.'

'Piss off.'

He laughs.

Chapter 27 – Sarah

The shelter has been done up with 'Happy Birthday' banners. Sarah hates parties, and a party to celebrate the first anniversary of a homeless shelter she hates even more.

The founder of the shelter, a baldy man wearing a suit that's expensive but designed to look casual, is in attendance, and it's like he's Bono or something, Sarah thinks, the way everyone falls all over themselves to talk to him. She's surprised to see the hippie man from last night with him, trailing along behind him, like a broken kite or something.

He and Alexandra don't even look at one another.

Isn't it well for them, these fat cats with their big wallets, all congratulating themselves on being so good to the less fortunate, Sarah thinks, as she watches the baldy man make his way to the top of the room. He holds up his hands for a bit of hush and people start to shush one another. Jenny looks excited for his speech, which sort of amuses Sarah. She's a bit naff, so she is.

This whole party would be much better if they served wine instead of fizzy orange, but when Sarah had asked, Bernie had told her that that would have been irresponsible because of 'addictions'.

Sarah supposed she had a point. Her mother would have drunk the place dry if she'd been here.

'To those of you who don't know me, I'm Liam,' the baldy man says, with a smile, and Sarah thinks that, for a bald man, he's not bad-looking. His smile makes people smile at him. He's the tallest man in the room. His voice makes him sound like a late-night DJ. 'It's fantastic to be here,' he says, 'to celebrate the first birthday of this shelter. I lived in Westport myself for a time, and to be able to help the community the way I was helped by the community as a boy gives me great joy.'

Sarah tunes out. Instead she watches the way the other volunteers and some of the social workers look at Liam as if he's some kind of saviour. Well, she didn't ask to be saved, thank you very much. She turns her attention to the hippie guy, wondering when he'll finally acknowledge Alexandra. She doesn't have long to wait. As Liam's speech drones on, the hippie guy sneaks a glance sideways and gives a slight eye roll as if to say 'what a load of bollix'.

Alexandra smiles like she agrees.

It's not much of a party, Sarah thinks.

Half an hour later, Liam is going around chatting to all the volunteers and making sure to talk to the unfortunates as well.

'This is Sarah and Jenny,' Bernie introduces them to Liam. 'They've stayed a few nights now.'

'Hi.' Jenny beams at Liam. God, she is so transparent. But she is only twelve. 'I love this shelter. Thank you for building it.'

'You've this fella to thank for making it what it is.' Liam thumbs to the hippie guy, whose name is Gareth apparently.

Gareth nods to them both.

Jenny turns to thank Gareth, and Sarah cringes for her.

'It's lovely to meet you, ladies,' Liam says, already looking past them. 'Enjoy the rest of the party.' And he's gone, Gareth trotting along in his wake.

Sarah watches as he dismisses Gareth, who, looking a bit fed up, leans against the wall. Alexandra hands him a cup of orange and they clink plastic cartons.

Liam has joined a woman who has just come in. She's high end but a bit frazzled-looking. Her face lights up when she sees Liam. Bernie goes up and air-kisses the woman.

Afterwards, Sarah climbs the stairs to bed as Jenny helps with the clear-up.

'You'd get a job in a kitchen,' Alexandra tells Jenny, who looks far too pleased with herself.

Sarah scoffs loudly so they can all hear.

Chapter 28

Westport is tourist mecca for this part of Mayo. A town that hums with life and food and drink and songs and buskers. Right now, at nine twenty, it's just gearing up for the night ahead. The buzz of conversation fades as I take the road to Croy. In minutes I'm enveloped in the silence of the countryside. At this time of night, I prefer to travel through Westport rather than taking the more isolated roads to get to Croy. It's only about ten minutes' difference and it's easier on the car.

I'm about half a kilometre from the house where the incident occurred when I'm flagged down by a guard who is turning back traffic on the road. He recognises me and waves me through.

I drive on, and about ten feet from the front garden, I pull in at the white and blue crime-scene tape, which, annoyingly, has been hung upside down. Again. How hard is it to hang bloody tape the right way up, I wonder, for about the millionth time in my career. It makes us look like a shower of incompetents with sloppy attention to detail.

I spot Mick who hands me a dust suit. 'The DI's orders,' he says. He looks a little ropy.

'Who the fuck hung the crime-scene tape?'

'I did.'

'It's upside fucking down,' I snap. He winces and I don't feel sorry. 'Where's William?'

'By the front door. I'll just sign you in.'

From what I can gather, it's just Mick, me, William and a few guards who've been ordered to flag down the cars. A woman, smoking a cigarette, sits on a wall, just outside the cordon. I assume she must have found the body. I join William at the door.

There's an orange 191 registered Fiesta parked by the front door.

'Take a walk through the house, Lucy,' William says, without looking at me. 'I'd like your thoughts. They're saying suicide.'

Which can only mean that he has his doubts. Which is why he has cordoned off the scene.

If it is a crime scene, I think, as I step through the front door into a wooden-floored hallway, at least it's an indoor one. Scenes like that are generally easier to manage: evidence is not washed away by rain or wind, and setting up a cordon is simpler as it doesn't have to extend as far. Inside a house, the environment is controlled, which allows the pathologist to give a fairly decent estimate of time and manner of death. Finally, if there's a shooting or stabbing, the walls and doors make natural boundaries so blood-spatter analysis is more straightforward.

If this is a murder, it will be an easier solve than the one I'm currently doing. But two in the space of a week, down here? Improbable.

The hallway is spotless, save for a puddle of water outside what must be the bathroom. In front of me there is what looks like a kitchen, the door ajar. I follow a safe path towards it, using my gloved hands to push the door a little wider. It's a small space, with a countertop and oak presses. A half-filled kettle, lid open, sits on the counter. The water inside is cold. Crammed into a far corner is a small table; large rubber-soled shoes lie underneath a chair. Leaving, I cross into a utility room, which smells of detergent. No clothes on the floor, nothing in the tumble dryer. Back in the hallway, I move to the living room. My skin prickles and the hairs rise on my neck. Plastic sheeting on the floor. Nuts and bolts and skeletons of radios aligned neatly on the plastic.

Jesus.

I tear my eyes away. There is an anglers' magazine on a low coffee-table opened on a page advertising the fish to be had at Ballin Lough. There are two bedrooms, one unoccupied, another with an opened suitcase, clothes in disarray, thrown all over the bed. And, finally, there is the bathroom. The door stands open, giving me a view of an overflowing bath of red water, the body of a large man immersed, his feet sticking out the end. He lies, face up, eyes open, slashed wrists exposed. Just beside the bath, a knife lies in a puddle of water. Blood has sprayed over the ceiling and walls and turned the water red. The man is in his late twenties at most, wearing jeans and a black T-shirt. A tattoo of a snake crawls from his fingers up his bare forearm. And, in a sudden flash, I know I've seen this man before. Somewhere. I know him. I do. I stand there for a few minutes, trying to place him, but the harder I try the more it evades me. Instead, I concentrate on the scene, on the strange quiet that accompanies death. I try to imagine what might have happened here and how. I bend down to look at his slashed wrists.

And then I know what I've suspected since I saw the half-filled kettle: this was no suicide.

★★★

I join William back in the garden. The air is still hot and sticky – the nights, these days, don't so much cool down as go off the boil.

He looks at me with raised eyebrows.

'It's not suicide,' I say.

'What's your reasoning?'

'Well, I had a close look at his wrists. There's just one cut. Joe always says that if someone intends to kill themselves there are usually a few trial marks before they take the plunge. Maybe he was pushed into the bath, but I doubt it – the suicide wouldn't look convincing with a massive lump on the head. He was forced in. Maybe at gunpoint? On top of that, he came on holiday with a packed suitcase. If he was thinking suicide upon arrival, he would never have packed a suitcase. And yes,' I interrupt William's next question, 'I do think it happened shortly after he arrived because he hadn't even unpacked – there are no toiletries in the bath-room. He was also in the process of boiling the kettle.'

'And?' William says.

'Whoever did it was looking for something. The clothes in his case were thrown all over the place. But on quick inspection, I think he knew his attacker because I couldn't see any sign of forced entry.'

'Good.' He nods. 'My thoughts too.'

'I think it's connected to our case,' I say.

'The radio parts?' William asks. 'It's a bit thin.'

'I've seen him before,' I say, 'I know I have, and it's recently enough.'

He looks at me, not willing to dismiss me but not fully onboard either. 'Let's get an ID first, then we'll see where we're going. I'll put a call into Joe. Get him down here. There'll be a murder conference tomorrow at nine in Westport,' he says. 'It's your area. You and Dan have been reassigned to it. I'll take Kev off the Achill team too.'

I gawp at him.

'I'm on the Abby Devine murder and, besides, Cig, there's a connection here. I know there is.'

'Until you can make it, you're on this case,' William says firmly. I open my mouth to protest but he bats me off like an irritating fly. 'Lucy, it's a week now since we found that girl. We've ID'd her, which was impressive seeing as she'd never been reported missing and was dead at least three weeks. We returned her to her family. As for the murder, we have a rough idea of her last movements, but we still have no place of murder, no motive for her murder, bar a loose one of robbery, which doesn't hang as she stated she was robbed a couple of weeks before her murder. We have no idea when she was murdered and no suspect, bar the brother who, frankly, doesn't seem the most likely. It was always going to be difficult with the trail cold. It's one we'll be lucky to solve. This here,' he indicates the house, 'it's fresh. We'll get whoever did this.'

'A bath full of water? That's not too good for forensic evidence,' I snap.

That annoys him. 'And a body in a lake for four weeks is?'

'A young girl, fourteen years old, was murdered.' I glare at him. 'She was stuffed into a suitcase and thrown into the middle of a lake and you're telling me that you're going to trust to luck to solve it?'

'I said no such thing.' His tone makes me flinch. 'You get away with a lot, Lucy. Don't push it too hard.'

It's a warning. One I'm sadly unable to take. 'I'll push as hard as I can for the people I'm trying to help,' I say, trying to keep my tone even. 'Mary Devine is depending on me to get answers for her daughter and I will. If it takes me months, I will.'

'Then you'll be working on your own time,' he says. 'Because this here, this is what you'll be doing for the next week at least.'

'She was a fourteen-year-old child.' Now my voice rises. 'If you had kids you'd—'

'Don't ever talk to me like that,' he says, face white with anger as he jabs a finger at me. 'You'll do what you're told and I won't hear another word. Have you any bloody idea what this means for me?'

'All I—'

'Two murders? Two murders? I won't get a fucking night's sleep, I won't get my days off. I will be twenty-four/seven grubbing about in the mud for the gougers that did this and I do not need you, my DS, arguing the toss. Have you got that?'

I stare at him. 'Yes,' I mutter, with bad grace.

'Get going now, Lucy.' William's tone is cold. 'As I said, you and Dan and Kev are off the Abby Devine case. I'll see you in the morning.'

I wake up at four a.m. because the face of the suspected suicide victim had popped into my dream. And suddenly I know where I saw him before.

The photograph in the hostel.

He was one of the hostel volunteers.

Chapter 29 – Day 8

By eight I'm up and raring to go. I've texted William with what I remembered about our IP but he hasn't replied.

I've drunk buckets of coffee and spent at least two hours googling. I'm wired – I can feel the crawling buzz under my skin that too much caffeine gives me. Most people hate it. I love it.

Luc wanders in just as I'm polishing off a piece of toast and pulling on my jacket.

It's not often we're alone together now. I wish I could sit and chat with him, but I need to make the murder conference in Westport, talk about how the two murders could be linked. And even though William is unlikely to reassign me I know this is a breakthrough.

I can feel it.

'Hey,' Luc greets me, shoving three pieces of bread into the toaster. He sounds a bit off.

'You all right?' I ask, knowing I should go, but the guilt of leaving him when he's so obviously down will haunt me if I do. 'I heard Sirocco crying last night?'

'She's getting teeth,' he says. He doesn't sound particularly excited at the prospect. He slumps into a chair. 'Is it meant to be this hard, Ma?'

My heart squeezes.

Something must show on my face because he immediately backtracks. 'Like I love Sirocco,' he clarifies, 'but sometimes . . .' He doesn't finish. Instead he indicates the coffee pot. 'Any left?'

I pour him a cup, not sure what to say. My mother would be way better at this than me. She'd give him solid sage advice, which he would lap up. I'll probably just make everything worse. But, damn it, I'm his mother, he has a right to expect something from me. I think back to the day when Sirocco was born, when he allowed me to hug him, and the certainty I felt then that I hadn't been too bad a parent. He might not see me the way I see myself. He might think I've got all the answers. I go for it. 'Luc, here's the thing,' I say, trying to be honest, yet inspirational. 'It is bloody hard.'

His face drops.

'But everything worth doing is,' I jam in hastily.

'Drinking a pint is worth doing. I don't find that hard.'

'Now you're being silly.' I smile, and he smiles back a little glumly. I sit in beside him. 'It will never be easy, Luc. She'll start sleeping through the night and get all her teeth, and just when that ends, she'll start to have tantrums and she'll say she hates you and she'll fight with you and . . .'

With every pronouncement, he looks a little more dejected.

Shit.

'And it will be hard,' I say, scrambling to put my words right, 'but you know what? She'll also love you with every bit of herself and cuddle you and kiss you, and you'll get joy out of seeing her grow and learn and make friends. It will become about her and not you.'

'Right.' The toast pops and he goes to butter it. His back to me, he asks, in a low voice, 'And what if she messes up like I have?'

'You haven't messed up.'

He laughs.

'You haven't,' I say, joining him at the counter. 'Your life just took a different turn. And when you and Tani had her, so did mine, and I wouldn't be without her, would you?'

'I just feel . . .' he shrugs '. . . I feel that my life isn't my own any more.'

'I hate to break it to you, sonny boy, but it's not.' I offer what I hope is an encouraging smile. 'Now, I have to go, keep the chin up – haven't you got me and your nan to help out, and Tani's parents if she ever talks to them again?' I'm hoping he'll tell me what's going on, but Luc is loyal. And I love it about him, but it's deeply frustrating. 'I'll have Sunday off,' I say impulsively. 'I'll take Sirocco, and you and Tani have a night away somewhere.'

'Aren't you working a murder?'

'I'll be off, I promise.'

'Thanks, Ma.'

I'll give my mam a call later, make sure he's all right.

The incident room is already full when I arrive. It's a bit fancier than the Achill one. I push my way through the throng to where William is talking to Ben. I stand patiently by, hoping he'll notice me. He finally does, with a sarcastic 'You made it, eh?'

'Any ID on the IP?' I ask.

'Adam Gray, living with his father in Dundrum, Dublin. We've informed the local lads, they've assigned a FLO and they're going to the family to break the news today. You can interview them later on.'

Another trip east.

'Anything else?'

'Not much. I took your point about him volunteering with that homeless shelter, so you can look into that when you go up today. Ciaran Brady, the Dublin DS, confirmed that Adam was the one volunteer they never managed to speak to. They were due to call on him later in the week. They're re-interviewing everyone today to ask about him. Now come on, let's get going.'

He walks up the room, me trailing behind, mind spinning.

The usual gang are assembled. I sit next to Dan, and Ben's on the other side of me.

'Mick is really in the shit with the Cig,' Ben says, laughing a little. 'Puked his ring up at the scene last night apparently.'

'It was a pretty bad scene,' I say back.

'Settle down,' William calls, interrupting the chatter, and as usual, people do settle down. He gets straight to business. 'Last night we had another murder in the locality,' he says. 'This comes on top of the one a week ago where we discovered the remains of a young girl in a suitcase in Lough Acorrymore. It was estimated that she had been in the lake up to three weeks. As of now we have a few irons in the fire and the investigation is moving forward. Jordy, you're still on the trail of the jewellery. I'd also like you to take over IDing the people who bought suitcases and cross-referencing it with the sale or hire of Peugeot 208s. Larry, have you got the lists on that?'

'Sure have, Cig. I dropped them to Jordy this morning.'

'And, Mick and Susan, I want hard evidence that our girl was at the hospital with her collarbone. I believe CCTV has come through from the hospital for the day in question?'

'Yes,' Mick says. 'And patient lists and we're making contact with them.'

A brief nod. 'So, on to the latest murder. I have reassigned Lucy, Dan and Kev to it for now. Last night the body of Adam Gray was discovered in a house four kilometres outside Westport in Croy. We do know that he was a volunteer in the shelter that Abby was last seen in, so there is a tenuous connection between this murder and Abby Devine's. However, they will be investigated separately for now.' William then gives a rundown of the scene yesterday, of how it was staged to look like suicide, and says that he and Garda Matt Bourke will attend the PM.

'SOCO are still gathering evidence at the scene and we should have some results from Forensics later today,' William goes on. 'Joe Palmer, who examined the body in situ, has sent through a brief report. Dan?'

Dan reads out Joe's report, which pretty much says what I told William last night. I feel a certain amount of pride in my deductive abilities.

Dan sits down and a guard who had been at the scene gives a rundown of the statement taken from the woman who'd found the body.

'Louise Roche, she's the owner of the property. She says that the house was originally booked by a woman who comes down every year, but that this year she had a death in her family and was unable to travel. She cancelled at the last minute and our IP booked it within the hour. Louise says she talked to him when he arrived and that he seemed nice but dim.' He looks up from his notes, and says apologetically, 'Her words. He didn't seem suicidal and said he was down for the fishing and for a break. I asked her if anyone else had keys to the property and she just said that keys go missing all the time, tenants lose them and that, but she didn't think anyone actually had another set of keys. That's it.'

'Good.' William nods.

The job sheets are given by the IRC with strict instructions on how the tasks are to be handled. Kev is told to talk to Louise about previous guests, to see if she can remember who had lost keys – she might even have a note of them. The door-to-door team is assembled by a trained sergeant. CCTV will be harvested from the local area, and I know that it will amount to sweet feck-all.

'Thanks, everyone,' William says at the end. 'And remember, assume nothing,' I think that's directed at me, 'believe nothing and check everything. Then check everything again. A, B and C. And C, A.'

The room clears, people filing out, unable to comprehend that, in just over a week, two people have met their deaths in this quiet part of the country. It'll be all over the news today. We'd somehow managed to keep a lid on the latest murder last night.

'Lucy,' William barks from the door, 'join me.'

'I'll get the car organised,' Dan says.

I thank Dan and join William at the door, my jacket over my arm, knowing I won't need it. The car will be a sauna on the drive up.

I follow William to his office. He sits down and indicates for me to sit too. I wonder will he say something about his outburst of the previous night. But no. 'Lucy,' he says, 'you're a good detective but the murder of a child tests us all. For God's sake, don't go colouring this investigation with assumptions.'

'I haven't done that.'

'I'm not saying you have, but the temptation is there. We need the team to follow the facts, not their hearts. While there is a link, and it's good to be aware of it, a few radio parts in a property and a volunteer job aren't enough right now to say they're connected.'

'I am aware of that, Cig. I was just pointing it out. It's an observation.' My voice is ice.

His eyes bore into me. 'Fine,' he says eventually. 'Now, to business.' He leans towards me. 'There will be a *Crimecall* appeal in the next few days for more information on Abby's murder. I'd like you to do it. You are the best authority on it right now.'

I am horror struck. I bloody hate doing those things.

'It'll be recorded,' he says, as if that should make me happy.

'Fantastic,' I mutter.

'You can go now,' he says, flicking on his computer and opening a file.

Dan is waiting for me, the air-conditioner running full blast. He's stocked up on biscuits and water for the journey. 'What did he say?'

'Not to assume anything.'

'I figured as much.'

'And he wants me to go on *Crimecall*.'

'Bollix.'

'Yep.'

I reckon Dan laughs all the way to Dublin.

Chapter 30

All I seem to do these days is interviews. But with each case, there's a certain number you have to get through. And Adam Gray's father is top of our list. The two lived in a small apartment in Dundrum, a nice enough area on Dublin's southside.

Though the building looks smart from the outside, the apartment where the Grays live is an absolute hovel. The air of neglect in the place makes Lugs Larkin's house appear positively cosy. The hall carpet is grey and stained and I can't tell if it's the apartment or the carpet that smells of dirt. Unwashed clothes are piled in heaps around the place, while incongruous pictures of kittens and baskets of flowers hang crookedly on walls that badly need painting. Mugs, plates, knives and forks trail from the table all the way to the kitchen sink.

'Sit down,' Mr Gray says, and his accent is pure Mayo, which makes my ears perk up. He takes a seat on a chair atop a pile of clothes. Dan removes some underwear from a sticky-looking green velvet sofa, worn shiny with the years, and sits facing Mr Gray. I remain standing in the space between the hall and the kitchen.

'We're sorry for your loss,' I say.

Mr Gray acknowledges the words by picking up a glass of what looks like whiskey from a battered coffee-table and downing it. 'We weren't close,' he says. 'My fault.' He pours himself another drink from a bottle by his chair.

'He lived here, though?'

'He did.' He thinks about that as he contemplates the drink in his glass. 'Boy was odd. Clever but stupid, not good for life, you know. He had a bit of a breakdown in his teens, never the same since. But his mother was a queen.' He glares at us as if daring us to disagree. 'She died three and a half years ago and I promised her I'd look out for him. I would have done anything for that woman. I've kept my promise but it hasn't been easy.' He looks at me, head cocked sideways. 'We were like two islands in an ocean.'

That explains the house. Two men grieving, the glue that kept them together.

'What can you tell us about Adam?' I ask.

'I tried hard to understand him, I did, but he wasn't like me. Wasn't like a boy, to be honest. All day in his room, tinkering about with stuff. The older he got, the odder he got. All through school he was picked on, bullied, made fun of, and he kept going back for more. He wanted friends so bad 'twas like a light on his head that said "Desperate". And, sure, that was all the vultures needed. I tell you now,' he leans towards me, glass clasped in his hand, 'I lost count of the number of times Elsie, that's my wife, tried to tell him to pull away, but he wouldn't listen. Easy led. He fell in love with anyone who showed him a scrap of attention. And once you were his friend, he wouldn't let go. There was no boundary with him. It was all or nothing. He broke his mother's heart. I tried to toughen him up but it made things worse.'

143

'Toughen him up?'

He rolls the whiskey glass between the flat palms of his hands and doesn't look at us as he says, 'I was hard on him, I suppose, but 'twas the only way. He wouldn't learn. Now look at him, he's bloody dead.'

'Did you beat him?'

'Aye, I did. I'm not proud of it.'

I let the emotion dissolve before saying, 'Did he work, Mr Gray?'

'Aye. As a doorman in some bar in town.' He screws up his face. 'McAdam's bar, I think it is. He probably just had to stand there and say nothing and that'd suit him, so it would. He's a big lad. If you didn't know him, he'd scare you off so he would. And if he was told what to do, he'd do it. And it was a waste. He was a clever lad.'

'If anyone had given him trouble, what would he have done?'

'If he'd been told to thump someone, he probably would have.' He takes a slug of whiskey, then adds, with a hint of bitterness, 'You know the way you can tell a dog to be "on guard" and that dog will defend to the very last even if it's the most placid dog? Adam was like that. Be a bouncer, Adam, and Adam would be exactly like what he thought a bouncer should be. I used to . . .' He stops, thinks about what he's going to say, then shrugs as if it doesn't matter any more. 'When the wife was out, I'd push him around, tell him to stand up for himself and always, always he'd cower away. He didn't trust me enough to believe me. But if a stranger offered him a scrap, he'd devour it.'

'How did he get the job?' I ask.

'That's the mystery, isn't it? Maybe they felt sorry for him. He's had the job a while now, though. I don't know much about his life, but I know he liked that job. He bought his car with his bonus a couple of months back and he was always taking off in it. Gave us both a break.' He waves the whiskey bottle about. 'Drink?'

We refuse and wait as he tops up his glass. He has the untidy look and the heavy eyes of a serious drinker. His lack of concern for his son is shocking.

'Was Adam away from home around July, Mr Gray?'

He looks at me oddly, not understanding why I'm asking. 'I'm not rightly sure. He'd go away on and off quite a bit, like I said.'

'All right.' I fish out two sets of pictures, one that includes James Devine and the other Abby. 'Would he have known either of those two?'

He barely glances at them. 'I never saw them with him, anyway.'

'Fine.' I tuck away the pictures, disappointed. 'I believe he volunteered at a homeless shelter?'

He splutters out a laugh. 'I doubt that. Volunteering would have meant being out even more in the world, so no, I would say that's wrong information.'

I let it go. Instead, I ask, 'Do you know of anyone who would want to hurt Adam?'

'Like I said, I . . .' Then, after a second, he frowns and says hesitantly, 'Well, there was this time, years ago, but it was a long time ago and . . .' He stops. 'No, no, it's nothing.'

'Let us judge if it's nothing,' I say. 'Tell us anyway.'

'Well, you can probably tell from the accent, I'm from the same part of the country as yourself, Guard. Just beyond Westport. We lived out of the town a bit and we were happy there. Adam loved it. But when he was about, oh,' he stares upwards, at his yellow ceiling, thinking, 'fourteen, I suppose, this girl, she was his friend apparently, a year or so older than him, well, she accused Adam of stalking her and scaring her and of trying to kiss her. Now, Adam was odd but harmless. He wouldn't know what harassment was, but if he liked someone or something, he could get a bit obsessive. And he'd taken a fancy to this girl, Ellie her name was. It was Ellie this and Ellie that all the time. Then she accused him of forcing himself on her. I mean, Adam? He was a child. My wife went to sort it out, but the girl's father, he threatened all sorts. And then people stopped letting their children talk to Adam. There was talk of prosecution. It all got out of hand. So, we moved up here. Adam was miserable but it was better all around.' There's a pause, before he says, 'People can be terrible. They see someone different and they persecute them. It was nothing short of persecution.'

It doesn't look good for Adam, though, I think.

'Would you have the name of that family?'

'John Walsh was the father.' He gives us an address. 'I don't know if they still live there. It was about fifteen years ago.'

'How did Adam seem before he headed off on his trip?'

'I don't know. He was driving me mad in the last few weeks, though. All I could hear was him tinkering about in his room with them auld radios he was always repairing, then pacing up and down, mumbling and not sleeping. Drove me mad.'

'Did he appear stressed, agitated?'

'You keep asking me this stuff. I don't know.' He slams his glass onto the coffee-table and whiskey splashes out. 'I don't know.'

'But you noticed he was pacing and mumbling and not sleeping. Was that normal for him?'

He shakes his head. 'Normally he slept like the dead. Even

146

when he got the job as the bouncer or doorman or whatever it was, if he was late in, he'd go straight to bed, clothes and all. But lately, he'd been . . .' He shrugs, unable to find the words. 'Once or twice I heard him shout out like he was having a bad dream or something.'

'And did you ever ask him if he was all right?'

A long silence. Then Mr Gray hunches forward in his chair, elbows on his knees, the whiskey glass in his right hand. He stares into it for an age. Dan and I stay quiet.

'No,' he says then, almost a whisper, the word filled with such regret that it catches me by surprise. 'No,' he repeats, with a shake of his head. 'I couldn't break it down, the barrier.' And he covers his face with his free hand and his shoulders start to shake. 'I never thought . . .' he says, his voice ragged. He takes a swipe at his nose, which is running. 'I never thought he'd go first.'

'It's all right,' Dan says, though it's clearly not. 'Take your time.'

'I'll make tea.' I pick my way through discarded clothes into the kitchen. It takes a moment to find the kettle under the detritus and even longer to locate a mug. A couple in the sink look usable. I scald them with boiling water, and a few minutes later, I place a cup of black tea in front of him, the milk in the fridge not looking or smelling its best. I hand Dan a mug too. He takes it dubiously.

'I put sugar in the tea,' I say to Mr Gray, 'But I'm not a doctor so it might not work.'

I'm rewarded with a shaky smile. 'I'm sorry. I don't normally . . .' He stops. Starts again: 'I think the worst part is that I never accepted him. And he knew it. I'd look at him and feel a failure. It must have hurt him. And now . . .' He takes a slurp of tea and gags, reaches for the whiskey. 'He must have been up to all sorts and I never asked. I never protected him.'

'Maybe he was just unlucky, nothing you could have done,' Dan says. He stands up. 'Any chance we can see his room?'

'Aye.' He gets unsteadily to his feet. 'This way.'

Dan treads on a half-eaten Mr Kipling cake. He holds one foot in the air, not sure what to do.

'It's fine.' Mr Gray waves a hand. 'Place is a kip anyway. Just wipe it on the carpet.'

With a pained look, Dan does as he is bade. He's a neat freak, is Dan. Fran, his partner, is the sloppy one. We follow Mr Gray out and he opens the last door off the hallway. 'In here,' he says.

Bright sunlight pours through the bedroom window and lends itself to the absolute weirdness and dazzle of the space. The whole room, walls, doors and ceiling, is covered with superhero posters: Batman and Robin, the Green Goblin, Spider-Man and Deadpool, Wolverine, Joker, Lex Luther and Kingpin. The poster that dominates the room and hangs over his bed is Voldemort from the Harry Potter books, the snake coiled around his arm. 'Jesus,' I whisper, pulling on a pair of gloves.

And there are radios everywhere. And bits of radios, the pieces all arranged on plastic sheeting on the floor, labelled as to what they are and what model they came from.

'Yeah,' Mr Gray says. 'He loved all that superhero rubbish. The boy never grew up.' He's recovered from his outburst of emotion and is back to criticising his son. 'He didn't care if they were villains or heroes once they had a superpower. And there are layers of posters here. There are ones underneath those, and ones underneath those again.'

'And the radios?'

148

'He fixed them,' his dad says. 'That's what he spent his days doing. He could fix anything. He could have made a living from it if he'd wanted. Watches and clocks he was good at too. But he loves the radios and the record players and that. Nerdy. Bought the parts online, put them together and sold the radios on or just plain gave them away. Good at maths too. Got an H1 in the higher paper in the Leaving.' He rolls his eyes. 'And he was a bouncer.'

We need someone to examine that plastic sheeting to see if it's the same sort that Abby was wrapped in. And we need those radio parts forensically examined too. There is one very manky-looking single bed. A brown chest. I pull open a few drawers and see underwear, some letters from banks looking for his business, car insurance and mountains of old photographs and albums.

'I can't believe he kept mementos of school,' Mr Gray says, peering over my shoulder as I flick through a yearbook. 'His school days were not happy.'

'We'll have someone in to examine the room and take away anything of interest that might help in the investigation, if that's all right?'

I only ask out of politeness.

'That's fine.'

'Did he have a laptop or a phone?'

'He did. But sure he would have brought them with him off fishing. He was never without his phone and laptop.'

I hadn't seen any in Louise's house.

I ask for Adam's number and jot it down. At the very least, we can get his phone records.

'Don't hesitate to call us if anything strikes you. Otherwise we'll be in touch with any news,' Dan finally says.

'Thanks.'

We leave him standing in the middle of his son's room.

'Christ,' Dan says, as we wait for the lift to bring us back downstairs, 'how does he live like that?'

'He's not living.' I walk ahead, forcing him to catch up. I have a need to get away from this impossibly sad place. 'Let's head to McAdam's bar. Then on to the shelter, see if we can talk to Gareth about him. He's looking like an interesting proposition. He knew both victims.'

'We need to establish a connection between Abby and Adam in life if we're to have a chance of linking the murders,' Dan says.

'We could go to Mary Devine and—'

'No.' Dan shuts me down. 'Ring Jordy and ask him to get someone to present Abby's family with a series of pictures, one of which is Adam, to see if they recognise him.'

I bristle. 'Who is the boss here?'

'You are, but think of me as your sensible self, the one that doesn't fuck up their job and piss their boss off by haring off on unnecessary journeys.' Dan unlocks the car and sits in. 'Right?'

I glare at him as I pull open the passenger door. 'Fran might love it when you come over all bossy and dominant, but I don't.'

'Just as well I'm not trying to shag you, then.'

I laugh. 'Just drive, arsehole.'

Chapter 31

There are several McAdam's bars dotted about the country – there's even one in Westport, which I've never been to – but the main one, the flagship, is in Dublin, right on the quays, near enough to the Bord Gáis Energy theatre.

The lounge is quiet, not many customers in yet as Dan and I approach a youngish barman, Asian, polishing glasses behind the dark wood bar. 'We're looking for the manager, please,' I say.

The barman barely acknowledges us. Instead, half lifting his head, he calls out, 'Miss Helen, two people here for you!'

'What do they want?' A person, presumably Helen, calls from a room somewhere. I spot a door a little way down behind the bar.

I flash some ID and the barman immediately scurries off to tell Helen that the guards are here.

'You can go on in,' he tells us, a couple of minutes later. 'She's in the office.'

I sense his flat gaze on us as we pass.

Helen is signing some documents behind a large, well-organised desk as we enter. Capping her pen, she puts the papers aside, stands up and shakes our hands. She's a woman who has worked hard on her appearance. I'd imagine she was one of those plain girls in school who discovered early on that, if she wore enough make-up and spent a pile of money on clothes and her hair, she could pass muster.

I am a total mess beside her. I only wear make-up to cover the worst of my scar. And even then it barely does the job.

'Guards,' she says, waving us to a seat, 'how can I help you?' Her dental work is perfect. Her voice rich and beguiling. A neutral accent, impossible to place. 'Can I get you a coffee?'

'No, thanks,' Dan says, much to my disappointment. 'We're here because we're interested in finding out about one of your employees. Adam Gray?'

'Yes, I know Adam.' She sits down, carefully folding her skirt under her as she does so. 'He's a doorman here now and again, or he was. He's been very unreliable lately.' There's an edge of impatience in her voice.

'Unfortunately, Adam is dead.' Dan gives Helen a moment to absorb the news.

For a second it seems as if she has to think about what to say. Then she gulps out, 'That's dreadful. Can I ask, how . . . or what . . .?'

'It's an ongoing investigation so I'm not at liberty to reveal details but you can appreciate that we need to know everything about him in order to understand what happened.'

'Of course.' She flaps a hand for him to continue. Her nails must be false. A fancy ring glitters on one finger. She's a woman who has done well for herself.

'How long has Adam been working here?'

'Since we opened. Three years on and off. He's a doorman but, as I said, recently he hasn't been the most dependable.'

'As in?'

'He keeps missing work and he appeared to be very stressed.' She pauses. 'I don't know much about him – he kept himself to himself – but I always got the impression that there was more going on in his life than we knew. Adam was . . . odd. He was a strange man. Some of the girls here wouldn't go near him but I always found him a nice enough fellow.'

'How did he get the job?' Dan asks.

'He came for interview and he was just so . . . eager. He really wanted to be a doorman. He reminded me of a kid who wanted to grow up to be a footballer. And I thought I'd give him a chance. It's not full-time, just something to give him money. And he worked out well until, like I said, recently.'

'Right. Can you tell me if he took any holiday leave in July?' Dan's deliberately side-stepping her observations, seeing if she'll bring it up again.

Helen presses buttons on her computer. Then more buttons. 'Here we are,' she says, swivelling the screen around. 'That's Adam's schedule,' she says, pointing. 'It looks like he did tell me he wouldn't be around to work from the first of July, which was a Thursday, to the fifth of July, which was Monday. So, a long weekend. He was apparently available all the time after that.'

Something in what she has said shimmers in my head, just out of reach . . .

'You say he seemed stressed?' Dan goes on, and the moment is lost.

'He was.'

'Any idea why?'

'I tried to ask him,' Helen says. 'But, as I said, he wasn't about much and he was a strange character. He didn't engage, just did his job and went home.'

'Why were your female staff wary of him if he didn't engage?'

Helen flushes a little. 'His oddness, I suppose, which sounds terrible. A couple of girls said he was staring at them, but really . . . it was just his way.'

'Can we talk to these girls?'

'It was a while ago. They've moved on now. I can barely remember who they were.'

'If you do, give us a call.' Dan passes over his card and she takes it. 'We also need contact details for your staff, for anyone who worked with Adam. Is there anyone you think who would wish him harm?'

'Harm? What do you mean? What happened to him?'

'We're not sure as yet.'

'When you said dead, I thought . . .'

'What did you think?' Dan asks.

'I don't . . . well . . . I don't know. Just not . . . Anyway, of course I'll print you out a list of my staff now.'

My phone rings and I glance at caller ID. It's Jordy. He wouldn't be ringing me if it wasn't important. 'I'll just take this. I won't be a moment.'

I leave Dan with Helen.

'Jordy,' I say, when I've found a quiet space, 'what's the story?'

His answer is preceded by a chesty cough that has me wincing. When he recovers, Jordy is straight down to business. 'I, eh, wasn't sure if it was you I should be ringing, like you're not on the Abby case now, but at the last conference—'

'What is it, Jordy?'

'I got images of that jewellery – you know, the jewellery from the robbery?'

154

'Yes, and?' My heart hops a bit.

'There were some very distinctive pieces that were never recovered. So, I checked all the usual sources, pawn shops and the like, and finally, I checked eBay for anything similar sold in the last two months. And I found a bracelet and a necklace sold this May that are a match.'

'Go on.'

'The account is in the name of a Jerome Smyth.'

'Do we know anything about him?'

'He's not come to our attention before. From what I could gather, he's twenty-one, and an arts student. He sells everything on the site, so there was a box of T-shirts going for fifty quid and Kev put in a bid for them. I don't know how to do that sort of thing. Anyway, we got them and told him we'd pick them up. Got the address that way. Turns out he lives in Blackrock, twenty-four Manor Park in Dublin. Now, here's the interesting thing. We found some social-media accounts for him, and guess what?'

'Hit me.'

'He's an old school friend of James Devine. They seem quite tight.'

'No way!'

'So, Kev dug a little more and get this. The Devines originally lived in Blackrock and only moved into Pearse Gardens in the last nine years. After the father left.'

'Beautiful.'

'What do you want to do?'

I think about it. Dan and I are up here for Adam's murder but, hey, if it's connected to Abby's, we might as well talk to the lad, seeing as we're up in Dublin anyhow. 'We'll arrest him under suspicion of handling stolen property. Ring Blackrock, tell them we're going to bring him in and to have a room ready.'

'Will do. Good luck now.'

'That's fantastic work,' I say. 'I'll make sure William is told.'

'Whatever,' Jordy says, not much caring. 'See ye when ye get back down.'

He promises to email me some jpegs of the jewellery before he hangs up.

When I go back into the office, Dan is winding up the interview with Helen.

She sees us to the door, wishes us luck with the investigation, and we emerge from the pub into blinding sunshine.

Dan peels off his jacket and slings it over his arm. 'They're predicting a storm at some stage next week,' he says. 'All this bloody heat.'

'I'd welcome one.' I tell Dan about the phone call from Jordy.

'That's great,' he says. 'Will we get him now? We can catch Gareth when we're done. It'll be on the way home.'

I'm glad he doesn't say it's not our investigation now.

'Give Gareth a call and set it up.'

Dan rings, chats briefly and hangs up. 'Gareth is in Westport,' he says. 'Has been since yesterday. What do you think of that?'

I remember that Gareth did talk about visiting the Westport shelter the last time we saw him. How odd that it coincided with the death of one of his volunteers.

Westport is only four kilometres away from where Adam was found.

Chapter 32

Google informs me that Jerome's house is the next left turn.

'Smell that?' Dan inhales deeply.

'What?'

'Money.' He smirks. 'How the other five per cent live, eh?'

Blackrock is an affluent suburb in South Dublin. Most people in this area have serious cash. I indicate and we turn onto a wide road with large detached period houses on each side. No two are the same. High-end cars are parked in long driveways.

Number twenty-four is at the end of the road. A handsome red-brick, double-sided period house. There's a BMW in the driveway. 'I'd imagine he's selling more than T-shirts,' Dan observes.

'Either that or it's his parents' house.'

We get out of the car and walk up the drive. There's a hush about the place, like the muffled sound you get in an expensive car. It's hard to believe that this street is just a turning off the main road. The garden isn't particularly well tended, but it seems not to matter: the house can absorb it. Dan rings the bell and the door is opened by a young man, wearing expensive sports clothes. His hair is artfully messy. He's got rich-boy good looks, smooth skin, perfect teeth and an air of confidence that comes with privilege. He offers us a warm smile, showing more of those shiny whites. 'Are you here for the T-shirts?'

Dan flashes him his card and makes the introductions. There is a moment when the boy flinches, but it's fleeting. Maybe I imagine it.

'Jerome Smyth,' Dan says, 'we're arresting you on suspicion of handling stolen property under the Criminal Justice and Fraud Offences Act. You do not—'

'Jerome, I almost tripped over that box in the kitchen,' an irritated woman calls, from somewhere in the house. Emerging into the hallway, she looks from her son to Dan and back again. 'What's going on?'

'It's the guards, Ma. They want to arrest me.' Jerome sounds like he might cry.

'What?' She hurries towards us on stockinged feet, carrying what looks like sludge in a glass. She's been doing yoga or something. 'What for?' Then, to her son, 'Jerome, what have you done?'

'I don't know.'

Dan continues with the caution. 'Do you understand?' he finishes.

'No. No.'

'We're arresting you over some jewellery you sold recently on your eBay site,' I say pleasantly.

Jerome takes a step back and I think, Bingo. He bloody knew it was stolen. But, of course, that's not proof. I caution him again.

'He sells everything on that site,' his mother says.

'Can you come now?' Dan says, ignoring her.

'Ma, they want me to go now,' Jerome says.

His mother seems to realise he has no choice. 'Go, baby. I'll ring your father. Don't say a word until we engage a solicitor for you. Go.'

And we're off.

A few hours later, Jerome looks a little lost, sitting opposite us with his solicitor in Blackrock garda station. Dan has introduced us, told him that the interview will be written down and recorded, cautioned him and informed him once more of the purpose of the interview.

Jerome, well briefed by his solicitor, knows that he has questions to answer but it doesn't stop the wounded look on his face. He reeks of privilege, and my back is up already, which I know is a bit judgemental.

'Would you like a drink?' I ask him, as I take a seat. 'Or a sandwich. I've a lad your age – he never stops thinking of food.'

'I'm grand,' Jerome says. 'I had lunch earlier.'

We chit-chat for a bit, talk about sport and cars, leading on to some general questions about his eBay, which, it turns out, he's very proud of, having built up quite the reputation as a wheeler-dealer. 'People trust me to give them decent stuff,' he says.

Finally, his foot stops tapping up and down and his hands relax on the desk.

'I just want to show you a couple of pictures,' I say. I place two in front of him. 'For the record, I'm now showing you Exhibits A1 and A2. A1 is an image of a gold bracelet with an opal inset, and A2 is an image of a diamond-studded necklace made to order in 1980 by a Mr Jim Deasy for his wife Carmel. 'Do you recognise these pieces, Jerome?'

He shifts about, glances at his solicitor, then mutters, 'Yes.'

'Tell me why you recognise them?'

'Because I sold them on my eBay last May.'

'Do you recall what date you sold them?'

'Late May, I think. Very late May. It'd be on my laptop.'

'Describe to me how you came into possession of these pieces, Jerome.'

'How I got them?' He shifts about on the chair and gears himself up.

'Yes.' Come on, pretty boy.

'Well, like I already said, I have a website but you know that already because you promised to buy T-shirts from me and you didn't.' His tone is faintly accusatory. 'I have to resell them now.' I think he wants us to apologise. After a moment, he goes on hastily, 'Anyway, basically, what I do on the site is I sell things for myself and on behalf of other less successful sellers. I have a shed–load of stuff to shift.' A moment of self-preening, which is nauseating. 'I make a good profit. People come to me and ask me to sell things they aren't able to sell themselves and I charge them a small fee. Anyway, that's how I got the jewellery.'

'What do you mean?'

'Someone asked me to sell it for them.'

'Who?'

'This girl,' he says, and there is something almost too casual in the way he tells us. Like he's practised it. 'I didn't get her name. She turned up on my doorstep with the stuff. She was just a kid. I have no idea how she found me.' A roll of his eyes. 'Maybe she bought something from me in the past or maybe someone told her about me. She said it was her mother's jewellery. She said her mother was sick and she needed money for medicine and she

160

wanted me to sell it for her. I asked her why she wouldn't go to a jeweller's, like I did ask, but she said she thought I'd make more money for her. And I'm a guy who trusts people. I didn't know it was stolen.'

'And then?'

'I sold it, gave her the money and kept a few bob for myself. Never saw her since.'

'Can you describe this girl?'

He gives an almost too accurate description of Abby. I place twelve photos in front of him, narrating for the purposes of the tape, and ask him if he can identify the girl for us.

'That girl,' he says, pointing to Abby.

'For the record, Mr Jerome Smyth has pointed at Abby Devine,' I say.

'Yeah.' He looks up at us. 'That's right.' Then, hastily, 'I never copped it was the same girl that was found in the suitcase but now you say the name I recognise her.'

And we're in.

'You must have been one of the last people to see her alive, Jerome. That's quite significant. What date did you pay her the money?'

He's wary now. 'I don't remember.'

I leave it a moment. 'It's important that you do because if you were the last person to see her—'

'I really don't remember.'

God, I love this bit, especially when they're as clueless as this idiot self-entitled kid. 'Thanks for that, Jerome.'

'No bother,' he says. He leans his arms on the table and runs a hand through his hair. I'd imagine teenage girls would fancy him like mad.

'You sell lots of things on your site. Would that be fair to say?'

'Like I said, I sell everything. Anything I can make money from.'

'Very enterprising.'

'That's what my father says.'

'Name a few things.'

He lists off an eclectic amount of stuff.

'And how often have you sold jewellery on your site?'

He shrugs. 'I don't know.'

'Never,' I tell him. 'I checked your site. No jewellery at all up until this mysterious girl knocked on your door.'

An interesting thing we spotted was that he sells radio parts too.

'There's always a first time,' he says.

'There is.' I wait a second, letting him relax, then ask, 'So, Abby Devine came and asked you to sell this jewellery.'

'Yes.'

'And you never met her before?'

'No.'

'She has a brother, James Devine, did you ever meet him?'

It's like watching a rabbit freeze in headlights. He hadn't been expecting that. Then he recovers. Swallows. 'Eh . . . it's ringing no bells.' He tries to look puzzled.

'I'm showing Mr Jerome Smyth Exhibit A3, a picture taken from his Instagram account.' I lay a picture in front of Jerome taken with a beaming James Devine. 'Can you hear that bell now?'

Jerome opens his mouth, then snaps it closed.

'Who is in the picture, Jerome?'

'Me and James Devine,' he mutters. Then, 'He was just in my school. I didn't really know him.'

I place two more photographs in front of him, showing the two of them together, laughing.

It takes a moment, but I can feel it coming.

He says, 'Am I going to be in huge trouble?'

'That depends on what you're going to say,' I tell him. 'And I have to remind you again that you're under caution.'

The longest pause.

'Right, well . . .' Jerome heaves a sigh and gazes at us hopelessly, as if he thinks we'll somehow rescue him '. . . it was like this. And this is the truth. I do know James, you're right. He used to go to my old school until he had to move. And I did meet up with him when he came out of prison, like – he wasn't a real criminal. He didn't sell drugs or shoot people. He's sound. And, anyway, hadn't he done his time?' He's not expecting an answer. 'We met up and went for drinks and that, and I told him what I was doing, and then, around April, he asked me would I sell some jewellery for him. Like there was no pressure or anything. I sort of thought it might be a bit . . . dodgy . . . like, where would he get jewellery, but I never asked. He needed the money real bad, he said, and I felt sorry for him. He promised me half. I wouldn't take it off him. He was a mate. So, I said, yeah, I'd sell it for him, that's what mates do for each other. Anyway, he brought it to me around the second week of May. He said if anyone asked, I should say his sister had given it to me. He said she wouldn't get into trouble the way he would.' He stumbles to a halt. In a sort of a whine, he adds, 'That's what he said.'

'Let's nail down a few dates here,' I say. 'When did James come to you with the jewellery?'

'I put it up for sale about two days after he gave it to me. You can get the date from the eBay site. Am I in trouble?'

'That'd be the twenty-second of May,' Dan says, ignoring him as he looks through his phone. 'So, you're saying two days before that?'

'Yeah.'

Which means James must have taken the jewellery from Abby around that time.

'And when did you give James his money?'

'I met up with him a week later and paid him in cash. It was over three thousand euro. I didn't take anything from it.'

'He said he needed the money. Did he say why?'

'No.'

'And you say he wanted to put the blame on his sister?'

'Yeah, it made sense. She was just a kid.'

'Were you in contact with him after that?'

'Well . . . yeah. Just on the phone. I haven't talked to him since his sister was, you know, murdered. I was freaked out about that.'

We can check his phone for calls to and from James, I think. Or check James's phone.

It's beautiful. So, James was in contact with Abby long after early May. He had taken the jewellery from her despite telling us that she had got rid of it herself. However, about misremembering when he last saw her, he cannot misremember whether or not he sold on that jewellery.

'To be clear,' I say to Jerome, 'you're admitting to selling jewellery you suspected might be stolen on your website.'

'Well . . . yeah, but it was for a friend and I made no money.'

'All right, Jerome. Detective Guard Dan Brown is going to

164

read back to you your statement, and if you agree with it, can you sign it, please?'

Dan reads the statement to him and he signs it. Dan and I sign it too.

We flick the recorder off and end the interview.

'What will happen now?' Jerome asks, looking from me to Dan.

For now, he won't be charged, because if he is, we can't re-interview him, though it's unlikely he knows much more. 'The gaoler will bring you back to your cell. You'll be released but down the line you'll be charged with handling stolen property.'

His tearful 'Aw, no' follows us out of the door.

When we emerge, a couple of detectives are waiting.

'You're lucky he was brainless.' One laughs.

'Most of them are.' Dan smirks back.

'Excuse me, I'm looking for my son. Is he out yet?'

This can only be Jerome's father. He's tall, athletic, with a long nose that's just perfect for looking down upon lowly detectives like me. I'll just bet he was one of the rugby stars at whatever private school he went to.

'He'll be out shortly,' I say.

'What's this I hear about stolen goods? Jerome would never dare—'

'I'm not at liberty to discuss it with you,' I say, walking past.

He blocks my way. 'I want to talk to whoever is in charge.'

'You're talking to her.'

A huff of a laugh. 'You've made a huge mistake. You'll be sent to police in the middle of nowhere by the time me and my legal team are finished with you.'

'Too late. Someone got there before you,' I say to Mr Smyth. Turning, 'Dan, let's go.'

'Right-oh, boss,' he says, falling in behind me.

I can hear the laugh in his voice.

Chapter 33

Back in the car, we call William with an update. I make sure to credit Jordy for the lead on the jewellery.

'I thought I made it clear you were off that case,' is the first thing he says after I've told him everything.

'Yes, but I mean we were up here and—'

'And you did your own thing.'

Beside me, Dan looks appalled.

'I suppose you could put it like that but—'

'I did put it like that. It is like that.'

I swallow hard. 'Yes. I suppose it is. But we were in Dublin and—'

'We'll talk about this when you get back,' he snaps. 'What's your thinking now?'

'Well, if Jerome is telling the truth and I think he is,' I say meekly, 'because he totally implicated himself, it seems pretty obvious that James lied to us for the second time. He must have tracked Abby down and taken the jewellery from her. Jerome was given the jewellery on the twentieth of May, which means that James had to have seen Abby around that time to have taken it from her. And that homeless girl Carla said Abby was roaring that

167

she'd been robbed, so maybe it was James. Did he assault her? She had a broken collarbone and James has a history of violence. And, to top that, he wanted to blame Abby for giving the jewellery to Jerome. Maybe he knew she wouldn't be around to defend herself. Maybe Jerome knew it too. I think we need to arrest James. The motive is there.'

My voice has risen despite myself. I think I've been a bit too passionate. William waits a moment, then says, 'Dan?'

'First off, William, sorry we went haring off, but we were finished our interviews up here and—'

'Your thoughts, Dan?' William's voice is steely.

'Right, well, I know there's a lot we need to still ask ourselves, Cig, but I'm with Lucy. James has been lying to us. I think at the very least we need to drill down into his story and either make him a person of interest or rule him out.'

Silence from the other end of the phone as William thinks some more. 'All right,' he says. 'He's been caught lying twice now. Arrest him first thing tomorrow and get a search warrant for the house. I'll get ye booked into Dubh Linn Hotel.'

I grin in satisfaction.

'And now, tell me, how have you actually got on with the case you were sent up to investigate?'

We give him a run-down of our interviews with Adam's father and Helen. 'Both say he was stressed, which would tally with him being involved in something,' I say. 'Any luck on prints yet, Cig?'

'Kev says by tomorrow for sure. He's asked for the print found in the blood on the plastic sheeting on Abby's body to be compared with anything that turns up on the plastic found at Adam Gray's murder.'

'Good.'

168

'Keep me posted.' A moment, then he says, 'Go in early on James tomorrow. We don't need him catching wind of Jerome's interview.'

And he's gone.

Later that evening, we get the news that the print found in the blood on the plastic sheeting Abby was wrapped in is a match for Adam's finger. So, we have a connection, which means Dan and I were right to go in on Jerome. And now we have a possible murderer in Adam, but no motive. And we have a motive for James but no forensics.

'To find out if James was involved, what do we need to know tomorrow?' I ask Dan that evening, as we're prepping for our interview.

Dan taps a pen on his teeth, thinking. 'At the very least we need to establish a connection between James and Adam,' he says. 'If there isn't one, if we can't find one, if we draw a blank on forensics, we can rule out James, because we know for definite Adam was there, which means we can rule out the jewellery as a motive. And if that proves the case we need to look a lot closer at Adam's life.'

'Good. So, tomorrow, we probe James on whether he did see Abby, which, let's face it, should be easy if we get his phone. Then we try to establish a connection between him and Adam.'

'Yep.'

I go to bed that night, satisfied that we know where we're going, but something niggles. Something we're missing. Something bloody obvious that I had almost grasped today when we'd been talking to Helen.

And though I lie awake most of the night, it won't come.

Chapter 34 – Day 9

After assigning an exhibits officer, I turn to the search team who have assembled in Pearse Street for the pre-search briefing. 'We're looking for anything that can tie James to the murder of Abby Devine or indeed Adam Gray. I want James's mobile phones and any laptops seized.' I hold up an image. 'Plastic sheeting of the type used to wrap Abby in. Any records that might relate to hiring a car, particularly in early July or in the past few days. Any jewellery from the original robbery five years ago. We'll need to examine his clothes, his shoes. I want everything bagged and tagged. Thanks everyone.'

We get into our cars and move out.

The look of horror on Mary Devine's face tears my heart open. 'We've come for James,' I tell her, when she answers the front door.

'What do you want with him?' She blocks the doorway, taking in me and Dan and the search team behind us.

'We're here to arrest James, and we have a warrant to search your house,' I say, keeping my voice as dispassionate as possible. 'It would be in your interests to cooperate, Mary.'

'I thought you were on my side,' she says to me, then turns to Dan. 'I thought both of you were.'

'We're on the side of finding out who killed your daughter,' Dan answers briskly, though I know he feels terrible about distressing her. 'Now, please, if you could just let us in.'

'Fucking pigs,' someone shouts from the garden wall. 'Wankers.'

'Mary, please?' Dan says. 'Don't make this difficult on yourself.'

'You're not coming in.' She shakes her head frantically and her eyes are desperate. 'No. No way. Not my boy.'

'What's happening?' James, in a T-shirt and boxers, appears at the top of the stairs. Seeing his mother upset, he takes the steps two at a time and comes to stand beside her in the doorway. He's a skinny, wiry little fecker. 'What's happening?'

'James Devine,' Dan says, 'We are arresting you under Section 4 of the Criminal Law Act on suspicion of the murder of Abby Devine. You—'

'What?' He gawks at us. 'Are you for real?'

'You are not obliged to say anything,' Dan talks over his protests, 'unless you wish to do so but anything you do say will be taken down in writing and may be given in evidence, do you understand?'

James looks to his mother, 'Ma, this is a load of bollix.'

'Do you understand?' Dan says.

'Of course I fucking do. You lot can't do your bloody job properly,' he snaps. 'So, you're making me a scapegoat.'

'You tell 'em, Jamesie,' someone shouts from outside. A cheer goes up.

'Jesus,' Dan mutters. Then to James, 'Go on up and get dressed. We'll wait.'

He throws us a poisonous look, gives his mother's arm a squeeze and slowly trots back upstairs. He'll take his sweet time, I reckon. Dan accompanies him.

'What have you got on him?' Mary whispers, looking terrified.

'I'm afraid we can't tell you that,' I say. 'I am sorry, Mary.'

She looks at me like I'm filth. 'Arresting him doesn't mean he's guilty, does it?'

'No, it means there's a suspicion about him. I've a search team here, Mary. You'll have to let us in.'

'He would never . . .' She shakes her head. 'He got mixed up with that awful boy Denis but that was after his father left and he went a bit mad and he's changed. He has. He would never . . .'

'We need to go in and search your house now,' I say gently, and with a small sob she moves aside and our guys push on by her. They will search every part of the house, being as meticulous as they can in teams of two. I stand in the hallway, waiting for James and Dan to come back.

They arrive down fifteen minutes later, James in a pair of garish green shorts, blue T-shirt, high-top runners and a baseball cap. He looks like something from an eighties American gangster movie. In the street, more people have gathered.

Dan pats him down, removes his mobile phone. 'You'll get a call at the station,' he tells him.

I cuff him, which causes his mother further distress. 'Stay between me and DG Brown,' I instruct him.

James, a little more scared than before, complies and we manage, amid jeers, to get him into the back of the car. He sits behind the passenger seat and Dan squeezes in beside him.

I drive.

'Do I need a solicitor?' he asks, after about five minutes.

'That's up to you,' Dan says.

James slumps back into silence.

When we reach the station, we have a conversation with the member in charge and James is soon cooling his heels in a cell, having been detained under Section 4 of the Criminal Justice Act.

Dan and I have only six hours to get an account from him or we'll need to seek more time from the super and that might not happen if we haven't made any progress.

The race is on.

Chapter 35

By two thirty the interview with James and his solicitor is well under way. I'm asking the questions because we reckon James will lose his shit easier with me than with Dan, and when people do that, they're liable to say anything.

I'm treading carefully, just as Dan and I agreed. The aim in the beginning is to build up some kind of rapport with the suspect, just to get them talking. James's gaze is hostile, flat. I'd say he'd like to hit me. His hands are clenched in front of him on the table. His breathing is heavy.

'All right, James,' I say, as pleasantly as I can, 'even though we've been through this before, what I'd like for you to do is to take us through, once more, the last time you saw your sister before she ran away.'

'I had nothing to do with her being murdered. This is crap. I'm saying nothing.' He folds his arms, leans back in his chair and regards me with a sneer.

'Fair enough. That's your right. If you're innocent, though, surely you'll want us to find the person who did it.'

'I am innocent.'

'Then help us. Convince me. Just answer our questions. When

was the last time you saw your sister before she ran off?'

He weighs things up, then says, 'I'm not sure. She wasn't always around so I never actually noticed when she was missing. It was just when I looked for the jewellery and it was gone that I put two and two together. But I can't remember for sure what day it was.'

'OK, thanks.' I pretend to think carefully about the next question. 'Can you take me through, in detail, as much as you remember about what happened after that?'

Once more he weighs up the pros and cons of talking. Come on, I think. Come on. It takes a few moments, but eventually, like an airlocked valve, his words spout out. 'You know I went looking for her after she disappeared, and I found her but all the stuff was gone. That was it. I never saw her again.'

'Take it slower. Where did you look for her? How did you find her? What did you say? That's all I want.'

He hesitates again. Then, 'She stole my stuff and I was panicked, like I already said, 'cause I didn't want it all coming back on me. I did not want to go back inside and so I went out looking for her. I told you that.' He heaves an exasperated sigh. 'I looked all over Dublin for, like, about four days. I don't know exactly. I had a photo of her, I showed it to people on the street and then one evening I seen her coming out of that hostel. The one on Moore Street. She was talking to this fella. Then he went and I goes over to her and she tries to run and I caught her and I held her hard and, anyway, the jewellery was gone and she wouldn't say where. I got real annoyed but, like, there was nothing I could do so I had to leave. Last time I seen her. I didn't say anything to me ma. She went out looking for her after but she couldn't find her. Then you lot turned up on the doorstep saying she was . . . dead.' He looks down at his hands. 'That's it.'

'And the man who ran you off?'

He jerks his head up. 'What?'

'When we talked to you last time you said this fellow in his twenties ran you off when you confronted your sister.'

A slow flush from his neck to his face. 'Did I? Right. Well, yeah, that fella she was talking to did, actually. It was a while back now.'

'You just told us you waited until he walked off before confronting your sister?'

'Yeah, well, maybe I didn't. It was months ago.'

'Maybe?'

'I didn't. He was there. He got aggressive. But the jewellery was gone.'

'Can you describe the man again?'

'No. I've forgot what he looked like.'

'Taller than your sister?'

'Well, yeah, obviously. She was tiny.'

'She was.' I allow that to sink in. I bite back my anger as the image surfaces of her in the suitcase. I have to remain calm. 'What age would you put on him?'

'Young. Tall. Hippie.'

While I immediately think of Gareth, I don't know if James is making this up now or not.

I make like I believe him. 'Good. Have you anything else to add?'

'Nope.' He runs a hand over his face and shifts in his seat. 'I did nothing to her, right.'

'You say you caught her and held her hard. Can you tell us what you said, what she said?'

'I said I wanted the jewellery, she said it was gone. I took

176

her bag offa her and it was gone. She was a bit out of it, to be honest.'

'I see.' I pretend to think about this. I run back over his story again and he nods away, agreeing that I've got it just right. I sigh, say regretfully, 'It's just that we have another witness who says that Abby was going about claiming she had been robbed.'

James stills, rallies: 'Maybe her drugs was robbed, all the crap she bought after she sold the jewellery.'

'Maybe,' I say. 'Maybe that's it. Now, for the purposes of the tape, I'm showing the suspect a picture, Exhibit A5.' I place a picture of Jerome on the table. 'Did you or Abby know this man?'

James leans forward and freezes. Slowly, he glances up at me. 'Eh . . . not sure,' he says, swallowing.

'This is the man on whose eBay account the jewellery you say Abby stole from you was sold.'

'Oh . . . right. Is that who she gave it to?'

'His name is Jerome Smyth. We've had a chat with him.'

James jerks like his string has just been pulled. Then a silence, as heavy and as sudden as a downpour, engulfs the room. After a second, he says, with a false cheeriness, 'Jerome Smyth. I do know him. Yes. And so did Abby. Maybe she sold them to Jerome. I know Jerome and I know she had a thing for him. Like, as a kid, when he'd be over in our house, he'd be nice to her and that. Maybe he offered to do her a favour, 'cause, like, that's what Jerome would do.'

Oh, neat. But not good enough.

At that moment there is a knock on the door. Just like we planned. It's one of the guards in the station. He apologises for the interruption, places a file in front of me and leaves. I give it a hasty flick-through and see that they've managed to crack James's phone records already and a number of calls and texts have been highlighted. And an identifying name written beside some of the texts makes my blood quicken. There is also a scribbled note inside the file, 'Nothing so far of significance found inside the house but early days.'

I close the file and rethink my line of questioning. If I play it right, I can snare him. Feigning nonchalance, I refocus on James. 'How do you know Jerome?'

'School. I used to live out that way.'

'Were you friends?'

'Years ago,' James says, 'then me, Ab and the ma moved away and I lost touch with him.' A moment. 'But, like, I know about his eBay account, everyone does. He tells everyone.'

'I see. When was the last contact you had with him?'

'I don't know.'

'He says he met you after you got out of prison.'

'I met a lot of people then. I was celebrating, wasn't I?'

'All right.' I tap the file that's just been handed to me. 'We have your phone records here, James. I'm going to terminate the interview for now while I have a better look at them.'

Disbelief and horror play out across James's face.

Dan reads out James's statement to him and asks him to sign it. We both sign it, too, before I gather my things and flick off the recorder. 'We'll be back after lunch. Some food will be arranged for you.'

As we leave, the gaoler takes James back to his cell.

Chapter 36

Prior to returning for the second interview, Dan and I have had a coffee and a sandwich and a chance to examine the quite honestly damning texts that were uncovered on James's phone. His solicitor arrives and asks to talk to us. I know him: he's one of the solicitors on the list provided by the state if a client hasn't one of their own. He's solid, and James is lucky to get him. Even though we don't have to chat with him, sometimes it can be helpful.

Thirty minutes later, Dan and I rejoin James and his solicitor in the interview room. The texts have made us re-evaluate our line of questioning. We can afford to be more direct now.

James looks a little more subdued, obviously beginning to realise the seriousness of his situation.

'Bearing in mind, James, we now have your phone records and we have talked to Jerome, is there anything else you'd like to add to your statement?'

'I did nothing to my sister,' he says.

I don't reply.

'I didn't.'

'Then help me out. What happened between the two of you? I just want the truth, that's all.'

He gives a huff of a sigh, almost despairing, and throws an irritated look at his solicitor. 'I did find Abby that time back in May and I lied, right? I lied. I was scared you'd blame me. Anyway, I saw her in Moore Street, like I said, and she was talking to this fella, and when he left, I went over and grabbed her. She had the stuff on her and she had no way of offloading it. The dealers wouldn't touch it. We didn't row, nothing. I done a deal with her. I told her I would sell it and we'd split the cash. I told her if she left and didn't come home, I'd give her money. She was stressing the ma out big-time. Me ma won't tell you but living with Abby was shite. Ma had breast cancer last year – she didn't need Abby's crap. Anyway, I took the jewellery and I contacted Jerome, I do know him, and he sold it for me. I gave Abby some money out of it. Jerome didn't know it was stolen. He's a good mate. Leave him out of it.'

That's unexpected.

'Describe how you got the jewellery from your sister?'

'She was happy to give it to me. It was either give it to me or dump it. Abby wasn't stupid.'

'And what date was this?'

'Around the middle of May.'

'And why didn't you tell us this before now? Why lie about it?'

'Because I didn't want you thinking I sold the stuff, did I? I don't want to go back inside.'

'You lied to us in a murder inquiry, James. That's a lot more serious than offloading jewellery you've already done time for.'

'I don't know the law, do I? I was scared.'

I divert for bit, it's easier to spot the lies then.

'I'm puzzled about something,' I say. 'Maybe you can help me.'

He says nothing.

'Why, then? Why did you suddenly, after six months out of prison, decide to sell the jewellery?'

'Didn't want it hanging around the house, did I?'

'You could have turned it in anonymously?'

'I could have,' he agrees.

'What did you do with the money?'

'I told you. I gave some to Abby, kept some myself.'

'You lost your job in Tesco around that time, didn't you?'

His Adam's apple wobbles as he swallows hard. 'How do you know that?'

Because the lads rang Tesco and anywhere else we could to check him out. I don't answer, though. He is such a fecking liar.

'Did your mother know about you losing your job?'

'Is this relevant?' his solicitor pipes up.

I push across the Law Society's 'Guidance for solicitors providing legal services in garda stations' with a raised eyebrow, and James's solicitor flushes.

'Did your mother know about you losing your job, James?'

'Nope.'

'You say you gave some of the money to Abby. Was she happy with her cut?'

His face drains of colour. He knows we know he's lying his arse off. Again.

'I didn't kill her,' he says to us, then turns to his solicitor. 'I didn't, I swear.'

'Can we go right back to the beginning, James?' I say. 'And start again? For the third time. And this time, tell us everything, all right?'

He brings the heels of his hands to his face and buries his head, rubbing his eyes. I think he might be about to cry. But he doesn't. He takes a few moments to compose himself. Then, inhaling deeply, he says, 'You have it all wrong. This is it, honest to God. Basically, it took me a while to find her after she left but I did and she still had the stuff on her. I caught up with her one day and we had a bit of a row. This fella ran me off, then I found her again, in Moore Street, and in the end, in return for a cut, she agreed to stay away. Only I never paid her, did I?' He says it defensively. 'I gave it to me ma so she wouldn't know I lost my job. Right?'

I wait. There is more. I know that from the texts. Dan flexes his fingers, tired of writing, and we all wince as they crack.

'I wasn't giving her money to shove into her veins,' he says, like he's being a hero. 'I told her that she had to get clean and I'd pay her off.' He hesitates, but he knows we've seen his phone, so there is no point in holding back. 'Then one night, she called me. She said she was going to come home, she was going to rob the place, she was going to tell the Ma I'd sold the jewellery. She threatened lots of stuff and I thought, you know, that she'd do it too. She was crazy . . . so I told her to meet me down by the docks. This was like probably end of May.'

I hold my breath, waiting.

'She came. I told her to get lost, that she was never seeing a penny of the money, and she was crying and begging me, saying she needed it to pay some debts or else bad stuff might happen but I told her no. I told her if she tried to rob Ma's house I'd report her.' He hesitates, perhaps trying to remember what exactly is on his phone. 'Maybe I said I'd kill her but, like, I didn't mean it. Then I walked off,' he finishes.

I turn to the page of texts. Pushing one in front of him. 'I have a text here,' I say, then read out, '"Exhibit A7. You broke my arm you toerag. I want money to get it seen to.'" I wait. 'That was at the start of June.'

Some sort of emotion flickers across his face. Shame? Annoyance? It's hard to tell. He shoots a guilty look at his solicitor. 'I didn't break her arm,' he mutters. 'She ran at me and I pushed her off and she fell. It wasn't deliberate.'

I read out another text. '"Exhibit A8. You pushed me and now my arm is broken. I have to get to hospital."'

'Stop! Can you just stop!' He covers his face with his hands. 'I didn't believe her, all right? She'd say anything to get money off you.'

'Did you pay her?'

'No.'

'We have a potential sighting of your sister in St James's Hospital on the seventh of June.'

He shrugs. 'I didn't give her any money and, anyway, she was homeless. She probably would have got it seen to anyway.'

'Did you bring her?'

'No. That time I pushed her was the last time I seen her.'

'Do you know this man?' I place a picture of Adam in front of him. 'Exhibit A6.'

'Yeah, that's the fella whose picture was in the paper the other day. He was murdered in Mayo. Yous aren't doing a great job down there, are yez?'

'Do you know him from anywhere else? Look hard now.'

'I know if I know someone. I haven't a clue. I told you all I know. I done nothing.' He looks at his solicitor. 'There, I've cooperated.'

'Abby sent a text to you that day she went to the hospital.' I read the line of text: '"You better pay me or I will tell Mam what you did."'

'I ignored that.'

'That day at the hospital was the last sighting of your sister.'

'Yeah? So?'

'Did Abby tell your mother what you did?'

He stands up. 'I've had enough of this. Jesus. You have nothing on me,' he says. 'You just have all this . . . this . . .' he waves his arm about '. . . superstition.'

It's a second before I realise that he means supposition. 'Can you sit down, please?'

He does so with a glower.

'We know that you have lied to us three times, so it's hard for us to believe you now. You admit that you assaulted your sister for the jewellery. It appears that you may have broken her collarbone. You lost—'

'I'm telling the truth now.'

'You lost your Tesco job because you had an altercation with another staff member that turned physical.'

To my surprise, instead of being angered, he laughs. It's a bitter sound. 'That bastard spent about six months taunting me about being in jail. And he hit me, too, but he didn't get fired. How can anyone bloody go straight if they come up against this crap all the time?'

He has a point, actually. 'Where were you on the fourth of July last?'

'How can I be expected to remember that?'

'You'd lost your job by then, hadn't you?'

'Yes. So I was probably out walking around looking for a job until it was time to come home.'

'Where would you normally walk?' I want to see if we can catch him on CCTV, rule him out of being in Achill.

184

'Anywhere and everywhere.'

'But mainly?'

'City centre, anywhere there was a job going, but it was shit. They all wanted me to submit my CV online.'

'Did you spend every night at home in July?'

'I did not kill my sister.'

'That's not what I asked. Did you spend the night of July the fourth at home?'

'If it was a Friday or Saturday, probably not.'

'It was a Friday.'

'There you go, then.'

He doesn't seem to realise what he's said. Maybe that's because he's innocent. Maybe he's just stupid.

'We reckon your sister was murdered that night,' I say.

'And I didn't do it,' he says.

His solicitor looks at us as though to ask if the interview is terminated yet.

'Fine.' I eyeball him, frustrated but trying not to show it. 'You are hard to trust, James. You've consistently lied since this investigation began. If you didn't kill your sister, you really should have shown willing to help us find out who did, but instead you've twisted and turned things—'

'Because no one trusts the guards. You'll just hang me out to dry if you can.'

Jesus wept. 'If you have anything else you'd like to tell us, James, now is the time.'

'I've told you everything.'

We let the silence drag on. We wait, more in hope than certainty that he will break. Finally, his solicitor asks, 'Are we done? Will you be charging my client?'

'Not now.'

Dan reads James's latest statement back to him and James signs it. Dan and I sign it too. I press the recorder. 'Interview with James Devine suspended at seventeen fifty.' I flick off the recorder. 'Thanks for your time, James. We'll be in touch.'

'Damn!' I say, when we're back in the car. 'I really thought we had him.'

'We have a whole pile of everything and a whole heap of nothing,' Dan says matter-of-factly, as I start the car. 'Back to the drawing board. Time to find more answers. Let's concentrate on Adam. That's the key now.'

I'm a little annoyed he can just accept that we got nothing out of this. I know it happens, I should be used to it, but something about Abby and her tininess has enraged me. I don't care what her brother says about her: she was a fourteen-year-old kid, with no clue about life or danger or anything.

Just as we pull onto the motorway, the phone rings. It's Larry. 'In a stroke of luck, we've managed to locate the Peugeot,' he says gleefully, before I can talk. It's rare that Larry lets any sort of joy bleed into his voice. 'Turns out it was rented under Adam's actual name, if you can believe it. That reads like a set-up to me, though maybe the man was that stupid. The company has the rental documents on file, so we'll be able to grab some prints from them, make sure it was Adam. We can also compare signatures. We're harvesting their CCTV too. The car was hired out for eleven days, including July fourth and fifth. We've requested that the car be tested for forensics, though it's been hired since Abby's murder.'

'That's brilliant.' I smile for the first time that day. What this also might mean is that the car was the one used on the night of Abby's murder and, if so, we have a date for the murder. And we also have another connection between Adam and Abby. 'Brilliant work, Larry. Have the results on the prints from the Adam Gray murder scene come through yet?'

'Yes, there were a number of them found, not surprising as the house was a rental. We ran James's prints against the scene but we didn't find anything. How'd you get on with him anyway?'

'Don't even ask.'

'Gouger,' he says, with a snort, and hangs up.

'What was your impression of James?' I ask Dan, after a second or two of silence.

'He might very well be innocent. Like, I know he's lied, but that doesn't make him a murderer. I can buy the fact that he doesn't want to go back to prison and I can also buy the fact that he sold the jewellery to protect his mother from knowing he'd lost his job. Those timelines fit. I can buy the fact that he lost it with Abby, too, and didn't kill her. And you know what else? When he said he didn't know Adam, I believed him. His reaction when he lied about not knowing Jerome was way different.'

That's a fair point.

'Maybe we need to start again, not forget about James but focus on the others.'

'Gareth?'

'Yeah. He had contact with both victims.'

I glance at my watch. 'Tomorrow we interview him as a matter of priority.'

'Absolutely.'

Chapter 37

The Cig is at the Achill station, so on the way back to my house that night, and feeling nervous, I drop in to talk to him. The station is locked to the public at this time but a small team is beavering away on Abby's case when I get inside. Jordy is on the phone, and Mick and Larry are poring over some CCTV. They barely acknowledge me. Susan is chatting to Matt, comparing PM horror stories, I think. It obviously hasn't affected Matt too badly as he's eating a take-out pizza with relish. They welcome me back like a long-lost aunt.

'How'd the PM go yesterday?' I ask him. 'All right?'

'We're just talking about Joe Palmer,' Susan says, making a face. 'Matt said that—'

'Is that Lucy?' William calls from his office. 'Come in here, will you?'

Susan and Matt react like startled mice, Matt almost choking on the pizza and Susan turning back to her computer. I suppress a smile.

Ten seconds later, I'm sitting in front of William. We eyeball each other. It's on the tip of my tongue to tell him that I was right to go in on Jerome, but he'd probably kill me. 'What have you got for me?' he barks instead.

Straight to business as usual. I give him a rundown of our day, finishing with 'We've asked the lads in Dublin to talk to the staff in McAdam's bar about Adam, and to re-interview the volunteers about him as well. Dan and I didn't get to talk to Gareth but we've rearranged it for tomorrow. We're also hoping to locate and interview the father who said that Adam harassed his daughter when he was a teenager.'

'So,' his voice is cold, 'you're actually doing the work on the Adam Gray investigation now, is that it?'

'We're refocusing the investigation on Adam now,' I say, as nicely as I can. 'We know his prints were found at Abby's scene, so it seems logical. We have James's prints on file and also his DNA so we'll be able to link him if anything comes up. We can also see if his phone pinged off any masts here in July.'

'Anyone in the picture for Adam's murder?'

'No.' I swallow. 'Not yet. We don't know enough yet to have any type of motive for his murder, bar third-party accounts that he appeared to be stressed about something. If he was stressed about Abby's murder, it might have been enough to drive people to silence him. But we don't know. I think the only way in is to see what the connection between him and Abby was and work from there.' I take a breath. 'I won't link them unless I can.'

'You'd better fucking not,' he says.

I nod. 'I won't.'

He holds my gaze. Then, deciding that maybe there isn't a lot more to be gained from giving me a bollocking, he pulls his jacket from the back of the chair and stands.

'I'm going for a pint. D'you want to join me?'

That's unexpected. I haven't had a pint with him since our last case together. That had been a good night: he'd loosened up and been quite the storyteller, but then again, the whole team had been on a high as we'd just solved our biggest murder case ever. Thinking back, it hadn't been half as complex as this one. All the strands we have, all the theories, but we have no proof of anything.

William is looking questioningly at me. I'll have to get a taxi home but it's been so long since I've sat in a pub with an adult that I can't resist. Even if it is one who has bawled me out twice in as many days. 'Coming.'

Ten minutes later we're in what has to be the crappiest pub in Ireland. William had invited the others along but they'd all declined. If he hadn't been going, they might have come along with me, but they're on unstable ground with William.

Despite the staggeringly awful ambience, the pub is quite full, attracting tourists who can't get into the other places or those who happen to think that a small pub with uneven flooring, rocky tables and beer-stained fabric seats is quaint.

I find a stained seat at one of the rocky tables as William goes to the bar to order the drinks. He comes back a few moments later with a pint of Guinness for himself and a pint of cider for me. We clink glasses and sit in companionable silence for a bit.

'I had to have a stern word with Matt this morning,' he tells me, apropos of nothing. 'It's why I brought him along to the PM. I didn't want the others to hear.'

'About what?' Matt is the most inoffensive guard you could meet. The locals love him and the old ones bake him cakes and invite him to dinner.

'Did you know he's seeing that awful journalist who works for the local rag? She got the exclusives on the last investigation?'

190

'Stacy?'

'Frizzy hair, big mouth?'

'Stacy,' I confirm. I can't see it – Matt and Stacy.

'It's been going on for a while. I met them last week in the supermarket in Westport. They were like a little couple.' He says it with a hint of impatience. 'And I know it's not my business but if there is a leak, he'll be number-one suspect, and she's already managed to get Lugs talking away about the black car he saw, and about you and Dan interviewing him. Did you read that piece?'

'I never see the paper,' I say, though my mother loves it. 'What was Matt's reaction?'

'He got quite stroppy,' William sounds surprised, 'said it was none of my business, that they're both professionals and that I had no need to worry.'

Good for Matt, I think. 'There you go, then.'

'Hmm.' He stares into his pint and I find myself wondering if he trusts anyone. If he actually likes anyone. If there ever was a someone. 'I'll be keeping an eye on him, though. He's an awful green eejit for a guard.'

'He's not,' I say. 'The locals love him, he's one of their own. I'd say he's as clued in as anyone. He'll know if Stacy has an agenda.'

'Journalists always have an agenda.'

He says it with such biting bitterness that I wonder how he'd been stung. I'd ask only I haven't drunk enough yet. And I want to keep my head, not have it bitten off.

'And by the way,' he says sharply, 'apologies for snapping at you the other night.'

I'm surprised. There is nothing remotely apologetic in his tone but I know he means it. 'You were right to,' I say. 'I overstepped.'

'That's true,' he agrees, with more enthusiasm than is

191

warranted. 'And you did it again yesterday. But still,' he takes a breath as if he's gearing himself up for something, 'I just, this case, it's—'

The sound of my phone derails the conversation. I put down my pint to scrabble through my pockets.

'You should always keep your phone in a designated pocket,' William says primly, and I throw him an exasperated look.

It's Mick. He specializes in calling when I'm with the Cig. 'Hello?'

'I've found Abby on the hospital video.' He sounds excited. 'Well, Larry dropped by and had a look. It's her. We're about to examine another bit of footage. Do you want to come back?'

'Mick says he's found Abby on CCTV hospital video,' I tell the Cig. Then I turn to the phone. 'Present it tomorrow, Mick. That's great work. What date was that?'

'June seventh,' he says.

I think about that. It seems strange that she'd go to get her arm attended to if she had any inkling that she was in danger. 'Is she alone?'

'That's what we're looking at now,' Mick says. 'I'll see you in the morning.' He hangs up.

'You can't say he and Susan aren't dedicated.' I observe William over my pint glass.

He observes me right back. 'They're doing it for you, Lucy. They like you, the whole lot of them. It's why you're on the team.'

And I think that that might just be the nicest thing anyone has ever said to me in this job.

Chapter 38 – Day 10

The following morning, Mick delivers the goods like a gift into a room hungry for information. 'If you could roll it there, Larry,' he says, with authority, standing up straight and looking for the first time as if he actually knows what he's doing. Susan is red with pride as she beams encouragingly at him.

'I hope this is good,' William mutters, but I know it will be. Larry would never involve himself if it wasn't. He's far too selfish.

Up on the screen, there is a black-and-white grainy image of an A&E waiting room. It's the usual depressing sight of people crammed together in misery. 'Now, here,' Mick says. 'This, we are certain, is Abby.'

A girl, tiny, comes into shot, her arm held a little gingerly. She queues at the reception desk and there follows an exchange between her and the nurse. Afterwards, the girl sits down on a vacant chair beside a woman with a little boy.

'We'll air this footage on *Crimecall* along with your appeal,' Mick says to me, and my heart jolts. Shit, they're recording me later today for that programme.

'Sure,' I say, trying to quell the panic.

'What makes you think it's Abby?' William asks.

'This,' Larry says. He zooms in on her jacket and we see her 'green earth' badge. 'The volunteer who remembers Abby gave a description of what she thought she was wearing. This badge stood out for her. It's not by any means a unique badge,' he goes on, 'but coupled with the jacket and her Converse runners,' he zooms in on her footwear, 'along with her slight frame and the fact that she had a problem with her arm, we're positive it's Abby. Anyway, rolling on.' He fast-forwards it and finally the girl is called into triage.

'There was nothing interesting in that footage, but it gets interesting when she comes back out,' Mick says. Immediately Larry plays the next bit of footage and we see Abby walk out and sit down again in a different chair, this time beside an elderly man.

'She'd had an X-ray and was told to go back outside and wait,' Mick explains. 'And, just for the record, the doctor noticed no burns on her upper left arm. Now watch.'

Abby sits, perched on the edge of her chair, like an animal about to take flight. Her foot bobs up and down and once or twice the elderly man glances at her. And then, quite suddenly, something catches her attention. She looks up, hesitates, stands and disappears out of shot.

'So, we rewound the footage,' Mick says, and Larry obligingly rewinds the CCTV to the part where Abby looks up. 'And you can see that something catches her eye in the direction of the front door. So, we ran the footage from the front-door area. Larry.'

More footage, this time from the other side of the waiting room.

'Abby freezes at two minutes past three,' Mick says. 'Now, a couple of seconds before that, this man walks into the waiting room.'

Onscreen, a tall figure comes through the door. Larry presses pause.

'It's at that moment that Abby looks up.'

'And have we identified who the man is?' William asks. 'Is it the brother?'

And in answer, Larry zeros in on the man's hand, on which can clearly be seen the tail of a serpent curled around a left index finger. 'We matched this to the image of the tattoo Adam had when he was found and they're identical. So, this is what happens after the man, let's call him Adam,' Larry says to laughter, 'comes in.'

The footage moves on and we see the man scan the room. He raises a hand in greeting. A girl crosses into shot and stands beside him.

'Abby eventually gets seen an hour later. The man stays with her the whole time.'

Larry lets the footage run for another few minutes. 'Notice anything?' he asks.

'Abby and the man are talking away to each other,' I say. 'They knew each other.'

'Yes,' Larry says.

We now see the girl and the man exiting the doors of A and E. They walk side by side in what appears to be silence. The girl wears a sling. The man points to the right, raises his hand again, says something to Abby and they move off.

The screen goes black.

'I think this piece establishes that someone else was waiting for the two of them outside A and E,' Mick says. 'Which also establishes that Adam didn't appear to be acting alone, and that Abby knew these people.'

'That's great work,' William says, and for once there is no irony or sarcasm in the remark. 'Larry, we have two cars of interest in this investigation, the black Peugeot, which was a hire car, and Adam's orange one nine one Fiesta. See if you can spot Adam's car near the hospital on this date. Anyone else?'

Kev's hand shoots up, 'I, eh, worked last night on Adam's scene. First off, I talked to Joe Palmer and tic-tacked with Forensics. So, Palmer reckons the time of Adam's death was between midnight and two in the day. Blood-spatter analysis has come back with the following preliminary results. Here.' He pops up a picture of the crime scene.

I notice Mick turn away.

'According to blood-spatter analysis, whoever assaulted him was standing here,' Kev points to a spot on the picture, 'and they know this because when Adam's right wrist was slit, the blood spray should have hit the walls and it didn't. It was blocked by something or someone.'

'So, the front of our assailant would have been covered with blood?' Susan says.

'Yep. Which was then carried through the house,' Kev says, and up pops a picture of barely discernible blood-spatter on the floor of the hallway. 'And out the front door.' Another blood spot. 'I talked again to Louise, the owner, and she says a set of white towels was left in the bathroom. One of these is missing so it's highly likely that our assailant used a towel to wipe blood from their hands or face. We haven't located that towel yet. An interesting thing is that the knife Adam allegedly used to kill himself with is not one Louise recognises.'

'That's great,' William says. 'Chase up details on the knife. Manufacturer, where it's distributed, then chase down all the shops.'

'I'm already on it, Cig,' Kev says. 'But the bit that's brilliant is that there was also a hair found in the bathroom that, get this, matches the hair found on Abby.'

The room explodes and I can feel my chest expand. It's like I can breathe for the first time in days. 'We have our link,' I say, over the hubbub.

'Quiet!' William snaps, though he's smiling, too, and throws me a quick wink.

'We have our link,' William says. 'We now know that there were others involved in Abby's murder and that this same individual, or individuals, were responsible for Adam's death. Was there any sign of forced entry?'

'None. There were no tyre prints of value, which is not surprising as the weather has been dry and the dirt roads are hard. There were a number of fingerprints found in the property, but as it's a rental, you'll get that. We've eliminated Louise's and Adam's prints and we've three unidentified decent prints that we ran through the system but got no hits. It's worth noting that James Devine's are not there. I'll keep at it.'

Absence of evidence doesn't mean evidence of absence, I think. He might have worn gloves.

William nods. 'Pat, where are we on the alibis for Adam Gray's murder?'

'All checking out so far, Cig. We did get one from Adam's dad and it's solid. He was seen by a number of residents in the apartment block as he came and went during the day. Dan and Lucy will talk to Gareth today and get an alibi.'

'And alibis for Abby?'

Pat shrugs. 'Aside from Adam, who was off those days, our only other suspect was James. Ben checked his phone against the towers here and nothing came back. So, nothing as yet. He could have turned it off, though. I double-checked Gareth's alibi for Abby's murder just because he's in the frame for Adam and the shelter sent on some work sheets that showed me he was working on those dates. It could have been doctored. Short of confiscating his computer, there's not much else we can do. And get this – he was alone in the shelter those nights aside from the clients. They're short-staffed in summer apparently.'

'All right,' William says, thinking. 'Our priority now is to establish a link between Adam and Abby. What happened that got them both killed by the same person? It appears they certainly knew each other, judging by the video. Was it just that he was bringing her to A and E on behalf of the shelter? Did they see something that day?' He gives them a rundown of our interviews with James and Jerome. 'We're not ruling them out,' he says, 'but James's story, despite the lies, hangs. Susan, Mick and Jordy, you're on Abby's case. That was good work on the CCTV. Have you got the hospital records yet?'

'Today,' Mick says.

'Talk to everyone, see what they can remember. Anything interesting, bring it to me. The rest of ye, I want ye to concentrate on Adam's case, but there will be a certain amount of crossover. Larry, any more on the CCTV?'

'Not yet, Cig. Just to say that there was no sighting of Adam's orange car on the island on the day we think Abby's body was dumped. That's not to say it wasn't there, just that it wasn't picked up at all – you know this place, CCTV is scarce. On the black car, it's being technically examined today. So Ger, who has volunteered to help in his week off—'

There's a bit of a cheer at this, and Ger Deegan, who'd been on the last case with us, stands up and takes a bow.

'Saint Ger,' Larry amends to more laughter, 'is going to help me and some regular lads with the CCTV from outside the hospital. According to the car-hire company, the Peugeot was rented for eleven days, including the dates we are interested in, so it neatly fits into our timeframe.'

'Great,' William says, pleased. 'Welcome aboard, Ger.'

'Thanks, Cig.'

'Right,' William continues. 'Jim has the job sheets for today. Pat, after you finish chasing down Gareth's alibi, if you can, start trawling through the things we took from Adam's house. Follow up everything, any phone numbers you find, all that kind of thing, you know the drill. Ben, see if you can trace Adam's phone from the records down here for that night.' He rattles off Adam's number as we all gawk at him. The man must have a photographic memory. 'Phone lines, who's on that?'

The lad on phones – I still can't remember his name, I'm not sure anyone can – raises his hand. 'Nothing, Cig.' He looks a bit demoralised. We can't have someone like that manning the lines, crap and all as it is. I'll talk to him after, I think.

'Lucy, can you prep a little for *Crimecall* and then when you've recorded the segment, can you tic-tac with the team on anything that needs to be checked out. I know you've a couple of interviews this morning as well.'

Jim gives out the job sheets, the completed ones are handed in and we're dismissed.

The guard manning the phone lines is Brian. I jam the name into my head so I won't forget it again. He's twenty and he's just graduated from Templemore. Originally from Cork, he was posted to Mayo and likes it well enough. But answering the phones has broken his spirit somewhat. 'They're all mental,' he confides in me. 'Seriously, everyone who has rung in is mental, like. The things they say, like.'

'You'll meet a lot of . . . unusual people in this job,' I hand him a coffee, 'and the phone lines are good training for that. Be respectful to them all, even if they're taking the piss. There's a reason they act like that. But don't think you're wasting your time. It can be invaluable. Listen well. That way nothing import-ant will slip through because even the smallest thing can unlock an investigation. And be encouraging, because if someone has important information, they won't give it up to a guard who sounds pissed off.'

He looks a bit shamefaced, 'That's a good point. I'll do better. Thanks for the coffee.'

'No bother.' I stand up and head back to the office I share with Dan, Larry and Ben. I meet Pat on the way to sign out Adam's belongings from Exhibits. There are boxes upon boxes appar-ently. In the office, Larry is scrolling through the CCTV, a huge burger in front of him. It's only ten in the morning, for feck's sake.

I start the prep for *Crimecall*.

Two hours later, having lashed on the make-up, put on my best blouse – the one I keep at work for good wear – and having sprayed some root spray in my hair to get rid of the greys that I really should have had done a few weeks back, I do my *Crimecall* piece from near Lough Acorrymore. It's recorded so any fluffs I make can be edited out, which relaxes me. It's actually a good interview probably because, despite all the warnings, I've become quite invested in the case. I talk about Abby, about her life, I ask for anyone who thinks they may have information about her to come forward. I mention that she was burnt on her upper arm: if anyone saw a girl with an injury like this, it would be distinctive.

Then I appeal for witnesses for Adam, I describe his orange car, ask if anyone saw him on his way west or if anyone talked to him at all. And that's when it hits me. What has been niggling at me since the Helen interview. I'm not sure yet what it means, maybe nothing, and yet . . .

'Detective?' the director calls. 'Are you all right?'

Shit. I've literally stopped talking! 'Yes, sorry. Can you edit that out?'

'For sure. Can we go again?'

And, finally, it's done. I breathe a huge sigh of relief and get back to doing what I'm good at.

I join Dan, who is helping Pat sift through the bits and pieces of Adam's life. It's a sad collection of football cards and fishing books and old photographs. Everything is worn and tatty as if he pored over them regularly, reliving whatever memories they contained. It's hard to believe that a killer who wrapped a girl in plastic and dumped her in a suitcase in the middle of a lake would keep photographs and lovingly label each one.

'Me and Mammy in Westport' shows Adam, probably aged around eight, and his mother, kneeling beside him, her arm around his shoulders. He looks like a happy kid, but shy, as he glances up through a tangle of fringe at the camera.

A picture labelled 'Mammy and Daddy, Westport' shows Adam's parents holding hands. They look to be in their mid to late thirties. She has her head back, laughing, and he is staring at her with naked adoration. There's only a trace of this man left now. Life is a bit shit the way it destroys people, I think, as I place the picture aside.

'Sad, eh?' Dan indicates the pictures.

'Yeah. Finding anything?'

'No. He was a bit of a whiz at the maths, though.' He holds up a picture showing Adam with a trophy for a 'Mathalon'. 'Funny that he never used it.' He looks at me. 'Are you going to Gareth now?'

'Yep.'

'I'll ask Kev to step in here. He's just on the phone to that knife manufacturer now.'

I wait until Kev arrives in and slides into Dan's seat. He rubs his hands. 'The perks of being a guard,' he snorts, 'looking at someone else's holiday snaps.'

Dan and I laugh.

'Had a bit of a breakthrough on the knife,' he says, as he pulls a load of pictures from the shoebox Adam has kept them in. 'It's exclusive to Musgrave's, so I'll talk to the shops today and see if they've records as to who bought those knives.'

'That's great, Kev.' I'm impressed.

'I'm not out to spook Gareth,' I warn Dan, as we leave. 'This is a friendly chat just to sound him out about Adam.'

'Damn!' he says, looking disappointed. 'I was looking forward to pulling his chain.'

'Fran might have a problem with that,' I joke, and he grins.

Chapter 39

Thirty minutes later, Dan and I are sitting at a bright yellow table in Home's Westport shelter. It's a replica of the one we were in in Dublin, the only variation being the posters on the wall of the dining room advising clients to 'Keep Calm and Keep Clean' or to remember that 'Every Day Has New Opportunities!'

Dan sniggers as he reads them. 'New opportunities to fuck up, eh?' He doesn't notice Gareth behind him, carrying the coffee.

'That, too,' Gareth says calmly, placing a cup in front of Dan, 'but there's always hope, you know.' He sounds like Gandhi.

'Oh, yeah, I'm sure there is,' Dan agrees. 'I wasn't meaning any disrespect.'

Sure.

'No worries.' Gareth pulls out a chair for himself. Today he's wearing what looks like sackcloth, his hair pulled away from his forehead in a severe bun. 'What's going on?' His expression turns serious. 'I heard about Adam. Still reeling.'

'It's awful, all right,' I say. 'Can you tell us how you knew him, how he ended up volunteering here?'

'Sure.' He sits astride the chair, takes a gulp of his coffee, which is in a mug that says 'Chill'. Putting it down on the table, he says, 'He came to the Dublin Home shelter about three years ago. He wanted to volunteer. We'd only just opened and I was glad of the help.'

'Was he in the shelter a lot?'

'Yeah, quite a lot. He was really dedicated.'

At that moment, a young woman arrives in, blonde and extraordinary-looking. She stops dead when she sees Gareth chatting to us. 'Gareth,' she says, 'I was just . . .' She takes us in. 'Sorry. Am I disturbing ye?'

'It's fine, Alex.' Gareth waves her on. 'You get what you want and I'll be out to you when I finish with these guards.'

'Guards?' Her eyebrows rise. 'Right.' She scurries over to a press behind the counter, bends over and pulls out a duster and some spray. 'No rush, no rush at all.'

'That's the lady who runs this shelter,' Gareth says, as she leaves. 'She's very good. Adam was a bit like that. Just . . . quieter.'

'Did you get on with him?'

'Aw, yeah. Like I said, he was quiet but once you got to know him, took the bother to know him, he was sound. Top fella.' He swallows hard and shakes his head. 'I can't believe it.' He sniffs back what I think is a sob.

I give Gareth a moment, then ask, 'When was the last time you saw Adam?'

He looks upwards, thinking. Rubs a long index finger across his brow. Adjusts the scrunchie on his bun. It's all so slow, measured, like a cat stretching. 'About a week ago,' he says eventually. He nods towards a retro-looking radio in the corner of the room, 'He dropped that in for me as an anniversary gift for the shelter. It's like his thing. Or was . . .'

'Nice,' Dan says. 'We heard he was interested in radios.'

'He was obsessed with radios.' Gareth sounds sad. 'Nothing he couldn't fix up. I just can't . . .' He shrugs. 'Who would do that to him?'

'That's what we're trying to find out,' I say. 'Now, this might seem an odd question, but bear with me. Did Adam ever have contact with Abby? She's the girl who was found dead just over a week ago on Achill.'

'I remember,' Gareth says. 'And, yes, if she came to our shelter, like you say, he probably did. Why?'

'Can you remember any specific interactions between them?'

'No.' Gareth sounds faintly annoyed. 'Why would I?'

'You said you saw him a week ago?'

'I did.'

'How did he seem?'

The question seems to give him pause for thought. His forehead creases. 'He was a bit . . . distracted, I suppose,' he says haltingly. 'And before that, he . . . Well, he was a bit all over the place. He missed shifts, actually, now that I think about it.'

'Did you ask him if anything was wrong?'

'No.' Then, almost as if it physically pains him to say it, he says, 'Maybe I should have.' Now he pulls off his scrunchie and his hair falls to shoulder length. He seems unaware of it. He rubs a hand across his forehead, massages his eyes. 'Sometimes we're so busy helping people that we forget the ones under our noses.'

What a do-gooder, I think, with slight distaste, though I suppose there are people who would say that guards are do-gooders too, only it never feels like that.

'There are suggestions that Adam was a little odd?'

Gareth freezes, and looks at me with slight hostility. It's a surprise coming from him. 'Who said that? Idiots. The man was quiet – he minded his own business. Yeah, he was a bit different, but you know what? He was kind.' He glares at us. 'He'd go out of his way to help the clients. He'd ferry them about left, right and centre on his days off. I used to tell him not to get too involved but he'd just say it was grand. I couldn't give a shit if people thought he was odd. He was a good guy, if people took the time to get to know him. You need to find out who killed him.'

'We'll do our best.' I eyeball him. He holds my gaze. 'Now, you said he'd bring people here and there. Where to in particular?'

'I don't know. One time he brought a girl to the hospital – she twisted her ankle. And he drove a boy home who'd run off.'

'OK. Can you remember the names of anyone else he might have offered a lift to or brought to hospital?'

'No, of course I can't.'

'Could you ask your clients? It might be important.' I don't tell him that on the last day Abby was seen alive Adam accompanied her to the hospital.

'All right,' he says, 'sure.' He hooks his hair behind his ear. 'I'll ask, but people on the margins, they don't like questions.'

'Thanks.' I stand up. 'We'll be in touch. Oh, and by the way,' I say as if I've just remembered, 'when did you arrive in Mayo for the opening of the shelter?'

He hesitates. 'The day of it,' he says.

He's lying. I can tell by the way his eyes slide to the side. 'Really?' I chance my arm.

He freezes, swallows, blurts out, 'Well, look, I came down the night before.' He darts a furtive glance at the doorway. 'That girl you saw earlier? We're sort of . . . well . . . together. But as I employed her to run this place, well . . .' he winces '. . . Liam wouldn't like it.'

206

'You stayed the night here?'

'Yes, but—'

'What time did you leave in the morning?'

'About seven, before I was seen. I was back here around four to organize the party.'

'Where were you between seven in the morning and two in the afternoon?'

'Am I under suspicion?' He suddenly sounds cross. 'I did nothing.'

'Where were you?'

'I don't have to answer.'

We wait.

'I was in my car, asleep, waiting to check into the hotel.'

'And what hotel was that?'

He names it.

Dan takes a note of it, then asks him to describe his car to us.

Just as Gareth is finishing, a tall, balding man, who appears to be in a bit of a hurry, arrives in. He glances questioningly at us and then at Gareth, who blanches.

'Hey, Liam, are you off now?' Gareth says.

'I am.' Liam looks to us again so I make the introductions. I know who he is: I've seen his photograph. 'You're a member of the board,' I say.

'Liam is chairman of the board,' Gareth corrects me. 'He makes all this possible.' He's babbling, licking up, I think.

'It's not just me,' Liam says modestly. 'There are others too. What seems to be the problem, Detectives?'

'One of your volunteers was murdered last week, as was one of your clients. We're investigating whether or not it has anything to do with the shelter.'

'Surely not,' he says, sounding surprised. 'I heard about Adam, of course. That was dreadful, not that I knew him but Gareth says he was a fantastic volunteer. He was to come to the party, I believe, but he never showed up.'

'Who invited him?'

'I did,' Gareth says. 'He told me he'd be fishing here for a couple of days so I invited him along.'

So, Gareth knew he was going to be in the area. Interesting.

Gareth had had the time to go and see him too.

I turn to Liam. 'And were you here for the launch?'

'I was. A wonderful night. Gareth has made these shelters better than we could have envisaged. We leave everything to him.'

Gareth shrugs, but looks uncomfortable.

'Great,' Dan says, and I can tell he finds all this praise-giving nauseating. 'We'll be in touch with any questions.' Dan hands both of them his card. Then says, 'Two murders in one shelter. That's not much of a recommendation for you, is it?'

I could bloody kick him.

'There was no need for that,' I say, once we're back out on the street and heading towards the main part of town. 'You didn't have to say that.'

'I know,' Dan says, looking about as contrite as a hired assassin. 'But that Gareth fella, he puts my hackles up.'

'Get onto Pat, ask him to check that alibi. Ask them to harvest CCTV from outside that hotel he mentioned, see if we can spot Gareth's vehicle in the car park. And talk to the girlfriend, check the times with her.'

Dan nods, taking it down.

'You saw that video this morning. Adam wasn't acting on his own. Someone he knew was there too,' I say.

'Yeah. But why? What are we missing?'

This conversation is cementing a thought I have, only I'm reluctant to say it out loud. So instead I ask, 'What's your thinking?'

Dan makes a face. 'Right, try this on for size. Adam makes a pass at Abby. She rejects him, blackmails him, threatens to report him. Just like she did with her brother. Adam panics, tells Gareth. Gareth's worried about the reputation of the shelter if Abby goes spouting off. That Liam guy has him freaked, you saw that right? So, Gareth and Adam warn Abby off. She won't listen, she ends up dead. Adam panics, not able for it. Gareth kills him.'

'Not beyond the bounds of possibility. But on the hospital video, it didn't look like Adam was the least bit interested in making a pass at her.'

'True.'

'And the burn on her arm? What's that about?'

'Yeah. Good points,' Dan says. 'I don't know.'

'Let's interview this John Walsh guy, see what he has to say about Adam harassing his daughter all those years ago. It might fly if Adam has form.'

'Sure.' Dan flicks open his notebook and reads out the addresses Adam's dad gave us.

I'll do this interview, I think, see how it goes, and if I still have that niggle, I'll tell Dan and see what holes he can pick in my theory. There are a lot of holes but my gut is telling me something I'll have to share.

But my gut has let me down in the past.

Chapter 40

John Walsh's address is just a short walk from Westport town. Dan and I abandon the car outside Westport station to take the stroll. It'll still be quicker than navigating the bumper-to-bumper traffic on the Mall. Though storms are predicted, there is no sign of them yet. The day is hot and sticky, and the heat lies heavy across the town. We stroll along the Carrowbeg river, up South Mall, dodging sweaty tourists, who are milling about the paths and the roadways, eating ice cream and sporting lurid sunburn. Kids, cranky in the heat, whinge and wail. Cars clog the road and the smell of food drifts out of the restaurants that line the way.

'Was there ever a summer like this before?' Dan pulls off his jacket and hooks it over his shoulder. 'I feel I'm being boiled alive.'

'D'you fancy one?' I indicate a smoothie bar on the opposite side of the road that I frequent when working from Westport. It's owned by an Achill man.

'A pint'd be better but, sure, go on.' Dan leans against the wall that runs alongside the river while I run across the road, dodging slow-moving traffic.

'Hiya, Declan,' I greet him, when I finally get to the top of the queue. 'An immune booster and a strawberry shake, please.'

'How's the law?' He chortles as he takes a fistful of frozen fruit and blends it. 'Busy solving those murders? That was shocking out in Croy. I know Louise and she's not the better of it. Was it a local fella that was killed?'

'No. He lived here when he was young but most of his life was spent in Dublin.'

Declan rolls his eyes, as if to say, what did he expect only to be murdered, living in Dublin? 'Here you are, now,' he says, handing over the drinks. 'Say hello to your mother for me. Tell her that I was up in Mary Laffin's during the week and she's on her last legs, the creatur. That'll be another wake before the month is out.'

'I'll tell her. Look after yourself, Declan.' I grab the drinks, in a hurry now and slam straight into a man behind. Pink strawberry juice covers a picture of a cow that stretches across his broad chest.

'Shit! Sorry!'

'Aw, it's grand.'

It's Johnny Egan in a tight T-shirt. The day just got a lot hotter. Johnny pulls a napkin from the counter and wipes himself down. 'On a day off, are you?'

I can see his man nipples. 'No, but even us detectives have to have smoothies.' I giggle. I never giggle and the sound is weird. And mortifying. 'Anyway,' I hold up the drinks, 'better get going.' And my voice is pitched a little high. Good God, I have to get out of there.

'How's Tani and Sirocco getting on?' he asks quickly, as I turn to leave. At my questioning look, he adds, 'It's radio silence from her.'

The admission costs him.

'They're grand,' I say, feeling bad for him. 'Though I think her and Luc are finding parenthood a bit tough. The summer evenings off drinking on the beach have been curbed.'

He laughs a little. 'No bad thing,' he says, and adds, 'Tani was always a socialite, just like her daddy.'

I remember that socialising. Nights on the beach with the gang from school. Me and my friend Megan, whom I haven't seen in an age. A blazing fire and drinks and singles of chips and the mountains behind. Oh, the things that happened in the hills. I flush with the memory. I think I'm sex-starved. 'I really have to go,' I say. 'I'll tell her you were asking after her.'

'Would you?' He sounds pathetically eager. 'Tell her I miss Sirocco.'

And then I do it. Against my better judgement. 'I'm minding Sirocco on Sunday, I'll probably take her to Keem beach. Be nice to spend some time with her.' I stop short of inviting him: that'd be just plain wrong. Instead, I bid him goodbye, and a few seconds later, I rejoin Dan on the other side of the road.

'Was Granny Lucy talking to Grandfather Johnny?' Dan asks, with a wink, taking the strawberry shake from me.

'Stop calling me that,' I snap. 'He was just asking after Tani and the baby. I told him I'll be minding her on Sunday for them.' I admit it because I'm looking for his reaction. I want him to nod casually and think it's no big deal.

'Feck off,' he says, stopping dead and gawping at me. 'You shouldn't have done that.'

'There's nothing I can do about it now,' I say with a shrug. 'So, what do we know about this John Walsh?'

'If he turns up at the beach and Tani finds out—'

'She won't. And chances are, if the weather is hot, he and Katherine might take to the beach themselves.'

'That's not their local beach.'

'He's missing his grandchild. Tani should talk to them.'

He throws me a look but says no more. Damn, I know he's right. I should never have said anything. I flirt with the idea of not going to the beach on Sunday, but what if that makes him come to the house and Mani finds out? She'd kill me. She likes Johnny well enough but she'd respect Tani's wishes. Why did I do it? Am I so pathetic that I want to win his liking by hurting Tani and Luc?

We turn left onto Newport Road and follow it, Dan remaining silent as I battle with the guilt. I could spin it and say I told him by accident if Tani does find out. And I feel bad at even thinking that. And then I think of the lies people spin down the station every day of the week without batting an eyelid and I bloody envy them.

Five minutes later, smoothies finished, we arrive outside a well-tended detached house in the middle of a well-tended housing estate. Just as we are about to head up the driveway a mother and two young children bounce out of the door, one of them yanking the other by the hand and the mother calling at them to slow down. All three stop when they see us.

'Hiya, Detective Sergeant Lucy Golden,' I say to her. 'Is this your house?'

'Yes.' A worried frown. 'What's happened?' Then, 'Lizzie, stop pulling Peter like that. And if I have to tell you once more, I won't let you go to the party, all right?' She turns back to us, eyebrows raised.

'Are you Eleanor Walsh?' I ask.

'No.' She frowns. 'But as far as I know, there were Walshes in the house before us. That was about eight years ago now.'

'Mammy!' Lizzie hops impatiently from foot to foot. 'Come on!'

'In a minute,' she snaps, making Dan and me jump. 'Sorry,' she says. 'But they drive me mad.'

'I know the feeling.' I don't really. 'Any idea where the Walshes went?'

'No. I think the man who owned our house died.'

'A man died in our house?' the younger child says. 'Where?'

'He didn't die in the house.' The mother shoots an irritated look at us. 'He just died and his family sold the house.'

'But where did he die?'

'In your bed, probably,' Lizzie says, and the boy shrieks.

'Thanks,' I say, but the mother ignores me as she drags her charges apart, grabbing each of them by the hand and pulling them up the street, her cross voice carrying back to us.

'Who'd be a parent?' Dan sounds amused. 'Will we try the neighbours, see if any of them has information on the family?'

'Might as well.'

The neighbour on the right is even newer to the neighbourhood than the woman in the Walsh house, but the other neighbour, an elderly woman, Mae, in her eighties, I guess, invites us in and plies us with orange and home-made sponge cake.

'That was a family and a half,' she says. 'The father was as mad as a brush. His poor wife killed herself and I don't think the fellow got over it.' She cuts us both a great big slice of cake and loads up our plates. 'Eat up there now.' Then, when she's satisfied that we will, she lowers herself into a chair and continues, 'Wouldn't let the children out of his sight. There were three of them. The two girls went off to Dublin, I could never tell them apart, and the son, he went abroad, I think. They ended up all

214

leaving him in the end. Oh, they came back for their share of the house when he died and, sure, weren't they at the funeral, but that was the last anyone around here saw of them.'

'Do you remember an incident with one of the children, Ellie, and a boy called Adam?' I ask. 'She—'

'Eleanor, now there was trouble in the making. She was out every night as far as I could see and the father going mad with her. Though I suppose you couldn't blame the child – they like a bit of freedom. And with her, I think it was like trying to keep a wild horse tethered up. She had this boyfriend, I remember, and that caused a lot of trouble.'

'What was his name?'

'Oh, that's going back a while.' She thinks, shakes her head. 'No. My daughter was friendly with her, she might know. I could give her a call, though she's off on one of these retreats or health farms or something where she can't take calls, but when she comes back, I will.'

'Thank you. Any idea where Ellie might be now?'

'None in the whole world,' she says cheerfully. 'Normally around here you would know, but they never really mixed with the neighbours.'

'Would anyone else around here have been friendly with Ellie?' I ask.

'They've probably all moved on by now, pet,' she says. 'And no offence, but I think you two would be better off investigating the other two murders that have happened here recently.' Nodding to our plates, 'Isn't that nice cake now?'

She's lonely, I think, so we spend another ten minutes with her as she tells us the story of the road and its residences and her life and how her husband died in a car crash. And of how the driver came to apologise years later. 'Aw, sure, I forgave him,' she says, 'what else can you do? He had the rest of his life to live and what kind of a life would it be if he felt he wasn't forgiven? He calls into me now and again, brings his children to visit, and it's nice, you know, when you don't have many visitors.'

Dan and I absorb this, letting the story settle, not wanting her to think we have to get moving, though we do. That's the thing about this job: you meet people who astound you. Whose bravery and selflessness are astonishing and yet who never get recognition for their acts of kindness or stoicism. 'Thank you so much, Mrs Lynch,' I say to her, after a decent amount of time has passed. 'We'll be getting out of your way now. Thanks for the nicest cake I've had in ages.'

'I have the recipe somewhere. Hang on now until I get it for you.'

She shuffles away into another part of the house and a few minutes later arrives back into the hall with a printout. 'The BBC website is very good for recipes,' she says. 'I get a lot of tips from there.'

'Thanks.' I tuck it into my pocket. The last time I baked a cake was back in third-year Home Economics.

She walks us to the door and bids us a cheerful goodbye.

'I'm not sure how helpful that was,' Dan remarks, 'but at least we've chased it up.' At my lack of response, he says, 'Earth to Luce, hello? I was just saying—'

'I have a theory,' I interrupt him, 'and it's much bigger than Abby's murder.' I take a breath and say, 'What if she was trafficked?'

Dan stops walking, turns to me. 'Go on.'

I speak slowly, trying to tease out the idea that has played around in my head the last couple of days. 'Young girl, homeless, clueless, drugged up maybe, stays in a shelter for a few weeks, gets to know the staff, trusts them, hurts her arm, gets driven to the hospital by Adam, who is working on behalf of the traffickers, and is never seen again.' I look at Dan. 'What do you think?'

Dan ponders it, chewing it, like a crust. 'Yeah. Maybe,' he says. 'And they have a policy of only taking the younger ones, the more vulnerable ones. Carla said that.'

'Yes.'

'But why murder her?'

'You heard what everyone said about her. She was spunky, didn't play ball. Maybe she wanted out. Maybe they discovered she was just too much trouble.'

'And murder Adam?'

'Maybe he was freaking out. He was obviously there the day Abby was murdered. We've heard he seemed stressed.' And then I voice it, the thing I remembered Helen saying. 'It would explain Adam's car.'

Dan gives me a puzzled look.

I pull him towards a seat by the edge of the river, speaking low and urgently, so we can't be overheard. 'D'you remember when we were interviewing Helen and she said that Adam's job wasn't full-time, just something to give him money? And Gareth just said that Adam was there in the shelter quite a lot?'

'Yeah.'

'And yet Adam's dad told us that Adam bought a car, a *car*, a one-nine-one car, with his bonus. I don't know of any part-time jobs where you can earn a bonus big enough to buy a car.'

Dan gives a low whistle. 'Good catch.' He sits up straighter. 'If you're right, I'm sure this isn't only going on in the Dublin shelter. How many branches have Home got around the country?'

I dig out my phone and ask Google. 'Seven. And Gareth oversees them all.'

'So, seven shelters trafficking young girls. It'd be easy enough to do. I mean, who misses young drug-users? It's par for the course for them to go off-grid. Abby wasn't even reported missing.' A moment. 'What we're thinking, then, is that Adam was on someone's payroll. He was enticing young homeless girls into sex work or domestic work or whatever. That he panicked when Abby was murdered and was then murdered himself.'

'Yes.'

'It's simple, it makes sense, but we have fuck-all to back it up.'

'Get an order and request Adam's bank statements.'

'I'll sort that now.'

I watch as Dan rings Pat – he's the paperwork whiz, great at applying for anything that demands form filling. And he knows the law backwards too. It's an art that should never be underestimated because any sort of misstep along the way can mean that crucial evidence is inadmissible in court. All the chains of evidence need to be impeccable.

'Great, Pat. Thanks. Make it a priority, yeah.' Then he adds, 'And, yeah, follow up on the alibis while you're waiting.' He hangs up.

We're silent for a moment.

'Who would recruit a guy like Adam?' Dan asks.

'He was easily led,' I say, though even to my own ears it sounds weak.

'Why would Adam let himself be recruited?' Dan asks. 'It couldn't have been money – you saw where he lived, his room.'

218

'It had to be because he liked the person recruiting him,' I say. 'And . . .'

'Gareth,' Dan gives a slow grin of satisfaction. 'He liked him.'

My thoughts exactly.

'Let's see how Adam's financials pan out before we talk to the Cig,' I say. 'You know him, he'll need more than just a theory.'

'We'll find it,' Dan says. 'If it's there, we'll find it.'

And then Dan's phone rings and it's Gareth.

'Liam lied to you,' he says.

Chapter 41 – Sarah

Someone drops a newspaper right on top of her head, as if she's invisible. Sarah opens her mouth to shout after them, then thinks, to hell with it, she might as well read the thing. She'd be on her own all afternoon as Jenny was leaving to chop vegetables in the shelter for dinner.

She's such a goody-two-shoes, Sarah thinks, unfolding the newspaper. Lurid headlines of a second murder in Mayo take up the first and second pages. She pretends to read as Jenny adjusts her hair, pulls her T-shirt down over the waistband of her spotty shorts and gets up.

'Bye,' she says. 'See you later.'

She doesn't know why Jenny helping out at the shelter annoys her but it does. 'Maybe,' she says, pretending to be engrossed in the story of a man found in a bath with his wrists slashed. She hates reading.

Jenny doesn't leave, perhaps sensing that all isn't well. 'Bernie and Alexandra think I'm a great worker,' she says, shifting from foot to foot. 'You should come too and they'll know that you are as well.'

'They're only being all chatty because they want to find out about you, Make you want to get a social worker who'll report you to—'

'No, they said I'm positive and dependable.'

'So why did Bernie want to know if you had a bank account the other day?'

Jenny flushes.

Sarah has her now. 'Because,' Sarah presses her point home, 'she wants to find out your address.'

'If you can't think of anything nice to say, don't say anything.' Jenny is properly mad now, not so certain of Bernie and Alexandra any more. Her small hands are curled into fists. 'You're just jealous because they like me better than you.'

'Bernie is going to hand you over to a social worker, that's what's going to happen.'

'No.' She glares at her and Sarah thinks she might cry.

'Off you trot,' she says, motioning her away with her hand, 'And don't cut yourself on them big sharp knives.'

'You can be so ... mean.' Jenny's voice rises. 'But you know what? You're just scared. You're scared in case something good happens because, oh, oh, oh, it might actually be a good thing and you wouldn't know how to handle a good thing and—'

'Shut up!' Sarah throws down the newspaper and stands up, facing Jenny. 'You shut up!'

'Make me!'

'I will, I'll—' She's so angry, her words won't come. Bam! She wants so much to hit her and—

'All right here?' A guard they hadn't noticed arrives up. He looks from one to the other.

They freeze before Jenny flounces off.

'Can you move on, Miss?' the guard says to her then. 'No loitering on the bridge.'

At six, she heads to the shelter for her dinner. She always likes to arrive a bit late because there's no point in being too eager: it's not as if she looks forward to it or anything. Plus, she doesn't want Jenny thinking that the row bothered her in any way. Because it didn't.

There are about fifteen people outside when Alexandra opens the door. 'Chips and eggs today,' she says.

That's Sarah's favourite. It's what her mother makes her whenever she cooks.

Inside, she scours the room for Jenny. No sign. Maybe she's in the bathroom. Sarah takes a plate and the volunteer who always dresses like she's going for a night out – Sadie – piles her plate with chips. 'Enjoy.' She smiles.

'Is Jenny here?' Sarah asks, as she helps herself to packets of salt. 'She said she was coming to chop vegetables.'

'We did no chopping tonight,' Sadie says. Then she calls across, 'Alexandra, have you seen Jenny? Sarah is looking for her.'

'I'm not looking for her,' Sarah snaps. 'I just wonder where she is.'

'She hasn't been in,' Alexandra calls back. 'I'm expecting her tomorrow because she said she'd help us with the dinner but I haven't seen her today.'

Sarah puts her plate down and the people behind her grumble. Sarah barely notices. 'She said she was coming here to chop vegetables.'

The two volunteers look blankly at each other.

'We never chop on a Friday,' Alexandra says. 'Maybe you misheard.'

'I didn't mishear. She said—'

'Will you get a move on!' the girl behind Sarah says.

'Will you fuck off!' Sarah says back.

The girl elbows her. Sarah upends her chips.

Sarah is told to leave and to come back when she can behave herself.

Aw, fuck that, she thinks. She may as well go and look for Jenny.

Hours later, there is no sign of her. Sarah is back in the doorway, unsure of where else to go.

Her phone rings.

It's her mother.

Sarah wants to hang up but she can't.

'Can you come home? I know we fought but I'm in a bad way here, Sarah.'

She supposes she might as well.

Chapter 42

We've managed to catch Liam before his trip back to Dublin. Though we tell him it's just a few questions, he looks annoyed at having his plans disrupted. I wouldn't say too many people challenge Liam over anything. It's probably why he's so successful. We've done a very basic Google check on him and apparently he has his hand in many businesses, is well regarded and has powerful friends. He's a son of Westport too, but he must keep a really low profile because I don't know anything about him.

'You told us you didn't know Adam?' Dan says, as we sit opposite him in an open-air coffee shop. Dan has his I-don't-like-being-lied-to face on. It scares most people, though Liam seems nonplussed.

'That's right.' Liam's tone is measured.

'We have information to say that you do, that you spent a while chatting to him the last time you visited the Dublin shelter.'

Gareth's words were that Liam and Adam appeared to be very friendly, that he was surprised they knew each other.

Liam looks at us as if we're bonkers. 'I chat to all my volunteers. It makes them feel valued, ensures they do a good job. I probably did talk to the guy but, sure, I'd forget.'

'I would have thought in your line of business that it was important to remember people.'

Liam folds his arms and seems to say a quick prayer for patience. 'Yes, but,' he heaves a sigh, 'he was a volunteer. They come and go all the time. I really don't remember him.' He offers us a smile. 'I'm sorry.'

I can see Dan wondering whether to press it or not, but in the end, he stands up. 'All right. Thanks for clearing that up.'

'No bother. By the way, who said I knew Adam?' The question is tossed out casually, but I can tell from the tone that he really wants to know.

'We're not at liberty to disclose that.'

Liam nods, but I can feel his eyes on our back as we walk away.

'Well, that went nowhere,' I say, when we're out of earshot. 'Do you think Gareth was on the level when he said Liam knew Adam?'

'The hippie little shit could just be trying to muddy the waters.'

'Yes, afraid we're about to finger him and his girlfriend.'

'Still,' I say, thinking of the annoyed look on Liam's face, 'it might be worth digging into the man, just a quick check.'

'We did. There was nothing, save for he's from Westport originally, like Adam, and that proves nothing.'

'Maybe they go back a bit or something.'

'Even if they did, Adam was hounded out of here, remember? If Liam knew that, do you think he'd associate with him?'

'Fair point. Right, where are we now?'

'We're pinning our hopes on your magnificent *Crimecall* appearance on Sunday night,' Dan says.

Oh, fuck!

Chapter 43 – Day 11

Sunday morning dawns as clear and as hot as every other day for the past seven weeks. Global warming is beginning to wear a little thin with me. Still no storms. I'd give anything now for a typical Achill day of rain punctuated by a few bright spells. I crawl out of bed, having barely slept because of the heat. I'd spent the restless hours running through how we might prove our theory and then bring it to the Cig. So far, on a preliminary check, Pat hasn't been able to find anything amiss in Adam's bank accounts. He's requested his father's now, a last-ditch attempt at finding the money, if there is money. We've had no success yet with the CCTV tracing Gareth's car on the route from the shelter to his hotel on the morning of Adam's murder.

The only news of note, Dan calls early to inform me, was that Adam's father's apartment had been broken into. He'd been so drunk he hadn't heard a thing. The kitchen had been disturbed along with Adam's room, though as we'd removed almost everything from it, there was nothing left to rob. I floated the idea that whoever it was might be looking for something. Weren't Adam's clothes tossed when he was murdered? And where have his laptop and phone got to? I request prints from the scene. Dan says he'll chase it up and, before hanging up, promises not to call me for the rest of the day.

My interview for *Crimecall* is airing this evening so perhaps that will shake some things loose.

But that's for tomorrow. Today, I think, as I blast myself with cold water, I have Sirocco to enjoy, her giggles and laughs and mini-tantrums. I feel good just thinking about it, the weight of the case shedding just a little. The only blot is that I've told Johnny I'll be at the beach, but there's nothing I can do about it now. Pulling on a pair of shorts and a T-shirt, I pad out into the kitchen, banishing my guilt to the back of my mind. My mother is up already, having a cup of tea. Sirocco sits in her high-chair slamming a spoon into her bowl of porridge and cackling with glee when it splatters up on her. It makes me laugh too.

I give the baby a kiss, pour myself a glass of water and tip some flakes into a bowl.

'Luc and Tani have been on already, wondering how the baby is,' my mother says. 'Anyone would think they didn't trust us.' She laughs gaily and guilt clatters me about the head. 'If you're bringing her to Keem,' she continues, 'you'd want to start making tracks before it gets too hot and too crowded.'

'I was planning to go about ten, I won't be too long. D'you want to come?' Please say yes, I think, then I might not feel so bad. I mean, if my mother and I ran into Johnny, it'd look a lot less suspicious.

'I can't.' My mother flaps her hand dismissively. 'No, no, I can't.' She sounds quite abrupt.

'Make sure now that you put plenty of sun lotion on her and do not let her pull her hat off. God help us altogether if that child gets a bit of sunburn.'

She's acting rather oddly but I don't have time to dwell on it. She diverts then to tell me that Mary Laffin died in the night, she read it on rip.ie. And weren't they fierce organised to have it up so quickly.

Maybe if I go early, I'll miss Johnny, I think. I cut off her ramblings about Mary Laffin when I say, 'I'll head off now. When I come back, we can go and grab some lunch.'

Fifteen minutes later, I pull into the car park on the hilltop over the beach, Sirocco grizzling in the back. I pause a moment when I step out of the car, just to gaze on the beach down below. Here is the playground of my childhood, a small cove, bounded on three sides by cliffs so that even on the wildest day it's an oasis of calm. The sea is that green-blue, and the sun sparkles and dances on the waves. Far out, I can see boats and surfers and hear the gulls, and something in me fills up. The weight of the case shifts on my shoulders and, for that brief moment, I can breathe.

Sirocco's grizzling turns into a full-blown wail. I take her out of her seat and show her the beach, though she's seen it before with my mother and her own parents. I tell her that this is the beach at the end of the world. This is where the road stops. This is the last beach before America. And she laughs into my face. I put her into her buggy and throw a rug and her bucket and spade underneath in the basket. Then, balancing the umbrella some way across her, I begin the descent.

Finally, I make it to the sand. It proves impossible to push the buggy any further, so I have to carry the baby, her buggy, the umbrella and the rug to where I reckon the most shade is.

Ten minutes later, I take her down the small beach into the water. As I dip her toes into the cold, she shrieks, making me laugh. Then she laughs too. She's a real water baby, just like her dad.

'She's loving that.' Johnny's voice from behind. I stiffen. And grow hot. Hotter actually. How did I not spot him? Some bloody detective I am.

I turn. 'Johnny, I—'

He holds up his hand, backs away a little. 'It's fine, I won't stay long. I know you probably regret telling me you were here.'

Yet he still bloody came. 'I shouldn't have.'

'No, but you did and I'm glad.' He beams unapologetically and hunkers down beside Sirocco, who I'm supporting by holding onto her armpits. Johnny's floppy hair falls across his face, 'Hey, little miss, how are you? Remember me? I'm Granddad Johnny.'

Granddad Johnny. It strikes me suddenly how old we're all getting. That this boy of my adolescent fantasies is a grandparent. I am what my mother is to Luc. Realisation is like a grief.

Johnny looks up. 'Can I?' He nods towards the water and I don't have the heart to refuse. He whips off his top, throwing it on the sand, and holds out his arms for Sirocco. I have to tear my eyes away from his slightly flabby six-pack. He's looks bloody gorgeous.

Releasing her to him, I watch as he leads her further into the waves. She yelps when the water slaps up against her fat little thighs so Johnny scoops her up and throws her into the air, then catches her. I laugh aloud as she shrieks in fear and delight. Johnny carries her further out, balanced high in his arms. I watch as he talks away to her, pointing out boats and birds and surfers.

'Your husband is very good with your daughter,' a woman says, coming to stand alongside me. 'She's having a great time.'

'It's my granddaughter,' I correct, a little flattered, then add, 'and the man is not my husband. But, yes, he's very good with her.'

I turn back and see Johnny encouraging Sirocco to wave at me, then he waves at me. Then he throws her into the air again. And it's so . . . I try to catch the word. Joyful, I think. It's bloody joyful and wonderful and right.

I don't see joy very often, not in my job, so I'm glad I've brought some measure of it into this day.

Finally, I don't know how much later, Johnny, Sirocco in his arms, sloshes his way back through the waves. 'I think I've tired her out.' He grins as he hands her over.

'She loved it.' I busy myself straightening the baby's hat, trying to avoid looking at Johnny's bare chest, which I'm sure he has waxed.

'Thanks,' he says simply. 'It's just so good to see her.'

'She liked seeing you too.' Sirocco is grasping for my hair and I try to pull away, causing her to jam a finger into my eye. I howl, which causes her and Johnny to erupt in giggles.

God, but that smile, I think, as I look at Johnny.

'Are you all right?' he asks.

'I'm grand.' My bloody eye is hopping.

He reaches over and untangles Sirocco's hands from my hair. I can smell his breath – I can taste it. Minty.

His forehead tips mine. He waits a second. I wait a second. Oh, God . . . His finger is tracing its way across my neck. Up my cheek. My scar—

I pull away. 'I'd better get Sirocco back. The sun is getting up. I'll be seeing you.'

'All right.' He salutes, unabashed. 'Thanks again.'

'You're welcome.'

I watch him stride off across the sand, pulling his T-shirt back on. Aside from feeling like a harlot, I think maybe I did the right thing by letting him see her, then that maybe I didn't. That I disrespected his daughter's wishes. But I think of the fun they had in the sea, of how much he loves this little scrap of a girl, and I know that it wasn't all wrong.

When I pull up to my house about half an hour later, my mother rushes outside to meet me. She only ever does this during emergencies or when someone has died whom she thinks I should know about. But she's already told me about Mary Laffin. Before I have a chance to ask what's wrong, she says, 'Now you're not to go mad. I won't have you saying anything.'

'About what?'

My mother attempts a nonchalant look. 'Katherine is here.'

'Katherine?' My blood runs cold. Has she somehow heard—

'I just happened to mention to her during the week that Luc and Tani would be away on Sunday and, sure, well, I never thought she'd call but there she is and—'

'You knew she'd call.' I'm trying not to laugh. God, we're a right pair of interfering bats. Then I whisper, 'I ran into Johnny on the beach.'

'Oh, well,' she actually manages to look annoyed, 'that's worse. That's way worse. Tani hates him the most.' She takes Sirocco from her seat and marches on into the house.

'How do you figure that out?' I follow her.

'At least I told you,' she says. 'You were sneaky about it.'

I can't argue with that, so I say nothing more until we are in the kitchen where Katherine is at the table, a big mug of tea and a slice of cake in front of her. She eyes me warily as I come in. 'I know this is a surprise but I just wanted to see the baby. I didn't want her to forget me.'

Be hard to forget Katherine, I think, as I pour myself a cup of tea. 'I'm sure you and Johnny are missing her.'

Katherine doesn't answer. Maybe she doesn't hear me. She gives Sirocco her full attention, making silly faces for her, but Sirocco, probably tired from playing in the waves with Johnny, is tired and cranky. I do feel a bit sorry for Katherine, then watch in disbelief as my mother spoons a little bit of ice cream into a saucer and hands it to her. 'Sirocco loves that,' she says. She eyes me, daring me to disagree. 'Loves it,' she repeats.

Tani and Luc have a ban on Sirocco eating sweets.

Jesus, and to think *I* was feeling guilty.

Katherine stays for about an hour and leaves, a little tearfully, just before lunch. 'Will you tell me when they go away again?' she asks, and my mother promises to do so.

I wait until Katherine has climbed into her taxi before I round on my mother. 'If Luc and Tani find out, they'll kill you.'

'If Luc and Tani find out, I'll tell them how selfish I think they're being,' she says. 'Grandparents need to see their grand-children. Anyway, you can't talk!'

She has a point.

'Now, where's this lunch you said you'd bring me on?'

Despite everything, we manage to have a lovely day, the three of us. I take the opportunity to drive us around the county, visiting and revisiting places I haven't been to in a while. I've been too busy working to fully appreciate the beauty of this brown and green sweeping landscape. The emerald seas, the majestic highs and lows of cliffs and ancient bogland. The food, the fish, the craic. The air hangs heavy and the day shimmers and all is good with the world.

Chapter 44 – Day 12

Even though I'm in early, William is at the Achill station before me. The door to his office is slightly ajar, so I knock gently and he tells me to come in. His bonsai tree has been moved to the far side of the office from its usual perch by the window. He brings that tree everywhere, and no one has ever had the nerve to ask why.

'Window too hot for the tree?' I ask.

He ignores the question. 'I believe you wanted prints from the break-in at Adam's. Kev got back last night. They're not a match for any others we have so far. Probably just a gouger seeing an opportunity.'

'Maybe,' I say, but I'm not sure. I feel that this case is bigger and deeper and wider than we've even begun to think. 'I've requested that Pat go through Adam and his dad's bank accounts. I think Adam was getting money from somewhere – he bought a car despite only working a part-time job that paid minimum wage. His father told us he'd had a bonus.'

'Interesting,' William says. 'What's your thinking?'

'That Adam had a source of income from somewhere that led him to be murdered.' I don't bring Abby into it. 'Just give me a day or two to find out more,' I tell him. 'Then I'll be in here begging to be let loose.'

He eyeballs me. 'All right.'

'I'm waiting to see if anything more conclusive comes out of my TV appearance last night.' I'd gone to Mary Laffin's wake just to miss it.

'I saw it,' William says, not meeting my eye. 'The night team said that the phones got a bit busier afterwards, so we'll see what surfaces today when we check them all up.'

I wait for him to make a comment on my appearance on the TV but he doesn't. Is that good or bad? I don't know. Usually there's a bit of slagging but then William isn't a man known for his cheery banter.

'Can I go now? I'll have a look at what's come in on the phones.'

'Sure.' He dismisses me, turning back to a file he's been reading.

Brian is still on a call when I check in with him. He sounds good on the phone, sympathetic and interested. 'I'll pass the message on,' he says. 'Yes, I have taken a description of the three-legged dog you think abducted her . . . Yes, a spotty dog. A Dalmatian, you think? . . . Right. Thanks.' He puts down the receiver and groans, stretching his arms into the air, interlocking his palms behind his head and closing his eyes.

'That sounded like a good lead.'

He manages a laugh. 'I was about to leave a note on your desk when I got that lunatic on the phone. I stuck around on the lines last night because I heard you were going to be on TV and you definitely woke them all up. I think it was the tree, actually. That was a good call.'

'The tree?'

'Yeah.' He doesn't elaborate, just laughs as if I should know and hands me a slip of paper.

'What's this?'

'A guy, a Mr Leo Blake, rang about thirty minutes ago. He sounded nervous and was whispering so I reckoned he was genuine. He was pretty evasive on the phone but he did say he might have information for you but he wanted assurances that he wouldn't be in any trouble if he talked.'

Now that sounds interesting. A man prepared to come in even though he might land in trouble. 'What part of the country is he from?'

'He's down here, actually, in Castlebar. I told him someone would call him today. He was very cagey.'

At least it's something. 'Anything else?'

'Yes, two people recognised Abby from the hospital footage. I passed them on to Susan and Mick.'

'Good work, Brian.'

'No bother.' He turns back to the phone, which has started to ring again.

'Hey,' Ben says, when I land beside his desk, where he's going through reams and reams of photographs, obviously giving Pat a helping hand with Adam's stuff, 'did you search the whole of Achill for that tree?'

'Sorry?'

He pops a Tic Tac into his mouth and grins wickedly. 'That tree. Oh, Lucy, you have a habit of fucking up, don't you?'

I slump into a chair, suddenly weak. 'What do you mean?'

He pulls out his phone and starts to flick through his pictures. Larry arrives in. 'Did you take a screen shot too?' he asks Ben.

'Bloody sure.' Ben sniggers and I look from one to the other.

'There you go.' Ben holds his phone towards me and I stare at it. At first, I can't figure out what they crack up at. I look quite well: the make-up even disguises the scar that runs down my face, my hair gleams and I look quite fit and trim, even though I'm not.

'I can't . . .' And then, oh, God. The bloody tree. What the hell is that? I peer at the screen more closely, holding it up almost to my nose to see better as Ben and Larry crack up laughing. 'Bollix.'

'That would be right.' Ben chortles, which sets Larry off.

The tree branch over my head can only be described as phallic, and when you see it, you can't unsee it. I hadn't noticed it during the recording the other day and the TV cameraman hadn't and, obviously, neither had RTÉ. I'd chosen the place because it was near to where Abby had been found and I'd wanted the beauty of the surroundings to haunt the viewer. 'You juveniles.' I shove Ben's phone back at him. 'No one else would see that.'

'Everyone did,' Ben sniggers, like a kid, 'which was great. People listened to you. The whole interview's been shared on social media and while it's causing a lot of laughs, people are paying attention to the case and it's getting more coverage than ever, so well done.' He winks at me in a thoroughly patronising way and I slap the back of his head.

'Sexual harassment,' he calls after me. 'Thank God I love a bit of harassment!'

'Probably because you're getting none at home,' I shout back. Then feel a bit mean, remembering that Ben's marriage had broken up a few months ago. The fabulous Marisa – as we'd all christened her – had run off with someone else, taking their two kids with them.

'Uncalled for,' he shouts after me.

I head into the kitchen to make myself a coffee. Jesus, once more I'd made a fool of myself on TV, but then again, if it helps the case and—

'Hey, Penis Tree Girl.' Dan ruffles my hair as he passes. I dodge out from under him.

'You told me you wouldn't watch it,' I say, feeling betrayed. 'You said you and Fran would be out.'

'Fran taped it. We couldn't stop laughing, but you know what? I reckon people aren't going to forget it.' He inserts a pod into the coffee machine and presses the button. The machine starts to burble, spitting coffee into his pristine white mug. Dan is the only one in the whole force I reckon who has a sparkling coffee cup. He's totally anal.

'I'm sure they won't,' I mutter glumly. 'According to Ben, it's doing the rounds on social media.'

Dan laughs some more and busies himself steaming the milk and pouring it onto his coffee.

I tell Dan about Leo Blake. 'D'you fancy coming along?'

'I thought I'd help Ben and Pat go through Adam's stuff. It's our biggest hope for a lead right now.'

He's right. 'Grand. See you later.'

Leo Blake, who sounds a little terrified, agrees to meet me in Newport, along the quay just before the entrance to the Princess Grace Park. Princess Grace had had family connections down here and this little woodland park was named in her honour. Better than having a Barack Obama Plaza/Garage, I suppose.

Leo has described himself well and, as I pull into a miraculously free space in front of the park, I recognise him at once.

Small, red-headed, freckled, with milk-bottle-white arms and legs, despite the heat. He's wearing baggy brown shorts, an oversized T-shirt and floppy hat. Hopping from foot to foot, he's a bag of nerves.

I lock my car and cross to him. 'Leo, hello, I'm Detective—'

'Yeah, yeah,' he says, darting furtive looks up and down the street, 'grand. Look, can we walk and talk? We can go into the forest. I can't be seen talking to you. Everyone knows you from the show last night.'

I curse myself. Of course they do. So much for poor Leo trying to keep this meeting low-key.

I half think of offering to send someone else to talk to him, but I don't. The guy is so jittery, he may not come back. I follow him into the forest.

'Before I start, I just want you to know that I've never done it since, that I'm not that kind of a person and that the whole episode has me haunted. Right?'

'Sure.' What is he on about? His whole manner is a bit frantic as if he's not completely stable. I wonder if I should be going into a forest with him. But my nose is at me and I couldn't leave now, not even if he produced a gun. Instead he pulls out a bottle of sunscreen and proceeds to plaster himself in it as we walk.

'Let's go through here,' he says, and I follow him up the narrow path and into the shade where it's blessedly cool. Because it's early, there are just two people in front of us, quite a bit away. I'd imagine in a few hours the place will be teeming with tourists, just like everywhere else. The scent of earth and dried grass assails me.

I'm going to hear what Leo has to say first, and if it's significant, I'll take a statement. It'll either be something completely bonkers or something very important.

'Right.' Leo comes to a stop in a small copse. 'Right,' he says again, tucking his sunscreen into his small haversack. And then he plunges in: 'Like I said, I'm not that sort of a lad but, you know, I was twenty-one last year and I had never . . .' he flushes hard '. . . you know . . .'

I can't put the words into his mouth. 'You hadn't what?'

'Been with anyone,' he mutters, his face flaming red. I think he might combust. 'Like, you know, in that sort of way.'

'What sort of way?'

'Sexually,' he says quickly, 'that sort of way, and it was bothering me terrible and all my friends were talking about their first times and tenth times and all that sort of thing and I was giving it all I had but I was just lying and I think they were suspecting it. So I decided, you know, to, well . . .' he flushes redder again which I hadn't thought possible '. . . to go to a, well, a sex worker.'

'All right.' Jesus. Jesus. 'And?'

'This was about a year ago now, during the music festival, but like, anyway . . .' He rubs a hand over his face, then winces as a great glob of unabsorbed lotion gets into his eyes. 'Aw, shit!' Blindly he scrabbles about in his haversack, takes out a bottle of water and starts using it like Optrex. I can only watch and think, quite uncharitably, that it's no wonder he hasn't had sex yet.

'Are you all right?' I ask, after a bit.

'I think so.' He sounds shaken. He blinks, cautiously trying out his eye. Blinks again. Heaves a sigh of relief. 'I'm grand. Now, where was I?' He thinks. 'Oh, yes, this whole experience, which I'd rather forget. Well, it happened about a year ago during the music festival in Westport. And it was so strange. I've thought about it ever since and when I saw you last night saying about, you know, the burn you think she might have had on her arm, well, it came back to me.'

'What came back to you?' I aim for casually interested. I can't scare him off.

'The girl I'd booked – you can do it all online, very handy really – well, when I got there, she came into me, like you had to hand in your phone first, go into the bedroom and then the girl comes in. It was like a bedroom of a normal house only inside they had all sorts of stuff, like red cushions and things I didn't know what they were for but they cost extra so I didn't go for that option. Anyway, there were three girls in the house and this man who was minding them I suppose. I didn't see them much, but I went down to the bedroom and the girl I booked came into me and I noticed that she had this, well, a sort of mark on her arm. On her left arm, here.' He points to the upper inside of his arm. 'It was a burn, I'm sure of it.'

'Did you ask her about it?'

'I did. Like, I was concerned. And she got a bit bothered, seemed like she would cry and that, so I got her a tissue and she said I just had to forget I saw it, that it was nothing, that if I said anything, she'd be in trouble. It was right up under her arm, hard to spot unless you knew it was there but I think she had a bit of an infection or something. I asked if she wanted some Sudocrem, because I had that with me, in case I might need it, you know. But the girl said no. We just had a chat after that. When I left, she was smiling.' He says it like he's trying to assure himself that he did the right thing.

'Describe that burn to me. Size? What it looked like? Exact position.'

'Well, it wasn't like a burn from, say, a fire that'd make a scar.'

His gaze lands on my scar and quickly turns away. 'This was more like . . . what you'd do to a cow.'

'A branding?'

'That's right. A branding. And it was about this big,' he makes a space of about two inches with his index finger and thumb, 'and it was a bit infected so I'm not sure what it should have looked like, but it was like a fence or something like that. Lines, maybe.'

My scalp prickles. 'Did you ask her what it was?'

'No.' He makes a face. 'I tried but she was up in a heap about me even spotting it. And I was up in a heap about spotting it and I felt bad about being there. She was only young. I wasn't expecting her to be that young. She was the same age as my youngest sister.'

My stomach rolls.

'All right, Leo. I'm going to ask you to take that from the top again and this time I'm going to write it all down. As in a statement. All right?'

'All right.' He goes through his story again, sounding even more nervous, and he nearly collapses altogether when I ask him to describe, step by step, how he'd booked the girl.

A pained look crosses his face. 'It was called Hotdates. It was, you know, not exactly an easy site to find.'

Does he mean the dark web? The site is probably not called that any more but I'm sure it can be traced and tracked, especially if we follow exactly what Leo did.

'I went on the web, found this site and there was like a search engine. Like daft dot ie or myhome dot ie where you could specify where in the country you were and what date suited you and what sort of a girl you liked. Sort of building up your fantasy date. It was very professional. And then when you put in all the information, pictures of girls came up. And you could choose one. None of them had a picture of any girls with burns. Not that I noticed anyway. And they all looked very nice.' He darts a look at me. 'I know it's a terrible thing . . . Anyway, I put in all the information, and the nearest I could get to what I wanted was this girl, Avril, I think she was called. She was operating from Westport during the first two weeks in July, for the music festival, they said, and I just had to book a slot. I booked two slots actually, an hour, just in case I wasn't sure how to do the business.'

I'm torn between wanting to knock his head off and feeling sorry for him. He's got an awkwardness about him that I suspect is offputting for women.

He then goes through the story of how he spotted the mark on the girl's arm, describing the exact position, and I ask him to sketch it as best he can, keeping it to scale. He takes my pen and notebook and hunches over it, finally producing a series of lines. I ask him to sign and date it and I record it as an exhibit.

Excellent.

On Abby, a piece of skin had been cut away in the exact position Leo has described. Maybe so that it wouldn't be recognised. I'd heard of that sort of thing, of tattoos to identify drug gangs, but I'd never come across it in this context.

I wait until a couple of walkers with a dog have passed us before I say, 'Leo, that information could be very helpful.'

'Good.' He doesn't seem as nervous now. Maybe it's been like confession for him.

'Where were these girls?'

'This house about fifteen kilometres from Westport. Sort of out on its own.'

'Would you remember exactly where?'

'I might. It was on the N59 on the road to Newport.'

'All right, here's what we'll do,' I say to him. 'I'd like you to show me this house.'

Leo is agreeable. He gets into my car and I pull out of the car park.

Finally, after I've been driving for a while, he points. 'Just there, I think. I remember I had to stop to vomit because I was so nervous, so yes, this was the house. Definitely. An Farraige, that was the name of it, I remember now, and I thought it was a bad omen at the time, really, because An Farraige means "the sea" and there's no view of the sea from it at all.'

Christ.

'You're quite sure that's the house?'

'An Farraige, yes.' He shuffles his feet. 'Look, I know I did wrong but I never even had sex with her in the end. In fact, I still haven't—' He clamps his mouth shut, slaps a hand over it. 'An Farraige,' he repeats.

The house is a low bungalow with a large garden that fronts out onto the road. It seems a strange choice for someone to run a brothel from. There are houses on either side, but not close enough that they would notice the comings and goings of whoever occupies the place.

Just then, in my rear view, I notice a car indicate and pull into the driveway. A man gets out, opens the back doors and two cute little girls tumble out, running and chasing each other, shrieking with excitement. A woman emerges from the passenger side and she and the man survey the bungalow for a moment. Then the man crosses to the boot and, opening it, pulls out suitcases.

It's a summer let.

The brothel was a pop-up. Here for the music festival and then

244

the girls are moved on to somewhere else. I wonder if whoever owns it has any records as to who booked it last year or in the past few months. If they can remember what anyone looked like. A long shot but worth pursuing.

I turn the car around, drop Leo off and head back to the station.

Chapter 45

William declares he can't remember a complaint ever being made about prostitution in the Westport/Newport area. 'Though if it was a pop-up, it may not have been noticed, especially with all the mayhem of a festival,' he muses. I give him a rundown of Leo's statement and he listens carefully, biting his lip. 'It explains a lot,' he says. 'It would certainly explain why the flesh was cut away from her arm. It would explain the way she disappeared out of Dublin to come here. It would explain the professionalism of the crime. It might also explain why Adam had extra money and why he was killed. Anything turn up on his financials?'

'Not yet.' And it's not looking likely either, but I don't say that. That money must be somewhere. And I need William on my side in this.

'Here's what we do,' William says. 'Get Mick to pass on the A and E hospital interviews to the lads in Dublin. Then tell him to follow, step by step, Leo's instructions for that sex site. Tell him to scour it for Abby's image.'

I jot it down.

'Also, Mick must have a list of missing girls from earlier on in the investigation. Get Kev and himself to check all those girls to see if they feature on Hotgirls too. Tell them to concentrate on any young girls that may have been homeless for a time before disappearing.' He pauses, thinking. 'If this is trafficking, we need to tread carefully, but so far we have nothing to go on bar the word of some young lad who wanted his hole. If we can spot Abby on a site or any of the girls that are missing, especially if we can prove that they, too, had contact with Adam, we may have a shot. But we need to find those girls first. Maybe even see if there's a tattoo on them.'

'Is it too risky to ask the volunteers in the shelter if they recognise anyone?'

'For now. I'd imagine if Adam was working as a recruiter from the Dublin shelter, they would have people working in all the shelters. Let's do some background checks first. Who are the funders for these shelters? Who recruits the volunteers? Put Susan on it, reporting to Jordy. We'll leave the rest of the team on the jobs they're doing at the moment.'

I open my mouth to protest but he waves me away. 'If it pans out, we'll move on it, but I can't justify uprooting the whole team on the say-so of some horny young fella.'

'Charmingly put, Cig,' I say, and he actually grins.

'This might be the break we need, Lucy, but we don't know yet. The pieces fit better, though. Abby was young, vulnerable. Someone offered her a chance to feed her habit and earn money. She agreed, was taken and branded, which is done to shock into submission. Somehow she stepped out of line and was murdered. From what we've heard about her, it wouldn't be surprising. If they're operating from down here, it might explain why her body was disposed of down here. Forensics on the car should be back soon, so we'll be able to tell if she was in it.'

'Yep.'

'Go on, hop it. Get me some results. I've the super and the bloody media breathing down my neck, wondering why we haven't even got a decent suspect yet.'

Chapter 46

It's not difficult to trace the owner of An Farraige. It's advertised on Tripadvisor and booking.ie and the contact details are the same. I arrange an interview with the owner, Grainne, for two o'clock.

She meets me and Dan in her own house, about two miles down the road from An Farraige. This one is called An Coilte, which means 'forest', of which there is none. Dan thinks it's hilarious.

'What can I do for ye?' Grainne's face is alight with excitement. Some people are like that, all agog at the drama of being maybe involved in an investigation. They tend to be helpful but sometimes a little too eager to please, so you can't take anything they say as gospel and they must be treated with caution. 'Will ye sit down, have a cup of tea? I have biscuits too.'

We let her whiz about her big airy kitchen, boiling a kettle, filling a teapot and placing biscuits on a plate. No point in interviewing someone when they're a bit hyper. Far better to let her calm down.

Finally, after about ten minutes of chit-chat, Grainne settles herself at the table and pours us all a cup of tea. The weather is way too hot for it but the biscuits look nice. Dan takes two and Grainne looks pleased. Then she says, 'I've told the children to stay out in the garden and play. Otherwise they'd be on top of the two of ye asking all sorts of questions about solving mysteries and that. I love all those shows on TV. Did you see the one about the serial killer on Netflix? Wasn't that awful now? The one where he chewed the ears off his victims and put them in pies?'

I'm fairly sure that series was fictional, but I let it go. 'We think you might be able to help us, Grainne,' I say instead.

'Anything,' she says, straightening up. 'What do you need to know?'

'Your rental house, An Farraige,' I say, 'we were wondering if you'd have any records of who rented it last year around the tenth of July, for the music festival.'

She looks disappointed that it's not a bit more exciting but says, 'I know without looking. It's the same people for the last maybe five years. The O'Sullivans and their girls. They stay for two weeks. They pay cash in hand and always leave me a little present. I think they're musicians or something, though I don't know for sure.'

'Have you ever seen them?'

'I met her, Jane O'Sullivan, in the beginning. She called to the house to pay me but now she just leaves the money behind in an envelope for me, along with a letter to book the house for the following year. This year was the first she didn't stay for the whole festival. At least, I don't think she did because when I went in to clean the place after their booking was up, the air was stale, like the windows hadn't been opened in a week, though they'd forgotten to close one of the bedroom windows, and there was a smell in the place.' She wrinkles her nose at the memory and takes a biscuit. 'I was a bit annoyed, to be honest.'

'What sort of a smell?' My heart quickens.

'She spilt bleach, she told me in her note. Something had got on the floorboards and she tried to take it out and one of the girls had knocked over the bleach. She did leave money for me to clean the place up. She's very—'

Dan is on his feet at once and on the phone. I press her for more detail. What does Jane look like? Accent? Age? Has she her phone number?

And, unfortunately, all she has is a name. She can't really remember her, but she was probably in her twenties and her accent, from what she can remember, is Irish. And she is gorgeous. Gorgeous Jane. At least, she was five years ago, she says. But one thing she does have is the note that Jane left. 'I need it back for the tax man,' she says, handing it over.

Yes! I bag it and label it and order Dan to get it to Forensics as soon as we can.

Grainne willingly lets us take her prints and some DNA to rule her out.

Less than twenty minutes later, an indignant holidaying family with two bawling children has been ejected from 'An Farraige' with Daddy threatening to sue the arse out of us.

I ask them for some elimination prints, but am told in no uncertain terms to feck off.

I do feel a bit guilty watching them drive away. There's no way they'll get a house or even a hotel room at this stage. Their holiday is ruined. One of the kids manages to twist in her seat and howl back at us from the rear window like something from *The Scream*.

Grainne is now going through a regret phase, seeing as her house is now the subject of a massive takeover by us and the SOCO team. 'They'll want their money back,' she says, about the departing family. 'And they'll crucify me on Tripadvisor.'

'We're designating your house as a crime scene,' I tell her calmly, 'because we suspect a crime might have been carried out in it.'

'This is Newport.' She draws herself up to her five feet three. 'We don't have crime down here.'

'We believe it was a murder.' Yes, I'm hoping to shock her enough to get rid of her.

'There was no one murdered in there,' she says. 'You'd get a sense if someone was murdered in a place and—'

'Who is this?' William asks impatiently, from behind me.

'I'm the owner of that house,' Grainne says, not at all intimidated by William, who, despite the heat, wears a suit. 'That's who I am.'

'Right. Well, Grainne, is it? You need to go. We have to get on with our job.'

She looks about to argue but, like a yappy terrier being faced down by a rough-looking Alsatian, she trots off meekly, tail firmly between her legs.

'She wouldn't go for me,' I say glumly, watching her depart.

William ignores that and sits on the wall that runs around the property. He pats for me to sit alongside him. Dan remains standing.

'What's the situation?' William asks me.

'According to Grainne, the smell was worst in the bedroom

252

around the side of the house, the one where they'd forgotten to close the window, so SOCO and the tech bureau are in there now, combing through everything. The only thing was, Grainne had the house professionally cleaned with the money this Jane person left her and Jane herself had done a clean-up too. I'm not sure what we'll find.'

'If she was murdered in that room, beaten up like we know she was, there will be evidence,' he says confidently. 'Every contact leaves a trace. And if we dust for fingerprints, we might get a match to one of the other scenes.'

The reality of it hits me all of a sudden. 'She was fourteen, William.'

'A cash cow for whoever was running this thing.'

I am nauseated. Sometimes it's easier to be on the trail of something than to reach the end. Because at the end you can finally lift your head and start to see the brutality of what you've been dealing with. 'If that's what was going on, I will crucify these bastards,' I say.

'I'll hand you the hammer and nails.' He stands up as one of the forensics boys beckons us from the front door. 'We found a bit of spatter in the back bedroom, all right,' he says, and I can tell he's grinning. 'Come and see.'

'If we've found the murder scene, we're cooking,' William says, as we don dust suits and slippers.

I sink into silence and keep my fingers crossed.

We follow the SOCO, George, as he leads us carefully across the stepping plates in the hallway and into the smallest bedroom. It has been darkened out and we can see the luminous smear of a blood pattern on the painted walls and wooden floor that someone evidently tried to clean. 'There was an assault of some sort in here,' he says. 'As you can see, an attempt was made to clean it up. They used bleach on the walls but didn't dare to use too much on the floors, so we should get some results from that. We've also found some small drips on the carpet in the hallway. There are numerous prints but that's not surprising. We'll process everything as quickly as we can.'

He leaves us and I stare about the small room. Is this the last place Abby saw before meeting her death? It's tiny and smells vaguely of damp. Traces of black fungus can be seen in the corner of the ceiling. Did her eyes focus on that? Did she think of her mother at all? And is this where Leo met the girl who had an infection in her wound? How old was she? Once again the enormity of what I'm involved in hits me. It forces itself down my throat so I feel as if I'm choking. I gasp slightly and William looks at me. I turn and walk out of the room.

I am shaking with anger.

He comes out in a bit and we stand together in silence.

Chapter 47

William briefs the team back in the station at around eight o'clock and asks for our progress so far. There is precious little. None of the hospital patients remembers much about Abby, the door-to-door has yielded nothing, and there are no results yet back on the Peugeot.

'Any progress on where the plastic sheeting was sourced for Abby's body?'

'It's a common one, on sale at every hardware shop in Ireland,' Kev says.

'And the knife?'

'I'm getting sales records from Musgrave's for the past three months. It was a popular knife.'

'In some good news,' Pat raises his hand, 'Adam's phone pinged off the tower at nine o'clock on the first of July. It pinged twice after that on the third of July. All were phone calls. After that, nothing. Now either his phone died, was turned off or he wasn't on the island any more, having disposed of a body.'

'What date was the music festival in Westport this year?' William asks.

'It started the third of July,' Pat says.

'The first of July was when An Farraige was let,' I say. 'So, he was around for that.'

'We need to check for his fingerprints in An Farraige, and if the blood found in the house matches Abby's DNA, we have our crime scene and a possible date. That, with the fingerprints on the plastic sheeting, will link him very firmly to Abby's murder, but Adam, by all accounts, is not a man to run a prostitution ring. He is a minion. I want Adam's life scrutinised in detail. How are the financial records coming on, Pat?'

'Nothing, Cig. All seems to be in order.'

'He was being paid. That money is somewhere. Scour his contacts for a Jane. Now, Adam's photographs and personal stuff?' William barks out.

'There's about three boxes left. Nothing so far.'

'Keep at it. Currently we have two persons of interest.' William points to the picture of Gareth hanging on the board. 'He knew both victims and he has no alibi as yet for the time of Adam's murder. We're harvesting CCTV to try to trace his car that morning. Records say he was working at the time of Abby's murder but they might have been doctored. We are currently investigating the shelter he runs on behalf of some board or other—'

'The Lomax Board,' Susan pipes up.

William looks surprised. 'Good, Susan. Do you have anything else on it?'

'It's headed up by Liam Russell.' She hands William a picture of Liam. 'I'm not sure if you want to add him as a person of interest. He oversaw the appointment of Gareth. I've tasked GENBSC,' she stops, winces, 'NGECB,' another stop. 'The Garda National Economic Crime Bureau,' she says. Then cautiously, 'GNECB to—'

256

Someone claps and she flushes.

'Enough,' William says sharply. Then, with a respect usually reserved for the likes of Kev, he says, 'Go on, Susan.'

She looks a bit rattled, thinking it might be a trap. 'Well, eh, I've asked them to look into the board further and they said they would so it should get fast-tracked.'

'OK, good.' William sounds insultingly surprised.

'Excellent,' I chime in, with a grin.

'Moving on,' William says, 'all the volunteers spoken to so far had good things to say about Adam and Gareth, but Gareth still needs to be fingerprinted and DNA'd. Tell him it's to rule him out of our enquiries. Does he have a Jane in his life? And recheck his alibi for the first murder, Pat. Make sure he was working the day Abby was killed. Person of interest number two, James, who fell out with his sister before she went missing and who admits to us that he was out of work and free to roam the weekend Adam and Abby were killed. He has been interviewed a number of times and we have nothing as yet to charge him with.'

'So, it's basically Gareth who's more in the frame,' Matt says.

'Yes. Mick,' William swivels on Mick, who flinches, 'how did you get on accessing that website?'

'We got in all right, Cig. We're going through the images now. Nothing so far, no sign of Abby. The girls appear to be very young, though, the right age.'

My head is bursting. This whole investigation is so tangled, so knotted, that I fear I might lose control of it.

'Can someone brief the night unit?' William finishes. 'Thanks. I'll be here at six in the morning. You know what ye have to do.'

***

Having handed over our job sheets, Dan follows me out of the room. 'Luce, Fran is in Keel at the Amethyst bar. I told him we hadn't eaten so d'you fancy joining us? You look hungry.'

'The mysterious Fran,' Larry says, from behind me. 'I quite fancy a meal out myself. Ben, d'you fancy coming to the Amethyst for a burger and a rare sighting of the Lesser Spotted Fran?' He grins cockily at us.

'I've the kids this weekend.' Ben joins us at the door. 'So, I'm off to buy all the crap I can find, then send them back to their mother totally wired.'

Ben had married way out of his league when he'd wed Marisa – we'd all known it, even him, I think. She was ten years younger than Ben, who looks ten years older than he is, he's so rumpled. And while Marisa swanned about like a contestant from *Celebrity Island*, Ben drank pints down his local. A more diverse couple was hard to find.

'Make sure and tell them what a bitch she is too,' Larry says, like he's offering sage advice. Ben agrees that he will, then slouches off. 'Well, I'll join ye, if I'm invited.' Larry looks expectantly at us.

'Dan?' I say. Now is his chance.

'I won't even try the Larry charm on her,' Larry says, and he's actually not joking.

'I'd love to see you try your Larry charm on Fran,' Dan says. 'Come on.'

And with Larry warning Dan that he might regret saying that, we head off.

Fifteen minutes later I pull up in the Beehive car park, opposite the Amethyst bar. The place is hopping. Bring back winter, I think, when it's much more sedate. 'Will we even get a table?' I ask, as Dan raises his hand to wave at Fran, who has been waiting for us outside the pub. He trots over to meet us. He looks as crumpled as I've ever seen him.

He and Dan, like Marisa and Ben, are an odd couple, but unlike Marisa and Ben, their relationship works. Dan, who on the outside appears fairly laid-back, is in fact not. He dresses as expensively as his budget will allow. Most of the time, he could be on a catwalk with his sharp tailoring. Fran, by comparison, though the better-looking of the two, always has the appearance of being thrown together. Today he sports sandals, horrendous patterned shorts and a yellow T-shirt with an image of a smiling surfboard. His overlong hair is tinted blond from the sun and pulled back from his face with a bandanna. He's a landscape gardener so he spends all his time outdoors. I'd love a job like that.

'How's things, Lucy?'

'A bloody mess. Yourself.'

'Aw, the auld fella is sick, so that's a worry but otherwise, grand.'

At that moment, Larry pulls up in his car. It's the biggest car he can afford and he roars into his space.

'Who the fuck is that?' Fran asks, in amusement, as we watch Larry get out and wave over.

Trotting towards us, Larry nods to Fran, turns to Dan. 'She not here yet? Has she stood you up?' A second. 'Does she even exist?' He laughs a little and inhales. 'Great night.'

'Larry,' Dan says, 'I'd like you to meet Fran, my partner. Fran, this is Larry, a work colleague.'

Larry's jaw drops as he does a cartoon double-take. It's not often he's caught on the hop like that. You learn poker face early on in the guards. I bite back a smile.

Still, give him credit, he recovers admirably, holds out his hand and tells Fran it's good to meet him.

The handshake is firm.

Dan sneaks a look at me and I wink back.

'Let's go inside,' Fran says. 'I got us a table. We can stick an extra chair on for you, Lar.'

Lar!

It's only after a few steps that I notice Larry hasn't moved. He's still gawping open-mouthed at the two men as they walk on inside.

'Close that mouth, you'll catch flies,' I say. Then add, 'And it's bad manners.'

A few hours later I'm on the way home. It's been a nice evening. Larry had been quite civilised and not made any off-colour jokes. Still, I feel oddly dissatisfied. I get that way whenever I'm with a loved-up couple. Right now, I feel my aloneness wrap itself around me so tight, it almost chokes me. I think of Rob as I drive, the sun setting in the west and turning the sea blood red. I think of how I'd taken us for granted. I'd thought he'd be with me for ever, that we'd have each other's backs. If only it had been true, I would have been one of those couples tonight. Anger at Rob swamps me, the way it does sometimes, and it takes a huge effort to damp it down. My thoughts turn to Johnny, another man who had let me down, though we'd both been young. And Katherine had been like a rainbow in the grey sky of nineties Achill, I admit. Still, if she hadn't arrived maybe Johnny would be mine now. Ridiculous tears sting the back of my eyes. Like a kid of six, I live with my mother and she's the one I tell about my day. I have no one that's all mine.

Plus, I have a scar that runs down my face, puckers my cheek. Who would ever want me?

I flick on the radio to distract me from these thoughts.

'What is it you think was going on?' Patsy Patten, the late-night DJ on *Achill Sounds*, asks his guest.

'I've no proof of this, Patsy,' an all-too-familiar voice says, 'but I think the guards found something very significant today. Apparently Detective Lucy Golden talked to the owner of—'

'Remind our listeners who Lucy Golden is,' Patsy says.

'She's the detective who caught the Night Caller. If you live on Achill or Westport, you'll see her around. A pale long sort of a woman with badly kept hair but a sharp mind.'

Badly kept hair!

How did Stacy find out about the house? News travels, I suppose. I only hope Matt isn't leaking information to her, because I'll show no mercy.

I pull into the driveway at ten thirty and the only one at the house is my mother. She's outside on the patio, in her pyjamas and slippers, enjoying the last bit of heat. I go into the kitchen. 'Where are the others?' I call as I poke my head into the fridge and pull out a bowl of salad and coleslaw. Grabbing a fork, I sit down beside her.

'They've gone to a friend of Tani's and taken Sirocco with them to show her off. She took her first step today.'

'No! Aw, lads.' My eyes fill. While I was at a murder scene, my little granddaughter was stumbling her way into this big messy world.

'Luc sent you a WhatsApp video,' my mother says. 'Didn't you get it?'

I pull out my phone and see that there is a notification. I find the video and press play, blinking back tears. Moments of joy, the pure kind, tend to have that effect on me. In the video, Sirocco is sitting on the dining-room floor, wearing only a nappy. Tani hunkers down near her and holds out her hands. 'Come on,' she says, in a high voice, 'come to Mammy.' This goes on for about two minutes before Sirocco grabs the edge of the sofa and pulls herself to standing. With Tani still encouraging her, she launches herself away from the sofa, takes two wobbly steps towards Tani and keels over. Tani catches hold of her and she and Luc cheer. In the background, my mother claps her hands. Sirocco beams, showing her bottom two teeth.

This is something that my grandchild will do every day for the rest of her life now. But it's miraculous. 'Isn't that wonderful?' I say tearfully, as I play it again.

'And she's only eight months. That shows intelligence and great sporting ability. She'll play for the Mayo ladies yet, you'll see. They'll get on better than the men, that's for sure. Now,' her voice dips, 'what you should do is forward that video to Katherine and Johnny. Tani refused to but you can just say you got it and didn't realise they were not to know.'

'That's called lying,' I say sternly. 'It can get you arrested.'

My mother makes a *pift* sound and rolls her eyes. 'So can with-holding information. Send the bloody thing.'

I do and, for good measure, I add the message, *Get your bloody acts together, get Johnny to sort out whatever it is with Tani or you'll both miss out big-time.*

'Nice,' my mother says approvingly.

Chapter 48 – Day 16

Dan and I sit in front of William. It's time for the good news, which I hope will inspire him to go along with what I think has to be done now. Like prepping for an interview, Dan and I have our objective and we've mapped out a path to try to achieve it.

The only thing is that William, unlike our suspects, is wise to our tricks.

'We've good news, Cig,' I say.

'You've got the results from the car?'

Damn. 'Eh . . . no. Tomorrow.'

'I thought Ben said it was due yesterday morning?'

'Yes but—'

'Fuck that.' He picks up the phone, dials the tech bureau and roars a bit. Dan looks at me. Not the best start. 'This afternoon,' William says to us, as he slams the phone down, 'that other wanker in Dublin tried to jump one on me. So, good news, eh?' He looks at us hopefully, hands interlocked on his desk. As ever, even in the heat of his tiny office, he still manages to look as if he's just stepped out of a cooler.

'Kev chased up Forensics on An Farraige. They fast-tracked it for us. The blood found at the house in Westport is a match for Abby's.'

'Well, well.' William sighs in satisfaction. 'Bloody great. So, we have a murder scene and a date, if the car matches up.'

'Yeah, and get this. There were fingerprints found in common at Adam's murder scene and at Abby's. So, the same person or persons was there both times. Those fingerprints don't match James's or, unfortunately, Gareth's. But someone was there. Someone aside from Adam was present at both murder scenes.'

'How decent a match are these prints?'

Dan shrugs. Fingermarks are hard. Ever since the Madrid bombing, they've lost a little of their sparkle. It's a subjective science and, though our lads are good, no one is infallible. 'Decent enough for court, we reckon.'

'And blood analysis? What can they tell us about what happened?'

'What with the attempted clean-up, followed by the professional clean-up, it's hard to estimate exactly what happened. There was substantial blood found in the bedroom, which indicates that that's where the murder took place. There was also blood found in the hallway, which they believe came from the shoes of the SO as he was leaving the house with the suitcase. Not a good enough match for shoeprints, though. There were also a number of unidentified marks, which could have come from anywhere.'

'All right,' William says, 'so what we have is that the house was booked allegedly for the music festival but was going to be used as a pop-up brothel. It was booked from the first to the tenth of the month. The car, which will be forensically examined today, was booked for the same time period. Something happened during this week, probably the third or fourth of July, and a girl was murdered. Adam and the car were called into service, the body was disposed of and the car left the island on the night of the fourth of July. It was returned on the day it was due back, so the murderer had time to clean it out. Four weeks later, the body is discovered, and a week later, the man we suspect was involved in the murder is found dead near to where her body was found.' He fires the details of the case at us like a hail of bullets.

'Yep,' I answer. 'Correct. Now, what Dan and I were trying to puzzle out, William—'

'You always call me William when you want something,' William interrupts.

'William,' I say again, and Dan bows his head, the good little boy, and I want to kick him. 'What Dan and I were trying to puzzle out was that we hadn't even considered Adam, hadn't even had him on our radar, until he ended up dead. All we had was a fingerprint we couldn't identify on some plastic.'

William nods. He always nods like that when he's interested. I start slowly reeling him in.

'And though we know from witness reports that Adam was on edge, he wasn't a suspect, so why kill him? It's not enough to say he would have cracked and confessed, because all we'd done up to that time was try to get an interview with everyone in the shelter. So, we think we spooked them. Something in our investigation that first week spooked them so they framed Adam, hoping to make it look like a suicide, hoping we'd go away.'

'And what is it you think you did?' William asks.

'The only things we did at that time were to interview Abby's family who, let's be honest, are not looking likely, but we also managed to track Abby to the shelter.' I let the words shimmer there. 'That's all we did before Adam ended up in that bath. And the lads from Pearse started interviewing all the volunteers.'

A second, and I can almost see the light bulb going off in his head. 'No,' William says. Then before I can protest, he says, 'I know what you want and . . .' he shakes his head '. . . we don't have enough.'

Oh, yes, he's walked right into it. 'But we do,' I say, prepared for this. I lay three pictures in front of him. 'At the conference this morning, you missed it—'

'I got caught up on a call about the assault in Galway.' He's busy looking at the photos. 'What am I looking at here?'

'According to Mick and Kev, who've been tracking those missing young girls, this girl, Samantha,' I point to a picture of a black girl, 'fifteen, went missing from Galway two years ago. She'd been homeless. Bunked off from a direct provision centre. This girl here,' I point to her, white, red-haired and freckled, 'Leah, Cig, she was thirteen when she went missing, and was reported missing a year ago from Dublin. And finally this girl here,' I place a picture of a stunning girl, long dark hair, dark eyes, skin as clear as the sky outside the window, 'this kid, Lou, was fourteen when she went missing from Carlow.' William says nothing. He knows I've got more. 'Galway, Carlow and Dublin. These are all places with a Home shelter.'

'Aw, Lucy, come on—'

I lay three more pictures in front of him. 'Remember you asked if any of the missing girls appeared in the hotdates dot com website? Well, this here is Samantha, this is Lou and this is Leah, the thirteen-year-old.'

The pictures are shocking. All the girls are naked except for a red thong, their heads thrown back in feigned ecstasy. William takes a brief look before closing his eyes and massaging his eye-balls with the heel of his hand. 'Fuck,' he says. And he means fuck that it was never connected before. Fuck that no one bothered to look for these girls, because who does? Who really does? The kids who live on the margins, they can disappear without a trace and no one notices. It's not even a ripple in the water.

I go on, pressing for home now, 'Each of these girls, Cig, I'm not sure if you can see it, but just underneath their arm, there is the smudge of what Kev reckoned might be a mark of some sort.'

'So, Kev asked for it to be enhanced.' Dan lays another picture down. 'He took what could be seen of the tattoo or branding, or whatever the hell it is, and got them all layered together. This is what we reckon it makes.'

William peers at it. He's quite shaken and he doesn't do shaken. 'It's a series of lines,' he says, looking up at Dan.

'We think it's a barcode,' Dan answers. He had figured that out, and once he'd said it, we'd all agreed. 'I worked a case once, Cig, where the handlers used to tattoo a barcode on the girls. It was a form of identifying them and also told the punter how much they'd be paying for a half-hour.'

'I remember that case,' William says.

'This partial matches the drawing done by the witness Leo Blake four days ago.' I lay a copy of Leo's sketch in front of him.

There is a silence.

I leave it alone. It takes enormous effort on my behalf, but Dan presses his foot on top of mine under the desk. Sometimes it's good to present the facts and stand back. Like lighting a fuse on a firework.

William is no firework, though. He's calm and measured and his eyes rake over the two of us. Finally, he sighs, like it comes from deep down in his shiny shoes, and says, 'Let's see what Forensics come back with on the car.'

That's good enough for me.

Dan and I head back into the incident room. As he and I settle ourselves in front of the boxes of Adam's photographs – we take it in turns to do that job – I notice a peculiar hush descend on the room. Dan senses it too. He looks up and people immediately turn away.

Oh, I think, half amused. Larry had held in his news for the last few days, but in the end the temptation had been too much, and he'd told everyone. Just like Dan hoped he would.

'Right.' Dan swivels in his chair to face the room. 'Yes, it's true. Yes, my partner Fran is a man. Yes, I'm gay. Now, can we all get on with our work, please, seeing as we are an enlightened country now and gay people can get married and all that shit?' He turns back to the desk, pulling a shoebox of pictures towards him and starts to rifle through them. His hands are shaking. I try to catch his eye but he avoids me. In the end I send him a text. *Well done*.

And he turns to me and offers me the tiniest smile.

A few hours later, Pat joins us sifting the pictures. Pat is one of those guys who tends to slip people's notice: he's quiet and methodical, and once an investigation ends, he's easily forgotten. But try to get bank or insurance paperwork without him and you miss him like a right arm. William knows this – he remembers these things. That's why he's so bloody good at putting teams together. 'I heard you're gay now, Dan,' Pat says, by way of a greeting as he sits down beside us. 'So, how'd ye both get on with the Cig earlier?'

'I've been gay for a while now, Pat, thanks,' Dan answers from his position at the window. 'And we got on good, I think.'

'He'll go for it.' Pat nods. 'I mean, unless he lets us go into the shelter, we'll be trawling through photographs and bits of paper for ever. GNECB told Susan this morning that they've drawn a blank so far. They reckon it could take them a couple of months to work it all out.'

'We have to force it,' I say. 'If those girls are in danger, we have to do something about it.'

Pat nods.

'Who is this Jane? That's what we need to find out,' Dan says, turning around.

'We've no guarantee that Jane is a real name. It's easy enough to book a holiday rental under a false name and pay in bloody cash. Sure who'd ever know?' As I say it, something hits me. 'Just a second, Dan. Find the number for Louise Roche for me, would you?'

'Who's that again?'

'The woman who owns the house that Adam's body was found in.'

Dan logs into the system and pulls up Louise's number. I dial it, and as I'm waiting for the call to connect, I reread the statement the guard at the scene had taken from Louise. Maybe it's nothing but I don't believe that. Louise answers, not sounding too friendly.

'If you're calling to apologise for the state your guys left my house in, it's about time,' she snaps.

Shit. 'I'm sorry, I don't actually have anything to do with that side of things,' I tell her, introducing myself, 'but I'll pass on the complaint. What I'm calling for is to ask you to clarify something you said to one of our members the night you discovered Adam Gray's body, if that's all right?'

'You want something from me. There's a surprise,' she answers sourly.

I ignore it and plough on: 'In your statement, you said that the house had been booked by a person who normally comes down the same time every year but then they had to cancel it.'

'That's right. Someone she knew had died.'

Abby, I think. Abby's body had been discovered in the lake by then and they couldn't risk coming down west to ply their trade so soon after.

'Would you have that person's name?'

'Jane something or other.'

Dan, who's been listening in, gives a fist pump.

'Would you have a contact number or email for her by any chance?'

There's a moment before Louise speaks. 'Isn't that funny? I don't actually,' she says. 'She comes with her girls, books from year to year just by leaving a note. The first time she booked, it was on Tripadvisor – that was about five years ago – but after that we just had an arrangement.'

The disappointment is massive, though not unexpected. 'How did she cancel? Did she contact you then?'

'Yes, by email.'

'Louise, I need to see that email. It's very important. Tell me, how did Adam Gray come to book the house?'

'He booked soon after. He said he'd heard about the house from Jane.'

The hairs rise on the back of my neck.

'He emailed, said he saw the reduced rate and wanted to book the house. I thought it was a bit sneaky and cheap.'

'Can we get a look at his email too?' I'd bet that is Adam's email. He was being set up and he didn't know it. 'What dates exactly had this Jane person booked the house for?'

'Same as always. Second week in August for the traditional music festival.'

'Louise, I need you to think carefully. Is there anything about Jane that stands out?'

'I only talked to her once, on the phone, after she said she'd like to book the house from year to year. Now she just leaves me a note with a present. She puts it on the table in the kitchen for me.'

'Is there anything about that conversation that you remember?'

'It was five years ago.'

'Her accent, her voice?'

'I – no. No, not really.'

'Would you have any of the notes Jane writes when she books your house?'

'I can look. I might have last year's if you want.'

'That'd be great,' I say. 'Finally, just one last thing. Seeing as you've never met Jane, have you any proof that she's a woman?'

Louise scoffs, 'Unless there's some bucko going about calling himself Jane she must be.' A pause before she adds, 'Though the world is gone mad so I wouldn't be surprised if it was a horse.'

Despite myself I laugh, then say, 'You've told me you've barely talked to Jane, you've never seen her, you just have an email signed Jane and a few notes. So, what I'm asking is, have you any actual proof that Jane is a woman?'

A long pause. 'She sounded like a woman,' she says.

I thank her for her time and inform her someone will be out to get the email from her computer and collect the note. After hanging up, I say to Dan, 'We'll send it to Dublin to see where it originated.'

He is about to reply when Larry, carrying a huge ice-cream cone, walks into the office. He looks from me to Dan. 'Send what to Dublin?'

'You, you miserable fecker,' I say. 'Thanks for asking if Dan and I wanted an ice cream.'

'You can both suck on mine, if you like,' Larry thrusts his cone in my direction and Ben guffaws from the doorway.

Larry has grown tired of being accepting, I see.

'Let me know when you both grow up,' I say, over their laughter. Just then the phone rings. I lunge across the desk and pick it up.

'We've preliminary results on that Peugeot. Have you got a pen?'

A half-hour later, I'm back in front of William. Traces of blood have been found in the boot of the Peugeot, which match Abby's, and fingermarks from the mysterious third party are in the car along with another set that were also found at An Farraige.

'We don't have a match for Gareth,' William says.

'He could have worn gloves. Cig, you know in your gut that that shelter is the epicentre of this. Please, give me a chance to prove it.'

He looks at me. 'You want to send undercover in to see what falls loose?'

'Yes.'

It seems an age before he finally nods. 'All right. I'll make a few calls.'

Chapter 49

I leave work with a lighter heart that evening. Finally, I have a clear direction in this investigation and William has signalled the powers-that-be are onboard. We'll be supplied with everything we need by tomorrow.

For the first time, I feel hopeful that finally we'll get to the bottom of this thing. That I will get justice for Abby.

However, there's nothing like family for crushing the joy out of an evening. I know as soon as I set foot inside the door of my house that all is not well. My cheery hello is met with a pissed-off sounding 'In here,' from Luc. I'd been hoping to come home to more videos of Sirocco and her feats of walking bravery. I'd shown one to Dan and Matt a few days ago but had taken the hint when Matt had said, in a bewildered tone at the end, 'I don't get it.' I think he'd thought it was some kind of WhatsApp joke.

Dan had tried not to laugh at his reaction, then told me a fraction too late that it was great.

In the kitchen, my mother sits at the table, looking quite chastened, which is not an expression she wears often. What the hell has happened? Luc is leaning against the counter, arms folded, his mouth set in a straight line. 'What's wrong?' I throw my bag onto a chair with a deep sigh.

'Did you send on a video of Sirocco walking to Katherine and Johnny?' Luc asks, with fury.

'Hello, Ma, want a cup of tea? How was your day?' I try to make light of it.

Shit, I think.

Luc eyeballs me. God, he looks so like Rob. I move past him and put the kettle on.

He's waiting for an answer. 'Yes.' I don't drop my mother in it by adding that it was her suggestion because I know I would have done it anyway.

'In fairness I told her to,' my mother chimes in.

Luc gives a laugh of pure annoyance. 'Tani and I told you both to keep your beaks out.'

'I don't remember being told I had a beak.' My mother sounds a bit irritated. 'But, yes, you both said you didn't want any contact with the two of them. But, really, Luc—'

'Really nothing, Nan,' he snaps. 'You betrayed me. You betrayed Tani. She's really upset.'

I have had enough. 'Betrayed is a bit strong.' I throw a teabag into my cup. On second thoughts, I throw in another. 'It isn't fair, Luc, to stop Tani's parents having access to Sirocco. It doesn't matter how badly Tani and her dad get on, he is still her—'

'All you both had to do was to trust that Tani knew what was best for her and Sirocco and leave it at that.'

I'm tempted to say that he and Tani are just two kids, but they're not. They're nineteen. I know the best thing to do is apologise, to say it won't happen again but, damn it, I don't think it's right.

'I have talked to Johnny and the poor man is in bits,' I say. 'And I'm sure Katherine feels badly rejected by all this messing about. Tani has to sit down with her parents and talk it out – and, frankly, Luc, your nan and I didn't ask to be caught in the middle of a family drama.'

'Aw, now,' my mother interjects hastily, casting me a panicked look, 'speak for yourself, Lucy. I'm sorry, Luc, of course Tani knows her own mind. But think about it. It was just a video. It's not as if we've given them access to the baby.'

God, the woman takes some beating. I actually flinch at the bare-faced lie. And half admire it too.

'No more videos,' Luc says.

'They deserve to know how their grandchild is doing.'

'No, they don't.' None of us has noticed Tani standing in the doorway. She's barefoot and wearing a red T-shirt of Luc's as a dress. It's huge on her. With her hair spilling across her shoulders, she looks fragile and breakable, and I'm reminded unexpectedly of Abby. 'My father especially,' she says, and her voice wobbles. Big tears slide down her face. 'He doesn't deserve to know anything about her.'

'Aw, babe, here, don't.' Luc wraps an arm about her shoulders, cuddling her to him as she swipes at the tears.

'They're right.' She looks up at him. 'It's not fair to ask people to do something they don't agree to without explaining.'

'You don't owe us an explanation,' my mother says, distressed by the crying. 'We'll abide by the rules.'

I actually think she does owe us one, but her tears, and the protective way Luc minds her, soften the detective need-to-know urge in me. So, despite my reservations, I nod in agreement with my mother. 'We will,' I say.

For a moment, Tani looks grateful but then she shakes her head, wiping her eyes with her fists. 'No, it's all right. I'll tell you. It might be good.' A glance up at Luc. 'Luc has been great.'

He smiles down on her.

In that moment, I feel inordinately proud of him. To hear him being praised by Tani makes me feel I did something right.

'You go and mind Sirocco.' Tani gives him a gentle push. 'I'll be fine.'

He gives my mother and me a warning glare from over her shoulder and leaves.

Silence. The kettle snaps off. We all stare at each other.

'Would a cup of tea help you along?' I ask Tani.

'Yes, please.' She slides into a seat, pulling her legs up under her. She says nothing more as I make tea for the three of us. Outside, the dark starts to encroach on the garden, shadows creeping in. I close the back door, not wanting the light to attract insects.

I hand her the tea and say, as gently as I can, 'Take your time.' I sit down opposite.

After a few seconds, sounding a bit shaky, she says, 'It's hard to tell you. I mean, I've wanted to since I came but I feel, you know, as if I'm betraying . . .' She tails off. After another few moments, she takes a deep breath and I recognise it as the decision to confess that it is. I've seen it many times over the years. 'About eighteen months ago,' Tani says, 'when I was in the middle of sixth year, me and Luc bunked off school. My parents were out so we caught a bus to my place.' A fraction of a second later, she tacks on, 'It was just for lunch and, like, innocent stuff.'

I'll bet, I think.

'Anyway, when we got there, the house wasn't empty.'

Oh, no, this is like a bad B-movie. I can see where it's going.

'My dad was there,' Tani says. She lifts the mug to her lips and takes a shaky sip. Then, without raising her gaze, she mumbles, 'When Luc and I walked in, he was coming down the stairs with this woman and they were holding hands and kissing and . . . it was disgusting.'

For feck's sake, Johnny, I think.

'That *is* disgusting,' my mother agrees, jumping up and pulling a piece of tissue from the kitchen roll. Handing it to Tani while patting her shoulder, she says, 'You must have had a terrible shock, *a stór*.'

Tani dabs her eyes. 'That wasn't the worst of it. That was only the start.' She puts the mug down and scrubs her eyes with the tissue. 'At the time, me and Luc just left. Later, Dad tried to convince me that she was just a workmate who'd come to fix his computer, but I told him Luc and I weren't blind. And then . . .' Tani blinks hard. Tears fall. She lets them. 'I never thought he'd be so mean.'

'Mean? How?' I'm almost afraid to know. To think I'd fallen for his superficial charm yet again, for his hangdog looks and his arse and his smile. What sort of a stupid idiot am I? I'd actually felt attracted to him. It's official: I am a terrible judge of men.

'He made me promise not to tell Mam. He said she'd go off the deep end, wouldn't be able to cope, that it was nothing and he would sort everything out. Only he didn't. He made me,' tears spill from her eyes, 'he made me an accessory. Is that the word?' She looks at me, and before I can react, she goes on, 'He got me to cover for him a few times. He'd say he was trying to break it off with this woman, then tell me he didn't have the time or it wasn't the right moment. He made me lie to my own mother. And the one time I told him I was done with it, that I was telling

Mam what I saw, he started to cry and say I couldn't do that. And I couldn't. Of course I couldn't. But I couldn't lie either, not to her, so I just . . . left. Took Sirocco here. Tried to avoid my poor mother.' She breaks down again and my mother faffs about with more tissues and tea.

I remembered in school, when Johnny had done the dirt on me with Katherine, me and my friends had christened him Johnny Rotten. How apt.

My mother hunkers down alongside her. 'Your father deserves a kick up the arse for himself.'

Tani splutters out a sad little laugh.

'He does,' I agree. And by Jesus, I think, I'll give it to him.

'I'm sorry I didn't say anything before now but my mother doesn't know and I feel bad other people knowing that she's being cheated on and not her. And because I can't tell her, like, all my chats with her are like living a lie and I can't stay there and do that. I just . . . I want it to go away.'

'And does your dad understand why you left?' I ask, just to be clear.

'Yeah, he does. But my mother thinks I'm being difficult. She says I'm selfish, that I should try to get on with him. I think he has her feeling sorry for him.'

Like I did.

'Is the affair still going on?' I ask. Getting my facts straight.

'I don't know. He says it isn't but he's been saying that for the last year and a half. I don't trust him.'

I feel sorry for Katherine and that's a first. 'Your mother has done nothing wrong in this.'

'Nothing wrong.' My mother takes Tani's hand and gives it a squeeze. 'Honestly, I cannot believe Johnny would do that.'

'He'll keep doing it until he's stopped. Him, getting you to lie
. . . it's appalling. Your mother needs to know. Honesty is best.'

'Lucy is speaking from experience,' my mother puts in with
the delicacy of a Trump statement. 'Her husband was a huge con
man and she only found out when she was investigating his case.'

'I know,' Tani says. 'He took all my mother's inheritance.'

I die a little inside. 'The whole incident almost killed me,' I
say, 'but in the end, I'm glad I found out. Your mother might feel
the same.'

'I can't tell her and my dad won't.'

'Let's just leave it for now,' my mother says, afraid we'll upset
the girl.

'You can stay here as long as you want, Tani.'

'And we'll keep our beaks out,' my mother adds.

'Thank you both so much.' Tani sniffs. 'Luc is so lucky to have
ye.'

That's one of the nicest things anyone has ever said to me.

Later that night, in bed, I do it. My mother would kill me, Luc
will disown me, but damn it, I will not stand by and let Johnny
Egan hurt his daughter and granddaughter.

*Can you and me meet? I have something to discuss. I'll have a window
tomorrow around two. I can meet you outside Centra in Newport?*

He texts back: *Will Sirocco be there?*

How stupid is that man? How the hell would I have Sirocco?
But I text back, *Try and stop her* 😊

He replies, *Meet you there.*

I give a thumbs-up.

Chapter 50 – Sarah

'The number you have dialled cannot be reached at the moment.'

Sarah stares at her phone in frustration. It makes no sense. She hadn't been going to call Jenny – after all it was Jenny had walked away from her – but it niggled. Jenny not turning up at the shelter, Jenny not ringing her, Jenny's phone ringing out each time she dialled.

Maybe she just didn't want to talk to Sarah any more. But, Sarah conceded, this was Jenny. Jenny was twelve and a total pushover. There is no way she would ghost her like this. Yes, she'd only known her a short while, but she had known her.

'I could have aborted you, but I didn't and it was the best thing I ever done,' her mother says loudly, as she enters the kitchen. 'D'you want a beer, Sarah?' She pulls a beer from the fridge and shakes it at her.

'I'm fifteen and I thought you were going sober,' Sarah says.

'I'm fif-teen, I'm fif-teen,' her mother takes off her voice. 'I know you're fucking fifteen, didn't I give birth to you? D'you want a beer?'

'No.'

Her mother pouts. 'You are a grumpy boots.'

'I grump because you just . . .' All of a sudden, it's like the whole world crashes down on her. This shit-looking kitchen, the peeling wallpaper and missing tiles, the broken cups, the dirt. It exhausts her. This bracing herself against life, the endless cycle of minding her mother, of trying not to care. Her voice cracking, she says, 'My friend is missing, I think.'

'Ooh.' Her mother looks sad as she slides like oil into the seat beside her. 'Your friend is missing?'

'Yes, and—'

'Can you get another one?'

For a second, Sarah can't understand what the words mean. She's spent a long time ignoring what words actually mean. Too hurtful most times, she has to block them out. Has to plaster on a personality that scares everyone away so they won't say anything at all to her. But now the careless way her mother talks about the only bloody friend she ever had stings like acid on a wound. She has to take deep breaths, so she won't cry out, so she won't actually scream right in her mother's spaced-out face. She stands. 'Goodbye, Mammy. I'm going to find my friend.'

'Good for you.' Her mother lifts the can, beer sloshing out. 'Go, Sarah.'

She blinks back tears. She hasn't cried since she was twelve and no one took care of her then either.

She will not let Jenny become her.

Chapter 51 – Day 17

The team are all assembled by the time I arrive the next morning. I barely slept as, after I'd sent the text, I'd spent the next few hours contemplating the fact that, yet again, I'd been fooled by a handsome sweet talker. What was it about me and unscrupulous men? I knew, though, that I had to sort it out, that Tani would never be in a position to do so, and that Johnny would drive a wedge between her and her mother if the situation continued. So, I'd decided to put myself in the firing line. Hopefully Luc would understand. Hopefully they all would. And after I'd made peace with that decision, thoughts of the case had taken over. I can feel the investigation narrowing down but I'm not quite sure where it's going to land.

William gives me a tight smile as I take my place alongside him at the top of the room. 'Nice of you to join us,' he says.

'You're welcome,' I snip back, not in the humour for his sarcasm. I know he's annoyed because Dan and I had outplayed him yesterday. We'd had all our ducks in a row and, my, how they'd quacked.

I rake my eyes across the room, making sure we have everyone.

'All here,' William says. 'You're the last one to show.' He stands. 'Settle down, everyone.'

Everyone gives their updates. Kev and Mick are going to talk to the families of the missing girls on the website today.

'Make sure and ask them if they ever went looking for their daughters on the streets, if they located them and where they were. Don't prejudice them against that Home shelter, for God's sake. Let them talk.'

'Sure thing.'

'Ask the families if the girls had bank accounts,' William says. 'Are these accounts still in use? If not, maybe a new one has been opened. We need to know if the girls have accounts in their names and where. I'd start with Bank of Ireland as that's where Adam's account was.'

'There was no suspicious activity in it, though.'

'I know,' William fights to keep the note of impatience out of his voice, 'but he was getting money from somewhere. He bought a car. Just check.'

'Right, Cig.'

'Then, Pat, if Kev uncovers accounts, check if you can get the orders drawn up to access the details.'

Pat nods.

'Susan?'

'Yes?' She jumps. 'What?'

'You can take over responsibility for looking through Adam's things until such a time as the GNECB come back with something.'

'Sure.'

'Follow up everything,' he says to her. 'No short cuts.'

'I know how to do my job,' she says crossly.

William stills. Mutters, 'Hmm,' and focuses on Brian. 'Did anything come in on the phone lines?'

'Nothing,' Brian says.

'That lead you got about Leo, that was great,' William says, and Brian flushes with pleasure.

After that there is nothing more of any significance until William stands up and a deep hush comes over the room.

'I do not want a word of what I am about to say to leave this station.' William eyeballs everyone, giving Matt a particularly long glare. Matt flushes but holds his gaze. 'As you heard, all of these missing girls disappeared in areas where there was a Home shelter. Abby, our IP, had been spending time in a Home shelter. Adam had been volunteering in a Home shelter. Because of this, we have instigated Operation Actor. Tomorrow, the National Surveillance Unit will send a specialist surveillance officer posing as a homeless girl into the Westport Home shelter. The operation will last for a week, maybe more. It will be run from the station in Westport.'

After William talks, an officer, Keith, from the NSU outlines the plan to the room. We hang on his every word. This sort of thing trumps interviews and trudging through photographs. 'Next week, the undercover officer will take up position on Westport Bridge, here.' Keith marks it out. 'She will wear a small camera in a cheap pendant. Because there is no car parking along the quay, there will be a team monitoring her from the station in Westport. A number of our officers will also take up positions on the street to keep an eye on her and to drop some money into her cup so that she can buy herself lunch. The object, of course, is for our undercover op to spend a few nights in the Home shelter and see what the operational set-up is. William?'

William takes over again. 'We believe, through the investiga-tion, that a number of people posing as volunteers are working for traffickers. Gareth is not in play at the moment as he's gone back to Dublin, so we believe there is another target there that has to be identified. Once the target is identified, we can begin surveillance, track their movements and who their contacts are. We will pull out our undercover op at that stage. Have we all got that?'

The buzz of conversation says it all.

'I will say again,' William's voice rises effortlessly, silencing them, 'if I hear wind of anything in the press, on the radio, I will personally hunt down whoever is responsible. Make no mistake, you will lose your job. This is a risky op. These people have killed a fourteen-year-old girl, and any leak will compromise our officer. Have you all got that?'

A bobbing of heads.

'Matt?' William asks.

An awkward silence ensues. Matt looks affronted. 'I am a guard, Cig. I take it seriously.'

'Unfortunately, your girlfriend takes being a journalist very seriously too,' William snaps back. 'Watch yourself. Go on, the lot of ye.'

I cannot wait.

At two o'clock, I'm watching the Centra in Newport from the safety of a spot on the other side of the road, beside Walsh's pub. At five past two, I spot him. It's hard not to because he's wearing those terrible shorts again. Someone must have told him they were nice or something. He also sports shades and a brilliant white T-shirt with a slogan on it. I can't read it from where I am. He leans his back against the wall, shoves his hands into his pockets and looks to all the world one happy man.

'Hey.' I deliberately approach him from the wrong side.

'Jesus, where did you spring from?' He covers his start with a lazy grin. 'Is this what a high-powered detective does? Tries to surprise people?' He looks about. 'Where's Sirocco?'

'I'm working. I'm on my lunch break right now and Sirocco hasn't yet got the hang of arresting arseholes so I left her behind with her mother.' He looks a bit taken aback at my frosty tone, but before he can react, I say, 'I'm going to make this simple for you. Either you tell Katherine about your affair or I will.'

'You've been talking to Tani,' he splutters, like a car that can't quite get going. 'She has it all wrong. She thinks I'm making her lie—'

'You are making her lie.'

'Aw, well, now, I'm not really. I just asked—'

'And I'm just asking you to man up, tell Katherine and face the consequences.'

'It would kill Katherine if I told her.' He scrabbles for purchase. 'You know what she's like. It's all about looking good. I can't bloody tell her.'

'You might have got away with not telling her if you'd ended things when Tani found out, but you dragged it on and on. Honestly, what sort of an eejit are you?'

'A terrible eejit, I know.' He winces. 'Katherine will kill me,' he says. 'She will kill me.'

I bite down a giggle. He's bloody scared. That's what it is. 'Then I'll know who to prosecute when we find your corpse floating in the Atlantic. Tell her.'

Just then my phone rings. It's the DS from Pearse Street. I answer and ask him to hold on a moment or two.

'Think about it, Johnny,' I say, as my parting shot. I hold up my phone. 'I have to go.'

THE BRANDED

As I'm turning, he says, 'You won't tell Katherine, will you?'
'I just might,' I say. 'You have a week.'
Of course I'm not going to tell Katherine.

Chapter 52

'Sorry about that. What's up?'

'We've had a bit of a development at our end,' the guard says. 'Not sure it'll be much use but it's curious.'

'Go on.'

'Adam Gray's father, Damien, was broken into recently.'

'That's right.'

'You'll remember nothing was taken. We believed it was either some opportunist or that this person was looking for something and didn't find it.'

'Uh-huh.' I push through the crowd, towards my car, a finger pressed in my ear, to block out the noise on the street.

'Damien rang the station this morning. He couldn't stand the thought that someone had been in his son's room so he began to strip the walls.'

I stop dead, people banging into me, but I hardly register their irritation. 'Did he find something?'

'Money,' she says. 'All glued onto the backs of the posters. Now, you can imagine, there are posters over posters, the money is stuck to them, it's bloody worthless, unusable. But it's there. Tens of thousands of euro. You found your money. We'll run it for prints, have a look at the serial numbers.'

I lean up against the wall, trying to absorb the information. 'But what was the point of hiding it like that? What use was it to him?'

'No use. I don't think Adam Gray was that interested in making money.'

An hour later, images of Adam's room have come through, swaths of torn and ripped posters with money glued to the backs. They lie across the floor and over his bed. Close-up of the money reveals that it's all euros. There is no pattern to the serial numbers on the cash either, so it's likely he got it at different times.

'That is so bloody weird,' Dan says.

'If you're not interested in money, why would you get involved in human trafficking?' I ask. 'What advantage was it to him?'

'Maybe he was just looking for excitement,' Ben suggests.

I raise an eyebrow.

'His dad said he was always easily led,' Dan says.

'These aren't strong enough reasons,' I say. 'What he was doing was wrong, and he must have known. When people do things that are so wrong, they are either just bloody evil, which I don't think he was, or they have much to gain. What the hell had he to gain?'

'We already think he liked whoever was working with him.'

'Gareth, maybe Liam,' I say.

'What I can't figure out is what the traffickers had to gain by choosing him.' Larry snorts. 'Aside from the radios and maybe the maths, he sounds as dim as a bloody thirty watt.'

That's true too.

I have a feeling if I can answer those questions, I can solve this case.

But the answers won't come.

Chapter 53 – Day 19

William has ordered us home to get a good night's sleep. He has warned the whole team that the next few days will be crucial, that some of us might be drafted onto the night shifts. The surveillance team are in charge and will report only to the SIO, which is William. Nevertheless, I'll be able to sit in with them and watch the operation unfold. I can't wait. I plan to stay and watch until I'm kicked out.

I pull my case from the wardrobe and shove a load of generic white blouses and black trousers into it. Boring work clothes. I think back to Stacy describing me as a woman with badly kept hair and realise, with shock, that she's right. The best I can say about myself is that I'm clean. As I add a pair of runners to the pile, I wonder when it was that I lost interest in how I looked. Maybe it—

The front doorbell rings.

My mother's quick, light footsteps cross the hall, and the front door squeals as she opens it. Then: 'Oh, this is a surprise.'

I freeze with the case half closed, listening.

'I'd like to speak to Tani, please.' It's Katherine.

I grow cold all over.

The voices become muffled. It'd look suspicious if I don't go and see what's up. Leaving the case where it is, I exit the room and, my stomach churning like an off-kilter washing-machine, I head to the kitchen.

Everyone is there. Luc and Tani are at the table, large glasses of wine in front of them, and all I can think is that Katherine will not approve of that.

'They don't drink like that every night,' I blurt out, as I enter, and everyone looks at me. 'Well, they don't,' I add defensively.

'Can't you see Katherine is upset?' My mother sounds faintly chastising as she hustles Katherine into a chair. Sitting her down, she asks, 'Would you like some of that wine?'

'No, thanks. I just want to speak to my daughter.' Katherine crosses one long leg over the other and tries out a smile. Tani looks terrified.

'Let's make ourselves scarce,' my mother says. 'Come on, Lucy, Luc.' She makes big whooshing motions with her arms.

'No, please stay,' Tani says. Then, to her mother, 'Please let them stay. They've been very good to me.'

My mother, Luc and I are frozen, not sure what to do now. Well, I know what I'd like to do: run away very fast.

'Fine,' Katherine says, not sounding at all fine.

It'll all fall down on me now. But what was the alternative? I lean against the kitchen counter, my hands suddenly sweaty.

'Go on,' Tani says to Katherine.

A moment of stillness. 'Your father told me everything.' She has a quiet dignity, which I can only admire.

My mother makes a face at me behind her back.

'Oh, Ma . . .' Tani whispers, crossing to her. 'I'm sorry.'

And then Katherine's slightly haughty façade crumbles and she dissolves in tears. My mother jumps into action, offering wine and tissues and tea in quick succession. Tani hugs her mother. Luc looks slightly shell-shocked, and I think about offering comfort but realise that it might be a bit rich seeing as I probably instigated this woman's discomfort in the first place.

'He said he was sorry.' Katherine blows her nose, then wipes it vigorously. 'He said he was consumed with guilt over it and that he felt he needed to confess and that he was responsible for you leaving and that he loved us more than life, but I told him to go. I told him I was done with him. Men are like dogs: if you let them bite you once, they'll do it again.' She blows her nose once more, gives it a good scrubbing before croaking out, 'I'm sorry, everyone. This is humiliating for me. This is not—'

'I think Tani and Katherine need to be alone. Come on, Mam, Luc.'

This time Tani doesn't object.

As my mother and Luc follow me out of the kitchen, I swipe the wine from the table.

And despite Johnny being a complete arsehole, at least he left me out of it.

That was decent of him.

Chapter 54 – Sarah

No one had seen her.

No one seems to care. It's like it's expected that Jenny might go off grid. But she's only fucking twelve, Sarah thinks. Surely that must mean something. But it hadn't when *she* was twelve, so maybe . . .

Even in the shelter, they take it with a grain of salt. Maybe she'd gone home. Maybe she'd moved on. There were so many maybes and not one of them was 'Maybe something happened to her.'

After three days of looking, of actually sleeping in the shelter at night just to see if Jenny will turn up, Sarah finally finds herself standing opposite the garda station in Westport. She has to gear herself up to go in because, in reporting Jenny, she might have to report herself and she doesn't want that. A laugh of pure joy snags on her thoughts. Just outside the station, a girl, much the same age as Jenny, has just been handed a present by someone with her. A big glittery affair done up with a huge pink and white ribbon. Sarah feels a stab of anger, so white-hot that it almost takes her breath away. These kids with their nice new holiday clothes and their smiley mothers. They're not going to be peeling vegetables in a homeless shelter or pickpocketing some stranger. It's not fair that Jenny has to.

She crosses the road, pushing rudely past the happy family, until she's right outside the station. Without thinking any more about it, she pushes open the door and finds herself in a small dim room.

A woman with big hair complains loudly about dog shit on the street.

'Hello?' Another guard beckons her forward.

Would Jenny want her to do this?

'Miss?' the guard says. He looks like the one who told her to move on the other day.

What if they sent Jenny back to that care home?

Still . . . Sarah crosses to him. It is the same guard. He looks questioningly at her.

Her mouth is suddenly dry. This is a guard, she thinks. He'd hardly believe her. Sweat pops out on her forehead, her hands get clammy, and her heart thumps.

'Sorry.' She turns and runs.

She needs a back-up. Someone serious. Someone they will believe.

Maybe one of the ladies in the shelter.

Chapter 55 – Day 20

The tech is set up in the incident room in Westport station and is hugely impressive. We are getting audio and visual feed from the camera that the undercover guard, Rosa, who is posing as our homeless girl, wears.

Rosa is a tiny, pretty thing, who looks a lot younger than her twenty-four years. They've chosen her because she's like Abby in appearance. Across the road from Rosa, another undercover agent is busking. He's very good and he seems to have attracted quite a large crowd. This is unfortunate for us as he has been fitted with a camera so we can keep an eye on Rosa. Right now, our view through his device is of a gang of people cheering and clapping along to 'The Wild Rover'.

Rosa looks thoroughly down and out, sitting on a square of cardboard at the bridge. People don't seem to notice her and those who do glance down quickly, then away. The odd few throw some money into her cup. Dressed in grey tracksuit bottoms and a tattered yellow T-shirt, hair matted, nails ragged, she looks every inch the young kid way down on her luck.

More guards from out of town are also on the street, keeping an eye on her, keeping an eye open for anyone watching her.

As the day moves from morning to afternoon, as the early mist lifts to be replaced once more by the relentless sun, we see, through her camera, the life and craic of a town in late summer going on all around her. Our view is street level, feet and sandals and dropped litter. It's a grind. We watch and make coffee, send out for sandwiches and smoothies, and watch.

'Stand by,' one of the guys on the street says. 'Young adult male, ten feet to the left of our girl, watching her.'

A sudden alertness in the office as five of us crowd around the feed. We can't see the young man from Rosa's camera, though from the busker's angle we spot a tall, thin individual, dressed in khaki shorts and a white T-shirt, looking at her from a few feet away. He takes a step towards her, pauses, seems to make up his mind and approaches her. In Rosa's camera, we see his tanned, hairless legs and a pair of blue flip-flops.

'Look up. Give us a dekko at his face,' William mutters, and almost as if Rosa hears, she adjusts herself and we can see that this guy has a hipster wholesomeness, similar to Gareth's. His hair is long, bleached blond by the sun, held back from his face with a Greenpeace bandanna, his face angular, sporting a beard that reminds me of a sad pot plant that refuses to thrive. His eyes, though, seem kind. But they'd have to be to attract the vulnerable. 'Hey, I'm Mike,' he says. 'Are you all right?'

Rosa says nothing.

'Just, you know, for your information, there's a pretty good shelter just around the corner. My girlfriend volunteers at it. It's open at six. You can get some dinner and book a bed there for the night. Or a few nights, even.'

Rosa remains mute.

'It's a grand place. They only take young people so it's not as rough as some other shelters.' Mike pulls a pen from a backpack he's carrying, then spends a few moments trying to locate some paper. He finally pulls out what looks like a napkin. Laying it on top of the wall of the bridge, he begins to write. Done, he holds it away from him, studies it, writes some more and finally, hunkering down, lays it in front of Rosa. It appears to be a map of how to get to the shelter. 'Just in case you're hungry at six,' he says. 'You're here, see?' He points to a place on the napkin and looks at her for a reaction.

She must nod, because he continues, 'Even if you don't want to stay, you can get a meal. My girlfriend, who's volunteered in a pile of these places, says it's the nicest.' He pushes the map towards her before hopping back up. 'Take care.'

'Follow him,' William orders. 'See where he goes.'

From the busker's camera, we spot one of our guys, tucking his paper in under his arm and setting off in pursuit of Mike.

'And get that napkin from Rosa. Be bloody subtle about it.'

Rosa takes up the napkin, pretends to study it as one of our guys bends to give her some coin. The map is popped into his gloved hand. He walks by.

And the time moves on with the slow drip of a melting iceberg.

As afternoon turns to early evening, Rosa leaves her patch to buy some water and a sandwich, then sits down again. Aside from the shop owners, who had regarded her with suspicion, no one takes much notice of her. People stand close to her, chat to one another over her, drop litter right by her, and one man, jogging, takes a flying leap over her so he doesn't have to break his stride.

It's bloody awful to watch.

At six, the busker stops singing. It's Rosa's signal to make her way to the shelter.

We have a van in position now, just up the road from the shelter.

For me, Dan, William and Ben, tonight will be an all-nighter.

Rosa has reached the door of the shelter when the member who'd been following Mike reports back that he seems to be just an ordinary Joe, job in a nearby Spar, still living with Mammy and Daddy and, right this minute, running up and down a GAA pitch with his local club.

'We'll still run his prints,' William decides.

On screen, we watch as Rosa puts out a hand and pushes open the door of the shelter. Nothing has changed since the day Dan and I talked to Gareth, except that now there is a picture on the wall of the volunteers.

'I want a screenshot of that picture,' William says. 'We can see if there is any connection between these volunteers and the ones in Dublin.'

This evening, a familiar woman is behind the desk. Dan gets there before me.

'Alexandra,' he says. 'Gareth's girlfriend. She's the manager.'

Alexandra is tapping away at the computer and initially doesn't see Rosa.

Rosa stands, saying nothing, watching Alexandra. Then she coughs. Alexandra starts.

Something flashes across her face, some emotion, I can't quite catch it. But then she laughs a bit, brittle. 'Good God, you put the heart crossways in me.' She smiles. 'Come in, you're very welcome.'

'Never trust a good-looking woman,' Ben says, with a hint of bitterness.

Rosa crosses to the desk. Now we've a close-up of Alexandra's chest and neck.

'Have you come to book a bed? We've four left . . . You have? Great. I'll put you down for one. I'll need your name, if that's all right?'

'Mari,' we hear Rosa say. 'Mari O'Brien.'

'And are you from Mayo? I'm asking because we're only allowed by law to give out beds to people who are registered here. Though between you and me, if we have any spare, we let them out.'

'Castlebar,' Rosa says.

Alexandra jots it down.

'Now we can assign you a case worker to help you. Does your family know where you are?'

A long silence.

Alexandra leans across the counter. 'If they're worried, you should at least tell them where you are, pet.'

The four of us hold our breath. William, who'd been peeling a banana, freezes. Is this it? Is this how they find out about their charges or is Alexandra just following a routine?

'I lived with my big sister, but now she's dead,' Rosa says.

Alexandra pulls away, dips down to look into Rosa's face. 'You're safe here for the moment,' she says. 'We'll sort you out. You're in room three.' She clicks some buttons and hands Rosa a card. 'Now, a few rules. The main ones are that we don't tolerate drinking, smoking, drug-taking. You cannot enter anyone else's room without an invitation. And if you're caught stealing, we'll call the guards. You'll find a full list on your bed. All right? Now go through there,' she points to the dining room, 'and get something to eat.'

Rosa moves off into the dining room.

'The die is cast.' William chomps down on what must be his tenth banana today. 'Let's see if anyone bites.'

There are about ten young people seated at the long table as Rosa goes and gets a plate of dinner from a volunteer at the counter. It looks pretty decent, some sort of a salad and quiche. No one speaks. All we can hear is the sound of cutlery clattering off plates. One or two more kids drift in, take their dinner and the conversation starts up. Some older people arrive and are fed, and at eight, the clear-up begins. Rosa has sat out the two hours in the room as people have come and gone. She has played with her food, stabbed at bits of lettuce and, finally, she allows her plate to be taken.

She makes her way upstairs, finds her room and enters. Before she has a chance to lock the door or throw her haversack across the bed, someone appears in the doorway. It's a girl who had been eating in the dining room, sitting two down from Rosa.

'Jenny had this room normally,' the girl says aggressively.

'So?' Rosa says.

'So, where is she? You took her bed.'

'Do you fancy Jenny or something?'

We all inhale sharply. The last thing we need is for Rosa to get in some sort of a dogfight.

'Fuck I do,' the girl says. 'I'm just saying. She's disappeared. You seen her?'

'Push it,' I hear William mutter. 'Go on.'

'Maybe I seen her,' Rosa says. 'What was she like?'

'You seen her?'

'Maybe I did. Does she have red hair?'

'No, brown,' the girl says.

'I seen someone with brown hair,' Rosa says. 'What else does she look like?'

'She's only twelve. Her hair is about to here.'

'To her shoulder,' Rosa says, for our benefit. 'Curly?'

'Straight. And her face is long and she's got crooked bottom teeth. Did you see her?'

'I don't know for sure. What was she wearing?'

'You're making an eejit of me. You never saw her.'

'I might have. What was she wearing when you last saw her yourself?'

'Red spotty shorts and a white T-shirt and blue runners. She got them all from a bag here. You see her?'

'Nah,' Rosa says. 'But I can keep a look-out.'

Dan has taken down the description, though if indeed Jenny is a missing person, it won't be listed yet or maybe not at all.

'No one seen her.' The girl bites at the skin around her thumb. 'I asked everyone on the street.' She sits on the bed. 'You been homeless long?'

'No, just the last month. Since I was on my own.'

Alexandra peers around the door. 'I'm going to turn out the lights now, girls, but I'll be at the desk until midnight if anyone needs anything. After that, you can find me in the last room down the corridor.' She gestures with a thumb. 'Hop it, Sarah.'

Sarah moves from the bed and we get a good glimpse of her. She has the hardened appearance of a kid for whom life has been nothing but brutal. That skinny, hungry look, the perpetual jagged motions of someone who can't sit still.

'Was Jenny in today?' she asks, on her way past. She runs a hand through frizzy hair. 'Or did anyone see her?'

'No,' Alexandra says. 'No one knows where she's got to.' She

301

smiles at Rosa. 'This one here is convinced something bad has happened to her.'

'Jenny would not just disappear,' Sarah says. 'I want someone to bring me to the guards about it.'

'Well, as I said,' Alexandra sounds like she's trying to hold in her irritation, 'if I thought she'd disappeared, I would go but people go missing all the time, Sarah. Now bed.'

'I'll ask Bernie when she comes back.'

'Do. Bed.'

Sarah glowers at Alexandra and stands.

The light snaps off, their voices fade.

Rosa locks her door.

Hours later, when the dark has stolen the light from the day and the only revellers left along the riverside are the drunken ones, Rosa's camera flicks back on with a ping.

William, who has been in the process of making us both a coffee, joins me and the surveillance crew at the desk. Dan and Ben have gone home: they'll take over tomorrow night. William places the coffee in front of me and offers around some bananas, which we all decline. The place reeks of his banana skins. We all watch the screen, me praying that Rosa won't do anything stupid. She's been told to find out everything she can without putting herself in unnecessary danger. It's amazing how cool the surveillance team are.

Very gently, Rosa opens her bedroom door. The corridor is dark, lit by a night light at the very end. The red flicker of an alarm pulsates in the corner of the ceiling, but the fact that Rosa has opened her door without triggering a bell shows that the alarm is only on the windows and external doors.

Nothing stirs. From down the hall, someone shouts out, but it must be in sleep because all goes silent again.

Rosa pads down the hall, she must be in her socks, and pauses at the top of the stairs. Then down she goes, missing the fourth step because it squeaks. She would have noticed that earlier.

She is now in the reception area.

On light feet she runs towards the desk, ducks behind it and lifts the camera to the picture of the volunteers. It's hard to make out, but then she takes the risk of turning on the light behind Reception. She leaves it on for a few seconds, then turns it off.

We get a screen shot.

One of the team prints it off and sends it to be compared against the one in Dublin in an effort to identify anyone in it.

My nails dig into my palms as the tension mounts. Don't be too anxious to prove yourself, Rosa, I think. But in the end, I know from experience, we all do what we all do.

Just as Rosa snaps the light off, step four creaks.

'Shit,' someone mutters.

'What are you doing?' A whisper from the dark. It's Sarah. 'Are you taking stuff?'

'No,' Rosa says. 'Nothing much to take. D'you fancy seeing what the biscuits are like?'

Sarah waits a second, as if assessing Rosa, then nods. They head into the dining room.

'Good read,' William says, impressed.

A few seconds later, the two are at the table, sharing a packet of ginger nuts. 'Have you stayed in this place a lot?' Rosa asks.

'In the past month a few times. That's why I don't understand . . .' She pauses. 'Like I had a row with her and all but . . . maybe she did go home. I thought you were her.'

'Nope.' They sit in silence, crunching biscuits.

'I never seen you on the street before,' Sarah says.

'I never saw you,' Rosa says.

Sarah shrugs but doesn't elaborate. After a bit, as if it's suddenly just hit her, she asks, 'What will they do when they find the biscuits gone?'

'Dunno.' Rosa stands, twists the top of the biscuits and puts them back into the press, 'They can't prove it was us took them.' A real guard's answer.

They tiptoe back upstairs. Her camera flicks off.

Day one down. And nothing.

Chapter 56 – Day 23

By the third day, my initial excitement has given way to slight panic. So far, nothing out of the ordinary has happened.

William, to my annoyance, sends me home that night. 'You've bloody been here three days straight,' he says. 'Ben is here now, and there's no need for all of us.'

'You've been here too,' I say back, not moving. The room is stale with the smell of bodies and the stench of over-ripe fruit. It's hot from the electronics. And, yet, I don't want to be anywhere else.

'I'm a DI, I can pretty much do what I want. You, however, can't. Home.' He thumbs in the direction of the door. 'Get some sleep, iron your clothes.'

From his position in front of the screen, Ben chortles.

'You can talk,' I say to him, taking in his crumpled Iron Maiden T-shirt and shorts. 'It's bad enough having questionable musical taste but wearing it as a T-shirt is bloody sad.'

'Bye-bye, Luce.' Ben wiggles his fingers at me, then turns away. 'What have we got, Cig?'

'Not much,' William says, joining him at the screen, effectively dismissing me. 'Though there has been a change of guard

305

on Reception. This one here,' he points to a woman we've learnt is Bernie, 'arrived today, replacing Alexandra. The clients seem to love her. We're running background now, but she basically ignores some of the rules, lets them leave the lights on in their rooms. She told Rosa that if she smoked she could have a sneaky one out of her window. Then she made Rosa promise not to tell Alexandra.'

'Grooming,' Ben says. 'Is that what you're thinking?'

'Well, we don't know. Alexandra is very reluctant to go to the guards about the missing Jenny. There's two of them in it.'

I stomp out, slamming the door on them. 'I'll be back tomorrow!' I call, in case they're in any doubt.

William pops his head out. 'Before you come here, first thing tomorrow check with the station in Achill, see how the rest of the investigation is going. If anything interesting shows, follow it up.'

Damn. Damn. Damn.

There's a chill this evening that hasn't been there the last couple of months, I think, as I step out of my car. Our bizarre summer must be coming to an end. Out beyond the road, I can see the Atlantic heaving, smell its spray even up here. The waves seem a little restless, a little bored with playing good. They look like they want to fling themselves onto the shore and smash against the rocks that line the coast. Out beyond, I can make out Clare Island, and further again, the smudge of Croagh Patrick, Ireland's holy mountain. It's a view I never tire of, and though the sky is always a mass of shifting lights and darks, the island and the mountain are constant.

There is no one at home. I hadn't told them I was coming back, and two quick phone calls with Luc and my mother confirm they're both away for the night. Luc's at a party and my mother's gone off to visit her friend in Galway. 'Don't look at the *Island News*,' she says, before she rings off. 'I would have got rid of it if I'd known you were coming home.'

Of course, the minute she says it, I hunt it down, where it's been thrown across the sofa. The headline blares, 'No Leads As Yet In Savage Murders'. It's Stacy, of course, and she does her very best to paint us as a shower of idiots.

I bypass her doggerel and flick through the rest of the rag. It really is terrible. The cookery page gives a recipe for scrambled eggs, and the fashion page shows some kid on the street talking about where she bought her clothes. Then there is the farming news, with prices of animals and pictures of sheep. There's a piece on fishing, and someone from the local angling community voicing his fear that, with the current water temperatures, fish will die. I turn to the back page, thinking that Stacy's story was hardly that shocking.

But it's the back page my mother must have been warning me about because Rob's picture takes up about half of it. The headline, 'Robert Ganley Photographic Exhibition for Ace Gallery'.

I spend a few moments in slight shock, and then, of course, I read it.

Robert Ganley, in an interview with this journalist, has expressed his delight and honour at having his work chosen for a showcase in the Ace gallery. 'This is a prestigious art gallery, and for them to think that my work is good enough is a huge boost to my confidence.' Robert Ganley has made his home just a few miles outside Castlebar in an isolated cottage, and it's exciting for this reporter to be invited inside. The front door leads into a small parlour, which is filled with beautiful prints of the Mayo coast and county. Most are stunning landscapes, taking in Blacksod Bay and the Ceide Fields. 'It's the most beautiful county in all of Ireland,' Robert Ganley says. And you can see the power of his love for it in every beautiful shot.

The exhibition runs from 1 September to 4 September.

'Wanker,' I say out loud. He had hated Mayo, hated anything to do with country living when I married him. He was a city boy, his words. He panicked in the wide open. He needed buildings and smoke and clutter. And now . . . He's so full of shit.

It makes me even more determined to turn up at his exhibition and throw his present back at him, tell everyone that he once said Mayo was where people came to die.

And that picture of him . . . arsehole with his serene big brown eyes looking appealingly at the camera, quirk of a smile, the flash of white teeth. Charm dripping off him, like fat off cooking meat.

And it's a testament to the terrible journalism in the *Island News* that the journalist didn't seem to know who he was. I'm sure half the island knows him – my mother's friends certainly will. Maybe it'll mean they won't turn up for his exhibition, and then I think that of course they'll turn up. They'll turn up for a gawk.

I take the paper and dump it in the bin.

And then, against my better judgement, I pull a bottle of wine from the press.

And that's when Kev rings.

Chapter 57

'What the hell are you still doing at work?' I ask Kev.

'Me, Mick and Susan all thought we'd stay on, like the sooner we can get Abby's murderer ID'd and those girls found the better. I know you're at home, on a night off, but I've a bit of news. I think we've found something interesting – well, Susan has. Can I send it through?'

'Sure. What is it?'

'I'm not saying because we want your opinion first. She found it in Adam's pictures and we reckon it's solid. But have a look you.'

'Send it on.' I screw the top back on the bottle of wine, ener-gised now, my mind thankfully disposing of Rob and all his lies, and refocusing on what is really important. A ping on my phone tells me something has landed. If it's a picture, however, I'll be better off looking at it on my laptop. I fire it up and it takes for ever to load. Accessing my work email, I see there's one from Kev with no message, just a photograph.

It's an old picture, slightly fuzzy, or maybe that's just the way it scanned. It's of six teenagers, all in school uniform, taken in Westport at the bridge. I immediately spot Adam right at the back, looking slightly awkward, the way he did in the picture of the volunteers in the shelter. He's taller than the others, gangly. Why has Kev sent me this? There were hundreds of pictures of Adam with various people. I blow the picture up and then something snags my attention.

The boy in the middle, he must be about eighteen, looks older than the rest. He's grinning broadly, his face open, smiling. He's also the one about whom all the others are orbiting. You can see they're not looking directly at the camera, they're casting looks in his direction. Maybe he's told a joke, but the focus is clearly on him. He's the best-looking, too, in a photograph of what are clearly oddballs.

To the side of the boy, hanging off him like a limpet, is a gangly girl with braces and fuzzy hair and . . . Jesus. No way. It can't be. But it is. The face has thinned out, but it's her. No doubt about it.

I turn back to the boy and suddenly I recognise him too. That must be who Susan spotted. Well done her. I'm not sure I'd have made the connection. He's lost a lot of hair. My stomach crawls with horror and realisation. And now it's like the snap of pieces coming together as I recognise a third person.

And suddenly I know why Adam did what he did.

And I know that this is them. These are the people we need to talk to.

One or more of these murdered Abby and was responsible for murdering Adam. I know it like I know my name.

All of these are probably involved in trafficking.

I need the proof.

It's up to Rosa now.

I call Kev. I tell him I'm coming back to the station. That we're going to do some all-night digging before we go to the DI.

Chapter 58 – Sarah

That Mari one is fucking odd, Sarah thinks. She's nosy, wants to know stuff, asks questions when Sarah doesn't feel like talking to her. She fucking seems to think that just because Sarah talked to her that first night they're friends. Sarah is done with friends. She doesn't need any more.

Mari sits in with her breakfast of porridge. 'I saw you talking to Bernie,' she says. 'I like Bernie.'

'Yeah.' Sarah tears a crust off her toast.

'Is she bringing you to the guards about Jenny?'

'Yeah, what's it to you?'

Mari looks hurt. 'Sorry. Just . . . well . . . that's good.' She turns back to her porridge.

Sarah feels bad now. She doesn't want Mari as a friend but, like, still and all . . . maybe Jenny was right. Maybe she is scared of good things. 'She's driving me in her fancy-pants car to Ballina,' she says, trying to make peace, 'because apparently Jenny was from Ballina so we have to go to that station to report it.'

'Right. Good luck with that.'

'I'm meeting her just up from here at two.' Now she can't shut up, Sarah thinks, but, like, she was so relieved it was happening.

It was, like, so hard to ask for help and now—

'Hi, Mari, love, can I have a word?' Bernie says. She looks pointedly at Sarah. 'I'll see you later.'

Sarah nods, stops, then says, 'Thanks, Bernie.'

Bernie smiles. 'Hop it. Go on.'

Sarah does.

Chapter 59

Me, Kev, Susan, Mick and Jordy work through the night, along with the lad from the night shift who has been drafted in. Piece by piece the information starts to pile up. At nine the next morning, there is still a heap of work to be done. I ring William and tell him we have a lead. And then I say, 'I'd watch Bernie. I'm not saying it's her, but we have reason to believe she's caught up in this.'

William whistles down the line. 'That's great because this morning at breakfast she made a point of talking to Rosa. Asking her what she liked, what she hoped to do, told her she could be anything then told her she'd have a word with her social worker, see what the story was. That she might have a job for her. Now, she could just be a helpful person but Rosa has put herself way out on the ledge now.'

I have a sudden image of a chick with no mother, cheeping loudly and attracting the attention of vultures. Something in me grows cold. 'I'll work from this end, Cig, and I'll be in touch later in the day.'

He rings off.

'All right, Kev, I need you to call around, find out who is the best person to identify the rest of those kids in the picture, get some extra information on the others. I'd start with the Saint Joseph and Mary secondary school in Westport. They're all wearing that uniform. Just ask if Adam Gray went to that school and would they be able to tell us about any friends he may have had. Jordy, chase up the rest of the forensics from both cases, put the boot in, try and get it for today. Susan, well done on spotting the face in that picture.'

She beams.

'Pat, how are we doing on the bank accounts of the missing girls?'

'According to Kev, three of them had accounts but no activity since they went missing. However, when I contacted Bank of Ireland they confirmed that in the last three years bank accounts have been opened under the names of seven of the missing girls on our list. Of course, some of the names are quite common, so I pushed, just for basic information, and what's really interesting is that when the bank looked into it all the girls had the same mobile number listed and they all had roughly the same address. Apartment Three, Apartment Three B and Apartment Four, all in a building somewhere out in north County Dublin. I'm getting the documents drawn up first thing.'

'Look those addresses up on Google Earth, see what type of a building it is.'

'Sure.'

'The rest of you, go and get some breakfast. Once we have names it's all hands on deck.'

My phone rings. It's William. 'Lucy, any more information on Bernie?'

'Not yet, no, why?'

'What's your gut say?'
'It says she's guilty.'
'Right. That's good enough for me.'
Without explanation, he rings off.

Chapter 60

An hour later, Kev and I drive to meet a teacher who has since retired. She remembers Adam well and has agreed to take a look at the picture for us. To my horror, she lives on Inishbiggle, a small island about fifty metres off the coast of Achill. Despite having been reared on an island, having lived on the beach as a kid, I am not a water baby. It is possible, at low tide, to drive there, but Kev won't hear of it. He wants to go across in the ferry, which is not a ferry: it's a small open-topped boat called a curragh. In winter, the currents here are treacherous but today all is calm, and Kev laughs and jokes with the boatman, whom I know, as he brings us across. I spend the short trip with my hands clenched hard.

'We're looking for Lilian Greene,' Kev says, as we step off the boat onto the small dock. 'She's just recently moved over.'

'Oh, yes, Lilian.' He pushes the cap back on his head. 'Walk yourselves up there, keep going until you come to the house with the red door. That's Lilian. She makes occupant number twenty on the island as of four months ago.'

Inishbiggle is tiny, almost abandoned, except for the few people who keep it going. The school and the post office are gone, it can be inaccessible in winter, but, my God, it's beautiful. Despite

316

spending the last two years on Achill after leaving Templemore, Kev is still surprised that people would live out here with nothing really in the way of facilities. In normal circumstances, I'd point out the various things to him as we walk. I'd tell him that, on a good night, the sky here blazes with thousands of stars, ones you'd never see anywhere else, but today, we're hurrying, trying to rush against the ticking clock.

The house with the red door is about a mile up the road. A tiny whitewashed two-bedroom cottage, set atop a small hill, commanding beautiful views from every window. Lilian answers our first knock and invites us to sit outside, in her tangled and overgrown garden, while she searches for her glasses.

'Nice place to live,' Kev comments, as she arrives back, glasses perched on her nose, 'even if it is a bit deserted.'

'It's nice because it's deserted,' Lilian corrects him, sounding every inch the schoolteacher. 'Now,' she looks at us expectantly, 'let me see this picture you've brought with you. I remember most children in that school, taught all of them back then as I was the only English teacher.' She takes the picture from me and holds it up to her face. She stiffens for just a fraction of a second, before lowering it.

'Let me tell you something about schools,' she says, 'before we get into the picture.'

I want to tell her to hurry up, but I can't compromise this.

'Schools are savage places where the different come to be sacrificed on the altar of popularity,' Lilian says. 'You probably know that yourselves. Most of them survive, it does them good, builds resilience, but for children who are not seen as cool, who look a bit odd, it's an isolating, miserable experience. And that's why this group was always so remarkable.' She taps the picture. 'That boy in the middle, Liam Russell, he was the popular one. As was his sister, Bernadette.' She points to the girl standing beside him. 'They came from money, inherited a lot when the parents died, I believe. In school, they were very popular with the other students. I mean, they had everything money could buy and buy it they did. And then, maybe in second year, Liam started associating with those other four children. He went out of his way to do it. I used to think it was nice of him, that he wasn't into the baying crowd, but then,' she frowns, 'one day I overheard him say something to one of them and it changed my mind. It was . . .' she winces '. . . I don't quite know how to put it, but it was . . . disturbing.'

Kev, who has been writing, leans forward. I shoot him a warning look.

'How so?'

'I overheard him say to Ellie, this girl here,' she points to the girl I met as Helen, manager of McAdam's bar, 'that Ellie should know her place. I mean, it was the way he said it, as if he was in charge. And I think he was. He seemed to gather those people to him, like a collection.'

He was still gathering them now, I think.

'I watched him after that, tried to make it hard for him, but there was very little I could do. Those children, without exception, were like plants with no water. Over the years, the group grew.'

'Any other names you can give me of people Liam befriended?'

She throws out a couple. Kev takes them down to check out.

'Was there ever any trouble between Adam and the rest of the group?'

'Oh, yes. They sacrificed him.'

318

The words send a chill right through me. I keep my voice level. 'How so?'

'That poor boy was besotted with Ellie. But Ellie was with Liam – I don't think she could believe her luck. Then Ellie's father got wind of the fact that she had a boyfriend. Now, that man was terrifying. His children lived in fear. He came to the school one day, cornered Ellie in a corridor and demanded to know who the boy was. He'd found condoms apparently. He had to be pulled off her. Ellie said it was Adam. By all accounts, that man made Adam and his family's life a misery after that, putting out rumours about what he'd done to Ellie, but I never believed it. Adam was such a bright boy, but he became a nervous wreck. It was very sad to hear he had been killed.' A pause. 'That boy there,' she points at a small, spotty, overweight young lad, hands behind his back, chest stuck out, 'that was Louis. He was a year younger than the others. He was gay and came in for a lot of slagging. Liam took him under his wing. I think Louis is in Carlow now – I know he moved away, anyhow. And finally, that's Fionn McGrath, I've met his nan a few times. We go to Knock for the pilgrimage and according to her Fionn manages a bar now. In Galway. He's doing very well for himself. Poor Fionn lost both his parents in an accident. He was brought up by his nan. Bought her a lovely little cottage there two years back, and she's very proud of him.' She hands the picture back. 'They were an odd collection of friends.'

'Thanks.' I tuck the picture back into my light jacket. 'I just have a couple of questions. What bar does Fionn manage in Galway?'

'Oh, now, that's asking me.' She screws up her face in an effort to remember, then says, 'I'll ring his nan and ask, sure.' She digs into the pocket of her shorts and pulls out a phone. 'I'll just say someone is wondering. The creatur will get a fright if I say the guards want to know.'

'Of course.'

The call connects, and Lilian spends a few minutes chatting away about the weather and how it's to turn, then says, 'D'you know what I was wondering? I met a woman in town last week and we got talking about your Fionn . . . Yes, Fionn. And she asked me what bar did he manage and do you think I could remember! Not at all! What bar is it? . . . McAdam's. That's great. I'll remember that for next time.'

As she chatters on, Kev raises his eyebrows and I nod. Then Kev takes out his phone and starts scrolling.

Finally, Lilian hangs up. 'McAdam's bar,' she says unnecessarily. 'There's one in Westport too.'

'That's great, and one more thing,' I say. 'Ellie had a sister, didn't she?'

'Yes, a twin.'

'What was her name?'

'Jane.'

A jolt of electricity shoots through me.

'Do you know where she is now?'

'In Dublin, last I heard.'

'OK, thank you.'

We stand to leave, Kev tucking his pen behind his ear and his notebook into the pocket of his shirt. Lilian shakes our hands and wishes us luck. 'He was a nice boy, Adam,' she says.

'There's a McAdam's bar in every town that has a Home shelter,' Kev says, as we make our way down the drive.

I think back to when Dan and I visited that day in Dublin. All the staff were foreign and young.

'Get Jordy to call out to McAdam's in Westport, see how the land lies. Just tell him to sit in and have a pint, maybe chat to one of the lounge staff. Tell him to take it as a normal lunch break.'

Kev makes the call as we wait for the ferry back.

I don't think I have enough to call William with just yet.

Chapter 61 – Sarah

Later that day, Sarah was taken. It was quiet on the street and she wasn't paying attention. She was rehearsing in her head what she would say to the guards, how she would make them believe her. Bernie had promised to help her along. It was a hot white day, though in the distance, towards the sea, there appeared to be a promise of rain.

She had just turned onto the street when a car pulled level with her. A man hopped out and ordered her to get in.

There was a woman in the back seat. The woman smiled at her.

Sarah did not trust smiles.

Or men.

They said something to her, she didn't hear, she made a run for it but the man caught her easily, held her gently, told her not to be afraid, but Sarah was.

She was bundled into the back and the street was empty again.

Chapter 62

Back in the station, I give them the names of the two kids we didn't know and ask them to check them out. I decide against interviewing Helen and Liam for now. There's no point in ringing any alarm bells yet. All we have is speculation, though I can almost taste their guilt.

'Liam and Helen sacrificed Adam once. I don't think they'd have hesitated to do it again,' I say to Larry. 'If Adam was panicking, who would be best to calm him down other than the girl he used to fancy?'

'Poor pathetic sod, you'd think he'd have got over his first love by now, eh?'

I ignore that because it makes me grossly uncomfortable. 'Ellie, a.k.a. Helen, never mentioned to us when we were interviewing her that she knew Adam of old. And Liam denied it flat out. That's suspicious. They're all in it, Larry. And Liam runs them all. He's recruited them, they've been in it for years.'

'You know what the Cig will say?'

'Right now, he'll say it's speculation so we need to dig some more. Susan, can you take over the phones, run Helen's number and see if she was down here on the fourth of July. And again in August. Check also for the mobile number being used by the bank accounts. Anyone got an address for Liam?'

'Yes.' Jordy ambles in at that moment, scratching his belly, a piece of paper in his hand. 'Nice food in McAdam's bar,' he remarks, apropos of nothing. 'Anyway, according to Land Registry, there are definitely two properties that can be associated with Liam, one in Dublin, out in the Naul, and another right here in Mayo, up the Nephin mountains, near Bunaveela. Very isolated, right in off the road. I've googled it but I can't get a proper visual. As far as I can make out, it's a house with some outbuildings.'

I sit in front of the computer, call up Google Earth, then key in Liam's address in Mayo. As Jordy said, it's a large area of land with a few outbuildings and a big square house. 'Did Pat look into where these homeless girls' bank accounts are addressed to see—'

'Is my name being taken in vain?' Pat, good humoured and calm as ever, arrives in. 'The bank just called. They're being very cooperative – I think they're shitting themselves, actually. They said they asked their own investigators to take a look and they've uncovered more girls with addresses to that group of apartments in Dublin, with the exact same mobile number. They also have girls with addresses in Mayo, Nephin and attached to another mobile number. They—'

'Is it this address?' I read out Liam's.

'Close enough,' Pat says. 'The bank said they'll send on the bank accounts as soon as they get authorisation. It should be possible in the early stages to access how the money was being spent in these accounts. Like, for instance, if there are a lot of expenses for food and nothing for accommodation, if the girls are moving about a bit, we can trace that in the accounts. If money is being transferred out of their accounts by a third party, we should be able to trace that too.'

'How many girls did the bank say?'

'So far, around twenty for the Mayo address and twenty for the Dublin address.'

I google the Dublin address. It's a tiny apartment block out in the Naul. There is no way any of those apartments would hold twenty girls. 'All right, here's what we'll do. I'll talk to William to see if we can get someone to—'

And then my phone rings and it's William. 'Rosa will be on the move later, around eight.' There's urgency in his tone. 'Bernie made her play. She offered Rosa a job this morning, as bar staff. She's bringing her to meet the boss later this evening.'

'That was quick.'

'Rosa had the perfect story. No one was going to miss her. Get your arse in here.'

'I've an update too,' I tell him. 'We haven't been sitting around doing nothing, you know.'

He laughs and I lay it all out for him, the photograph, the grooming, the bank accounts of the missing girls, the other accounts the bank says they've found.

He listens carefully, asks a few questions and then fires out a list of jobs for everyone. 'Mick, look into those girls when you get the names from the bank, see if they've been listed as missing too. Larry, see if you can find Helen's address and track down any vehicles registered to her. Run that against the CCTV in the hospital car park. See if we can conclusively rule out Gareth through CCTV as well. I'll ring Dublin, Galway and Carlow, see if we can get eyes on Helen, Louis and Fionn. Let's not spook them for now.' He rings off.

'All right.' I look at them all. 'You know what has to be done. Go for it.'

Chapter 63

I'm with William in an unmarked van with tinted windows and we're parked just up from the Westport shelter, waiting for Bernie to come out with Rosa. I'm on edge and yet part of me, the part I barely understand, can't wait to get going. Because we've no idea what we'll be facing, only those of us authorised to carry a gun are involved, along with members of the Armed Response Unit. It's six in the evening, rush-hour is in full swing. Summer is coming to an end in the west. The tourist season is winding down and already the streets are quieter, the evenings darker. The air temperature has dipped markedly and it's a relief. The heat in the van is bearable – last week we'd have suffered big-time.

'We had someone tail Bernie last night,' William tells me, as he throws his jacket into the back. 'She didn't go straight home. Instead she called to four houses scattered around the county. We're running the owners down now.' He bends over and pulls a very unappetising squishy banana from a pack resting at his feet. 'Want one?'

'No, thanks.'

He peels his own, takes a bite and goes on. 'She lives in a

326

modest enough semi-d on the outside of town but I'm sure when we start digging, we'll turn something up. The thing that will bring them all down is if we can trace the money. Good work on the photograph.'

'That was Susan. She recognised Liam from doing background on the shelter. Why do you eat so many bloody bananas?'

He's mid-bite. He looks at me a little affronted. 'Because they're nice.'

'Not ones that are about to decay.'

'They're my favourite type.' And he takes another bite.

I shrug and look out of the darkened window. The sky in front of us has turned an unnatural bruised purple. Behind us, the sun spills over-bright light onto the street.

'Aw, Christ,' William remarks, peering out. 'I think we're in for a downpour.'

'We've got a problem.' Dan's voice crackles over the radio. 'Bernie has made Rosa change her clothes. Apparently, she has to look more respectable for the job. We've lost the camera, though we still have fuzzy audio as Rosa has insisted on bringing her clothes with her in a bag.'

'It's too risky. Did someone tell her she can't go?' William is halfway out the door, but just then Rosa and Bernie exit the shelter. Rosa wears black leggings and a black T-shirt. Her hair has been washed and is pinned back. She looks even younger than she did when I met her.

William climbs back into the van, cursing.

'We'll stick close,' I say, though this is not ideal at all.

The two women get into a small BMW a few spaces ahead and Bernie pulls out.

William indicates and slides into the traffic after them.

We follow Bernie as she leaves the Carrowbeg estate and heads right onto the Castlebar road. The traffic is moderately heavy. She passes Father Angelus Park, takes a right onto the North Mall, following the Carrowbeg river, then takes a left towards Newport. The road here is clear enough and we allow some distance to build between Bernie's car and ours. We are two back from her. Dan reports that so far the conversation in the car is chilled.

Bernie follows the road all the way into Newport where we hit some minor traffic again. We cross the Newport river and keep on the N59.

On the radio, we hear Dan firing updates on our position to other cars in the area.

We clear Newport, about three cars behind Bernie now. The town gives way to houses and fields and then Bernie takes a sharp right, just off the N59. Suddenly we're off the main road and climbing. It's just her car and our van now and we keep well back. The road here is narrow, just big enough for a single car to pass comfortably, fields to one side, stone walls to the other. In the distance, the humps of mountains and large hills are etched in stark contrast by shafts of light pushing through to the rapidly darkening stormy sky. Fat drops of rain start to land on the windscreen. The wind picks up and the van shudders slightly. The narrow road changes, it's now bounded by trees, sunlight flashing in and out, creating patterns on the road, rain hitting the van when we clear the shelter of branches. It's an odd thing, the sun and rain vying for space. Suddenly, without indicating, Bernie pulls into a tiny, overgrown grassy road on her right and stops the car. There's another waiting – we see it as we pass the junction. We can't possibly pull in beside Bernie as to pass her and continue on up the grassy road would be to risk recognition and maybe harm Rosa. William calls in our position with a description of the waiting car. 'Black Ford Mondeo,' he says. 'A one-nine-one. We're turning back to follow as soon as we can.'

We drive for about twenty seconds before William satisfies himself that the black Mondeo isn't coming our way. 'Shit,' he says, and turns our van around in what, quite frankly, is a danger- ous enough move. Then he fires back off in the direction we've just travelled. When we reach the turn-off Bernie had pulled into, there is no sign of either car.

'Bernie obviously delivered her charge and turned back, and the Ford has taken Rosa. Most probably up this way,' William says.

With that he guns our van forward onto a rutted, grassy road that doesn't look like it sees much traffic. We start to climb more steeply now, up and up, no sign of a house or of any cars in front of us. William drives on faster as I clutch the sides of the seat, calling out updates to Dan.

'She's with a man now,' Dan says. 'We can't make out what they're saying.'

The road twists and turns, the rain grows heavier and the sky darkens. Inside me, there is a growing unease that I can't explain. Like a shadow that's just out of reach. I glance sideways at William. His hands are white on the wheel, his mouth set in gritty determination. We cannot lose Rosa, we cannot lose her. Where the hell is the black car? A sudden shift in the clouds sends an edge of sunlight flashing onto something in the distance. 'There,' I point. 'There.'

The car is ahead of us by some distance and William takes off after it. We can't afford there to be any more turns: we need to keep it in sight. Dan notes our position and relays it back. Now that we can see the car, we can hold back a little. The road crowns the top of the mountain. To our left, far below, is a large lake, and on our right, scrubby bits of bogland, stripped for their fuel. And still we go on.

'Shit,' Dan says suddenly. 'Hold back a bit.'

'Why?'

'The road you're on, it ends. There is only one way in and one way out of the place you're going and it's that road. I'm looking at Google now, you'll drive for another two kilometres or so and end up in a yard with about five white sheds all with green corrugated roofs.'

At least we won't lose Rosa, but we can't keep driving or we'll be spotted.

'Where is Liam Russell's house in relation to here?' William asks.

Dan takes a moment but eventually comes back, 'About ten minutes away, on the road yez were on originally.' Then, 'What do you think, Cig?'

William pulls the van in, though there is no way to hide it, unless he plans on driving it down the cliff face. The wind and rain are a lot heavier here because we are on exposed mountaintop. Sheer sheets of it pelt the windscreen and outside the pretty bog flowers, heather and grassy hillocks bend beneath it. I wonder if Rosa's car has pulled in or if they're still ploughing their way forward to the sheds at the top of the mountain.

'We can't go in without being spotted,' William says, almost shouting to be heard over the howl of the wind. 'We can hold on provided Rosa isn't in any danger. What's her status?'

'Nothing to report now, but she's still in the car.'

'All right. Lucy and I will try to get as close as we can to those sheds without being noticed. Keep everyone on standby in the area. If we need backup, I want it here pronto. Get a search warrant drawn up for the place – we might need it. I'll keep the radio on me.'

'Will do.'

William drives the van on for another bit, getting as close as he can to the end of the road without making our presence known. Of course, if someone decides to come back down the road, we'll be discovered. A sudden crack of jagged lightning makes me jump. For a second, the whole area is lit up like daytime.

'Fuck,' William says, slowing,

The lightning is followed by a boom of thunder so loud the ground seems to shake, and another crack of forked lightning zigzags along the ground. William pulls the van to a halt. I check Google. No signal. The land ahead and to the left of us is bleak and desolate, the peat bogs of County Mayo.

'I think we're about five hundred metres cross-country from the top of this road,' William says. 'If we leave the van here, we can cross that bog and I reckon the sheds will be just around the bend there. Once the other units come, we can block off access to this road. But we'll need them to be discreet for now.' He relays this to Dan.

I'm glad we're going to head towards the barns because every instinct in me is screaming now not to leave Rosa alone there. 'You ready?' William asks. He pulls on his jacket and thumbs to the back of the car. 'I've a couple of rain jackets as well in the boot.'

Of course he has. That's why he's my boss, as he'd no doubt tell me if I said anything.

We get out of the car and are immediately soaked in what might best be described as a lukewarm bath of rain. Lightning flashes again, thankfully sheet lighting this time. Thunder booms across the mountainside.

'God rolling his beer barrels again, eh?' William says, and I glance at him, amused, despite the tension.

He hands me a rain jacket. 'Zip up or you just might drown.'

We pull on the jackets. William takes a torch from the boot as well and shoves it into his pocket, though it's unlikely he'll use it as we'll be seen. Then, William leading the way, we crouch low and start a slow trek across the bog. I remember Dan chasing the Night Caller across bog and a sudden chill steals over me. 'Watch out for bog holes,' I say. 'Test the ground first. It can surprise you.'

William turns to me. 'Would you be better at it?'

I take the lead. The thing about bogs is that they're always wet, no matter how dry the weather. Even if you don't hit a bog hole and sink up to your waist, you can get sucked into the mulch and lose a shoe or slip and fall. The safest way to cross is to identify the dry tufts of grass that stick up and aim for them. And you have to do that without being led off course. It's like chess: you have to be able to see about five tufts ahead. Right now, with the darkness of the storm and the blinding rain, it's hard to see my way at all, but I'm quicker than William so that's something. It takes about half an hour before we begin to ascend the steep hill, my legs aching. Up and up until we round the turn in the road, and when we do, we spot the sheds about fifty metres in front of us. We dip, lie flat on our bellies on the sodden earth, the rain finding its way into our jackets, down our necks and into our shoes. The sheds are exactly as Dan described: five, arranged in a circle, the front doors all facing into the middle of what is probably some kind of a yard.

William takes a small pair of binoculars from the pocket of his jacket and holds them to his eyes. Is there nothing he doesn't have in there?

'Of all the nights in all of summer,' he says, 'it has to piss rain on the night we need it not to. Can't see a bloody thing.' He jams the binoculars back into his jacket in disgust. He presses the radio. 'Dan, what's the status of backup and Rosa?'

'Backup is assembled and ready to assist once they're given the order. Rosa is inside. We have no audio now – they've obviously taken the clothes from her. And—'

A sound pierces the darkness, short and sharp, and when it's over, I don't know if I even heard it. But William turns to me. 'Did you hear that?'

And it comes again. We scramble forward, ten metres now.

'What was it?'

And again.

Someone is screaming.

'Assistance needed,' William calls into the radio. 'Get the lads up here now. Get the road out blocked off.' He looks to me. 'Let's go.'

Crouching low, him following me over the last part of the bog, we soon find ourselves at the back of the sheds. Light spills out from the window, set in the centre of the back wall of one. We stand either side of that window. Smoke from a fire inside catches my throat and I fight not to cough. William draws his gun and I draw mine, hoping I won't have to use it. I have never fired a shot in all my years as a detective, except at the range. He indicates that I should approach the shed from the left and he will approach from the right. We'll see each other when we reach the front of the building, the part that faces the yard.

A voice reaches us, muffled and anguished, the words indistinguishable. My stomach lurches, like a boat on a stormy sea.

A man's voice, louder. Still hard to make out. The scream again.

The temptation to storm in is overwhelming, but loss of control could mean a loss, so William and I move rapidly but cautiously in opposite directions, backs to the wall, guns pointed, traversing the length of the barn. I reach the edge, whip around, ready to fire, but no one is there. I take it more slowly now. The opposite wall of the other barn provides shelter from the wind and rain and, as a result, I can't afford to make any noise. Now, my training kicks in and I block out everything except making my way safely to the front door of that barn. I'm on autopilot. I dip low and creep as softly as I can along the width of the building, finally arriving at the edge.

Now I can see a section of the courtyard. Right in the centre, a large dog is lying on his forepaws in a kennel. He appears to be chained to a boulder. I make a move. He stirs, sniffs the air, crawls from the kennel and gets to his feet, head cocked sideways. Can he smell me? Just beyond him is the car we'd seen Rosa get into. I can't make out the registration from here. Across the yard, light spills from the window of another shed and I think I can make out the sound of voices being carried on the wind. Low voices. Other than that, everything else appears to be deserted. There doesn't seem to be anyone occupying the other barns. I take a breath, brace myself and whip around the front of the barn.

Nothing. The dog spots the movement, though, and growls, then snarls, pulling on his chain. William rounds the building on the other side and, as the dog grows ever more frantic, William raises his arm and together we run towards the door. The dog is howling. William and I stop either side of the doorway.

'What the fuck is wrong with that dog?' someone inside says. 'Richie, go out and see what's happening.'

Footsteps cross the floor inside and the door is opened. Richie, a small, wiry teenager, steps into the yard. 'Shut up,' he shouts. And then he spots William, who has his gun pointed. He swallows hard. William puts his finger to his lips and points at me. Now Richie turns to me. I indicate that he should move towards me and get down on his knees.

'What the fuck is going on out there, Richie?'

'N-n-nothing,' Richie stammers, going down on his knees and holding his hands out for me to cuff him.

'Police.' William bursts into the room as I snap one cuff on Richie and the other on a drainpipe, all the while hastily cautioning him. Then I follow William inside.

In the distance, sirens can be heard, growing closer.

The barn is bright after the darkness of outside. Rosa is tied to a chair in the middle of the floor, hands bound behind her back, legs bound to the chair, a rag stuffed into her mouth. Tears pour down her face and I see that the underside of her arm has been branded. A man holding a branding iron has his arm about her neck. 'Keep off with yourselves,' he says, his eyes feral. 'I'll brand the bitch's face if you come any closer.'

'If you touch her, I will lay you out,' William takes a step closer, his gun not wavering. 'There are guards right now about to take the rest of these buildings. The road away from this place has been blocked. You don't have a choice.'

The man tips the hot iron onto Rosa's face and she howls in pain.

MARTINA MURPHY

Light footsteps behind me. I swivel around. 'Stop right there.'

A man drops a wooden plank he'd been holding, raises his arms. Outside the dog barks and thunder breaks, further away now. 'Get up against that wall.'

The diversion is enough for the man to toss the branding iron in William's direction. Rosa's chair topples over, taking her with it. The back of her head slams down onto the concrete floor and the crunch is sickening.

The man makes a dash for the door, William in pursuit. He makes a grab for him, catches a fistful of his shirt and yanks him back, causing him to lose his footing. William sidesteps, letting him go, and the man, arms cartwheeling, falls backwards. He tries to scramble up but William is on him, an uppercut sending him flying against the wall.

'Don't fucking move,' William shouts, pointing his gun at him.

Where is the backup?

Outside we hear voices. Panic. The dog howls.

Someone starts the engine of the car in the yard.

Fuck!

Rosa is motionless on the floor, her arm and chin already blistering. I am swamped with the realisation that this was my idea. If anything should happen to Rosa, it is my fault.

Chapter 64

Thirty minutes later, the place is swarming with guards and ambulances as dazed women and men are led from the only other occupied shed in the yard. They are young, a mix of races, all with the small brand on their inner arms. I am in a sort of twilight, the high of saving these people very much diluted by the fact that Rosa is being treated in the ambulance across the courtyard. She has regained consciousness but is very confused and has vomited.

I just want to hear that she is all right but I'm almost afraid to go over and ask. She's only a kid. I think my life will crumble if I've been responsible for putting her in danger.

Around me, blue flashing lights illuminate the land for miles around. The rain has eased, softer now, and the storm has passed. I shiver despite the blanket the emergency services gave me.

'You all right?' William, looking in complete control, joins me. Then, without waiting for an answer, he says, 'We've issued a media blackout and Dan is getting search warrants signed tonight.'

I watch one of the ambulance men jump down from Rosa's ambulance and wonder where he is going.

'She'll be all right,' William says, without looking at me. 'It's just bad concussion.'

'And a facial burn.'

He looks at me, understanding flooding his face. 'Yeah, that's regrettable but—'

'Don't bloody say it's part of the job,' I snap. 'Just don't. It's horrible and—' I'm suddenly choked up. I wave a hand. 'Just don't.' My facial scarring had devastated me for a long time. Whatever looks I'd had had been taken away in that split second when that woman had gone for me. And yet, at the time, I thought I deserved it. Payback for Rob and what he'd done. I felt that the sacrifice of my looks should atone for my stupidity, should show everyone that I was a real guard, prepared to face real danger. But it hadn't made it any easier to bear.

'I'm . . .' William stops, not knowing what to say. There is nothing he can say. Instead, he points to where the forensics team are heading. 'They've found what they think is a freshly dug grave and a body in one of the sheds. It looks like they were in the process of burying someone.'

I rub a hand across my face. Sometimes I'm not sure I can bear this job any longer.

'That fucking bastard, he knocked me down!' The man who'd branded Rosa is being led towards a garda car. He jabs a finger in William's direction. 'Punched me in the face before he cuffed me, he did. I know my rights. He used unnecessary force. Police brutality.'

'Shut up,' a guard says, as he sits him into the back of a squad car.

We watch as he's driven away, both of us, I think, wishing William had hit him harder.

Chapter 65

'What the fuck is going on?' Sarah says, as the man and woman who'd pulled her off the street come in with a bar of chocolate and a Coke. She nods towards the offerings. 'You can fuck off with those.'

The man smiles a little and leaves them on the table anyway before sitting opposite her.

'I don't believe you're the police.'

'We are,' the man says. 'My name is Ben Lively. I'm a detective. This is Julie, a social worker.' Then he goes on to tell her that bloody Mari in the shelter is really called Rosa and that Bernie is trafficking kids through it. 'We knew you were to meet Bernie – we picked it up on the video. We had to stop you without compromising our agent. I'm sorry if we frightened you.'

'Did you catch Bernie then? Did she have Jenny?'

There is a pause so deep that Sarah wants to hide from it. 'I'm afraid,' the detective says, 'Jenny has passed away.'

'Passed away where?' Sarah asks. And then reality lands, like a punch. 'Dead?' she whispers.

'I'm sorry,' the man goes on. 'It looks like she got an infection in a burn on her arm. We have to investigate it, but they think sepsis . . . I'm sorry.'

Sarah blinks, swallows hard. 'She was twelve,' she says. 'She was only fucking twelve.' She wants to roar at this man, to tear the room down, but a tear runs down her face and takes her by surprise. And then another and then more and then so many she can't keep up with them.

The woman hands her a tissue.

Chapter 66

We're interviewing the smaller fish first, building up a picture of what happened and how, before we go in on Liam and Helen. At the moment, we have very little evidence on which to charge them. Helen says she didn't know Abby – how could she have known her? – and that on the day Adam was killed, she was in Dublin city centre.

There is footage to prove it, too, which has seriously dinted our case.

All we need is a lever. Still, now that we know where to look, we can slowly try to put the pieces together.

For now though, Forensics has just thrown up something quite interesting on Richie, which might help with our enquiries. His foot is tapping up and down – he's a bag of jangling nerve ends.

'D'you know what I have here, Richie?' I ask conversationally, after about thirty minutes of chit-chat and denials.

He looks at me with scared eyes.

'Fingerprint results from the break-in at Adam Gray's house. They are an exact match to yours. Can you explain that?'

He flinches. Shifts on his chair. I can see his brain trying to think of a way out. 'I – I've been in Adam's room loads of times.'

We'd prepared for that in our interview strategy.

'Not according to his father. He said no one ever went in there. He doesn't recognise you either.'

Richie's foot taps out a more agitated beat and his solicitor glances at him once or twice in irritation. Then he blurts out, 'All right. I did it. I broke into the Grays' place.'

'Go on.'

'I'm not a bad person,' he whines. Then, after a pause, 'I was told to break into his room. I had to look for a zip drive or iPad or something electronic. Then I had to make it look like a regular burglary by trashing the rest of the place.'

I take a moment to compose myself. I want to smash this guy's head into the table. Mr Gray had lost his son and this gouger was robbing him and, on top of that, lining up girls to be trafficked. I take a hard look at his long, spotty, adolescent face. Is it youth that makes him so careless of others or is he just a shit?

'So, eh, that's it,' Richie says, growing uncomfortable with the silence, I think. 'That's all.' He makes to stand.

'Sit down,' I snap, and even Jordy jumps. 'Who told you to break into Adam's room?'

His eyes widen and he shakes his head. 'Aw, no . . . I don't remember.'

'Look, if you broke into a room under duress, I get that. You don't seem like the sort of person who would just go and rob a bereaved man.'

'I'm not. I'm not a bad person.'

'So someone told you to break into Adam's room.'

'Yeah.'

'You'll have to give me a name or you'll be seen as the wanker who—'

'Helen. Her name was Helen.'

Beside me, I hear Jordy inhale sharply.

I keep my voice level. 'You say this was Helen's idea?'

'Yes.'

I pass across some photographs. 'Can you identify Helen here?'

He points to Helen Walsh.

'For the record, the suspect has identified Helen Walsh. Did Helen say why she wanted this zip drive?'

'You don't ask Helen questions,' Richie says. 'You just do what she says. Her and—' He stops. 'You just do it,' he says.

'How exactly did she phrase her request?'

He screws up his face. 'She told me to come up to Dublin, I suppose because no one might know me, and she gave me an address and said . . .' he pauses '. . . "Trash the place, especially the bedroom. Look for a zip drive and get it to me."'

'When exactly was this?'

'Just before Adam's death made the news. I didn't even know he was dead when I said I'd do it. She wanted me to go that night, but you lot were crawling all over the place by then so I had to wait a day or so. There wasn't much left to trash by the time yous had been,' Richie says. 'I didn't do a lot of damage, really.'

'Shut up,' I snap, and wince. That is not a phrase recommended in any guide for interviewing witnesses and suspects. 'How did Helen seem when she asked you to do this?'

'Pretty seriously pissed.'

So whatever it was, Adam had hidden it from her. But we had been through Adam's room and, aside from the photographs that had led us to where we are now, there was nothing. We'd gutted that room – we'd even taken the radios and bits of radios and examined them. One of the lads in Forensics, who was a bit of a radio geek himself, had said that Adam must have had a huge talent for it: how he'd got some of those pieces working was impressive. I wonder if I should ask the team to have another look through his stuff. Get it all brought up from Exhibits and go through it. Maybe, though – the thought shimmers in front of me – maybe when Helen went looking, when we went looking, the object she'd wanted had already been removed. Maybe somehow Adam had known, had tried to use it as a bargaining tool.

Oh, my God.

'Can I go now?' Richie asks, in a whiny voice, breaking into my thoughts.

'No.' I stand up, trying to dampen down my excitement. This might unlock everything. 'You'll be taken back to the cell and I'll get one of the boys to bring you your lunch.'

He is led out.

'Come on, Jordy,' I say, as he looks up, startled. 'We've somewhere to be.'

Chapter 67

Jordy agrees that what I'm thinking makes sense, so thirty minutes later, we pull up outside the cordoned-off Home shelter in Westport. There's a guard on duty and he lets us in.

Jordy follows me, panting and wheezing, through Reception and towards the dining hall. Behind me, I hear him splutter out a laugh. 'Begod, that poster makes me want to hurl.'

'Well, there are more, so I hope you didn't eat too much breakfast.'

He laughs again.

I push open the door to the dining room and, to my relief, the radio that Adam gifted to Gareth is still sitting on the little table in the corner of the room. It's the only thing I'm aware of that had been removed from Adam's room before we did the search. And, according to Gareth, whom I'd rung about it, it doesn't work. It never worked, which is odd. With all Adam's apparent skill, he should have got it to work, surely.

Jordy pulls on a pair of gloves and hefts up the radio, putting it into a clean exhibit bag, which I'm holding open. Something inside it rattles and we smile at each other.

'Bingo,' Jordy says.
I hope so.
And then Mick rings and I think, Jackpot.

Chapter 68 – Two days later

Two days later, Dan and I are finally ready to face off against Helen. Larry and Ben have been given the dubious pleasure of interviewing Liam.

Helen is already in the room when we arrive, sitting at the table with her solicitor.

I cannot bloody wait.

'Hello, Helen,' I say, placing my files on the table and taking a seat opposite her. 'Would you like a tea or a coffee before we begin?'

'No. I just want all this ridiculous nonsense sorted. I'll sue the lot of you after this, my good name being dragged through the mud.'

'This interview is being recorded, and may I remind you that you are still under caution. For the purposes of the tape, the interview of Helen Walsh is being conducted by Detective Sergeant Lucy Golden and Detective Guard Dan Brown. In attendance is solicitor Ruth Erris.'

Dan lounges back in his chair, pen in hand, looking relaxed and at ease.

'All right, Helen, we're interviewing you first in connection with the trafficking of people for the purposes of exploitation.'

Two hours later, after she has twisted and turned and denied, accusing all the people who have ID'd her, all the people in the sheds who identified her from our photographs, of lying, I make my move.

'As you know, Helen, we searched your house after your arrest and removed a number of items. I'm going to show you some images now and I want you, for the purposes of the interview, to identify them for me, if you will.'

She eyeballs me, hard.

I push a picture in front of her, 'Exhibit LB2, a blue Noelle Brown designer dress, size ten.' I list the make and the style. 'Yours?'

'Yes,' Helen snaps.

I go through various other items of clothing, including a red scarf and a few pairs of shoes, including a pair of blue and red sandals. She admits to owning them all. I then move on to two phones we found in her house and she agrees that, yes, they belong to her as well.

'And would you use both phones?' I ask.

'Yes.'

'Anyone else use them?'

'No.'

'Why two phones?'

'One was personal, the other was business.'

'I see.' I place some bank statements in front of her. 'Exhibit LB3,' I say. 'Do you recognise these, Helen?'

'Should I?'

'They are bank statements opened up under the names of various ladies who have accused you of trafficking them.'

'So?' But her voice falters.

'The phone number associated with these bank accounts is for this phone here.' I tap the image of the 'business' phone taken from her house. 'And you've admitted that it is your phone.'

She says nothing, just stares at me.

'Were you in charge of a trafficking ring, Helen?'

She considers her options. 'It was Liam's idea.' A moment. Then she says, 'We thought we were helping them. Giving them a new start. They were bloody penniless, for God's sake.'

'Go on.'

And the story pours out of her. She manages the business side, meets the girls on their first nights. There is no mention of Abby or Adam.

Time enough.

We go back to interview her again in the afternoon. Having got the confession of trafficking out of her, we are now focusing on the murder charges.

Helen is outraged. 'I didn't know either of those two people. Adam merely worked for me on and off.'

'Can you remember where you were on the night of the third of July, Helen?'

'I was working. You saw my timetables.'

Lovely.

'Exhibit LB4.' I place the school photograph in front of her. 'Can you identify the people in this picture, please, Helen?'

Her mouth drops open when she looks at it. She brings her eyes to meet mine and I see it, the way she gathers herself in, before returning her gaze to the picture. She hadn't expected it. That much is obvious. 'Adam,' she breathes. 'Oh, my God, Adam Gray? I didn't realise. He never said . . .'

I wait.

'You're saying Adam my bouncer was Adam my childhood friend?' she says. 'I didn't realise . . . Oh, God, was he stalking me?'

She's lying. She knew him, we all know it, but unfortunately Dan and I have to prove it.

'The one and the same Adam.' I nod. 'His father identified you from an array of pictures I showed him.'

'I had no idea.' Helen gives a tinny laugh, 'I gave Adam a job because I felt sorry for him. I had no idea that he was Adam from my schooldays. He certainly never told me. And it makes sense, because he was weird around me. As far as I know, Liam had no idea who he was either.'

'How do you mean weird around you?'

'Stalkerish. I never told you that because he was dead and it would have made no difference, but now it all makes sense. He was stalking me.' She gasps a bit in horror. 'Was he involved in a murder?'

I ignore the question. 'Do you recognise this car?' Once more, I list the exhibit number as I place an image of the Peugeot on the table.

A second. I know she's wondering if we've placed her in it. 'Yes,' she finally says, 'yes, I do. Adam hired it one weekend and took me for a spin. He was obsessed with me, always trying to show off.'

'I see. Exhibit LB7. Do you recognise this suitcase?' I lay the picture of the blue suitcase in front of her.

'I bought one like it a couple of months ago but then it was stolen.'

'I see.'

'I think Adam stole it. He was in my apartment, for a staff party, and then it was gone. I did ask him about it but he denied it.'

God, she's good.

'How would you explain the fact that fibres found on Abby Devine, before she was wrapped in the clear plastic, match items of clothes in your wardrobe.'

'What items?'

'These items.' I point to the blue dress and the red scarf she's admitted to owning.

'I had those clothes in the case the first time I used it, I suppose.'

'What you're saying is that you were in the car that Abby travelled in, you owned the suitcase that Abby was found in and that some of your fibres from your clothes were found on Abby but that you had nothing to do with her murder?'

'Yes. I never knew that girl. And, besides, anyone could own those clothes.'

'Dan?' I say, and Dan lays a picture on the table in front of Helen. I narrate for the purposes of the tape, 'Detective Dan Brown is showing Helen a photograph of Abby Devine. Exhibit Number LB1.' The picture shows Abby in the red thong, her hair thrown back, the name Mz Luscious emblazoned sideways across the photo. 'Computer Forensics put a lot of work into retrieving files on your computer, Helen, and they found this.'

Helen barely glances at it. 'Maybe she was one of our girls. I didn't know them all personally.'

'This picture we now know was uploaded onto your website on the first of July and guess when it was removed and shredded?'

Helen eyeballs me. 'I have no idea.'

'The very night that Abby was murdered. How did you know she was murdered that very night?'

'I didn't.'

'How do you explain the picture being shredded?'

'I can't.'

'And this,' I push another page towards her, 'Exhibit LB9.'

'I have no idea what I'm looking at.' She folds her arms.

'This is a list of phones that pinged off the tower in Keem between the third and fourth of July. That's your phone there. The one that is linked to the bank accounts. So, if you own the phone and were the only one who used it, you were here that weekend.'

Her face pales. But she rallies: 'That does not prove murder. It does not prove that Abby Devine was with me that weekend.'

And I wait, let the silence settle, eyeball Helen, who eyeballs me back.

'But in your alibi you told us you were working in the bar. And yet, this phone, which you admit to using, was most definitely not in the bar.'

Nothing.

'Why would you lie if you'd nothing to hide? Also, sorry, forgot to mention it. Those items of clothing you identified as belonging to you, we found Abby's blood on the blue and red sandals.'

The words drop into the room.

'Fuck. You.'

Inside, I'm smiling. I love the slow stalking of suspects. Giving nothing away, I say, 'We'll move on now to the murder of Adam Gray on the eighteenth of August.'

'You're stitching me up.' She changes tack. Her eyes fill with tears. 'I don't know anything about that! I didn't know him well. I wasn't there. I was in Dublin until well after four.'

'Exhibit LB10.' I lay down another picture. 'Do you recognise this girl?'

'No.'

'She recognises you,' I say. 'Her name is Sarah Muldoon. Sarah had a near miss. Your friend Bernie was all set to drive her to Ballina to report her friend Jenny missing. God knows what could have happened if we hadn't taken her off the streets, eh?'

'This has nothing to do with me.'

'It has. You see, Sarah alleges that she was at a function, a first birthday party of the homeless shelter in Westport – Adam had been murdered earlier that day – and she says at the end of the evening she saw you with Liam. And Bernie. She alleges that you all seemed to know one another very well.'

Helen draws herself up. I can see the fury behind her eyes, the anger that all this should be going against her. 'No.'

'This young girl identified Jenny out of an array of pictures and guess what? We found Jenny dead in those sheds that Liam owns.'

'No.' Helen shakes her head. 'Who is this girl? What has she against me? I didn't kill anyone.'

Dan stands on my foot under the table. This is the litmus test. 'So, tell me, what was the last thing Adam threatened you with as he lay dying?'

Her reaction is instantaneous. She rears back off the chair, her mouth open. Then realising that she's played her hand, she tries to rein it all back in. 'I don't know what you mean. I wasn't there when he died. I was in Dublin city centre, shopping. I told you this.'

Dan and I have agreed that if she had a violent reaction to the question, we'd stand up and leave, let her stew. The truth of it is that we do have footage of her in Dublin, yet the way she has just reacted, tells us that she was with Adam when he was murdered. We need to re-examine that footage to see where the lie is.

'We'll leave you to reconsider your position,' Dan says.

As the gaoler takes her back to the cell, she looks a little scared.

The team, except Ben and Larry, who are still interviewing Liam, gather around to look at the CCTV footage of Helen. Ger rewinds it to the day in question. 'It's lunchtime,' he says, 'so, really, she'd have been cutting it fine to make it down to murder Adam. You can see her coming in here.'

Dan and I have reviewed this numerous times since Larry located it, and I'm hoping today some fresh eyes will crack it open.

Within seconds we're looking at a busy, bustling GPO with queues at the counters, people posting letters or parcels, claiming Lotto wins, tourists having a look at where the Easter Rising started.

'There she is.' Ger points out Helen coming in through the main door. 'We've also got her on the street, but this is the clearest image we have.'

Helen looks a bit rougher than the Helen I'd met in the bar, her hair awry, wearing baggy but comfortable clothes. She dodges the crowds and joins a queue, finally reaching the top. We watch her banter with the teller, both of them smiling before he passes her something. She signs it and passes it back. Then she leaves.

'Again,' I say.

And we watch it again.

'So weird,' I say. 'Her reaction just now and yet . . . how could she have—'

'Em . . . I don't think that's Helen,' Susan pipes up from somewhere at my shoulder.

We all turn to look at her.

William raises his eyebrows.

At that, she flushes. 'It's just . . . well, I was there when she was brought here, when she was arrested, and she looked high-end glamorous. I just . . . well, those clothes, they don't look like something she'd wear out shopping.'

She's right. She is so right.

'Were any clothes like that found in Helen's house?' I ask. 'Scan the exhibits.'

I get Ger to rewind the video again.

And then I notice it. I think back to when Dan and I met her first and she was signing papers in her office.

And suddenly it clicks. 'Susan, you little gem,' I say. 'You bloody little gem!'

I pick up the phone and make a couple of calls.

Chapter 69

Helen gives us a tearful but accusing stare when we arrive back in. Once more we go through the process of switching on the recorder, cautioning her, asking her if she'd like to say anything in relation to the murder charge of Adam Gray.

'No.'

'You still maintain that Adam was just a bouncer?'

'Yes. I was only doing him a favour employing him.'

'You still maintain that you were in Dublin on the date of his murder.'

'Yes.'

As I narrate, Dan runs the video footage of Helen being led into the garda station on the day of her arrest. 'Can you confirm that this is you?' I ask.

'Yes.'

Dan then plays the video footage of Helen in the GPO. 'Can you confirm that this is you?'

'Yes, that is me.'

I push a piece of paper and a pen across the desk towards her. 'Can you sign your name, please?'

And it clicks. A moment before she says, 'I'm ambidextrous.'

'Then write your name with both hands.'

She pushes the paper back towards me. 'No, it's ridiculous.'

'Are you refusing?'

'Yes.'

There is no need to push it. I change tack.

'Tell us about your siblings, Helen.'

'I've a brother and a sister.'

'We've confirmation from two sources that your sister Jane is actually your identical twin,' I say. 'Would that be right?'

'I was in Dublin the day of that boy's murder,' she says.

'In fact, Mae, your old neighbour, says it was almost impossible to tell you two apart.'

'I did not kill Adam Gray.' She starts to sniffle. Her solicitor passes her a handkerchief.

'I'm going to show you Exhibit LG1, a zip drive. This zip drive was found inside a radio that Adam Gray gave to Gareth Wilson three days before he died.' My voice is casual, studying her reaction.

She stills, her gaze riveted by the innocuous piece of hardware in front of her.

'Why would Adam do something like that, Helen? Hide this inside a radio?'

'I don't know.'

'This zip file contains links to bank accounts of all your girls, along with details of various shell accounts, which we have no doubt will be linked back to you and your accomplices. Adam Gray was not just a bouncer, was he? He wasn't just a volunteer. He was your accountant.'

'Liam was in charge of all that.'

'We have a witness who says that the day after Adam's murder, you asked him to break into Adam's room and take everything from it. He was to look for a zip drive.'

Her mouth works, as if she's trying to speak but the panic and fury is jumbling what she wants to say. Her eyes narrow. 'No,' she says eventually.

'And, oh, yeah.' I push towards her a copy of the note Helen had written to Louise. 'In Exhibit LB1, fingerprints found on a note retrieved from a Louise Roche match yours, even though you seem to be calling yourself Jane quite a lot. Not a great way to use your twin, is it? The same fingerprints were also found on a note written to Grainne booking her house.'

She says nothing.

Now I place exhibit CB3 in front of her. 'A serrated carving knife, used in the murder of Adam Gray. Do you recognise this knife, Helen?'

'No.'

'It's a carver, sold only through Musgrave's. That's a store that catering companies use a lot, isn't it?'

She swallows hard,

'The curious thing about this knife is that Louise Roche did not identify it as coming from her house. So whoever killed Adam brought it in with them. Exhibit LB4, a credit-card statement of purchases made for McAdam's bar, Dublin, from Musgrave's. I am showing the suspect the receipt for a knife bought in Musgrave's a day before Adam Gray was murdered.'

'So?'

'Despite a thorough search of your house and bar, no knife identical to this one from Musgrave's was located. So, the question must be asked, what happened to the knife you bought?'

In unison, Dan and I stand.

'We'll give you a few moments to absorb all that.' Dan speaks for the first time.

We watch as she is escorted back to her cell.

And I exhale.

Chapter 70 – Sarah

Sarah places some flowers on Jenny's grave. There aren't many because Jenny had no one in the whole world to give her flowers. Everyone belonging to her was either dead or had fecked off.

And she'd still believed that people were good.

Sarah swallows hard, blinks back tears. She can't stop crying now.

I've gone into foster care, she tells Jenny in her head. I'm giving it a go. I'm going to stop hating everyone, because you were right . . . I was scared.

She takes a step back and her foster mother gives her a tiny smile.

Sarah smiles back a little.

Chapter 71 – Six days later

It's the first of September and the weather has cooled significantly, almost as if that long hot blistering summer was a dream. I'm looking at my reflection in the hall mirror, trying rather unsuccessfully to put the finishing touches to my make-up. I probably should have got someone to do it for me. Or bought new stuff. I'm not quite sure my three-year-old lipstick is up to the job.

On the plus side, my new hairstyle and clothes look quite nice.

'You're different.' Luc makes a face as he walks by. 'What happened?'

'She's made an effort to look good,' my mother says, and she can't hide her approval. 'She's got some lovely new clothes and had her hair done.' Then, to me, 'Will you be all right on your own?' She reaches up and fusses about, patting away a stray hair, fingertips brushing over my scar.

'I'll be fine.' I pull away. 'I'll be fine.'

'Poor Dan. What was it happened again?'

'Fran's father died. He had been sick but still . . . it was quite sudden.'

'Was he an old man?'

'Younger than you,' I tell her, with a grin, and she wallops me.

361

Luc is peering inside the bag I'd left on the hall table. 'What are you doing with Sirocco's present from Dad?' he asks.

'Giving it back to your father.' Then at Luc's look, I add, 'What?'

'It's Sirocco's present, Ma.'

The words slap me about the face. He hardly wants to keep it?

'It should be me who gives it back,' he says. 'She's my daughter.'

And with those words, the bittersweet feeling of hitting a new landmark with my boy crashes over me. From his first steps as a youngster, to his first day in school, his first communion, his first year in college he has been moving away from me. It's a wonderful sort of grief. All I can do is what I did back then, what Luc and Tani did for Sirocco the first time she walked: all I can do is encourage him and be there if he falls. He's a man now, a father. He's willing to take responsibility for confronting his father on his daughter's behalf, and it moves me something rotten. Blinking back tears, which I know will horrify him, I take the present and press it into his hands. 'He's opening a photographic exhibition in Westport tonight. I'll drive you.'

I park about sixty metres from the gallery, the sky threatening rain. We hop out and I pull an umbrella from the boot and put it up. Luc looks at me as if I've just offered to shield him with a dead cat. 'I'll pass on that, Mam,' he says, then adds, 'I don't need you with me. I might call on a couple of the boys for a pint afterwards, seeing as I'm here.'

'I'll come as far as the door,' I say. I want to go in with him so hard it hurts. I want to be there to protect him in case Rob says something to hurt him or throw him off balance. But this is not an interview I can control. This is not something I have a gut feeling about. This is raw and messy and uncertain. 'Just . . . don't take any soft soap from him. Or any crap.'

'I won't.' He's irritated now.

As we near the gallery, I spot William loitering outside. At least, I'm fairly certain it's him. This version of William has ditched the shirt and tie and wears jeans and black Docs, a royal blue T-shirt and a black jacket. Despite the clothes, he still looks like a guard.

'I didn't know you were into photography,' I say, as he peels his back from the wall and crosses to me.

'Hey.' He nods a greeting to me, then focuses his attention on Luc.

'William, this is my son, Luc. Luc, this is my boss.'

They shake hands.

'I'm going in, Mam. Don't be here when I come out,' Luc says, and it's an order. Without waiting for me to offer any more unwanted advice, he's gone.

'That's me told,' I say, with a smirk, to William. 'Aren't you going in?'

'Not unless you are. Dan told me about tonight. He asked me to come over and have your back.'

That Dan should think of me, that William should offer to take his place and both of them knackered after a hard investigation causes a lump to form in my throat. God, I'm an awful mess. I think I'm just tired after everything. 'That's . . .' I take a breath. I have no words so I settle for 'Thank you.'

'You're welcome.' He pushes open the door. 'Well?'

'I'd better not. Luc is returning the gift himself on his daughter's behalf. I just drove him here.'

'Good man, Luc,' William says approvingly.

He makes no move to go. We stand there then, not quite sure how to proceed. I say, 'I'm sorry for . . . you know . . . snapping the night at the sheds. I was just . . . I . . . felt . . . bad for her, you know.'

'Aw, sure I knew that.' He starts to walk and I fall in beside him. 'And it's not easy, seeing that stuff, especially . . .' His eyes flick across my face.

'Yeah.'

'Word is she'll be grand. A bit of a skin graft and that.'

'Good.'

'D'you fancy a pint?' he asks. I must look surprised because then he says, 'Well, you look like you took some trouble to show your ex-husband what he was missing, be a shame to waste it.'

'I didn't get dressed up for that gouger.' I'm indignant.

'Sorry, I just—'

'This hairstyle is for me. And, yes, I'd love a pint, thanks.'

He smiles a little, unsure. 'Right. Then let's go, Lucy Golden.'

The rain is a steady patter and I hold the umbrella over the two of us as we walk, side by side, up the narrow street. He's taller than me, so it's difficult.

'May I?' he says, taking the umbrella.

The smell of food is carried to us on the air from the restaurants that line the riverbank. Some brave busker is hammering out a tune. A young girl is begging, a little bowl in front of her. She can't be more than thirteen.

I pull a twenty from my purse and hand it to her.

Eyes wide, she tucks it into her back pocket, saying nothing. We move on.

After a moment, William says, 'We can only do our best, Lucy.

We can't beat ourselves up over everyone we can't save.' His gaze bores into mine. 'And we did good. You did good. All right?'

I know that that has to be enough, but it's hard. 'All right.'

'It might interest you to know that Helen folded, like a bad poker player, last night. Larry found her car on CCTV at the hospital the day Abby was there. You can see Adam and Helen in the front seats and someone in the back. She told us everything, names, dates, places, the lot. Says Liam wanted to road-test Abby and that she bit him and he lost it. Liam's cracked too, blamed it all on Helen, arrogant bastard. We've a long way to go still but, God, it's a bloody good start.' He pushes open the door of Matt Molloy's. 'Buy me a pint and I'll fill you in.'

And he's off, talking shop, with me hanging on every word, asking questions. Back on familiar ground. In tune.

It's enough.

Glossary

AFIS	Automated Fingerprint ID System
APT	Assistant Pathologist
Cig	Short for Cigre. A common nickname for Detective Inspectors as Cigre means 'inspector' in Irish. Pronounced Kig
DDU	District Detective Unit (unmarked cars)
DG	Detective Guard
Debs	A graduation dance attended by sixth-year students before they go on to college
DI	Detective Inspector. Often referred to as 'Cig'. *Cigre* being the Irish word for 'inspector'. Pronounced Kig
DS	Detective Sergeant
GNECB	Garda National Economic Crime Bureau
IP	Injured Party
IRC	Incident Room Co-ordinator
NSU	National Surveillance Unit
SIO	Senior Investigating Officer
SOCO	Scene of Crime Officers
SO	Suspected Offender
TE	Technical Examination

ACKNOWLEDGEMENTS

Thanks to EVERYONE who purchased my last book – *The Night Caller*. I have never had such a reaction to anything I've written before and it was much appreciated. It gave me the confidence to write *The Branded*.

Thanks to the usual suspects – my family, Colm, Conor and Caoimhe, the world's greatest cheerleaders.

To my mam and dad, for being just great, basically.

To my siblings – Claire, Seamus, Eithne, Treasa and Aoife, and to their other halves, Tony, Dearbhla, Paul, Simon and Jules.

All my nieces and nephews and godchildren – Jenna, Tom and Nathan.

My in-laws, for being lovely and championing the books.

Thanks also to my friends – I would not survive without the walks, chats, coffee and moaning 😊

Thanks to my agent Caroline and all at the Hardman Swainson literary agency – you are brilliant!

And to all at Little, Brown and Constable – Krystyna Greene, a lovely, lovely editor. We have not met yet, but I know I'll like you! Thanks to Hazel Orme, copy-editor extraordinaire, Hannah Wann, Rebecca Sheppard and Zoë Carroll.

Thanks also to the Hachette Ireland team – especially Siobhan Tierney, for arranging the book signings, and thanks to Mark Walsh from Plunkett PR for doing a great PR job.

To my early readers: Claire, a great editor; Caroline Hardman for her invaluable suggestions; and also to the detective I have been lucky enough to persuade to read my early drafts. Thanks for putting me straight on procedure and giving this book a real *Line of Duty* vibe.

Thanks to Kevin Clarke for his input and for answering my questions.

Thanks to all who interviewed me about the last book, those who reviewed it and to all the bookshops but *especially* the local bookshops in Maynooth – the aptly titled Maynooth Bookshop and also to the staff in Easons Maynooth. I appreciated the support so much.

And finally, while I love the book writing, it is a lonely road sometimes, so I want to thank all those who worked with me on a group writing/drama endeavour: *FRACTURED – a family, a nation, a dream*, the world's longest-running and largest podcast! It kept me sane and yet beautifully stressed during Covid. Thanks especially to Lucina Russell, the most amazing arts officer for championing the idea, and to my fellow writers, Claire Joyce, Joe Bergin and Brendan Farrell, who also did sound engineer. It was a pleasure.

And as usual – thanks to YOU, dear reader.

PS I have not mentioned Covid at all in this book because it's set in the near future and I am at heart an optimist!